Dear Reader:

When a Del Rey e[...] likes enough to publish, we call it a Discovery, [...] our readers that there's a new voice out there to celebrate. No guarantee—just a conviction that something new is always worth the risk. One day, we hope, each new author's name will come to be recognized by eager readers as a guarantee in and of itself: a sure bet for a good read.

Scott G. Gier is a name that, to me, has already come to guarantee a sure thing. His Discovery novel, *Genellan: Planetfall*, was one of my favorite books that year. Rarely have I seen gritty, down-and-dirty military action blended so seamlessly with truly poignant emotion. Action, adventure, romance, tragedy, and both planetary and personal victory—it was all there! And my enthusiasm only grew when I read Scott's second book, *Genellan: In the Shadow of the Moon*.

Now I'm proud to introduce the third Genellan book: *Genellan: First Victory*. If you've been enjoying the series so far, you won't be disappointed to see how the story is developing—I guarantee it. If you've never read the earlier *Genellan* books, you'll still be able to pick this up and understand what's going on—and I know you'll find yourself rooting for the good guys, wringing your hands at the machinations of the bad guys, and caring desperately about the outcome for the people of Genellan. I guarantee it!

If you like military science fiction with sympathetic, believable characters—both human and alien—and a touch of romance, *Genellan* is for you. I guarantee it. In fact, we at Del Rey feel so strongly about this book that we're standing by our convictions: *Genellan: First Victory* is officially GUARANTEED to be a great read (see last page for details). Try it: You'll like it!

Welcome to the world of Genellan!

SCIENCE FICTION
FANTASY

Happy reading!

Shelly Shapiro
Executive Editor
Del Rey Books

By Scott G. Gier
Published by Ballantine Books:

GENELLAN: Planetfall, Book 1
GENELLAN: In the Shadow of the Moon, Book 2
GENELLAN: First Victory, Book 3

GENELLAN:
First Victory
BOOK 3

Scott G. Gier

A Del Rey® Book
BALLANTINE BOOKS • NEW YORK

A Del Rey® Book
Published by Ballantine Books
Copyright © 1997 by Scott G. Gier

All rights reserved under International and Pan-American Copyright Conventions. Published in the United States by Ballantine Books, a division of Random House, Inc., New York, and simultaneously in Canada by Random House of Canada Limited, Toronto.

http://www.randomhouse.com

Library of Congress Catalog Card Number: 97-92210

ISBN 0-345-40450-5

Manufactured in the United States of America

First Edition: November 1997

10 9 8 7 6 5 4 3 2 1

To Patty, my wife

ACKNOWLEDGMENTS

I would like to thank Dr. Dan Perkins, my first reader, editor, and accomplice in learning to write.

I would like to also thank Ms. Alice Chan for her Chinese language assistance.

CONTENTS

PROLOGUE

PRISONERS OF TIME

Pake descended into a furious haze. She hauled on the bleating packer's lead, her rag-wrapped fingers stiff with cold. Iron dust gusted sideways, scratching the woman's weather-beaten skin. The wind tugged at her head wrapping, a dingy rag giving feeble protection to high cheekbones, buttresses to Mongoloid eyes of black adamantine. The bloodred sun slanted downward, groping for a demarcation of land and sky. There was no horizon, only a nether distance of fiery orange.

Marking the valley's bottom was the furred glow of the smelter. Its roaring hellfire, rattling conveyors, and thundering ore-crushers were enfeebled by the wind's jealous scream. Pake's growling stomach served its own notice. She pulled a flapping packer hide about her distended belly and yanked the packer's lead. The animal balked, planting its hooves. The dusky beast tucked its stubby, red-crusted muzzle into the lee of its cargo of cactus-wood. The dull, fat-humped species had survived eons by turning from the wind.

Wielding a metal truncheon, Pake beat the brute, her exertions allowing the wind to rip the ragged scarf from her face. The packer, mule ears drooping, relented to the human's superior purpose. Pake, spitting grit, leaned on the rope to keep the animal plodding forward. A tress of gray-streaked jet streamed in the gale.

They were almost home. The terrain moderated, gradually rounding to broken flatness. Plaints of other packers drifted on the wind. Her animal lifted its head, cracked open lash-filtered eyes of rheumy white and gave a sand-stifled honk. It increased its pace, no longer needing tension on its lead. Animal and

1

master came to a sandy-bottomed, steep-sided wash. Pake hugged its rising lee, the cold, burning wind blasting over her head. She walked in a dim tunnel of hissing dust. A wrist-thick sand snake sidewindered from her approaching feet.

Pake came at last to an erosion defile. She clambered up the smooth cleft through which water had not trickled for longer than she could remember. The sweet spring's precious yield was captured at its source and used to irrigate the village box gardens. Thoughts of water made Pake's throat well. Pake spat into her filthy hand and rubbed saliva on her crud-crusted forehead. Thus anointed, she prayed, and climbed.

Gone almost two days, Pake was exhausted. She had scaled the valley wall, higher than ever before, gleaning deadfall from cactus groves in the mountain vales. She had climbed above the swirling sands, above even the range of the cactus, high enough to glimpse hardwoods on the ridges. Precious hardwood. She had seen rock goats bounding across the sheer faces, and in the night had heard banshee screams.

A brooding cluster of adobe huts materialized. Their low profiles were dominated by a dragon-backed ridge, dimly silhouetted against sanguinary twilight. Another form, an unnatural shape contrived of technology, sublimated from the dust-ridden dusk—an Ulaggi field station. Its streamlined tractor was huge, its great studded treads higher than Pake was tall. Not an ore-hauler, this tractor pulled but a single unit. It was an inspection module.

The burbling rumble of an auxiliary lifted above the wind. Pake smelled its exhaust. A searchlight flashed into being, a coruscating tube of light, fixed at its source, its brightness textured with driven dust. The light tube ended in an attenuated oblong of white light. The dazzling ellipse darted unerringly over red gravel. Helpless in its glare, Pake shielded her eyes. After several seconds the searchlight shut down.

Ulaggi mobile stations came every ten days. Pake grunted with irony. The iron-ore shafts were not the only tunnels into which the Ulaggi peered. In the morning, all fertile women of the village would obediently present themselves to alien medical technicians.

The arrival of this particular tractor aggrieved Pake's soul; this visitation promised an ominous milestone, for Little One's menarche was arrived. Her daughter would be expected to join the women. Pake trembled, not with cold. She fervently wished, for the thousandth time, that she had had the courage to murder her offspring.

In darkness Pake stumbled up the village alley. Knees protesting, she arrived at her own nodule of mud and straw. Swirling gusts could not purge the odor of cook fires fed with cactus-wood and packer dung. Her demanding stomach, a constant in a life of unremitting misery, growled again. Her packer bleated, anxious to join its herd mates, and anxious to be fed. Hunger—the curse of the living.

Pake threw her bedroll and rucksack over her shoulder. Where was Little One? Little One always came out to help. Pake untied the faggot bundles and allowed the precious fuel to fall against the mud wall. She released the packer's girth and lifted the cross-tree from the animal's hump and hefted it toward the door. She would not leave the hardwood frame outside, certain to disappear. Growing angry, Pake ducked into the lee of the hut, lifted the latch, and pushed open the door with her scrawny buttocks. She dragged the saddle frame inside.

"Feed the packer," Pake grunted, her throat protesting its coating of dust. "Bring the cactus-wood inside." Overhead, hides interwoven between thin roof beams fluttered softly.

"Mama," Li-Li sobbed. Li-Li, her youngest, never cried.

Pake turned, suddenly frightened.

She caught their sweet, musky scent. A wall of dark-helmeted Ulaggi hulked between the mother and her daughters. Four squat forms with massive shoulders, wide hips, and big feet filled the cramped room. Three were black-suited guard-males. The fourth wore the tan ground suit of a reproduction technician. The technician seized Pake in a viselike grip. Pake averted her eyes and sucked back a scream. Time froze. Small things became suffocatingly acute. Red dust sifted downward, visible motes dancing in the flickering candle flame. Drifts of russet powder dusted the thick plastic table, its once garish yellow sheen abraded over time to sanded buff. Ulaggi boot marks—obscene, fan-shaped imprints patterned by hobnails—overlapped the floor of her home. There was grit in Pake's teeth, the taste of iron in her throat; anger welled in her heart, but the emptiness in her belly dominated all sensation.

"Move you!" thundered the technician, in a ghastly parody of her language.

Pake retreated, falling back into the biting wind. Her head covering streamed into the gale, loosening her hair to thrash her face. The wind was not loud enough to mask Little One's sobs. Pake dared not look back. Collecting her tresses and twisting them under control, she stumbled downhill. They came to the hulking station. The boarding ladder was not deployed. The technician boosted Pake roughly to the head-high hatch landing. She crawled along a grit-filled catwalk, taking shelter in the lee of the entry lock's weather baffle. Wind howled through the railing.

Dim amber lights came on. A guardmale clambered onto the landing, using one arm to hoist himself upward. In his other arm, clasped to an obscenely broad chest, was her frightened daughter. Pake held out her arms, but the guardmale knocked her aside and strode past. The technician came next, pushing Pake before him.

A hard blast of warm air emanated from the lock, exploding dust from the enclosure. A translucent membrane clamshelled over them, its bearing surfaces protesting contact with cold grit. The inner door *whooshed* open. Pake was pushed forward again. Once inside, the guardmale and the technician disappeared to the right. Pake's last glimpse of her innocent daughter was a dangling bare foot.

A guardmale yanked on her packer hides. Pake disrobed, as she had many times before. Compliant as a whipped dog, she hung her limp rags and sat on the cold bench. They were always made to wait naked. More guardmales stood near, leering and joking.

This time there was no wait. A guardmale stood her up and pushed her into a sanitation closet, slamming the thick door. A hard spray exploded on her filthy body, needles of steaming caustic. Pake kept her eyes closed. The acrid assault stopped. A mist encompassed her, slippery and warm. A pause ... the hard spray again, this time water, precious water. Stinging jets combed her body, starting at her head and working to her feet. Shielding her eyes and breasts with her elbows, Pake grabbed her hair and wrung out bloodred water.

Too soon the water stopped. The door opposite hissed open. Pake moved against a flow of cold air into an examining room, her skin puckering into gooseflesh. A reproduction technician, no taller than she but as wide as he was tall, awaited. This technician had large, variegated eyes, with brown irises marbled with putrid blue. His skin was a moist, translucent nacre, with veins and pulsing arteries prominently revealed. Muscle mass was also clearly distinguishable, constantly shifting beneath thin dermal layers. An older male, Pake perceived; she could tell by his milky eyes and sagging features; his nose was a drooping slab of mottled flesh. His expression was not unkind. Pake steeled herself, finding courage.

"Why now?" she asked. "Why not in morning?"

"Emergency," the technician muttered, pushing her onto her back. He spoke her language, horribly accented.

"Emergency?" she asked, emboldened.

"Shaft explosion. Mine Three. Injuries," the technician said more loudly, with less kindness. He probed her body, fondling her with thick fingers, but gently and swiftly. He positioned her before a machine.

A rush of static came from the box on the wall. And then some Ulaggi words. An Ulaggi guardmale growled in response. More words crackled back, some she understood.

"Why you wait for me?" she dared to ask.

"Boy child," the Ulaggi grunted, touching her distended belly.

For this Pake was perversely glad. They would take the boy from her. Mothers never saw their sons die, only their daughters. Daughters became mothers, and mothers died many times—a death for every stolen male child; a death for every daughter cursed too soon with womanhood.

"Also, better you here . . ." the technician continued, "when daughter is sowed."

The cycle starts anew. Pake had been the youngest of five daughters, and still only a child when they took her mother away for the last time. She could not remember her mother's face, but knew her mother's stories, repeated as litany by her older sisters. Wondrous thing, her mother had known another planet, another world, another life. But even those magical tellings had grown dim.

"Wait you," the technician grunted. "For daughter."

Pake dropped to the bench and closed her eyes. Another rush of static came from the radio. She winced and lowered her head into her callused hands. Her oldest daughter, no longer a child, would be pregnant. With her first baby. Of many.

Pake would take Little One home. She would hug her. It was all she could do.

SECTION ONE

LIVING IN FEAR

ONE

TO KISS A TIGER

"Make ship ready for jump exit," *Eire*'s boatswain of the watch droned. "Tether down. Tether down. Now jump exit."

Fleet Admiral Runacres, on the mothership's flag bridge, monitored a kaleidoscopic array of status screens. The Tellurian Legion First Fleet task force, eight motherships and three auxiliaries locked in gravitronic matrix, approached destination coordinates, designation Pitcairn System.

"Jump exit thirty seconds," the tactical watch officer barked.

"All ships alpha-alpha," Commodore Wells boomed, a little too loudly. Even Runacres's imperturbable operations officer was showing the strain of being this deep in the Red Zone.

"Very well," Runacres replied, floating into his acceleration tethers. He rechecked battle armor integrity on his helmet headup. A metallic taste flooded his throat—a familiar sensation, felt prior to every jump exit. Not fear, but something proximate, a precursor to the inevitable flood of adrenaline.

"Ready to launch corvettes," Captain Wooden, the corvette group-leader, reported. "Screen command is Eagle."

"Carmichael's got the point again," Runacres remarked.

"Best pilot for the job," Wooden replied.

Runacres had no dispute with that claim. Jake Carmichael was the ace of the fleet; in fact a double ace, with eleven kills: six konish interceptors and five Ulaggi—the only two-race ace in the fleet.

"Launch on my command," Runacres ordered.

"Aye aye, Admiral," the corvette group-leader responded.

* * *

On the cramped flight deck of *Eagle One*, Commander Joyman K. Carmichael monitored screen tactical, interrogating unit status telemetry. A steady stream of controller chatter cluttered the flight ops circuit.

"Osprey," Carmichael demanded over command grid-link. "What's happening with your number Two? I'm reading a main power lock."

"Roger, Eagle," returned the sharp voice of Mick Wong, Osprey Squadron skipper. "Two is down. My Five bird is spinning up. Give me twenty seconds."

"Negative. Peregrine will take Osprey's screen sector," Carmichael commanded, simultaneously revising assignments on the tactical order of battle. "Osprey is now Alert Five. Acknowledge."

"Peregrine, screen sector six," answered Tonda Jones, Peregrine Squadron's commanding officer, her rapid reply cracked with anticipation. Osprey acknowledged electronically.

"All systems on line, Skipper. Energy reservoirs at maximums," Carmichael's second officer reported from her engineering console located aft of the pilot stations. "All screen units are marshaled."

"Very well," Carmichael replied. "Setting six gees."

"Six gees," Carmichael's copilot acknowledged.

Carmichael tightened his tethers and tried to relax. The image of Sharl Buccari, somber green eyes glowing like fired emeralds, coalesced in his mind. Carmichael wanted desperately to hold her strong, warm body.

Would he live to touch her again?

From the flag bridge mezzanine Runacres looked "down" on the flagship's operational bridge. Captain Sarah Merriwether, ensconced in the command station at the center of *T.L.S. Eire*'s control deck, was surrounded by her battle watch. All hands moved with calculated deliberation.

Runacres used his retinal cursor to bring up the flagship captain on his secure channel—a jump-exit ritual. A ritual indeed; how many times had they jumped into a new system, leaping blindly from hyperlight, logically anticipating yet another solar system barren of life's spark, yet hoping to chance upon intelligence, and fervently praying that whatever intelligence they found did not annihilate them?

"Jump exit twenty seconds," the tactical officer reported.

Three standard years had lapsed since the Legion's last contact with the Ulaggi—at Hornblower, where Runacres had lost eight corvettes to the screaming Ulaggi horror. And two years before that, Oldfather, where a task group of Legion motherships had been destroyed, along with the entire Oldfather Three colony—over two thousand spacers and colonists murdered. But the worst collision had been the first, over three decades earlier—at Shaula, where the Asiatic Corperation's hyperlight fleet and four thousand souls had been annihilated, without a survivor to explain how or why.

Runacres's standing orders were to make contact with the malevolent aliens and to establish peaceful intercourse. Units of the Tellurian Legion Fleet had penetrated ever deeper into the Red Zone, slicing hard across the u-radial gradient. To no avail. Even with hyperlight translation capabilities, the galaxy was immense. Human exploration had spanned but a sliver of its encompassing expanse.

"You're looking a mite peaked, Admiral," Merriwether drawled. Runacres shifted his gaze to his communication vid. Through the transparent perfection of her visor the Rubenesque ship captain's varicose cheeks were cheerfully rosy. Crow's-feet exploded with droll profusion from the corners of her large blue eyes.

Runacres grunted.

Merriwether's attention momentarily left the vid-cam. "Weapons," she barked. "Battery Four optics are still low temp. What are you doing about it?"

Runacres, not up on weapons tactical, was not privy to the reply.

"Look smart, man!" Merriwether commanded.

"What say your bones, Sarah?" Runacres asked.

"At the moment it's my bladder that's talking," she replied gruffly.

"Old age," Runacres muttered.

"Speak for yourself, space-sailor," she huffed. "All due respect."

Runacres harrumphed and attempted a smile. They silently stared into each other's eyes.

"Godspeed, Sarah," he said at last, his usual plea.

"Smooth sailing, Admiral," she answered.

"Jump exit ten seconds," the tactical officer reported.

The ten second advisory tone sounded. Runacres switched to flag tactical and reestablished vid-link with his ship captains. Their helmeted visages formed a grim constellation. All mothership skippers electronically acknowledged fleet tactical sequence; all ships were programmed into the battle plan.

The five second tone sounded.

There was nothing more to do or say. Would it be the disappointing sterility of a dead system? Or a fight for their lives?

Four seconds . . . three . . . two . . . one. A familiar nausea gripped Runacres. And then came the high-pitched vibration set against a deeper, wallowing oscillation. His peripheral vision swam with gray. The admiral forced his eyes to remain open. He focused on navigation parametrics, fighting to quell the panic that always lurked just beyond reason. Outputs were nominal. It was just another jump. Just another jump.

It was over.

"We're out," Commodore Wells pronounced. "All ships alpha-alpha. Impulse drives are engaged. Grid matrix is secure."

The formation was stable. Ship's status boards processed a flood of new data; the only tangible reference to sublimate from the sensory chaos was the planetary icon for Pitcairn Two.

"Launch communication buoys," Runacres commanded. "Commence full-spectrum broadcasts. Science, all sensors full active."

"Broadcasting on all frequencies, all sensors active, Admiral," the science duty officer replied.

"Very well," Runacres said, studying the gathering signal data. Minutes ticked by. Would the Ulaggi heed their pleas?

"Launch the screen," Runacres commanded.

* * *

The hangar bay outer doors flew aside with gut-sucking speed. Carmichael stared at star-struck blackness. Low on his viewscreen, the system star glared with irritating brilliance. Carmichael's visor darkened automatically. Launch alarms sounded. Flight ops interrogated his ship, designating his corvette first to launch. Carmichael acknowledged. Docking grapples released with a rippling vibration. Launch sequencing lights flashed. Cleared to launch!

"Launching," the copilot announced.

Carmichael used his retinal cursor to activate the maneuvering alarm. He laid his forearms in their acceleration rests, fingers poised over communications and control buttons. He hit the kick-switch. A dull *thunk* reverberated through his ship, and the massive corvette was catapulted through the yawning opening, pushed with increasing force from the cavernous hangar bay, into the infinite blackness of space. Carmichael relished the press of acceleration and sank easily into his seat. He allowed his eyes to close.

"Corvette away," his copilot announced.

Clearance diodes flickered amber to green. The huge geometry of the mothership fell astern. Carmichael pulsed the port quarter thrusters; the corvette's tail slewed smartly to starboard.

"Clear angle," the copilot reported.

"Mains," Carmichael barked, firmly setting throttles. "Six gees."

The corvette leapt on course, gaining velocity at a lung-squeezing rate.

"*Eagle Two* is out ... Three ..." The second officer reported. "Four ... Five ... and Six. Eagle flight is out of the barn."

"Very well," Carmichael replied. He was back in space, in his corvette, jumping into an unknown system. He found himself thinking once again of Sharl Buccari.

"Sector one picket is formed," the second officer reported.

Angry with his lack of concentration, Carmichael shoved his vagrant thoughts aside and monitored the tactical holo-vid.

Icons representing Raven Squadron maneuvered into position. His old executive officer, Wanda Green, commanded Raven. Good old Brickshitter. From other motherships came more corvettes, spreading into assigned stations in a three-dimensional formation across the programmed threat axis.

Concentrate, Carmichael admonished himself. *Concentrate.*

"Intruder alert," the bridgemale reported.

Cell-Controller Jakkuk sensed the alien presence.

"Humans, Jakkuk-hajil," resonated Cell-Controller Kwanna's telepathic assessment. Pokkuk Merde der Jakkuk relished her sister cell-controller's vibrant fear-pleasure. And her own. The intruders were impossible to ignore—an electromagnetic cacophony exploding across all transmission spectra. The interlopers' signals were localized and channeled into the axionic links of the Ulaggi neural-fusion network. In perfect sync, the cell-controllers each brought their six ship-mistresses to alert status.

At long last, contact again. Jakkuk's *g'ort* stirred exquisitely. The cell-controller luxuriated in the ecstasy of incipient danger. Jakkuk also sensed the bridgemale at her side. She opened her eyes. The perspiring bridgemale recoiled; the he-worm's milky-gray flesh drained of color and his stubby fingers fidgeted annoyingly. Jakkuk emerged snarling from the dendritic interface. Her *g'ort* vanished, the exquisite emotion submerging into the insipid sea of self-restraint. The bridgemale, sensing Jakkuk's return to rational control, sighed involuntarily. Jakkuk wanted to break the male's stubby neck; anger rushed in to fill the void left by the dissipation of her fear. Sublime, intoxicating fear. Sensual fear.

Jakkuk surfaced completely into the conscious realm. Fleet Dominant Dar, black braids drifting like coiled snakes, waited for her to report.

"Dar-hajil, there are intruders," Jakkuk barked, snarling with malignant joy. "Eleven alien interstellars, mother! The humans have come to us." The cell-controller shut her eyes, seeking to recapture a vestige of her fear. A tantalizing spark of ecstasy still glowed.

"Yes," Dominant Dar hissed, hajil complexion flushing copper to bronze. "Most accommodating. They come far . . . to visit."

"Too far," issued a slithery, monotonic inflection. Karyai, the white-robed political, entered from her underway chamber and floated possessively across the bridge.

"Do we attack, mother?" Jakkuk beseeched her dominant.

"Honor is ours, Karyai-lakk," Dar declared. "The humans have come to us. They deserve our attention."

"It is written," the political chanted. "Glorious death awaits the serene and patient warrior."

"Honor is ours, mother," Dar replied, golden eyes narrowing.

"Honor is ours, Dar-hajil," Karyai replied. The political was tall, even for a lakk, forcing the hajil officers to crane up at the gray-faced mother's long features.

"Eleven human ships, mother," Dar reported. "Does the Empress's proscription stand? We did not seek this encounter. They intrude upon—"

The lakk silenced the fleet dominant with an impatient flip of her spidery hand, then stroked her long jaw. Dar waited, her countenance professionally vacant.

Jakkuk wanted to scream.

"Humans come to this system at their peril, daughters," Karyai said at last. "They belong not. Proceed as you desire. I will speak for the Imperial tribunes."

Dar nodded, her knife-edged upper lip lifting into an obscene smile. Jakkuk sensed the dominant's rising passion, a febrile blossoming. The cell-controller's emotions resonated gloriously.

"Maneuver your cell for direct contact, Jakkuk-hajil," Dar ordered. "Kwanna-hajil will act as anvil. Fist a'Yerg to mount a frontal attack. Make battle link. Honor is ours."

"Yes, mother," the cell-controller responded, slipping back into her dendritic interface. "Honor is ours."

Jakkuk's telepathic link with the other star-cruiser cell was immediate and impassioned. *Attack!* Cell-Controller Kwanna's resurgent *g'ort* telepathically intertwined with

Jakkuk's in resonant harmony—a sensory embrace of exquisite magnitude, lacking only physical contact. And blood.

TWO

WE ARE HERE

"Something's happening," Wells said quietly.

Runacres studied the screens. The main status plot struggled to integrate the onslaught of data, glowing magenta darkening to indigo around the celestial symbols for sun-star, planets, and moons. Runacres's motherships formed a solid cluster of data. A coordinated sprinkle of corvette icons debouched from his star-ship wombs like pollen from flowers. Areas around the planet flickered with nonrandom activity.

"We have coherent signals!" the tactical officer barked.

Runacres jerked his vision to the situation screens. In orbit around the second planet, icons representing unidentified objects materialized with scintillating, attention-dominating auras.

"Science, what are we seeing?" Runacres demanded.

"Almost certainly Ulaggi ships, Admiral," Captain Katz reported. On Runacres's console the science duty officer's image was replaced by the dark features of the fleet science officer. Null gravity was not kind to Katz's countenance; jowls and wattles shifted and shivered like gelatin. But his words struck like hammers, and his black eyes did not waver. "Electromagnetic emissions in all critical reporting spectra. Cohesive and patterned."

"We've found the infernal hive!" Wooden, the group-leader, said.

"Definitely not," Katz answered. "We have localized transmission nodes on the second planet and its satellite. Estimate it to be a colony, not a home planet. First sensory pass yields planetary analysis of at least an alpha-four class, definitely life-supporting."

An alarm sounded.

"We're being scanned," the science officer announced calmly.

"They know we're here," Wooden muttered.

"That's what we wanted, isn't it?" Merriwether interjected. "We're screaming at the top of our electronic lungs."

"We have up-Doppler on at least ten large-types," Wells reported.

Runacres was not worried. The closest contacts were months of sublight travel away. He had ample time to investigate the alien system, time to beg for cooperation. Time to escape.

"Set battle cruise—" he started to say.

A proximity alert sounded. On the main status plot, icons representing the ships of his fleet suddenly sprouted crimson threat haloes.

"Admiral, unidentified contacts exiting hyperlight at fifty thousand kilometers!" the tactical officer announced.

Months were reduced to mere hours.

"They've jumped subsystem!" Wells boomed. "We have positive unit-parameter match."

"Contacts designated contact group alpha. Six mothership-mass units, designated alpha-one through -six," the tactical officer announced. "Confirmed hostile. We are being targeted."

"Commence jump checklist," Runacres barked.

A subsystem jump of such short duration was a tremendous feat of physics and navigation. Runacres's already considerable respect for his adversary increased severalfold. His trepidation escalated proportionally.

"Aye, Admiral," Wells responded, attacking his operations console. "Jump coordinates Genellan lima-two, category one offset. Ten minutes and counting."

"Do they answer our hails?" Runacres demanded, knowing the answer.

"Negative," Katz responded.

"Thunderation!" Runacres roared, clenching his fist.

"Where are the screamers?" the group-leader growled.

"Fast-movers!" the tactical officer reported.

"Speak of the devil," Wooden said. "Adjusting threat axis. Admiral, request permission to launch all alerts."

Runacres stared at the status plot. A tight cluster of hostile icons had broken from the main body. Ulaggi attack craft would be in weapons range within the hour.

"Negative. Recall the screen," Runacres ordered, his stomach turning hot. A gamble. "Commodore Wells, accelerate the checklist. Let's get out of here."

"We'll lose termination accuracy, Admiral," Wells counseled, his fingers flying. An alert sounded.

"Get us back to Genellan, Franklin," Runacres ordered.

"Aye!" Wells responded.

Carmichael saw the new contacts a split second before the tactical alarm sounded. Smaller contacts, alien attack ships, boiled from the bellies of the interstellars. The fight was on.

"New threat axis," he broadcast, punching in assignments. "Reorienting the screen. Raptor takes the point. Merlin and Nighthawk sectors two and four. Raven and Peregrine sectors one and three. Eagle will be maneuvering reserve."

Squadron commanders acknowledged with tactical laser. Carmichael checked his ships. The corvettes of Eagle Squadron were already forming into battle spread. He initiated a command vector; his formation maneuvered as one, all Eagles slaved to his course and speed.

"We have recall, Skipper!" his second pilot reported. "Jump count has commenced."

Carmichael blew air from his lungs. "Belay my last," he broadcast. "Fall back to the grid, by the numbers. Eagle and Raven are rearguard. Let's move."

He received electronic acknowledgment.

"Check tactical," his copilot reported. "Got more of them. Listen to them. Good God, Commander, listen to them."

"Pay attention to your firing circuits," Carmichael said, his jaw tight: his blood running cold. He listened to the haunting screams

"BOOO-CHARRY! BOOO-CHARRRY!" Destroyer-Fist a'Yerg screamed, her *g'ort* rampant. "BOOOOOOO-CHARRY!"

Ulaggi destroyers, in three-ship formations, lanced through space. Destroyer-Fist a'Yerg, the destroyer attack commander, screamed the name of her adversary. Joining a'Yerg's ululations, in hellish disharmony, were the orgasmic battle screams of her triad leaders. Blood lust!

The roonish attack commander's rational self reined in her libidinous alter ego, not gently. A'Yerg's *g'ort* screamed all the more viciously, desperately, yet silently, for her frightened animal suddenly had no voice, no muscle, no power. The roonish warrior trembled with ecstasy, basking in the flames of her *g'ort*'s residual terror. The animal, sensing its renewed hold, surged into being, forcing forward the destroyer's throttles. A'Yerg mercilessly quelled the rising passion, pounding her *g'ort* back into the recessed lobes of their shared braincase. A'Yerg's first duty was to do battle. She retarded her throttles, enabling her attack force to take assigned positions.

A brassy tingling intruded on a'Yerg's consciousness, a command signal from the cell-controller. Jakkuk-hajil's intrusion was formal, guarded, yet imperious. The attack commander enjoyed playing with the cell-controller's defenseless emotions, but now was not the time. Roonish warrior was she, and battle was joined. The cell-controller provided a'Yerg with coordinate projections. The attack commander acknowledged and ordered an adjustment to the attack axis. Satisfied, a'Yerg allowed her animal to scream once more into the universe.

"BOOO-CHARRY!"

Runacres shivered at the eldritch cry.

"For God's sake!" Wooden roared.

"New contacts!" the tactical officer reported. "Contact group bravo. Six hostile heavies coming out of hyperlight.

Twenty thousand kilometers, sector two. Probing fire. Shields unaffected."

"We're bracketed," Wells reported.

"Admiral! Admiral!" Captain Katz broke in. "We're picking up something else—a plain language broadcast. In Chinese. Nonhuman voice patterns. Multiple repetitions."

"What?" Runacres demanded.

"In Chinese, like the Buccari engagements at Scorpio and Hornblower," Katz returned. "Translation: 'We wish to talk. Hold position.' "

"Say again!" Runacres demanded, dumbfounded. Were they really going to talk? Had he at last broken through?

"It says—"

"Contact group alpha is jumping again!" Commodore Wells's transmission overrode the science officer.

Runacres jerked his gaze to the vanishing signals. A crushing realization dawned: he had suddenly realized how Ketchie's task force had been blasted into eternity at Oldfather.

"Listen!" someone shouted. The horrible, brain-chilling screams increased dramatically, permeating the tactical frequency. Buccari's name was horribly rendered to the universe. Diversions! More diversions.

"Group-Leader," Runacres boomed, "are your corvettes in the grid?"

"Affirmative, Admiral," Wooden replied.

"Emergency jump," Runacres commanded. "Panic overrides now."

"Panic overrides, aye," Wells echoed, hands flying.

A pulsating gong hammered their senses. Threat alarms burped into life.

"Heavy contacts sector one, close aboard!" the tactical officer shouted. "It's contact group alpha!"

"They're coming down on top!" Wooden shouted.

"Maximum power to shields," Runacres ordered, staring helplessly at contacts forming above the firing cones of his main batteries. There was no time to maneuver ship. Their only hope was to escape into hyperspace. Was there time?

"Fifteen seconds," Wells reported. "All links firm."

Threat alarms brayed futilely. Acquisition and fire-control computers screeched maneuvering advisories. Shield sensors pulsated ominously. Hostile icons materialized with dismaying clarity.

"Ten seconds," Wells reported, his voice like iron.

An eternity. Yodeling banshee wails haunted the alarm-filled cacophony, a discordant bedlam. Again Buccari's tortured name rose above the din like a cork bobbing in a storm.

"Secure that frequency," Runacres ordered.

"Aye, sir," responded the tactical officer. The unholy screaming was squelched.

"Five seconds," Wells reported.

"*Corse* is getting pounded!" shouted the tactical officer.

Status images revealed *Corse* to be at the focus of burgeoning enemy battery fire. Her icon blossomed with casualty parameters; telemetry indicated her shields were gone. *Baffin* was also taking fire.

"Three . . . two . . ." someone shouted.

The nauseating vibrations of hyperlight swept Runacres like sweet summer rain. He held his breath. Would the grid matrix survive the attack, or would they stumble out of the jump, still in the clutches of the Ulaggi? Or worse, would they eject from hyperlight light-years from any star, without the ability to reform a grid?

The unsettling vibrations continued. There had been no catastrophe. They had made it. The Tellurian Legion First Fleet was once again in the gravitronic womb, safe but for the relentless passage of time.

And in time the transition vibrations ceased.

"Report," Runacres shouted, ripping off his helmet. Perspiration exploded from his hairless head, shimmering about him like a halo.

"All units except *Corse* alpha-alpha," Commodore Wells reported. "*Corse* has category one thermal damage. Her shields were fried and her hull penetrated. Captain Foxx's damage control teams have stabilized the situation. *Corse*'s grid-link is secure and redundant. *Baffin* suffered a shield blowout, but no penetrations. No other serious damage reported."

"Group-Leader?" Runacres demanded.

"Except for one hell of a rough ride, all corvettes are unharmed and captured in the grid," Wooden reported. "Recovering by squadrons now."

"Injuries?" Runacres demanded.

"*Corse* has two dead," the tactical officer reported. "Four remediated fatalities. Another two dozen serious injuries, and a load of radtox cases."

Runacres tightened his jaw and glanced down at his comm-vid. Merriwether's image stared up at him.

"More deaths," he said.

"Consider instead how many were saved, Admiral," Merri-wether counseled.

He nodded, the reality of what he had just witnessed hitting like a club. He closed his eyes and swallowed his fear. The Ulaggi interstellars had performed a deadly accurate, sub-system hyperlight jump! A fantastic tactical weapon.

"Except for *Corse*, all ships stand down from General Quarters," Runacres ordered.

Wells acknowledged.

"How did their ships stay together?" Merriwether asked.

"How did their crews survive spatial displacement?" Runacres replied, struggling to formulate a counter to the enemy's overwhelming maneuvering advantage.

"Robot ships?" Wells offered.

"I don't think so," Captain Katz joined in. "Signal patterns from the ships indicate a biological entity . . . Admiral, I've just been shown another plain language intercept, also in Chinese."

"Go," Runacres replied.

Katz hit a button. "Analysis indicates," he continued, "this transmission originated from the planet proper."

A recorded transmission filled the silence: "*Aw dei hai doe. Aw dei hai—*"

"It translates as follows," Katz said. " 'We are here. We

are . . .' Just the one sentence and the partial repetition. The signal was obviously interrupted."

"Your assessment, Captain?" Runacres said.

"Human voice pattern, Admiral," Katz replied.

"Human!" Runacres exclaimed.

"Ninety-eight percent probability," Katz replied.

"Survivors of Shaula?" Wooden ventured.

"Or their children," Merriwether interjected.

"I have an analysis on the sensor sweeps compiling, Admiral," Katz said. "Planet profile, the works. We took a reasonably good scan."

"Later," Runacres said, ordering his growing list of priorities. "I've got *Corse* and her crew to worry about now."

"Aye aye, Admiral," Katz replied, signing off.

"Transit time," Runacres demanded.

"Genellan lima-two in forty-four standard days," Wells replied. "We'll be coming in wide. Estimate ten days of sublight to orbit."

"Let's hope the bastards don't follow us," Wooden said.

"One crisis at a time," Runacres replied, but he worried about the same thing. This battle likely had another chapter to play. Ulaggi ships had followed him on jumps in the past.

"Set the transit watch, Franklin," he ordered.

"Aye aye, Admiral," Wells replied, pulling the helmet from his massive bald head. His ebony skull was silvered with a patina of perspiration. A senior operations watchstander floated up to relieve the commodore at the operations console.

"Group-Leader, have a corvette ready to take me to *Corse*."

"Aye aye, Admiral," Wooden replied.

Runacres rubbed his eyes and opened a private circuit to his flagship captain.

"Losing my nerve, Sarah," Runacres exhaled.

"Discretion is the better part of valor," Merriwether replied, her mottled pink features drawn with the press of command. "We were about to be vaporized."

"I am so weary of stuffing my tail between my legs," Runacres grumbled. "Someday we will have a go at them."

"Be thankful you still have a tail to stuff," Merriwether drawled.

He glanced at his comm-vid. Merriwether's three-dimensional countenance, acceleration-battered and space-worn, filled the small screen. Her sweet smile was a tonic.

"One of inferior breeding might presume your statement awkward, if not amative, Captain," Runacres said.

"Six weeks to Genellan orbit, Admiral," Merriwether replied, her voice dropping to a husky whisper. "Get some rest, space-sailor."

She used her tactical override to disconnect.

A last roonish shriek died wistfully among the stars.

Gone. The aliens had jumped. Jakkuk's blood coursed hotly through distended veins; her primal instincts screamed for pursuit. Battle on near even terms had been joined; there was no honor in retreat. Jakkuk strained to embrace her retreating passion, treasuring the last vestiges of her *g'ort*'s wanton urges.

Cell-Controller Kwanna's feedback-demanding telepathic link jolted Jakkuk to rational action. Jakkuk's tenuous fear-animal whisked into the recesses of her mind. Frustrated, Jakkuk concentrated on Kwanna's telepathic link. Her sister cell-controller registered the alien's departure radial. Jakkuk measured its intensity and direction and accepted the report. If only the tribunes would authorize pursuit and reconnaissance.

Jakkuk pondered the Imperial tribunes' reluctance. The Imperial fleets remained locked in defensive positions in the Kar-Ulag and Tir-Ulag systems, while the rebels under Dominant i'Tant held rein over I'rd-Ulag. I'Tant's huge ships had intimidated the tribunes, but this was a threat from outside the empire. Now that humans had penetrated so near the home worlds, surely the Empress would signal action.

"Blood, but roons are insufferable," Kwanna communicated, an implicit plea for assistance. Jakkuk joined her sister cell-controller in transmitting a telepathic recall, compelling the roonish attack craft to return to their interstellars. She fended off the insinuating emotional reflections that inevitably came from roonish pilots returning from battle, their *g'ort* high, their blood lust unsatisfied. The cell-controllers liberally employed the power of the dendritic interfaces to quell the emotional chaos. The destroyer pilots begrudgingly acquiesced, muzzling their howling alter egos and setting course for rendezvous.

Jakkuk allowed a portion of her awareness to monitor her physical surroundings. A brooding silence on the bridge had continued for too long. The smoldering tension between the fleet dominant and the political was palpable. Unquestionably both hajil and lakk desired to pursue the aliens, to punish the humans for their brazen foray into Ulaggi spheres, to destroy them before they became too powerful. Had roons been in charge, there would have been no hesitation; a roon always ran down the foe. For a roon, victory without annihilating the enemy was a tasteless meal.

"They have offended our boundaries," Dar growled.

"Return your ships to support orbit, daughter," Karyai slithered. "The ore harvest will be completed."

"Our blood is hot, mother," the dominant remonstrated.

"Your mission is clear, daughter," the political sneered.

"They have come—"

"It is written: 'Impetuous courage is the way of the beast.' "

An insult! The dominant inhaled magnificently.

"Attend," the lakk hissed.

THREE

DAWN ON THE CLIFFS

Far below, the Great River thundered. Spirit-lamps, their orange globes haloed with shreds of windblown steam, cast a dismal luminescence.

"Farewell, brave husband," Gliss chirped, ebony eyes glittering with amber reflections.

"Farewell, mother-of-my-offspring," the warrior replied.

The sable-furred beauty blinked; her double-lidded, red-rimmed eyes squeezed forth more tears. Gliss attempted to avert her gloomy demeanor, but Brappa tenderly held his wife's knobby head against his own, transmitting a vibrant symphony of affection. Gliss responded in kind, at once stimulating, loving, and forlorn.

Brappa pulled away. His wife smiled, showing rows of razor-teeth white against crimson maw. The warrior was overcome with her beauty.

"My love," Gliss whispered.

Gently pushing from his wife's embrace, the hunter bounded upon the flower-bedecked wall before the chasm. His gaze rested one last time upon his home. Beyond his mate, Greatmother Upolu restrained his unfledged offspring at the stony threshold of his abode. Brappa would bid his oldest sons farewell on the morrow.

"Farewell, my life," Brappa said, diving into the mists.

His return to the stars begun, the warrior glided through morning fog, echo-ranging along the rugged cliffside, past steaming vents giving welcome relief to wind-chilled droplets accumulating on his snout and wings. Brappa was grateful for the long-leg body armor; its hard surface repelled moisture.

The stubby deathstick holstered at his hip impeded wing movement far less than bow and pike.

Constellations of mist-dimmed spirit-lamps flitted past, marking the abodes of cliff dwellers. These were incidental to navigation, for Brappa's sonic sensors etched the vertical terrain into his brain. Ahead was the lift platform, its metal-edged decking returning distinctive echoes. The elevator moved upward, hoist chains grinding. Brappa adjusted his trajectory, beating his great membranes with slow, powerful strokes. Cliff dwellers riding the conveyance sensed Brappa's sonic probes and made room for the hunter's graceful touchdown.

Folding his wings, Brappa turned to face the impending day, visible through rents in the mist. The small moon, a lumpy crescent climbing above a perfect horizon, heralded the dawn. A glittering raft of stars yet danced, but their number fast dwindled.

Under the scrutiny of fretful steam users, the lift reached the topmost terminus. The tunnels converging upward were clogged with hunters, young and old, dressed for battle. Guilders, taller than hunters and without weapons, also trekked for the plateau; Brappa observed steam users, gardeners, stonemasons, and fishers moving along in small clusters. Ahead, winding up the main ramp to the surface, was the procession of elders. Those most ancient guilders were surrounded by apprentices bearing luminous spirit-globes.

Brappa hoisted himself through a guarded sentry egress and clambered past duty barracks, murder-ports, and deadfalls, to exit a sally port. The warrior, confronting the mind-numbing precipice of the river chasm, climbed nimbly onto a stone parapet. The hunter waddled along the plateau's rim, his talons marring a patina of frost. Other warriors scrambled over the edge before and behind Brappa, their pikes and knobby heads silhouetted against the dawn.

Sherrip, clan of Vixxo, awaited, along with Croot'a, clan of Usoong. Both wore dark green armor and holster, hallmarks of the star-warrior.

"A day for the ages," Sherrip chirped.

"A tale for all time," Brappa continued the litany, inspecting the parade common, where two score and ten sentries were formed into ranks. The young warriors-to-be, their rite of passage about to commence, were armored in stained leather still of golden hue. In ranks beyond the sentries, equipped in carapaces of green and carrying deathsticks, were hunters already trained.

"All is ready, Brappa-son-of-Braan." Croot'a saluted.

Brappa returned the salute, showing teeth. Croot'a departed to join the ranks.

"Where is Toon-the-speaker?" Brappa inquired.

"Toon and his apprentices have the honor of accompanying the elders," Sherrip replied. "It is not often the elders top the plateau."

"No," Brappa replied, allowing his senses to absorb the moment. Over the scuffling and murmuring, Brappa heard the burbling stream, swollen with snowmelt in its headlong rush from the plateau lakes. Forty spans distant, the rill tumbled into the void, spraying its pulsating fluid to the winds.

But it was the mountains, soaring in cloudless skies, upon which Brappa's attention focused. He gazed at the granite giants as if for the first time. And for perhaps the last. The western range, spread across the horizon, distant snowcapped pillars, symbolic, magical, beyond the wing of any hunter. The hoary crags defined more than a boundary to their realm; the unchanging mountains symbolized the essence of nature's invincibility. To the cliff dweller, the mountains, like the stars, were godhead. Or at least once had been. The coming of the long-legs had shaken timeless faith. Long-legs flew over mountains. Long-legs flew among the stars.

And so now had cliff dwellers. Brappa-son-of-Braan had himself traveled the incomprehensible spans, had gone to stars not visible even from the heights of the plateau. The warrior's mind struggled with unsettling implications. Were there no longer gods?

As Brappa contemplated his existence, sunrise touched the growler-toothed pinnacles. Against a sapphire sky the sunstar's hot glow kissed the western spires and, like a sheet of molten gold, flowed downward, rippling lower and nearer, defining glacier-hung defiles, at last finding the plateau's central karsts. As would a sentry on watch, Brappa about-faced to the east.

Across countless spans of taiga still shrouded in hazy darkness, a fiery limb broached the firmament, rising between twining volcano plumes. Brappa's near field was clouded by tendrils of steam rising from the river chasm. The curtain of mist suffused the sun's rays into a prismatic veil of gold.

"Dost thou sleep whilst standing, son-of-Braan?" Craag-leader-of-hunters asked, startling Brappa.

Chagrined, Brappa turned to face the tall warrior chief, uncle to Gliss, his mate. Craag, splendidly scarred and battle-wise, wore the leather amulet of his rank. With Craag was old Kuudor, clan of Vixxo, ancient captain of sentries and grand-sire to Sherrip. Kuudor wore a winter growler pelt over his crippled, furless shoulder.

"Rising winds," Brappa chirped, bowing.

"The sun also rises," Kuudor screeched. "It is time."

"It is time," Brappa agreed, looking to the long-leg camp.

Over the gurgling stream came low-pitched groans and grunts, clatters and scrapes, the unmistakable sounds of a long-legs awakening. The long-leg bivouac stood beyond the stream defile. Cook fires burned without smoke, small orange flickerings redolent of mysterious chemicals. Long-leg hovering machines squatted in the distance.

"Oh, man, it's cold," Nestor Godonov complained, forging through the fog of his own exhalations. Pulling up the hood of his expedition parka, the science officer crawled from his tent. Shivering, Godonov stepped into his boots and slammed home the ankle couplings, activating the biosystems. He stood erect, his chilled toes relishing thermal feedback. Frosted taiga crunched underfoot.

"Beautiful!" a familiar baritone shouted.

Godonov turned at the exclamation, causing his punished neck to twinge. Major James Buck, Hunter Company commander, bareheaded, stood staring reverently to the east, his sharp features catching the sun's first rays. The major's camp kit was cleanly torn-down and packed out.

Bleary-eyed, Godonov tried to focus. The horizon had changed. He realized he was seeing thousands of cliff dwellers in silhouette against the golden dawn, their pikes, shortbows, and knobby heads as still as stone.

"Wow," he mumbled, kneading his back muscles.

"We'll make a marine out of you yet, Nes," Buck said, his deep pitch belying a rail-thin body.

"Not voluntarily." Godonov chuckled, turning to work on his gear. Actually, he had never felt so strong, so vital. The science officer had lost weight; his spacer's belly was transformed into flat muscle; his cheeks had hollowed. A lush set of umber handlebars bridged his upper lip, and a variegated brown-blond beard swirled elegantly from his lower jaw.

He bent to the task of packing out his gear. From across the camp Sergeant Chastain laconically harried the troops, the noncom's soft basso more effective than any whip. Godonov hastened his tear-down.

"Cliff dwellers make damn fine grunts," Buck declared.

"Whereas science officers do not," Godonov replied, collecting his gear. "I'd rather do vermin research on Hornblower Three."

"Ho! What's this?" Buck said.

Obscured by the sun's low rays, a globe-lit procession rose above the plateau's edge. Hunters stood aside, allowing the cluster of taller guilders to wend its way to the rocky hillock above the sentry common.

"Council elders," Godonov replied. "Get the men moving. We're late."

"Mr. Godonov," the familiar voice rumbled. "Do you need help?"

"Eh . . . thanks, Sarge," Godonov said, turning to see thick, pistonlike legs, pedestals for a massive chest and shoulders. Sergeant Chastain was one of Buccari's Survivors, one of the very first humans to land on Genellan. Sleepy brown eyes twinkled from a cherubic face blushed rosy red—a two meter tower of muscle. The marine wore only field fatigues and beret. A field ration steamed in his ungloved hand.

"You should eat, sir," Chastain said. "I shut down the mess."

"Thanks, Jocko," Godonov replied, seizing the food before his rumbling stomach jumped out of his mouth.

While the science officer gulped his breakfast, Chastain packed out the remainder of Godonov's camp kit. Buck stood there, shaking his head.

"Marine life. Piece of cake." Godonov laughed. "You finally about ready, Major?"

"Form 'em up, Sergeant," Buck ordered, laughing.

Brappa fidgeted, although a human would not have detected the cliff dweller's minuscule twitches. Elders approached, only seven, the other four too infirm to make the cold climb to the plateau. Koop-the-facilitator no longer led processions; the fisher's ultimate journey was near. In Koop's stead strode ancient Craat-the-gardener, wearing emeralds and garnets. Behind the elders came Toon-the-speaker and his apprentices. Brappa pondered yet again: how would his hunters protect guilders in space?

Toon-the-speaker, in a sad parody of a march, broke from the procession and led the half-dozen apprentice-speakers onto the sentry common. Each wore dark green armor and a holstered deathstick; each also carried a long-leg communication machine and a small knapsack over atrophied flight membranes. Once the sloppy rank was in place, Toon-the-speaker rejoined the elders.

"I bid thee long life," Craag addressed the elders, bowing deeply, spindly four-digit hands palms up. "Thy presence honors us."

"Rising winds, Craag-leader-of-hunters," the irascible Craat screeched, nodding curtly. Without preamble, the elder turned to Brappa and Sherrip. Brappa shot Craag a look of commiseration.

"Rising winds, Brappa-son-of-Braan and Sherrip-son-of-Vixxo," the elder chirped. His croaking salutation was transmitted sonically across the common for all to hear. "Brave spawn of brave sire, thy veins carry the blood of heroes. Our hearts go with thee, warriors-of-the-stars."

Brappa and Sherrip bowed deeply.

"Thou assign us great honor, ancient one," Brappa replied.

"Toon-the-speaker, pursuer of knowledge," Craat continued, turning to the shovel-nosed guilder. "Thy courage and the courage of thine apprentices is perhaps the greater, for thou art not by nature warriors. May thou come to great wisdom."

"Our knowledge is thine," Toon replied, bowing. His communicator slipped from his sloping shoulder.

"Proceed," the elder shrieked.

A whistling lifted from the massed hunters.

Craag screeched from the top of the hillock, silencing all voices and stilling all movement. The leader of the hunters raised high his pike. Second-year sentries commenced a ceremonial tattoo, pounding granite with tuned metal bars.

"The long-legs come," Kuudor chirped sardonically.

Brappa turned to see Big-ears and Sharp-face stride from their breaking camp. The long-legs hurdled the stream and jogged up the rocky incline, their breath trailing in great puffs. Stopping at a respectful distance before the elders, Big-ears bowed hunter style, five-fingered hands held wide, palm up. A hood covered the unsightly cartilage protrusions characteristic of his race, the trait for which Big-ears had been named.

The long-leg warriors, with Giant-one towering at their head, had formed ranks. Moving at double-time and with commendable precision, the green-garbed long-legs, to the delight of sentries and hunters, took position behind Brappa's warriors, barking cadence and slapping their deathsticks.

"Now it is time," old Kuudor chittered, limping with impeccable dignity toward his formation of graduating sentries.

"To our positions, cohort," Brappa chirped at Sherrip.

Brappa and Sherrip marched across the sentry common. As he paraded past the young hunters, Brappa looked into their proud eyes. Times had changed: These sentries would not collect salt and growler skins; these sentries would go to the stars.

* * *

Godonov watched the old cripple and then Tonto and Bottlenose waddle to positions in the middle of the clearing. The science officer inspected the sea of black eyes and leather wings crowding the plateau rim. Pikes and bows prickled above the horde, a field of blades.

He brought his attention back to the wizened, white-furred elder—a gardener, by his jewelry. It was not the same leader Godonov had seen on previous occasions; that had been a fisher. The black-eyed ancient was tall even for a guilder, rising above Godonov's chin. The obscenely ugly creature's white-furred head was much rounder than a hunter's, his snout shorter, blunter. The elder looked at Godonov as if the human smelled bad. Captain Two, the heavily scarred hunter leader, screeched again, raising a tooth-filled maw to the sky.

Lizard Lips appeared at Godonov's side, punching industriously on the Legion communicator. The shovel-nosed guilder displayed the device with no little exasperation.

MORNING GREETINGS. FOLLOW, the icons comanded.

Godonov bowed hesitantly and turned to follow the guilder. Sentries banging on the rocks provided a marching beat, but Lizard Lips shambled to his own accommodation. Godonov concentrated on maintaining interval. As they took positions before Lizard's apprentices, Captain Two screeched again. The tattoo ceased. An unnatural silence descended on the mobbed common. The burbling stream became audible, and the wind freshened with the rising sun.

Captain Two stood alone and silent atop the hillock. Pivoting, the hunter raised his wings to embrace the four winds. At each cardinal point, Captain Two screamed hauntingly. The mob stirred and joined in, merging thunderously with Captain Two's harmonics. The hairs on Godonov's scalp bristled with emotional electricity. A powerful resonance rattled the air. The science officer's sinuses vibrated. Dust elevated from the ground—a compelling sensation, hope and fear commingled.

The harmonic crescendo abruptly ceased. Again, stream noises came to Godonov's senses, as did the soft thumping of blood coursing through his veins. Godonov glanced about; all cliff dwellers, tooth-filled maws agape, black eyes unblinking with obedient rapture, were focused on Captain Two. The hunter leader screeched fiercely and thrust his black pike downward. The crippled old hunter, only a few paces away, whistled piercingly, making Godonov start. The drummers initiated a quick beat, and the sentries sidestepped with talon-clicking precision. The cliff dwellers mobbing the periphery chirped raucously in time.

Captain Two screeched again, brandishing his pike, this time in Tonto's direction. Tonto sang out. The rock pounders redoubled their efforts, adding ringing flourishes. One by one Tonto's older warriors stepped forward, marching in time to the frenetic timpani. Each green-armored hunter marched into the sentry formation and took position, forming interleaved ranks with the leather-armored sentries.

The sentry common roiled with nervous movement and sounds. Captain Two raised his arms. Silence fell, the gurgling of the stream once more ascendant. Captain Two screeched lustily, and the cliffside was drowned in a ritual bedlam. Godonov recognized the discordant patterns of the hunter's death song. All warriors present sang for death, for a death of honor, for a passage to final peace. The death song was a hunter's plaintive acknowledgment that life was short, that he would fight to the limits of his strength—and that when the time came, he would be ready to die, to become one with his world.

The hideous screaming built level upon level. Captain Two raised his pike, and the din swelled to a crescendo. The drummers initiated a march tempo with side beats and flourishes. Bottlenose joined Tonto at the formation head. The mob parted before them, and the hunters marched over the cliff edge, deploying their membranes with explosive power. The formation followed, one rank at a time, to the whistling shrieks of the multitude.

Tonto and Bottlenose set their wings on fresh updrafts and circled over the chasm. Their formation swelled with new flyers, the ranks sliding outward until a large vee was formed. The entire complement on the wing, the company of star-warriors veered to the east, allowing the rising winds to push them from the plateau.

The shrieking from those hunters left behind increased in shrillness. Masses of winged cliff dwellers poured off the plateau edge, leaping out over the river chasm and heaving upward on currents rising stiffly against the face of the plateau. A billowing, screaming horde of black bodies soared upward, tribute to those about to travel the stars. The wavering vee of Tonto's star-warriors faded to a faint line above the eastern horizon while the rest of the hunter population swirled upward, darkening the sky.

"Sergeant Chastain," Buck shouted. "Load 'em up!"

As Chastain barked commands, Godonov brought his eyes back to the parade common. The procession of elders shuffled away. Lizard Lips chirped loudly. The steam user and his apprentices stared at the science officer expectantly.

"Go with Giant-one," Godonov waved his hands, flashing a hybrid cliff dweller sign language.

Lizard Lips, chittering constantly, waddle-trotted after the marines. The apprentices, with little uniformity of motion, followed. Godonov watched the marine ranks pound with martial precision toward the helos, with the whistling cliff dwellers sauntering in their train. He laughed and craned upward to take a last look at the oily column of hunters screaming overhead.

"C'mon, Nes," Buck said, slapping the science officer's shoulder. "We just got fifty more cliff dwellers to train."

"We're getting good at it," Godonov replied.

FOUR

TECHNOLOGY TRANSFER

From the observation blister on hyperlight battleship *House Ollant*'s command bridge, Tar Fell stared into the depths of space. Genellan lay ahead, a brilliant opal set in star-splattered ebony.

"Firing!" commanded Magoon, Tar Fell's flotilla commander.

Salvos of energy resonated his flagship. Razor-thin lines of blue-white destruction converged in a vicious thermal enfilade from hyperlight battleships *Star Nappo* and *Thullolia*, all passing precisely through a computer-generated point in space. The fourth ship in Tar Fell's battle line, the hyperlight cruiser *Mountain Flyer*, maneuvered to gain a clear field of fire. Angry flickers emanated from that ship's forward optics turrets.

"All ships on target, Armada-Master," Flotilla-General Magoon shouted proudly.

Armada, pah! Tar Fell thought. Four hyperlight-anomaly ships did not constitute even an understrength flotilla. The Thullolian suppressed his grim impatience. More ships would come. Spaceships took time to construct, and hyperlight crews took time to train.

Tar Fell surveyed the solar system. Beyond his nascent armada, well clear of firing angles, was the immense bronze and silver geometry of a Planetary Defense Force energy battery. Holding loose formation with the PDF defense station, and minuscule in juxtaposition, was the torus-encircled cylinder of the Tellurian Legion mothership *T.L.S. Novaya Zemlya.* The joint task force, human and kone, was en route to

37

Genellan, charged to ferry the first PDF station into Genellan orbit.

Establishing the defense station in Genellan orbit was important, but Tar Fell felt the urgency of a greater mission; his ships were on a momentous shakedown voyage. His task force, once integrated with the Tellurian Legion First Fleet, would jump into the infinite distance—the first hyperlight deployment by konish ships. Tar Fell's emotions welled with anticipation; his joy and fear bladders discharged profligately. He cared not.

"Simulate emergency jump," broadcast a human voice. The human female sang the konish northern dialect with an enchanting liquid inflection. "Full emergency radical maneuvers."

Magoon, eye tufts limp with exasperation, turned toward Tar Fell. The armada-master nodded curtly at his flotilla commander.

"Signal for emergency jump," Magoon rumbled. "Reform grid matrix."

Maneuvering Klaxons sounded. Yet another drill.

Tar Fell pushed off from the station-keeping blister and made for the technology bridge. He floated into the brightly illuminated compartment. Konish technicians and scientists in the primary chamber stirred uncomfortably at his presence. Planetary Defense Force officers and ratings under training came to attention.

"Resume your duties," Tar Fell rumbled, looking through the carbon-glass partition into the human section. Tar Fell observed Scientist Dowornobb, Captain Ito, and Citizen Sharl in the liaison chamber, intent upon some instrumentation. They talked rapidly and simultaneously in the human tongue; too rapidly, the autotranslators were garbling. The human technicians, noses wrinkled and hands waving in front of their faces, labored at their consoles. Dowornobb, hulking over the humans, gesticulated wildly, russet brow tufts as rigid as iron.

The scientist suddenly took note of Tar Fell's presence and dove for the connecting lock. Citizen Sharl glanced up, her intensely green eyes flashing with excitement. Her white, round head was covered with a burr of the darkest auburn. The diminutive human female favored Tar Fell with a smile, dimpling the pearly scar that ran from temple to nose. She also pushed for the hatch. Tar Fell felt a peculiar sense of warmth.

Scientist Dowornobb, still shivering from the morbid chill of the human atmosphere, squeezed through the connecting airlock. Dowornobb, an astrophysicist and astronomer, was an immense konish commoner, as massive as Tar Fell, thrice the size of a large human. Citizen Sharl and Captain Ito easily floated through the lock together, both donning transparent face seals. The delicate aliens wore white and charcoal underway suits.

"General Magoon begs for respite," Tar Fell thundered. "Captain Ito, your fervor for training is unsurpassed."

The diminutive moon-faced being touched his earpiece, concentrating on the translation. Captain Ito, although taller than Citizen Sharl, was slight of stature, even for a human male. The fragile alien's almond eyes were a brown so deep as to be almost black. A tall stubble of jet had reclaimed his wide, round head and broad brow. Ito had spent more time on konish ships than any other human, laboring with human and konish engineers to refit PDF ships for hyperlight travel. Tar Fell's respect for the small alien rivaled his feelings for Citizen Sharl.

"Time-ah be . . . small, Armada-Master," Ito said in halting konish, his voice surprisingly deep, his accent comical. "Drill no from me. Citizen Sharl make drill."

"Citizen Sharl," Tar Fell rumbled, "is a taskmaster."

"Your crews do well, Armada-Master," the human female said, speaking konish flawlessly. Her accent was charming, but her captivating eyes were like spears. Citizen Sharl's skull was wrapped tightly, with skin so pale as to seem translucent, except for the opaque whiteness of the scar. She had tiny round ears and the sharp, mobile features of her miniaturized race.

"But not well enough?" Tar Fell replied.

"There is not a crew in the universe," Citizen Sharl replied, "that cannot improve, Armada-Master."

"Armada-Master," Dowornobb blurted, "I have a discovery."
Ito, brow furrowed, concentrated on each speaker.

"A theory," Citizen Sharl amended. "Although with every
passing minute I become more convinced."

"I have tuned the entire PDF sensor network to collect
hyperlight disturbances," Dowornobb rumbled, "and analyzed
the outputs using newly derived regression transforms. Peculiar, statistically conforming gravitronic flux patterns have
been detected that may well portend the imminent emergence
of gravitronic wave-riding bodies from hyperlight—"

"Master Dowornobb," Citizen Sharl interjected, "is predicting Admiral Chou's hyperlight arrival, both time and
position."

"Gravity, is that possible, Master Dowornobb?" Tar Fell
responded. "Are you not predicting the future?"

"Perhaps," Dowornobb mused. "Travel along universal gra-
dients creates a flux resonance. The closer the disturbance, the
greater the amplitude. I have focused on Admiral Chou's estimated exit point. There is a measurable disturbance, and it
grows!"

"It is difficult to say who is teaching whom," Citizen Sharl
said. "Scientist Dowornobb has taken the foundation we have
provided and created an entirely new field of hyperlight
mathematics."

Tar Fell pondered this development. That konish scientists
were capable of extending hyperlight technology was no surprise. Konish technical endeavor antedated human civilization
by a millennium. Kones had traveled the planets of their star-
system centuries before humans had gained their own moon,
and yet the kones had failed to discover the secrets of hyperlight. A confounding frustration! Centuries earlier the planet
Kon had been brutalized by marauding aliens, likely the same
aliens encountered more recently by the humans. The kones
had reacted by girding their planet with powerful defense
stations, and by creating a systemwide network of intruder
sensors.

"Contacts emerging from hyperlight," reported a technician.

"Location?" Tar Fell demanded.

"Need you ask?" Dowornobb harrumphed.

"Earth transit jump exit, Armada-Master," replied a technician. "We are receiving transponders. Eight motherships and a convoy of five settlement freighters. It is the Tellurian Legion Second Fleet."

Citizen Sharl gasped. Captain Ito's mouth dropped open.

"Pah!" Dowornobb exclaimed.

From atop fluted towers in scattered agrarian hamlets, luminescent yellow sirens sounded an all clear. The steady blare drifted across grain fields and echoed from the yellow, neo–art deco edifices of New Edmonton (NEd), Genellan. At camouflaged positions on the savannah, in cultivated rice paddies, and among the fountains of NEd's central park, heavy gauge energy batteries submerged beneath their albedo screens. Optics shields and heat dissipation gills smoothly retracted into concrete emplacements.

Commander Cassiopeia Quinn, standing on her office balcony, watched as the colony's inhabitants stood down from the invasion alert. The Legion administration building overlooked a sprawling new city. Sharl Buccari Boulevard curved delicately to the south, across the newest section. Where the avenue approached the promenade along the city's main river, a tall stone obelisk commemorating the first Kon-Earth Accord speared into the sky, the focal point of the vista.

NEd's denizens streamed from underground bunkers, preparing for another cycle of settler assimilation. Quinn, the Tellurian Legion's settlement administrator, surveyed the city—the city that she had built, yet a city still nascent. Precise rows of austere apartments, tinted in soft yellows ranging from canary to saffron, lined the wide boulevards on each side of New Edmonton's central park, awaiting Admiral Chou's download. The prior occupants of the tenements had been resettled to residential quadplexes or to agrarian hamlets fringing the city.

As sirens warbled to silence, Ambassador Kateos and Governor Et Silmarn came through the airlock from their pressurized diplomatic chambers adjacent Quinn's office suite. The gigantic kones joined Quinn on the balcony, dropping to all fours to avoid the lintel. A humid, salt-scented breeze lifted a lock of silver-blond hair across Quinn's face. She captured the wayward tress and slipped it under the rim of her forest-green beret. Quinn stared southward, across rolling terrain toward the distant ocean. Stately, heavy-bottomed cumulus marched from west to east, their shadows flowing over wind-rippled fields like animate stains.

Cassy Quinn trembled with excitement.

"Will-ah our meager defenses make-ah a difference when the attack-ah finally comes?" Et Silmarn rumbled in thickly accented Legion. The planetary governor's grainy, burnished-gold complexion lifted to the warmth of the sun's direct rays. Long, russet eye tufts lay smooth over the noblekone's bovine brow, curving splendidly around great gibbous eyes of liquid brown.

"Pray let us hope we never find out," Kateos stated, her Legion without accent. The female was much smaller than the noblekone, yet still larger than any two human males.

"The PDF defense station that Tar Fell brings to us will make an immense difference," Quinn said.

"One station is not-ah enough," Et Silmarn boomed.

"It is a start," Kateos said. Both kones wore Genellan suits but carried their breather helmets under tree-trunk thick arms. Kateos was a commoner, although her broad features had been tanned nut-brown. The towering kones were excited. Their emotion glands sputtered constantly, surrounding them with a sweet and bitter essence, despite the sea-scented breeze.

Quinn's thoughts were dominated by delightful anxiety. Her state of mind had little regard for the depressing fears of invasion. Her admin unit warbled. The human acknowledged.

"Admiral Chou is downlinking, Commander," the settlement duty officer reported. "Transmission delay is under one point five. Uploading standard reports and requests at this time."

"Very well," Quinn replied, switching channels. Transmission delay under one and a half seconds—impressive. With each subsequent HLA arrival, the fleet's navigation precision increased. Admiral Chou's settlement freighters would be in planetary support orbit in less than forty-eight hours; the advance party corvettes would arrive within eighteen. Her anticipation elevated even higher.

"Good morning, Admiral. Quinn, over," she said, spinning on her heel and heading back inside. Kateos and Et Silmarn dropped to all fours and followed. The transmission delay lapsed as Quinn walked into her office suite. There, she confronted Artemis Mather, the Legion chargé d'affaires, bustling in from the anteroom. The large-boned woman was all handshakes, smiles, and salutes, waving emphatically to the kones. Kateos and Et Silmarn returned the waves politely, if without enthusiasm.

"Good day, Commander Quinn," Admiral Chou finally replied. Chou's large square head filled the three-dimensional vid, his acceleration-battered features placid as usual. Quinn sat down at her comm station and struggled for composure. Her vid-cam winked as it focused.

"Your signal status indicates no emergencies," the admiral continued. "Have you anything to report? Over."

"Negative, Admiral," Quinn answered. "Colony status is excellent. Over."

Three seconds lapsed as transmission bursts streaked to and fro over the intervening distance.

"Then I commend to your authority two thousand settlers, Commander," Chou announced. "Permission to download. Over."

Quinn looked to the ambassador. Kateos nodded, her expression unreadable. As Quinn returned her attention to the comm-vid, she made passing eye contact with Art Mather. The chargé's dimpled smirk of satisfaction was not attractive.

"Affirmative, Admiral," Quinn responded. "Ambassador Kateos is with me now. Facilities and foodstocks for two thousand settlers are in place. We are ready for immediate downloading."

"Excellent," Chou replied. "I anticipate the first drop to commence in seventy-two hours. Obviously, I wish not to be in planetary support orbit any longer than necessary. Commander Quinn, there is one other matter ..." the admiral continued, his epicanthus-shrouded eyes closing to amused slits. "There is an individual in this download—"

Quinn's elation leaped skyward and took wing. He was back. She felt her professional demeanor dissolving.

"—uh, Nashua Hudson by name, medically retired from our ranks. I believe you might be suffering some impatience in his regard. Mr. Hudson wishes to be a member of the advance party. Will you accede to his demand? Over."

"Permission granted, Admiral," Quinn replied, fighting for her dignity. "Over."

"Very well." Chou laughed. "Mr. Hudson wishes to speak with you. It was a pleasure seeing you again, Commander. I look forward to landing once again on your beautiful planet. Chou out."

Hudson's hairless image immediately filled the screen. Quinn struggled for her next breath. They had given him back his face, a beautiful face—radiant, cadmium-blue eyes, full lips, and a man's nose, long and strong. A face made whole. A face, oh, so young.

"Hello, Cass," Hudson said, a familiar voice deep and strong, and she remembered how young he was. Quinn's hand flew to her cheek. She felt her own wrinkled, sun-hardened skin. Years of space travel, years of on-surface planetary exploration, years of life, had taken their toll. She was a scientist; she understood facts. She had grown old.

Soaring spirits plummeted. Would Hudson still love her?

"Where's our daughter, Cassy?" Hudson continued. He smiled, and in his smile she perceived the answer to her question.

FIVE

SHARL BUCCARI

Advanced awareness of hyperlight arrival!

Lieutenant Commander Sharl Buccari exchanged glances with Captain Isamu Ito. Ito's dark eyes widened with amazement. It was intolerably warm on the konish technology bridge, but a chill ran down Buccari's spine. The significance of Scientist Dowornobb's discovery was impossible to fully comprehend. At a minimum, fleet tactical defense doctrine would be revolutionized. What else? Only the future would tell.

"Armada-Master," Buccari said, turning to Tar Fell. Dowornobb remained absorbed in his data. "Scientist Dowornobb's discovery must be protected. You must instruct your technicians—"

"Worry not about my technicians," the silver-clad behemoth thundered, eye tufts lifting.

The giant floated closer, his great bulk a most persuasive argument. Tar Fell was angry; the tang of his loosened emotion intruded into Buccari's mask, watering her eyes.

"Gravity!" Tar Fell continued. "These are konish discoveries. Will human technicians preserve konish secrets?"

"No! No!" Ito shouted in konish. "Have-ah no choice. Must-ah trust each other. Must-ah!"

Tar Fell and Buccari turned at Ito's outburst, struck by the officer's vehemence. Dowornobb glanced up at the outburst.

"A common enemy and mutual purpose make for good marriage, yes?" the konish scientist offered. "And trust, of course."

Tar Fell's demeanor relaxed. The giant's gash of a mouth twisted into a crooked smile. His eye tufts settled.

"So, Citizen Sharl, now we are married," the behemoth rumbled.

Buccari bowed, pulling her forehead to the metal deck. As she straightened she laughed openly. The towering kone, easily four times her mass, laughed majestically.

"Armada-Master," Buccari said, staring into Tar Fell's grainy, bovine face. "The Second Fleet's arrival presents an opportunity to test Admiral Chou's defenses and Colonel Et Lorlyn's interceptors. Your permission to lead a simulated attack?"

"Of course, Citizen Sharl," Tar Fell rumbled. "Perhaps, in your absence, General Magoon's ship crews will get some rest."

"That is up to Captain Ito," she replied, floating to a command console and entering mission orders. An alarm sounded. She turned to Ito and saluted. In Legion she asked, "By your leave, sir?"

"I assume we will see you next on Genellan?" Ito replied, taking a handhold and snapping off a sharp salute.

"With your permission, yes, sir," she answered. "I should like to spend some time with my son before Admiral Runacres returns."

"Citizen Sharl," Dowornobb thundered in konish. "I cannot go with you. Admiral Chou's arrival data is critical; it must be thoroughly analyzed. Ambassador Kateos must be, ah ... briefed on these developments. Please deliver to her my regards."

"Ah," Tar Fell thundered. "Deliver also my respects. Master Dowornobb, will Ambassador Kateos accompany us when we perform the hyperlight jump? It will be a momentous occasion."

"She will come," Dowornobb asserted. "Even if it means enduring space travel."

"Enduring my presence, rather," Tar Fell boomed.

"She speaks well of you, Armada-Master, and very often."

Dowornobb laughed, a sound akin to an avalanche. "No, it is only space travel that my mate abhors."

"Kateos will do as she pleases," Buccari said, pushing off from a thrust plate. As she dove for the nearest lateral bore, she glanced back to see Tar Fell with a mountainous arm enfolding Captain Ito's slight form. She was not worried; if any human could manage the headstrong armada-master, it was Sam Ito.

The capacious passageways of the konish battleship were designed to accommodate massive anatomies. Perspiring freely, Buccari knifed through the torrid environment, bouncing around filleted angles and kicking off bulkheads, dodging and overtaking dozens of konish spacers, many of whom insisted on being used as cushions or springboards for her maneuvers. She was anxious to ferry the planetary defense platform into position. By itself the PDF energy battery would not be enough to defend the planet, but it was a start. The Ulaggi were coming, sooner or later. It was only a matter of time.

Fears of invasion were pushed from her consciousness. Even Dowornobb's discovery refused to hold position in her thoughts. She was eager to return to Genellan, to see her son. But also, and she forced herself not to be too excited, she anticipated the arrival of the First Fleet on its swing back from deep space. Admiral Runacres would remain in Genellan orbit for at least a month, for delousing, before returning to Sol System. She wanted to see Jake Carmichael, to feel his strong arms. She grew even warmer.

Arrival in the interceptor bays broke her reverie. The hangar-bays were immense. *House Ollant,* in addition to a complement of fuelers and tugs, carried two full squadrons of attack craft. Legion motherships carried but a single squadron of corvettes. PDF interceptors, stacked in staggered tiers like bullets in a magazine, were hard-chinned, midnight-blue craft, sleeker than a Legion corvette and twice the mass.

Condor Two, white and bulbous, pocked fore and aft with maneuvering ports, sat at the near end of the docking stack, looking like a tugboat nestled up to a school of giant sharks.

The corvette's ungainly form filled Buccari with bittersweet pride. In the Tellurian Fleet's first engagement with the konish Planetary Defense Force, Buccari, as copilot and firecontroller, had destroyed three konish interceptors. Since then she had accrued an additional six Ulaggi kills. Only Jake Carmichael had more victories, but Carmichael had had his corvette blown out from under him. Buccari had saved his life.

Kill counts gave Buccari little satisfaction. Trepidation overwhelmed all emotions, for each victory was a tick of the statistical clock; it was but a matter of time before an outcome turned against her. The Ulaggi won far more often than they lost.

Buccari repressed old memories and new fears and focused on the present. In the vast hangar-bay cavern, flight crews, pouring from the ready rooms in a coordinated ballet of motion, swarmed aboard their ships, their ponderous bulk diminished by distance and juxtaposition to titanic geometries. Buccari analyzed her trajectory and pushed off directly for her corvette, mindful of the massive aliens hurtling about. Drifting across the hangar bay, she patched into the corvette's intercom.

"*Condor Two* flight deck, Buccari here," she snapped. "Status."

"Five minutes to pressure dump, Skipper," Lieutenant (jg) Ted Thompson's deep, fluid voice replied. "*Condor Two* ready for launch. Holding final."

"Continue your count," she ordered. "On deck in thirty seconds."

"Aye, Skipper," Thompson replied.

"Hoot hoot," Lieutenant Sean Flaherty piped in. "Welcome back, Skipper. You don't mean we're actually going to launch. We've been lashed down for so long, I thought we'd fused to the cradle."

She made contact with a grapple truss, using her boots as shock absorbers. A handhold lattice enabled her to parallel the clifflike surface of her corvette.

"Good to be back, Flack," she rejoined. "I just hope you haven't screwed up my 'vette too much."

"That hurts, Skipper," her copilot replied.

"A'begging your pardon, Captain," came the sweet tones of Chief Marigold Tyler, *Condor Two*'s weapons officer. "Tis not often can I report such a positive example of leadership. Mr. Flaherty has been a fine officer in your absence."

"Good grief, Gunner! Flaherty's even got you shilling for him," Buccari responded. "Now I am worried. Mr. Silva, how goes Engineering?"

"Power plant and firing circuits are four-oh, Captain," the corvette's taciturn engineering officer replied. "Welcome back, sir. And Mr. Flaherty did a good job, sir."

Buccari double-clicked her transmission key. The slab side of the corvette was interrupted by the swelling contour of the starboard lifeboat blister. Its man-hatch gaped wide, the threshold illuminated with white light—a pleasing brightness next to the jaundiced ambience favored by the kones. Chief Boatswain's Mate Winfried Fenstermacher, in brown docking hood, waited for her.

"Be frigging glad to get off this frigging sweat box," the wiry little man muttered, offering an indifferent salute.

"That's two of us," Buccari seconded, pushing off from Fenstermacher's shoulder, a spacer's sign of trust and friendship.

"We going home, Skipper?" Fenstermacher asked.

"For a little while, Winnie," she sighed, moving into the airlock.

"Can't hardly wait," Fenstermacher moaned, stepping in with her. "Damn, I miss my family. Sometimes I wonder if I did the right thing. MacArthur's Valley's a tough place to leave a wife with a kid."

"Yeah," Buccari agreed.

" 'Specially . . ." Fenstermacher mumbled, manipulating the hatch controls, "you know, with all them lonely men around Hydro."

The lock sealed.

"You did the right thing, Winnie," Buccari said. "The fleet needs you, and I need you. Now, get your head back in the game, Chief."

"Aye, Skipper," Fenstermacher replied, recovering his panache.

Buccari might assure Fenstermacher, but she could not assuage her own guilt. At least Fenstermacher's daughter had a mother. Buccari had left her son alone. No, not alone. Nancy Dawson, and Leslie Lee, and the other Survivors were taking care of her son. And Greatmother, the old huntress, was fanatically dedicated to protecting the boy. No, her son was not alone. Still, Buccari's guilt would not go away.

Dammit, someone had to fight the Ulaggi. The goddamn bugs. Even her dreams were dominated by the Ulaggi and the nagging fear of invasion. She wrenched her thoughts back to operating corvettes.

They cycled through the lock. Buccari pulled off her docking hood, her lungs welcoming the temperature drop. Glory Nakajima greeted them in the EPL bay and rattled off a succinct report. Buccari left the boatswains in the upper EPL bay and pulled herself through the hatch to the crew deck. It was empty, all hands at launch stations. She pushed into the tight galley and charged a power-bottle with hot coffee and two nutrition bladders with suit-goop. Her stomach growled. Next she floated to her locker and disengaged the flightsuit from its recharger, loading the bottle and bladders into their suit magazines. She stepped into the supple armor, sealed her helmet, and used her visor headup to check status on environmentals. The sound of her own breathing was loud in her ears.

Buccari propelled herself through the top-forward hatch, into the main transverse passageway. She slammed her gauntlet on the flight deck palm switch. The hatch irised open, revealing a compact flight deck cluttered with arrays of consoles, gauges, and switches—a worn gray womb softly illuminated by diodes of varied hue and intensity. She floated on deck. Flaherty, in the copilot's station, turned his helmet slightly and tossed a cavalier salute. Thompson, at the second-pilot station, was intent on the checklist. He glanced up and smiled, white teeth gleaming against his mahogany complexion. Buccari grabbed the overhead grips and pushed feet first into the pilot's station.

"Status," she demanded, activating primary tethers. Back and hip attachment points snugged down. Someone very tall, probably Thompson, had been sitting at her station.

"Hangar-bay dump commencing," Thompson reported.

"Primary and secondary checks complete," Flaherty reported. "All go. Tertiary checks holding. Colonel Et Lorlyn has established data connects. Commander Raddo is already away."

"Very well. Continue," she replied. And then: "Compute . . . command. Pilot Buccari. Station . . . reset."

Her station elevated and moved forward, giving her an unobstructed view out the forward viewscreen. Maneuvering controls came into reach of hands and boots. She clasped the massive, button-festooned throttle and set power for six gees. She used her eye cursor to select a suite of transmission frequencies. She noted the tactical holo-vid looping through self-test. She terminated the test and verified calibration. All the while the master checklist scrolled down her console screen, advancing under Flaherty's and Thompson's joint management.

Horns sounded and yellow crash beacons pulsated maniacally. Pressure dump was complete. The huge hangar-bay doors clamshelled open with stunning speed, and diodes flashed green on her primary control annunciator. The launch light illuminated. She used her eye cursor to sound the maneuvering alarm.

"Attack leader," came the voice of the konish launch commander, synthesized into Legion, "initiate operations."

"Attack leader commencing launch," Buccari broadcast, hitting the release authorization. *Ka-thunk,* the docking grapples fell away. Launch lights sequenced.

"Launching," she broadcast on the corvette's intercom.

Condor Two jolted into motion, propelled by a launch piston.

"Corvette away," Flaherty announced. "Hoot!"

Clear of the static reference of the konish battleship, all sense of motion abruptly ceased. Billions of stars, pinpoints of brilliance, hung motionless in fathomless velvet. Buccari smoothly applied a vertical power coupling, twisting the corvette nose-high to the launch plane. Genellan's luminescent disc swung into view.

"Clear angle," Flaherty announced. "Et Lorlyn's birds are up and out. And linking."

Buccari, bringing her attention inside, checked the tactical holo-vid. Icons representing konish battleships spewed smaller icons, a liquid swarm flowing into trail behind her, taking well-ordered intervals. Colonel Et Lorlyn's interceptor was dead on her heels, pulling *House Ollant*'s squadrons behind him. From *Thullolia* and *Star Nappo* streamed more strings of icons.

"Six gees," Buccari broadcast. "Buster."

She double-checked her throttle setting and hit the ignitors. *Condor Two* leaped forward, accelerating once again, this time sustained by the thermal imperative of the corvette's main engines.

"Hoot . . . h-hoot," Flaherty grunted. "Condor's up."

Buccari checked tactical. From the direction of *Novaya Zemlya* came a division of four corvettes trailed by a fleet fueler. The Legion formation converged on her track. Buccari established laser link with the lead corvette.

"Condor lead, *Condor Two*," Buccari broadcast. "Hand off to you."

Zak Raddo acknowledged electronically. With economy of maneuver, the commanding officer of Condor Squadron assumed his position as strike leader and first wing commander. Buccari established her position as second wing commander, and Colonel Et Lorlyn, the konish tactical commander, assumed command of the third wing. The trailing interceptors and corvettes organized into four-ship clusters and took formation on their assigned wing guide. Within minutes three strike wings, each with twelve attack craft and four fleet fuelers, were formed.

"Eight hours to strike radius, Skipper," Thompson reported.

"Very well," Buccari replied. "Set the cruise watch. Everyone consume a battle ration. I want all hands off watch in their sleep cells. Flack, I'll take the first two hours."

"Skipper," Tasker, the communications technician reported, "you've got a backlog. Message traffic's coming in pretty steady."

"Any action?" she asked, staring out at the planet. Genellan had grown perceptibly larger, a sublime chunk of life floating in the infinite inhospitable emptiness.

"Couple of zingers from Second Fleet," Tasker replied. "One from a civilian named Hudson."

Nash was back!

SIX

REUNION

Hudson stared at the telescopy output, memories welling.

Genellan, so like Earth when viewed from space, and yet profoundly different. The brilliant planet, a global wilderness, pristine and untrammeled, rolled beneath the corvette. Fabulous nine-thousand-meter mountains, majestic glaciers, steaming caldera. Amazonian rivers, lakes, and seas churning with fish and monsters unknown; prairies alive with musk-buffalo and Genellan horses. Field dragons and whip-tailed nightmares; snow lions and behemoth bears; eagles with fifteen-meter wing spans, and mountain flyers . . . mountain flyers. Cliff dwellers—hunters and guilders. Intelligent life.

Genellan. So different from teeming, exhausted Earth.

The advance party had not yet completed its first orbit. The domes of Goldmine Station on the continent of Imperia, the main konish logistics base, had passed beneath their track twenty minutes earlier. Below them now was the vast continent of Corlia. They chased the terminator, arriving with the dawn.

"It's like having Plymouth Rock named after you," the corvette's science officer remarked.

"What's that?" Hudson asked, staring breathlessly at the survey lab's broadscan output. The powerful instrument was isolated on a familiar landmark—the plateau. The steaming, lake-topped table of basalt fifty kilometers in diameter was clearly visible, starkly illuminated by the low sun angle. Unmistakably defining the plateau was the graceful semicircle of a magnificent watercourse—the Great River.

"Hudson's Plateau," the officer muttered. "You'll go down in history like Neil Armstrong and Lou Hata."

"Sergeant Shannon and his marines were the first ones on the ground, not me," Hudson muttered, suddenly sad. Shannon, MacArthur, Commander Quinn, Bosun Jones, Rhodes, and all the others; they were all dead. Dead. Hudson himself had nearly died on Genellan—more than once. Genellan was a beautiful planet, but she was not tame. That any of *Harrier One*'s crew survived was a miracle of luck and leadership—of Sharl Buccari's leadership and the incredible good fortune of befriending the cliff dwellers.

"How much longer?" Hudson asked, linking his helmet visor to the powerful optics. His melancholy was displaced by anticipation. He manipulated the slewing controls, driving the magnified image past the volcanoes, along the braided river until the wiggling channels converged into a single turbulent waterway. It was spring on the wilderness planet, and the Great River was swollen with white water. There, at right angle to the river! MacArthur's Valley, a cleft in the mountains, much of its length filled with an alpine lake. A chill tickled Hudson's spine. He slewed the image to the southern end of Lake Shannon and went to full magnification. Despite the shimmering vibration, he made out the cove. The settlement palisade was still in shadow, but he could see Hydro; the Legion village on the lakeshore had grown.

Hudson was nervous, maybe even frightened, but at the same time he was very happy. He was almost home. But he would not go directly to MacArthur's Valley. That enormous pleasure would come later. Hudson's destination was thousands of kilometers to the south, where the Great River found the ocean; where the only other civilization on the continent was to be found. There, on the Equatorial Sea, were two burgeoning cities, twenty kilometers apart.

Ocean Station was situated at the mouth of the Great River. The konish city had originally been an undomed, part-year science facility, before the humans came. It was now the nexus of konish-human relations. All konish governments had established embassies under its expanding domes.

To the west of Ocean Station humans had constructed a spaceport on the ocean dunes. Inland from that facility they had built their primary settlement, calling it New Edmonton. NEd would be his planetfall. Cassy Quinn was at NEd. And there, too, was his daughter, Emerald Hudson Quinn.

"Reentry next orbit," the science officer reported. "Better get your gear on board the apple."

Hudson pushed off for the EPL bays. Everything he required was on Genellan.

The double sonic boom rattled windows and fixtures. Artemis Mather barely noticed. The Legion chargé d'affaires doggedly sifted the daunting backlog of message traffic downlinked from the arriving task force. Mather plowed through interminable messages from the Tellurian Legion State Department, many redundant and self-referring, most overcome by events, not a few patently inane. She searched for responses to her own correspondence sent to Earth six months earlier. Those she found were insipid or neutral, generating more questions than answers. The hyperlight transit delay was infuriating. There were classified plans for increased immigration, and administrative orders from the Colonization Board demanding the impossible. And countless pleas from well-connected friends and associates for assistance in obtaining emigration status.

"Fools," Mather muttered.

"Beg pardon, Art?" said Jadick Jones-Burton.

Mather's administrative assistant flaunted a silk cravat and diamond stickpin, the uniform of their mutual professional society. More garish jewelry, some of it genuine, sparkled from the man's delicate earlobes. The entire ensemble was set off by his sleek, shiny, too-black coiffure. His eyebrows needed work. Mather was glad she did not have to play that game; her tight curls were naturally black as pitch.

"Just reciting some poetry, Jad," Mather replied with a perfunctory smile. Jones-Burton smiled sweetly in return. Jones-Burton wanted her job.

Mather winnowed out her high priority traffic. Much of even the flash precedence traffic was time-atrophied drivel. The communiqué most highly classified was the triple-encrypted missive from Secretary Stark beseeching her to discover when the kones would accept a formal ambassadorial legation. The kones had insisted on dealing through Commander Quinn's office, instead of the Legion State Department. Buccari's work, no doubt. Mather knew she would have to humble herself and make another petition.

"Have you scanned St. Pierre's latest?" Jones-Burton asked.

"Heard about it," Mather said. Reggie St. Pierre was becoming more than a nuisance. "Fomenting to restrict immigration. Something about calling a constitutional convention."

"Sounds like he's running for office," Jones-Burton said. "Did you know he's put in a request for permanent residence at NEd?"

"I did not," Mather replied, pondering the implications. St. Pierre was Buccari's spear-carrier. He promulgated her slow-growth propaganda on the network link. He was infuriatingly effective, too; his independent news had ten times the access ratings of the Legion net service. The last thing Mather needed was St. Pierre talking to NEd settlers face-to-face on a full-time basis.

"Your meeting with the Ransan delegation this afternoon," Jones-Burton said, "should I postpone it?"

"Whatever for?"

"Admiral Chou's advance party," Jones-Burton said. "You did hear the reentry, did you not? Will you be going down to the spaceport?"

"I'll go to the landings when the settlers come down," Mather replied. "There's nobody of importance on that apple. Quite the contrary. Nash Hudson's on board."

"Nashua Hudson, the Survivor? I've read about him— Buccari's buddy. He was pretty messed up, wasn't he?"

"Yeah," Mather muttered, scrolling through her message traffic. "He's been fixed, but not the way I'd like."

* * *

Quinn, as nervous as a schoolgirl, stood on the ramp of the spaceport's main roll-out runway. Screeching sea birds wheeled overhead. A cool breeze rolled off the ocean, bringing with it the booming of surf. Emerald Quinn, a lanky three-year-old with close-cropped flaxen hair, skipped about the elephantine legs of Ambassador Kateos. The kone, with startlingly quick reactions, reached out and seized the tiny human, submerging the screaming child in an Olympian embrace.

"The ambassador has-ah more fun than-ah your daughter," Governor Et Silmarn rumbled.

A score of kones were waiting for the EPL's arrival, technicians and scientists befriended by Hudson during his winters spent under konish domes. All wore Genellan suits, most with their helmets on. The ambassador's land-cruiser, a bus-sized vehicle articulated at its midsection and mounted on six monstrous low-pressure tires, was parked nearby. From time to time kones would retreat to its oppressive interior to escape, what was to them, the planet's painful damp chill.

Cassy Quinn wore expedition shorts and a light sweater.

"I am so happy," Kateos gushed, setting Quinn's child on her already running feet. "Citizen Hud-sawn is such a good friend. He has suffered so. But now he is returned, and his scars have been repaired. This is a day of great joy."

Quinn smiled despite her nerves. She monitored the landing frequency on her multiplex. The pilot of the endo-atmospheric planetary lander reported the base leg of his approach. She scanned the skies, knowing exactly where to look. There it was, a black mote against the crystalline sky, growing larger—like the lump in her throat.

Her admin unit beeped.

"Quinn," she acknowledged.

The voice of her operations duty officer spoke softly in her ear, requesting Quinn's assistance on the never-ending requirements of managing a colony. As Quinn issued a series of commands she watched the silver EPL slide down the glide slope, stubby delta planform and multiple horizontal stabilizers growing distinct. A fragile undercarriage appeared beneath the fat bullet, silent except for airbrakes whistling in the slipstream. The apple flared and kissed the runway with twin puffs of white. Spoilers slammed into position, and the EPL was past them, rolling out on the long runway. A yellow ground tractor, anticollision beacons flashing, moved into position.

The EPL coasted from the runway, and the tractor took it in tow. The lander was nosed around and pulled, with excruciating deliberation, back down the taxiway. Quinn's excitement transformed into elation. A sea eagle, soaring high overhead, screamed with visceral abandon. Quinn wanted to scream with it. She grabbed up her daughter and hugged her vigorously.

After a fluttering eternity of heartbeats, the tractor positioned the apple in its parking slot and disconnected. From the cockpit the pilot threw a nonchalant salute at the waiting group. Ground-power trucks and cargo dollies appeared. Quinn's admin unit beeped again. Shifting her squirming daughter in her arms, Quinn acknowledged.

"Commander," her duty officer reported, "medical needs a—"

Quinn stopped listening. The EPL's cargo hatch hissed upward and a tall man in a tan underway suit skipped down from the apple's hold. He looked about and saw her! Hudson broke into a sprint, on restored legs, like the athletic young man that he once and still was. Quinn set down her daughter and stumbled into an accelerating trot, spreading her arms.

He was so tall. They collided with passionate fusion. Hudson swept her from her feet, his lips pressing hers, both their faces wet with tears. Quinn's beret fell to the ground, and her admin unit babbled incoherently. She felt Hudson's warmth, his strength, his beating heart.

"Where is she?" Hudson demanded hoarsely, allowing Quinn's feet to touch the ground. They turned to see Kateos approaching. The immense konish ambassador, bending to walk on three of her limbs, led Quinn's tiny daughter by the hand. The shy and delicate elf with corn-silk hair grasped the single fat finger of the cow-faced giant. Kateos's eye tufts were erect with joy; her cloying, bitter emotions tinged with sweetness intruded on Quinn's awareness. Mercifully, it was blown away by the sea breeze.

"Nash," Quinn almost sobbed, "this is Emerald, our daughter."

Hudson, lips parted, dropped to his knees. The child halted and cut her eyes, putting a finger in her mouth. Suddenly she hugged Kateos's leg, glancing sideways through a fall of white silk.

"I'm your father, Emerald," Hudson said, holding out a hand.

The child looked at the proffered hand. "I know," she mumbled into the alien's leg.

"Can I have a hug, sweetheart?" Hudson whispered, his voice breaking. "I've come a long, long way for a hug. From you."

Without speaking, the child threw herself at her father.

"Oh, God," Hudson sighed, standing erect, daughter in arms. He turned, smiling, to Quinn, ecstatically shutting his eyes. She moved close, and the man embraced them both.

"Oh, Nash!" Quinn exclaimed, her joy rampant. "I missed you so."

"We-ah all missed Citizen Hud-sawn," Et Silmarn boomed. The forest of monoliths that were kones crowded close, blocking out the light, overwhelming Hudson with their affection. Elation glands discharged audibly, and despite the nearly airtight Genellan suits, the bittersweet odor was almost debilitating. Quinn stepped in and extricated her daughter, moving upwind as the giants surged forward, gently touching Hudson's repaired face and thundering their approval of the cosmetic workmanship. Hudson, eyes and nose running from noxious vapors and happiness, shouted out names and clasped shoulders as he recognized old friends.

Hudson came at last to Kateos, both smiling hugely. He glanced once again around the assembled crowd of kones, his face suddenly revealing perplexity and disappointment.

"Kateos, where is Dowornobb?" he asked in perfect konish.

"I was looking forward to showing your mate my handsome new face."

"Master Dowornobb sends his fondest regards," Kateos replied, her Legion fluid and precise. "My mate has expressly directed me to inform you—despite my vehement diplomatic protestations—that whatever improvements have been made to your person, they serve only to redefine the universal meaning of 'ugly.' "

Hudson laughed and threw himself at the ambassador's broad expanse, making a futile effort to cast his arms about her. Kateos extended her own great arms and overwhelmed the tall human in an exuberant embrace, lifting him effortlessly into the air.

"This is a wonderful day, Katy," Hudson rejoiced, his feet returned to the ground. He turned, seeking Quinn and their daughter. Quinn, braving the konish emotional emanations, walked back into Hudson's embrace. It was indeed a wonderful day.

"But there is another person missing," Hudson said, "that I should like to see."

"Citizen Sharl," Kateos boomed, speaking for everyone.

SEVEN

INVASION ALERT

Genellan expanded to fill her viewscreen, a brilliant dun and blue body aswirl with clouds. Buccari checked tactical. Admiral Chou's motherships, still over thirty hours from support orbit, were maneuvering in good order, shielding the freighters from the approaching attack force. The ghosted planetary icon swelled as a backdrop. Field lines for the planet's gravity well grew closer together.

"Screen units are coming out to fight," Flaherty reported.

"Roger," Buccari acknowledged. Elements of Admiral Chou's screen slanted from defensive positions in a preemptive effort to disrupt the attack. Revised tactics were suggested by the battle computer; contingency programs activated. Commander Raddo, leading the first wing, broke off from the primary attack vector and adjusted to the counterattack. Buccari's command annunciator flashed, designating her attack lead. Et Lorlyn acknowledged the guide shift.

"New vector. Five gees, ten seconds," she broadcast on laser link, setting throttles. Flaherty hit the maneuvering alarm.

Buccari checked tactical again. She refined her heading with a burst of nose thruster. Et Lorlyn acknowledged. Satisfied that her telemetry had reoriented the attack force, she hammered ignitors.

"H-Hoot," Flaherty grunted.

Ten seconds lapsed. The acceleration timed out. Buccari glanced at tactical. Both attack wings remained in good order, the konish interceptor pilots demonstrating high levels of proficiency. Some of the konish pilots had been flying in space longer than she had been alive.

"Energy reservoirs recovering," Thompson reported.

"Engagement range two hours," Gunner Tyler reported. "All weapon systems energized."

"Bogies are reacting," Flaherty grunted.

Buccari watched the Second Fleet's screen maneuver to the new attack formation. Commander Raddo's diversion was already causing disruptions.

On board *House Ollant* newly installed HLA activity alarms sounded. Scientist Dowornobb shook his head. The gravitronic flux anomaly was still there, perhaps even increased.

"Is wrong?" Captain Ito asked, floating over to observe.

"Uncertain," Dowornobb replied. "I am detecting a disturbance, but . . ."

Dowornobb modified his search parameters again, broadening scan angles, filtering out background disturbances caused by local gravitation fields. The Planetary Defense Force's detection network, a systemwide web of sensor arrays, had been programmed to scan against Dowornobb's search parameters. The scientist reinitiated the search. Detection alarms sounded immediately.

"It is too sensitive," said Scientist H'Aare. "The sensor arrays are not having time to report back. It should take hours, not seconds."

"I agree," Scientist Mirrtis said. "Local gravitational fields are in constant flux."

"Perhaps," Dowornobb allowed, adjusting filtering parameters once again and initiating another scan. The sensor alarms sounded. Captain Ito floated closer, watching and listening intently. The gravitronic flux anomaly was still there, and measurably more pronounced. It was not in the correct coordinates for an impending hyperlight exit, but it was alarmingly close to their trajectory.

"You must report this," Ito said sharply in Legion. "Quickly."

Dowornobb looked at the human officer. The tiny being's dark eyes brooked no argument. Dowornobb opened a circuit.

"Inform the armada-master," Dowornobb said. "I have data that anticipates another hyperlight arrival."

"We're lit up like a fusion-flux laser," Thompson declared.

Fire-warning Klaxons screamed. Buccari checked tactical. Her corvette had been acquired by at least three Second Fleet motherships. The vanguard of her attack formation, although strung out more than she would have preferred, had outflanked pursuing screen units. Et Lorlyn's wing was streaming behind hers, his flank vulnerable to Admiral Chou's corvettes. Too bad.

"New attack vector," she broadcast. She made a heading adjustment, selected her target, and pushed her throttles to the limit detent. "Nine gees, five seconds."

"Big hoot," Flaherty acknowledged, hitting the maneuvering alarm. "Optical lock on *Madagascar*."

"All units are answering," Thompson reported.

"Buster," she announced, pressing the ignitors. Tethers tightened; acceleration grips secured her wrists within reach of the finger controls. The corvette lunged explosively for the shining planet. Buccari tightened her abdomen and grunted air into her lungs, fighting the pressures that compressed her heart and lungs against her spine. Her eyeballs quavered in her skull. Her vision tunneled to grayness.

Five seconds later the acceleration ceased, giving the sensation of a sudden stop. She checked tactical. Her attack force had flanked the screen. Much of Et Lorlyn's wing had also eluded the outer perimeter defenses. A flight of picket corvettes held intercept position, but they would soon be overwhelmed by attackers.

"Simulate firing decoys," Flaherty gasped.

"Roger," Buccari replied.

"Shields hot and hard," Thompson reported.

"Simulate barrage-firing kinetics," Flaherty reported.

"Ten seconds to cannon range," Gunner Tyler reported from weapons.

"We are taking simulated battery fire," Thompson reported. "Gaming computer says our shields are gone. Securing shields."

"Five seconds," Gunner updated.

Buccari watched the big picture unfold, evaluating the performance of the attack forces under her command, as well as analyzing the viability of fleet tactics. Attacking a mothership formation with a corvette group was suicidal, at least for the greater part of the attacking force. Given enough strike units, some attackers would eventually penetrate the long-range defenses to get close enough to deliver ordnance, but how many attack pilots should be sacrificed to get a mothership? She laughed cruelly. As many as it took, was the only possible answer. They were at war.

"Hard lock! Hard lock!" Flaherty reported. "Stand by to fire!"

"Flush it," Thompson moaned. "We just got cindered. Umpire says we're out of the game. Resetting transponder squawk."

"So frigging close!" Flaherty moaned.

"We're dead," Buccari said. "Secure firing circuits."

Weapons and engineering acknowledged. Buccari employed maneuvering thrusters to deflect her corvette's trajectory from the melee and settled in her tethers to observe the rest of the drill. One after another, her attackers were classified as destroyed, their altered transponder beacons signifying their impotence. Simulated fire from Admiral Chou's big guns ripped the strike formation apart, but the cumulative sacrifice was having an effect. Mothership energy weapons could not fire continuously. The big interstellars rotated as they engaged, to clear new batteries, but the attack had saturated the sector. Remnants of Et Lorlyn's interceptor wing were making it through, engaging motherships in close. Suddenly *Madagascar*'s transponder squawked inop. And then *Hawaii*'s. Two motherships classified as destroyed. Not damaged— *destroyed*. Buccari's neck turned cold. Nine hundred simulated casualties.

Only three of Et Lorlyn's attacking interceptors were still

operational; three out of an attack force of thirty-six, and those units would surely be destroyed trying to retreat through the shattered screen—thousands of simulated deaths, attackers and defenders combined. This was only a drill; in a real attack, they were forever dead, all of them. Had this been real, she would never again have seen her son.

"Exercise is over, Skipper," Tasker said, coming up on the comm circuit. "Admiral Chou signals 'Bravo Zulu to all hands. Well done.' "

"Rog'," she replied, shaking off her fatalism. "Tasker, notify Colonel Et Lorlyn that he has wing command. Send Condor our orbit ETA."

"Aye, Skipper," Tasker responded.

"Flack," Buccari exhaled, "you've got the ship. Genellan PSO, sixty-degree trace. Best speed. Mr. Thompson, schedule a plug."

"Aye, Skip," Flaherty responded. "Time for a little shore leave."

"At least until First Fleet shows," she replied, loosening her tethers and her mind. Soon she would see her son, and Nash Hudson, and Cassy Quinn and Kateos, and all her friends. She would see the new school in MacArthur's Valley and the—

"Skipper," Tasker announced from communications. "Broad-band zinger. Armada-Master Tar Fell sends. General recall."

"Golly mama!" Thompson whispered. "It's an invasion alert!"

"I've got the ship," Buccari barked, sounding the maneuvering alarm. "Flack, marshal the strike wing! Mr. Thompson, get us a tanker, *Now*. Command precedence."

Her flight crew acknowledged. She used her eye cursor to open the range on tactical. Tar Fell's flotilla had moved closer to the planet, but his task force was still three thousand klicks from orbit. *Novaya Zemlya* and the PDF battery remained in company. There was nothing else on the screens. What was prompting Tar Fell's urgent warning?

And then she remembered Dowornobb's discovery.

"Contact coordinates are displayed," Thompson said. She studied the holo-vid.

"Wrong! There's nothing there!" Flaherty replied.

"Mr. Thompson, where's our tanker?" Buccari demanded.

"I'm on it, sir," Thompson replied.

"Everybody and their brother low on fuel and spread all over the damn system," she brutally castigated herself. "I've hung the frigging fleet out to dry."

"What?" Flaherty protested. "There's nothing there."

"There will be," she said. "Strike status?"

"Everyone's headed in the same direction," Thompson reported. "*Condor One* is guide. Et Lorlyn's wing will form on us."

"Very well," Buccari acknowledged, maneuvering to the rendezvous vector. The planet disappeared from the viewscreen. Her stomach lifted into her throat. Genellan—and her son—would have to wait. *Please don't let there be an invasion,* she begged.

"Emergency signals!" Tasker reported over the intercom.

Buccari jerked her attention back to tactical. There it was, at the indicated coordinates: the icon for a fleet panic beacon.

"What the—" Flaherty gasped.

"It's First Fleet, Skipper," Tasker reported. "Coming out of hyperlight, reporting battle damage and casualties. Admiral Runacres indicates high likelihood of enemy pursuit."

"Setting vector for intercept," Buccari announced, her heart pounding. "Two gees, twenty seconds." She adjusted throttles to the anemic setting allowed by her fuel state.

"Tanker, Mr. Thompson," she growled, grinding her teeth.

"Aye, Skipper," her second officer responded. "On new vector, tanker rendezvous in thirty minutes."

"Buster," she said, hitting ignitors. The corvette surged politely forward.

"Okay, Skipper," Flaherty said after the acceleration had timed out. "So how the hell did we get an invasion alert before a jump exit?"

* * *

"Jump exit complete," Commodore Wells reported.

"Very well," Runacres replied, exhaling.

He relaxed too soon. A proximity alarm sounded. Runacres gripped his arm supports.

"We're targeted, Admiral," the tactical officer gasped. "Multiple first-order energy systems. Range closing. Firing radius in two hours."

Threat warnings blared.

"Prepare for emergency rejump!" Runacres exclaimed, still in the thrall of hyperlight's insinuating nausea. A panic jump off a panic termination was a recipe for disaster. Interstellar navigation was too fragile; they would go groping into the void.

"Aye, Admiral," Wells replied soberly. "Emergency destination coordinates Magellan Three, lima-one. Commencing countdown. Fifteen minutes."

"What is happening?" Runacres thundered. His ships had just exited hyperlight. There had not been sufficient time for in-system batteries to locate and lock on. His own acquisition computers were still struggling to integrate the flood of data. Who was targeting them? How had they locked on so quickly?

"Targeting contacts bear zero-zero-three-niner," the tactical officer announced. "Range thirty-eight thousand kilometers. Identifying konish ships . . . and fleet transponders. Positive ID on *Novaya Zemlya*, in company with a PDF defense station. Also, positive ID on konish battleships *House Ollant*, *Star Nappo*, *Thullolia*, and the cruiser *Mountain Flyer*."

"Infernally close," Runacres barked, daring to be relieved. "Secure jump checks. Maintain grid-links."

Wells acknowledged, and Runacres exhaled hugely, still staring anxiously at the firming status plots. Icons representing additional contacts coalesced closer to the planet.

"Identify contacts in close!" Runacres demanded.

"Second Fleet transponders approaching Genellan orbit," the tactical officer reported. "Numerous fast-movers, corvettes, and konish interceptors."

"Launch the screen," Runacres ordered, his gaze moving from the fleet dispositions to the nether regions of the status plots, searching for indications of hyperlight arrivals. Where were the Ulaggi?

"Aye aye, Admiral," the group-leader acknowledged.

"Genellan high standoff, Franklin," Runacres ordered. "Full speed. Set the cruise watch. Maintain battle stations until we've completed delousing."

"Full speed to HSO, aye," Wells replied.

"Voice contact," the tactical officer reported, "with Armada-Master Tar Fell, Admiral. Embarked *House Ollant*."

Runacres cleared his comm screen. The kone's broad, pebbly-skinned countenance was displayed on the vid image. Sam Ito floated at the armada-master's shoulder.

"Fleet Admiral Runacres, my ships are yours to command, over," Tar Fell growled, his terse message synthetically translated into Legion.

"My deepest professional respects, sir," Runacres replied. "Your ships are now under Tellurian Fleet command. Stand by for orders."

Commodore Wells, monitoring the exchange, acknowledged electronically and immediately began issuing rudder orders to konish ship captains. Tar Fell turned to Captain Ito and the two conducted an earnest, off-line conversation. Runacres was impressed by Tar Fell's unequivocal actions. Surrendering command was a profound decision; surrendering command of an entire task force of new ships to an alien fleet commander took tremendous courage. It spoke well for the future—assuming there would be a future.

Runacres, satisfied with Commodore Wells's dispositions, brought his attention back to the comm-vid.

"Armada-Master, would you indulge me with a status report?" Runacres requested, glancing back to the tactical plot. *How much time had they to prepare their defenses? Where were the Ulaggi?*

"I defer, Admiral," Tar Fell boomed after the translation delay. "Timeliness and accuracy of communication are of the essence. Captain Ito will report for me."

The diminutive officer, sorely in need of depilatory treatment, replaced the giant at screen center.

"Admiral, you caught us in the middle of an integrated fleet defense drill," Ito responded. "We were simulating an attack on Second Fleet units."

"That might explain how you were able to target us," Runacres said. "Admiral Chou is also in-system?"

"Second Fleet is entering planetary support orbit with the next settler download. Tar Fell's hyperlight task force, with *NZ* in company, is escorting a PDF battery to Genellan orbit—"

A PDF energy battery!

"Is the energy battery operational?" Runacres preempted. The weapons radius of a konish planetary defense station outstripped any Legion mothership. Runacres prayed that it also outranged the shipboard batteries of the Ulaggi. He glanced again at the detection screens. Nothing. Yet.

"Yes, sir," Ito replied. "But sir, there is more to report—"

"Sam, we met the Ulaggi at Pitcairn," Runacres said, searching the status boards. "And we were maliciously rebuffed. I anticipate the bastards will come out on our heels. I must delay the balance of your briefing for a more propitious moment. Runacres out."

Runacres returned to his battle plans, contemplating his meager options. Commodore Wells had ordered the fleet into a standard defensive posture with the battle-damaged *Corse* removed from the line and clustered with the auxiliaries.

"Franklin," Runacres ordered, "designate the PDF battery as formation guide. It will be our mainstay."

"Aye, Admiral," Wells replied. "Admiral Chou has aborted his approach to PSO. Second Fleet units are elevating to high standoff and reforming grid."

"As would I," Runacres replied, staring at the boards, waiting, forcing himself to breathe. The security alert on his command console illuminated. He authorized the transmission. It was Ito, his image reduced to two dimensions and his voice garbled by encryption filters.

"Yes, Sam," Runacres acknowledged heavily.

"Admiral Runacres," Ito petitioned, "Scientist Dowornobb has demonstrated the technical ability to anticipate hyperlight arrivals. That's how we were able to target you so quickly."

"The hell you say!" Runacres blurted.

The entire complement of the flag bridge turned at the admiral's exclamation. Runacres struggled to contain his emotions. *Was this the counter to the Ulaggi maneuvering advantage?*

"What is more, Admiral," Ito continued, "Scientist Dowornobb has no indications of an imminent hyperlight arrival. Your wake is clear, sir. For the moment."

My wake is clear! Runacres stared for long minutes at the officer's vid image. He had known Sam Ito for decades, and had never, ever known the competent officer to misspeak.

"Full staff briefing on the first watch, Captain," Runacres commanded, at last permitting himself the luxury of breathing slowly.

"Tar Fell should attend, sir," Ito said pointedly. "The discovery belongs to the kones."

"Of course, of course," Runacres replied. "I want Buccari there, too ... and Carmichael, and all the usual suspects. Admiral Chou can monitor on the secure net. We have a great many things to discuss."

"Aye aye, Admiral," Ito acknowledged, bracing.

Runacres signed off, wanting to believe. Trying to hope.

"Stand down," Runacres ordered, easing off his helmet.

Your wake is clear. Never had he heard four more beautiful words.

EIGHT

INCOMING TIDE

Nash Hudson closed his eyes and inhaled the humid, full-bodied essence of a new day.

"Too bad the invasion alert screwed up the download schedule," Quinn said, strong hands on the steering wheel of the all-terrain.

"Too bad," Nash agreed, laughing. They drove south in the predawn, toward the ocean, on the crowned, fused-gravel road. The sun, still reposing beyond the peninsula range, shot shafts of gold through the towering rearguard of a passing front. Ahead, a storm-textured ocean gathered the morning's shifting colors, transforming it from somber slate to a promising shade of sapphire. Hudson remembered the road as a rutted, muddy trail through endless wild grasslands teeming with grass-dogs, gazelles, poppers, and other species of innumerable count. Now the ten-kilometer hard-surfaced connector was a necklace of cultivation, beaded with adobe-walled hamlets.

"I'm exploring the geological properties of the coastal littoral," Quinn deadpanned. "It's on the science schedule."

"Exploring, right," Hudson allowed.

"Once the downloads start, I won't have a free moment for six months," Quinn said, steering the truck through a descending turn. A compact field of oil derricks, dipping and rocking in ceaseless kowtow, came into view, along with a refinery and fuel farm. A hot blue burn-off flame flickered to yellow and orange. A few kilometers later the road doglegged inland and traversed a steep-sided promontory. As they crested the high ground, NEd's spaceport spread before them, the tower beacon blinking white-white-green. Amber lights near the thrust diverters flashed with staccato urgency. A takeoff was imminent.

"While you're working with the new settlers, I'll have Emerald all to myself," Hudson said, leaning back to look at his daughter, asleep, curled up on their camping equipment. "We'll stay out of your way. Maybe fly up to MacArthur's Valley. We aren't helpless, Mom."

Hudson felt strong and confident, ready to face the wild planet and all its uncertainty, but as he gazed on his sleeping daughter he realized that he was also responsible for the safety and future of a child. His confidence wavered.

"Unlike many of our settlers," Quinn said, sighing. They passed the spaceport turnoff. The hard-surfaced road turned to dirt. She slowed the all-terrain vehicle.

"The cream of enlightened civilization," Hudson said, laughing humorlessly. "The political and intellectual elite. We should make them spend their first winter in a homestead cabin in MacArthur's Valley. Get them recalibrated to reality."

"Half would die of the conditions," Quinn laughed, "and Sharl's Survivors would feed the rest to the nightmares."

"Might help the gene pool," Hudson said, shaking his head.

"The nightmares' gene pool," Quinn said, laughing.

"What's the headcount?"

"This download brings the total on the ground to over twenty-two thousand," Quinn said, ". . . not including fleet technical personnel and Legion staff. That's another two thousand. And wait until you see the immigration projections that State is trying to jam down our throats. New Edmonton's exploding. Even MacArthur's Valley has more than a thousand inhabitants—human inhabitants. There are probably twice that many cliff dwellers living in the valley."

Hudson shook his head.

"You won't recognize MacArthur's Valley," Quinn said. "The guilders have built fish farms in the lake shallows, and Hydro's a regular boomtown. Settlers finagle their way north, even though we try to keep them south."

"Why do they go north?" Hudson asked. "Life's tough up there."

"Two types of settlers go north," Quinn replied. "One group's answering a religious calling. Tookmanian's Church—Maggie's Chapel everyone calls it now—has become a shrine. Sharl Buccari's cabin's a shrine, too. Sharl's a saint in their eyes."

"She's a saint in my eyes, too," Hudson said. "It's worse on Earth. Wholesale Buccari-worship cults have started."

"Poor Sharl."

"She can handle it," Hudson said. "Who else is going north?"

"Prospectors. Gold and precious minerals are falling out of the mountains like dirt, and it draws a bad crowd, mostly Legion contract workers at the refinery. I've tried restricting travel from NEd, but the Legion embassy staff and I don't see eye-to-eye on that particular issue, or on a great many other issues, for that matter."

"Mather still in charge?" Hudson asked.

"Your friend and mine," Quinn replied.

"Why don't you send her home, like you did Stark?"

"State Department would just replace her with another one of their sleek-headed power geeks." Quinn sighed. "The devil you know . . ."

"Stark is the Tellurian Legion Secretary of State now. Can you believe it?" Hudson said.

"Need I say more?" Quinn replied.

"What's Sharl say?" Hudson asked.

"She's busy," Quinn replied. "What can she say?"

"Sharl could stop it, Cass," Hudson said. "She could go to King Ollant and ask him to forbid any more human settlement. That's what I would do. Why screw up another planet?"

"Watch it, mister," Quinn admonished. "I'm in charge here, and you are impugning official Legion policy."

"How long are you going to do this, Cassy?" Hudson asked, reaching over and stroking Quinn's neck. "Give it up, and let's move north."

"I've a daughter to raise, Nash," Quinn said firmly.

"*We* have a daughter to raise, Cassy," Hudson replied. "And we can raise her in MacArthur's Valley. You have a planet to explore, Cass. You're a scientist, not a politician."

"I'm in charge because King Ollant refused to deal with another Legion ambassador like Stark—"

"You're in charge because Sharl insisted on it," Hudson said. "Sharl should stop the immigration. Then it won't matter if you resign."

"Sharl won't," Quinn said. "And she shouldn't, Nash. Genellan is humanity's greatest hope. If I step down, it means turning NEd—and your precious MacArthur's Valley—over to one of Stark's ambassadors and to Legion civil administration. Do you want Art Mather to run the show?"

"A horrible prospect," Hudson agreed. As they spoke, a heavy-lifter blasted from the spaceport, shaking the ground and illuminating the countryside with a fiery dawn. Emerald was suddenly leaning over Hudson's seat, frantically hugging his neck with both skinny arms. Hudson lifted her into his lap. Together, they watched the pillar of fire climb into the sky, accelerating with sight-defying pace. The gracefully curving fireball arced out of the planet's shadow; its contrail found the sun and bloomed with phosphorescent purity. Thundering detonations rumbled into silence.

"Are you going away again, Daddy?" his little girl asked.

"No, hon!" Hudson said, squeezing his daughter's arm.

"This is where she found you," Quinn replied. "She thought we were taking you back."

"I'm not leaving you ever again, sweetness," Hudson said. "Keep driving, Mom. Get us away from this place."

The road ended, dwindling to a set of ruts that too quickly became a game trail over grass-thatched bluffs. Quinn stopped on a sandy point above a wide beach. They watched the sun lift above the clouds, Hudson holding a happy towhead. Broad rays of golden morning splayed across sea-misted skies. Hudson looked at Quinn just as a warm bar of light touched her face. She smiled, and Hudson's heart expanded. He hugged his daughter, trying to contain his joy.

Morning light washed the seashore. Swells curling to the

shorebreak lifted from a metallic-blue ocean and were transformed magically to wavering tubes of emerald translucence.

"Sun's up and the tide's almost run out," Hudson said with a growl. "Get this buggy moving."

"Yeah, Mommy," Emerald shouted. "Move your buggy."

"Strap in," Quinn chastised her comrades.

All harnesses secured, Quinn stomped on the accelerator, tossing back twin gouts of sand and grass. The ATV hurtled over the high ground's edge into a steep sandy swale. Quinn ogred the vehicle through a mogul field of rolling dunes, twisting and turning over unstable terrain, until she arrived on the flat beach. Gunning the engine, she drove past the high-water mark. Once firmly on the low tide hardpack, Quinn accelerated, driving the vehicle in and out of the thin wash of exhausted waves, splashing rooster tails into a light offshore breeze. The tide was at full ebb and the forever wide beach was streaked with a glittering labyrinth of runoffs and tidal pools. A sea-heavy breeze lifted Quinn's hat. It flopped madly, held around her neck by a chin strap. Her silver-blond hair flashed in the morning sun. Hudson lifted the hat from her head and shoved it under her thigh.

"Don't get too far out," Hudson shouted.

"I've got a sand anchor rigged on the winch," she replied, laughing. "I've been stuck out here too many times to count."

"I'm jealous. What're you doing on my beach?"

"Exploring. I'm a geologist, remember?" she replied. "Actually I was looking for that island you used to talk about so often."

"Did you find it?"

"You tell me when we get there," she answered.

"Look," Hudson announced, pointing into the distance. "Sea cows."

A hundred meters ahead a sprawling army of giant sea mammals floundered across the sand, making for the ocean's edge. Quinn slowed and turned behind the herd, not wanting to cut them off or get too close. The maned and tusked males, two tons of muscle, could charge with astounding speed and unbridled ferocity. Mixed in with the brindled mammals, pockets of ivory seals gamboled, small in comparison with the sea cows, but many times larger than any man. A raft of gray seals could be seen offshore, porpoising through the shorebreak with blurring speed.

"Look!" Quinn shouted, pointing.

Hudson followed her direction. A pod of black predators, immense and orcalike, streaked below the clear surface, dorsal fins cleaving the emerald water, chasing the seals. The pursued animals lifted into the cresting waves and torpedoed into the air, spume-streaked comets of white. The seals, barking and bleating, made land, and the whales, spraying fountains of foam, continued along the shorebreak.

"Wonderful!" Quinn shouted over the rush of air. Shoreward, an overcast of canary-yellow birds lifted from a tidal marsh and circled overhead in screeching cacophony.

"We can always go back and get Art Mather and her toadies," Hudson shouted back.

"Aarrrggh!" Quinn bellowed into the wind, easily eclipsing the sound of the breakers rolling in on the slack tide. Emerald, delighted at her mother's joy, raised her own small voice in shrieks of pleasure. Hudson laughed, and the beach blurred by. In time a cluster of islands broke loose from the coastline. They slowed to ford a river emptying across the beach.

"We made it," Hudson said. "Spit's still visible. I got fresh water in the truck. Go for it."

Quinn arced the Jeep along the curving line of the sandbar, splashing through the rolling froth of an incoming wave. The island was connected to the mainland by a three-hundred-meter, tide-washed sand spit. Quinn accelerated madly through the shallow wave wash, slewing and spinning over loosening sand, steering determinedly across the ephemeral bridge.

"No problem!" Quinn shouted as the ATV hauled up on the dry perimeter of the island.

"No problem!" Emerald shouted.

It was a large island. It took five minutes to drive to the far side. Quinn at last drove across a sandy headland and stopped the truck in a grove of bent cypress. A sun-dappled lagoon opened before them. Off the headland a string of smaller islands, islets, sandbars, and reefs dotted the lagoon's mouth, many connected by spits of water-washed sand.

"Chief Wilson told you, didn't he?" Hudson said.

Quinn exhaled smugly.

"Are we here?" Emerald asked.

"Almost, babes," Hudson replied, lifting her from the all-terrain. "But we have to hurry."

Hudson's island was one sandbar and two islets farther offshore. They would have to wade while the tide was low, floating their supplies on an inflatable raft. Time was of the essence. The waves of an incoming tide thundered against the outer reefs.

NINE

QUESTIONS

Buccari's emotions tumbled about.

Eire expanded in her viewscreen as Flaherty hand-flew the docking approach. The graceful golden toroid of the flagship's habitation ring revolved slowly overhead. *Condor Two* slid into the groove.

She was disappointed, but she was reconciled to another delay before seeing her son. Buccari arranged her thoughts for Admiral Runacres's meeting. Conspicuous among those thoughts was the implication of Scientist Dowornobb's discovery; an entirely new technical vista had opened. Yet a greater curiosity—inciting fear—was the news of the latest encounter with the Ulaggi; ominous rumor of the aliens' inter-system jump at Pitcairn had spread through the fleet. Joy collided with fear and sadness, for persistent among her thoughts, requiring near-constant squelching, were sweet thoughts of Jake Carmichael.

"Skipper, you've got a zinger from flag," Tasker reported from communications, breaking her reverie.

"Roger," she replied, checking her comm file. There were three new messages. She scanned them on her visor headup. The flash priority was from Group-Leader Wooden requesting her presence immediately upon arrival; she acknowledged. The second message was from Flagship Captain Merriwether, requesting Buccari join her for dinner. Buccari gladly dispatched a consenting reply.

The third message was from Jake Carmichael. It said simply: "Marry me, Booch. Nothing else makes sense."

Buccari's heartbeat quickened.

"Three hundred meters," Thompson reported.

"Three hundred meters," Flaherty acknowledged, glancing at his pilot. "You okay, Skip?"

"Huh ... uh, yeah. Pay attention to what you're doing," Buccari admonished, more to herself. She cleared her mind; she had work to do.

"This approach is in the bag, Skip," Flaherty replied.

Ahead, the curving rectangle of the hangar bay yawned darkly from the white, debris-pitted shaft of the operations core. Trajectory-guidance lasers winked red, amber, and green in concentric oscillation around the amber bull's-eye defining the docking path. Parallax lasers provided continuously updated velocity differentials. Reluctantly squelching her euphoria, Buccari inspected Flaherty's flight path on her digital headup. Her corvette was dead on velocity delta and centered on docking trajectory.

"Main engines are subcritical," Thompson reported.

"Hooks out, optics cold," she reported. "Docking checks complete."

"Roger checks," Flaherty replied.

Her copilot drove the corvette rock-solid down the docking chute.

"Paddles, *Condor Two*," Flaherty reported. "Meatball. Manual."

"Roger ball, Two. Manual approach," the controller dryly acknowledged. "Cleared to dock."

"Two cleared," Flaherty replied, reducing forward momentum with a pulse from the nose thruster. *Condor Two* entered the buffer radius; from that point on, all momentum retardation would come from the verniers.

"Hey, check out the PDF bullet," Flaherty said.

Buccari looked up. Through *Eire*'s massive hangar bay gantries and past docked corvettes, she could see the unmistakable lines of a konish interceptor, midnight-blue and sleek, parked in a heavy-lifter bay.

"Fifty meters," Thompson reported.

"Rog'," Flaherty acknowledged, deftly correcting a high drift.

The corvette's nose eased past the yawning lip of the hangar-bay door. Luminescent yellow receiving arms made contact with the corvette's hardpoints, latching on and governing the ship's drift. The corvette moved forward, no longer under its own power. Docking grapples seated with emphatic vibrations. The corvette was once again an integral part of a mothership.

"Secure the ship, Flack," Buccari said, disconnecting from her station. "I have an appointment with the brass."

"How long we here, Skipper?" Flaherty asked.

"Long enough to get a wardroom meal and a grease job," she replied. "Maintain a two hour alert. Mr. Thompson, see if Mr. Silva needs any downtime and let me know."

"Aye, Skipper," Thompson replied, busy at his station.

Buccari floated through the flight deck iris and dove into the crew decks. Fenstermacher was the only crew in sight, the others still at docking stations.

"Damn, Skipper," the boatswain whined. "We ain't ever frigging going home." He floated in the galley hatch, without helmet or docking hood, a squeeze tube in his bare hand.

"I don't want to hear it, Winnie," she snapped. "Get your ass into a docking hood and get to work."

She turned her back and stowed her flight deck gear in its recharging unit, then donned her matte-gray, black-trimmed underway suit and a docking hood. She pushed through the EPL hatch with Fenstermacher, sour-faced and pulling on his docking hood, at her heels. Boatswain Nakajima labored at the ship's primary replenishment station. Fenstermacher joined her, receiving a glance evenly mixed with empathy and impatience. Buccari cycled through the personnel lock, leaving *Condor Two*'s crew to prepare for the corvette's next launch.

First things first. Once in the hangar bay, Buccari pushed upward through the towering corvette stack into the flight crew manifold; pressure differentials sucked her upward to level ten and into an egress chamber. She selected flight ops medical and debouched into the receiving ward, joining other corvette pilots funneling into the depilatory sequencer. The attack drill had taken the spacers from their motherships for two days, causing them to miss the twice-daily treatments. For Buccari, it had been almost two weeks. She drew stares, but then she always did. She was a legend.

Her turn came. She palmed the ID plate, and a vacant scanning chamber opened. She entered and a battery of optical analyzers locked on, following her every movement. Buccari jettisoned docking hood, underway suit, and thermals, securing the clothing in a transport cubicle. A positive pressure iris hissed open, and she glided naked into the queue. Sonic skinsloughers oriented to her anatomy. Fan-beams activated, tingling her skin as they dug away dead dermal cells. Suction limpets simultaneously vacuumed away spalling layers of epidermis. The fan-beams whined down, and a membrane clamshelled and locked about her. Her tight environment was pressure-filled with a snowstorm of pungent gas-liquid. Reflexively, if unnecessarily, she held her breath.

The tank emptied instantaneously. She was gently ejected from the immersion stall and propelled through an air curtain. Medical scanners hummed as she swept by. A soft tone sounded, and a gentle fog of oil caressed her. She was ejected through the final filtering membrane. Her grease job was over.

Her clothes, redolent of antiseptic, awaited. Her hair and dead skin were gone, eradicated. Her body was perfectly clean, perfectly smooth; her thermals slipped luxuriously over lubricated limbs. Her skin was translucent alabaster, all vestiges of Genellan's sun sloughed away long ago. She smelled like a spacer. Her vision was wider, brighter, the fuzzy near image of her lashes and eyebrows removed from her peripheral vision. She floated out into the dark-blue passageways of flight operations.

"Hey, Booch!" shouted a delightfully familiar baritone. Bart Chang, emerging from Eagle Squadron's ready room, sailed gracefully for her. She braced against a thrust buffer and used both arms to absorb the collision with her tall Academy classmate.

"Hey, Bartlett," she replied, embracing the pilot's hard body. "Heard you had another run-in."

"Had the bugs right where we wanted them," Chang replied

with requisite bravado. False bravado. His mobile features lost their happy facade before his sentence was finished. He was distraught.

"What happened, Bart?" she asked.

"Sharl, they screamed your name!" Chang cried.

Buccari's stomach expanded hotly upward. The memory of Ahyerg's horrid tones forming her name at Hornblower and again at Scorpio rushed forward. So Ahyerg was also at Pitcairn. Or had her name become an Ulaggi battle cry?

"Screw that," Buccari snapped back. "What happened?"

"We were maneuvering to engage. Eagle, Peregrine, and Raven were on the point. Big Jake had screen command. I was on his wing." Chang separated to arm's length, his demeanor frighteningly somber, his deep voice breaking. "The bugs were screaming . . . getting close. Most we'd ever been up against. They would have chewed us up, Sharl, but the admiral reeled in the screen and we skipped. It was a rout."

"Damn," was all Buccari could answer. She envisioned Carmichael leading his pilots into the meat grinder—again. Her pulse quickened.

"The bugs jumped in-frigging-system, Sharl!" Chang whispered. "Their BUFs got up on top in close and started doing jackhammer brain surgery on *Corse* and *Baffin*. We're lucky Runacres pulled the plug so damned fast. Damned lucky!"

She stared into her friend's face. Bart Chang was one of the happiest humans she had ever met, but all she saw in his liquid brown eyes was fear.

"Dead meat, Sharl," he moaned. "We were dead meat."

Buccari's neck turned cold. She pulled her friend into her arms. How many more of their mates would die? When would Bart Chang die? And Carmichael? Before or after her?

"I gotta go, Bart," she said at last, pushing away. "I've got a meeting with the group-leader."

"I know," Chang said, his infectious smile limping back to its usual station. "Commander Jake sent me. Follow me."

Carmichael! Buccari's heart awoke. Blood pounded in her throat and she grew warm. In her mind she could smell him, feel his arms holding her to her wide chest. She shook off the daydream. Chang arrowed straight for *Eire*'s axial transport tube. Together they floated into an up-bore and latched onto slow-speed tractor lugs. Once stabilized, and seeing no obstructing traffic, they dove up the bore.

Level two, the end of line, came quickly. Chang deftly grabbed a braking bungee, and Buccari took hold of her comrade's underway suit, their momentum dissipating precisely as the exit hatch dropped to eye level. Buccari followed Chang through, kicking off a thrust buffer at the main bridge hatch and jackknifing upward to the level one entry. Security robots tracked their approach, and the hatch to the flag offices hissed open before them. Chang floated through and pressed the palm plate for the group-leader's underway cabin. The door signaled clear. They pushed through the iris—into Caesar's foyer. At each august threshold Chang's demeanor stiffened. Buccari felt the same intimidating ambience.

They entered the group-leader's underway cabin, a compact two-room suite. It was crowded; also present were: Wanda Green, Raven Squadron skipper; Zak Raddo, her own squadron commander; and Jake Carmichael, Eagle Squadron. She made eye contact with Carmichael. His rugged features formed a hopeful smile, but his eyes were dog-sad. She forced herself to look away, acknowledging the other officers.

"Ah, Buccari!" Wooden nearly shouted. "The Ulaggi were looking for you at Pitcairn."

"So I heard, sir," she replied, doing everything she could to avoid Carmichael's worried stare. No wonder he was sad. He was afraid—for her. For all of them.

"This will be quick. The admiral is waiting," Wooden announced. "I asked permission to make these announcements. It's not something you should hear through the rumor mill."

The pilots waited silently. Unable to prevent herself, Buccari looked at Carmichael. His soft brown eyes embraced her, adored her. Her heart reached out to the tall, wide-shouldered officer.

"You're all aware," Wooden continued, regaining Buccari's attention, "there are two HLA battleships coming off the ways within the year: *Avenger* and *Intrepid*. Admiral Chou has brought with him crew detailings for these ships. Those officers assigned to billets aboard the new ships will leave for Sol-Sys with Admiral Chou. First Fleet command changes are effective immediately."

The group stirred as one. Promotions and new postings, Buccari thought. What was in store? She glanced at Carmichael. He was staring at her, his eyes pleading. He already knew.

"I am not at liberty to divulge all command assignments, but Captain Knox, skipper of *Terra del Fuego* is to become commanding officer of *Intrepid*. I will relieve Captain Knox as skipper of *TDF*."

"Congratulations, Captain," Wanda Green boomed. The others enthusiastically seconded Green's endorsement. Buccari joined in, but with a faint heart. Buccari and Carmichael locked stares. The group-leader position was vacated. She guessed what was coming. Her jaw ached. Buccari realized she was grinding her teeth. Wooden held up his hand.

"Commander Carmichael," Wooden continued, "er ... Brevet Captain Carmichael will replace me as First Fleet strike operations group-leader. Congratulations, Jake."

The clamor increased severalfold. Carmichael was genuinely liked by all, and fiercely respected as a pilot and a leader. Carmichael ripped his eyes from Buccari's and acknowledged the spirited congratulations.

Oh, how things had changed. Buccari's heart grew leaden. Carmichael was once again her direct commanding officer.

Wooden held up his hands, impatiently commanding silence.

"Wanda Green, at Jake's insistence, returns to Eagle Squadron as commanding officer. Commander Chang will be her executive officer."

"You're sausage, Bart." Zak Raddo laughed. The assembled officers gave Chang a boisterous round of condolences.

"Zak Raddo," Wooden continued, silencing them, "has been designated executive officer for *Avenger*."

"Bend over, Zak!" Green shouted, to the delight of the

group. Buccari was happy for the hard-charging squadron commander. XO on a new battleship was a sure ticket for big-iron command, and one of the toughest jobs in the fleet. Buccari recaptured Carmichael's gaze. His lips tightened into a poor semblance of a smile.

"Last, but certainly not least, Lieutenant Commander Buccari is promoted to brevet commander. She will take Zak's place as Condor Squadron commanding officer."

Squadron command! Buccari did not hear the cheers. She stared at Carmichael. A brutal slap on her shoulders brought her back to reality. She turned to face Wanda Green's beaming countenance and outstretched hand. Buccari reached out and received the iron-hard grip of her old XO.

"Welcome to the thankless club, Booch," Green's gravelly voice boomed. Wanda Green was a head taller than Buccari, generous of hip, and in all ways prodigiously endowed. But it was because of Green's Vesuvian temper, not her Valkyrian proportions, that she had earned her nickname. Buccari knew Wanda Green's heart to be even grander than her temper.

"Thanks, Brickshitter," Buccari replied, torn between the gratifying achievement of squadron command and wrenching emotional turmoil. She managed a smile. "You, too. You've got the Eagles."

"Ain't it great, Booch?" Green said, laughing. They were surrounded by the other pilots. Chang, displaying a champion smile, floated up to shake hands. Green, shorter than Chang, but heavier, slapped his hand aside and pulled him into her expansive bosom. Chang's smile grew impossibly larger, but he was not daunted in returning the hug.

"Okay, XO," Green boomed, shoving Chang toward the hatch. "That's the last hug you get from me. Now get your pretty butt back to the ready room, and tell those Eagle weenies to enjoy their last few moments of peace. The Brickshitter's coming to make their lives miserable."

"This meeting's over," Wooden announced. "Carmichael, Buccari, your presence is requested by the admiral. Follow me."

Wooden pushed off and arrowed from the compartment, followed by the others. Buccari started for the hatch, but

Carmichael grabbed her elbow. They were alone, if only for the instant.

"Sharl," Carmichael begged, holding onto her. "Marry me."

"Oh, Jake," Buccari cried. "I was . . . ready, but—"

"What's wrong?" he almost shouted, the muscles of his jaw working. "What's stopping you, Sharl?" he repeated. A plea.

"You're my boss, dammit," she remonstrated, pulling from his grasp. "I'm just another pawn on the board, Jake. You'll have to send me out to die, and I'll have to go. You can't marry one of your pawns . . . Captain."

Carmichael floated before her, hands clenched. "No, Sharl . . ." he pleaded. "Please. We may not have much time. One of us could die—"

"Don't say that," she snapped.

"Sharl . . ."

"C'mon . . . Jake. Admiral's waiting," she said softly, pushing into the passageway. She blinked tears from her eyes, leaving a fairy's wake of tiny silver spheres.

TEN

ANSWERS

Runacres was fascinated—an answer to his prayers.

"A phased-detector array can-ah be deployed on a mothership grid-ah," Dowornobb explained in thick Legion, presiding over a technical briefing in the flagship's science information center. "The greater the fleet grid-ah dimension, the greater the gravitronic parallax."

"And the more detectable the incoming gravitronic flux," Captain Katz added. The science officer, his beret canted askew, stared reverently at the data—an instrumented reconstruction of the fleet's arrival into the konish system. Commodore Wells's massive form floated above the display, demonstrating slight consideration for his own personal dignity.

"A shipboard detection array cannot provide the omnidirectional sensitivity of the systemwide PDF network," Dowornobb said.

"But it can provide some warning?" Wells asked.

"Yes," Dowornobb replied.

"We can orient the detectors to scan fleet vertical," Merriwether said. "Perhaps now we'll have time to cover the battery firing cones."

Runacres glanced at Merriwether. The mothership captain, intent on Dowornobb's excited narration, floated at the admiral's side, brushing against his shoulder. Runacres felt her excitement, her warmth. Thunderation but she was stubborn! Merriwether had turned down command of the *Avenger*, the lead battleship in the new line, insisting on participating in First Fleet's return mission to the Red Zone.

"There will be other ships to command," she had calmly replied. Runacres was immensely angry with his flagship skipper, and strangely gratified.

"How far out can a fleet array detect an incoming contact?" Captain Ito asked. The diminutive human stood at Armada-Master Tar Fell's side, like a small child. The other kones, Flotilla-General Magoon and Colonel Et Lorlyn, hulked in the corner, uncomfortably cramped in the human ship. All kones, except Dowornobb, wore environmental suits with helmets installed. Dowornobb, wearing a dun cloak of spongy material, frequently inhaled from a breathing unit.

"If-ah you know the direction from where it-ah comes, quite-ah far," Dowornobb replied. "I think some day it-ah possible to have several hours of warning, perhaps even days."

Runacres brought his uneasy thoughts back to the briefing. If Dowornobb's breakthrough had generated any euphoria, it was short-lived. The Ulaggi could still outmaneuver him with local jumps. Even if he knew from where the aliens were coming, Runacres realized, the Ulaggi would still control the pace and place of battle—overwhelming advantages.

A security alarm sounded. All screens went blank. The hatch cipher-lock clicked open and Captain Wooden floated in, followed by Carmichael and Buccari.

"Ah, Cit . . . ah, Cit-i-zen Sharl," Tar Fell thundered in brutally accented Legion, startling everyone. Runacres could not recall the konish commander ever speaking Legion before. "I-ah berry sorry not-ah you see you child-ah. Duty-ah first, yesss?"

Tar Fell, eye tufts rigid, looked to Ito for approval. The tiny human smiled largely at his hulking student. Buccari floated up to the armada-master, said something in konish, and bowed her head in respect. The giant was much pleased by Buccari's words.

"Always in command of the situation," Merriwether whispered.

Runacres nodded. The import of the exchange was not lost. Tar Fell, a Thullolian commoner, was the most powerful political and military leader of Kon's southern hemisphere.

King Ollant IV, ruler of Kon's Northern Hegemony, owed his very life to Sharl Buccari. Buccari had captivated konish planetary leadership, both northern and southern hemispheres, commoner and noblekone.

"Second Fleet's up, Admiral," Wells said. Admiral Chou's blocky visage appeared on the main vid-screen, the image reduced to two dimensions on the high-security channel.

"Good day, Norm," Runacres announced, bringing the meeting to order. Humans took stations on the left side of the briefing dais. The four kones, as wide as ten humans, overflowed the right. Ito steered Tar Fell to a position next to Runacres, in range of the primary vid-cam.

"Good day, Admiral," Chou replied. "My respects to Armada-Master Tar Fell."

"Thang you, Ad-ah-miral Norm-ah," Tar Fell boomed, and then looked about in embarrassed puzzlement. The humans were laughing. Ito slipped to the behemoth's side to explain.

"Status of settler download, Admiral," Runacres demanded.

"Evasive action cost us a week of positioning time, and no little reaction fuel," Chou reported, speaking slowly and pausing frequently to permit the translation programs to keep pace. "Download freighters are approaching PSO now. If the revised schedule holds, all twenty downloads should be completed within a standard month. Over."

"Thank you, Admiral Norm," Runacres said with exaggerated stiffness, drawing a good-natured rumble from Tar Fell. "Getting the settlers down to the planet will be our highest priority. First Fleet, augmented by Tar Fell's task force, will provide HSO cover.

"The next topic," he continued, "is the timing and destination of the konish hyperlight excursion. Tar Fell, Captain Ito has briefed me on the impressive progress of the konish technical teams. When will your task force be prepared to jump?"

"Gravity, we-ah can jump-ah today," Dowornobb boomed.

Tar Fell darkened at the breech of etiquette. The impetuous scientist lowered his head. The armada-master reverted to konish, speaking in thundering, clipped syllables.

The synthesized translation came from table speakers: "Scientist Dowornobb . . . has accurately stated my sentiments. Konish ships and crews . . . and konish scientists . . . are anxious for this historic event . . . to transpire. As are the humans who have assisted us. I commend Citizen Sharl, Captain Ito, and the technology transfer team . . . for their unselfish dedication to this effort."

"Well spoken, Armada-Master Tar Fell," Runacres replied. "My officers have related to me similar sentiments. Your trust pays us the greatest compliment possible. We have become . . . shipmates."

A pause, as Tar Fell considered the response. The kone looked to Ito. The human spoke softly in konish. Buccari laughed discreetly.

"Ah! Good-ah words . . . ship-ah mates," Tar Fell rumbled. The room fell silent.

"Armada-Master Tar Fell, would you brief us?" Runacres finally said.

"The status . . . of the Konish Planetary Defense Fleet," Tar Fell said, speaking slowly in his own tongue. The translation program thundered, "PDF battleships *House Ollant, Star Nappo,* and *Thullolia* . . . and PDF battlecruiser *Mountain Flyer,* are fully trained and equipped for hyperlight. Four additional battleships and as many cruisers . . . will be converted by the end of the sun-cycle. Eight new-construction battleships . . . are scheduled for completion during the subsequent sun-cycle."

Runacres's euphoria dared to rise. Another battlefleet within two years. Would it be soon enough?

"Armada-Master, when may we expect another PDF energy battery to be deployed to Genellan?" Wells asked.

"Uncertain," Tar Fell boomed. "There is argument . . . among konish governments on this subject. Many fear the defenses of Kon are degraded. It is a valid concern."

Runacres nodded. Until Genellan was ringed with the high-energy weapons, as was the planet Kon, defense of the planet was problematic. The Ulaggi maneuvering advantage outweighed all other considerations. Runacres could not blame the governments of Kon for having similar perceptions. Their planet had been savaged before.

"The timing and destination of the first konish jump has been determined," Runacres announced. "Tar Fell, your task force will accompany Admiral Chou on his return to Sol System. Admiral Chou, if you will deliver the President's invitation."

All assembled turned to the vid.

"Mr. Socrates Duffy," Admiral Chou announced, "President of the Tellurian Legion, has asked me to extend a personal invitation to Armada-Master Tar Fell and his ship crews to be his guests on Earth. The leaders of our government are anxious to establish direct communications with konish leadership."

Tar Fell listened carefully to the translation. "I am honored," he replied. "But there has been no mention ... of Admiral Runacres's battlefleet returning to Earth. Admiral Runacres, what are your intentions?"

"I am afraid there is important work to do," Runacres said. "Dangerous work."

"Then I confess disappointment ... at not being included," Tar Fell thundered, his emotion not tempered by the translation. "I wish my crews ... to become fully battle capable. I wish to fight at Citizen Sharl's side."

The briefing room's human occupants stirred uneasily. Buccari blushed magnificently.

"And-ah I wish to test-ah in-transit hyperlight theories," Scientist Dowornobb boomed. "I-ah have ideas that-ah need testing. This could-ah be of great-ah assistance to your mission."

"Of course," Runacres replied. "However, Tar Fell, I must insist you comply with my president's wishes. My mission will be no place for first jumps. However, I fully intend to test Scientist Dowornobb's hyperlight theories, or what we understand of them."

"But-ah I must-ah go—" Dowornobb boomed.

"Admiral Runacres," Tar Fell interrupted thunderously, "despite my disappointment ... I defer to your judgment. It will be a momentous event ... for konish ships to visit your planet. But I am most curious about your mission. Please continue."

"Bring up the Red Zone," Runacres ordered.

The briefing room darkened. Admiral Chou's visage dissolved from the main projection area and was replaced by a scintillating holo-view of the galaxy. The viewer's perspective zoomed inward, toward a brilliant crimson dot that expanded to become a hollowed oblong, and still larger to become a region, its sanguinary brilliance diffusing and becoming transparent. Not stopping, the viewer's perspective penetrated the holo image, more slowly now, until most of the celestial view was highlighted in red glow. Galactic universal radials and coordinate frameworks, razor-thin lines of gold, hashed through the holo image in graceful arcs.

The Red Zone was the area of highest alien contact probability. Sol System, marked by a tight blue sphere, lay just outside the Red Zone's perimeter. The scale of the display revealed no movement, but Runacres knew Earth was moving closer to the Red Zone with each passing minute, as the galaxy inexorably swirled on its axis, realigning universal gravitronic radials, the avenues of hyperlight travel. That the Ulaggi would one day visit Sol System was not in doubt.

The konish system was another bright blot of blue, decidedly inside the threat area. Farther inside were the Ulaggi battle sites, marked with yellow spheres: the first contact at Shaula System; the annihilated colonies at Oldfather and Hornblower; and Scorpio; and lastly, the deepest alien-contact point within the Red Zone, Pitcairn System. Also marring the depths of the red-shaded volume was a lobed region of ghostly white: the region estimated to contain the Ulaggi home planet.

"The encounter with the Ulaggi at Pitcairn Two," Runacres continued, "was brief and violent. There we learned, with near tragic consequences, that the Ulaggi have the ability to perform an accurate in-system jump of less than thirty thousand kilometers."

The briefing room buzzed with awe.

"With no apparent spatial trauma to material or organic structures," Captain Katz added, muting the audience murmur.

"They came out shooting," Merriwether growled.

Runacres allowed her words to sink in, then continued. "Our scientists maintain that what the Ulaggi did at Pitcairn is impossible."

"Of course they-ah are wrong," Dowornobb rumbled softly.

"All too obviously," Runacres said. "However, during our retreat from Pitcairn, I was burdened with the certainty that our fierce adversary possessed an insurmountable advantage. I perceived no offsetting tactic, no hope . . . but now I am much encouraged by Scientist Dowornobb's discovery. And even more encouraged by his indications of more advances to come. So encouraged, I am planning a return to Pitcairn System forthwith."

An uncertain silence filled the room.

Tar Fell spoke for everyone. "To what purpose?" his translation boomed.

"What I am about to disclose is classified Top Secret," Runacres said, looking solemnly about. "At both Hornblower and Scorpio, Commander Buccari had engagements with an alien who communicated in Chinese. Commander Buccari, were you aware that your name was once again shouted into the void?"

"I've heard, sir," she exhaled, rubbing her forehead and glancing sideways at Carmichael. Her expression, Runacres thought, was decidedly morose for someone just promoted in rank and elevated to squadron command status.

"Those Chinese language intercepts," Runacres continued, "confirm that the Ulaggi captured members of the AC fleet at Shaula. We now have tenuous evidence to suggest the presence of imprisoned humans on Pitcairn Two. Captain Katz, would you continue?"

The holo-vid of the Red Zone dissolved and was replaced with a three-dimensional presentation of a dun planet.

"This is our composite of Pitcairn Two," Katz said, "rated alpha-three, mainly on atmosphere and temperature spread. Point nine-seven gee. About thirty percent high-saline ocean coverage. It is a desolate planet, arid and windblown over much of its lower elevations. There are wide temperature extremes, but there are places and times when the planet would be quite pleasant. It is rich in iron and iron compounds. Planet specs are available. We shot off no fewer than a dozen planetary reconnaissance probes. If we ever return, and if the Ulaggi don't purge the satellites, we'll have a great deal more information."

"Habitation status," Runacres demanded.

"Pitcairn Two has been colonized," Katz continued, "but sparsely. Signal intercepts from the surface, as shown, were widespread and low volume. These sites are geologically consistent with resource exploitation activities—ore and mineral mining, perhaps."

Dozens of intercept icons appeared, scattered across the globe.

"Play the intercept, Captain," Runacres ordered.

"At jump exit plus forty-three minutes, just after the Ulaggi had attempted to decoy us, we intercepted the following transmission." Katz pushed a button at his briefing station. A voice broke the static, a frightened voice, a child or a female:

"Aw dei hai doe. Aw dei hai—"

The signal ended abruptly.

"It is Chinese," Katz said. "Cantonese, to be precise, with an unidentifiable inflection, probably caused by three decades of isolation. Our computers assign it to a female anywhere from eighteen to twenty-five standard years. It translates: 'We are here! We are—' We feel confident that the voice we heard was a genuine human voice, either a survivor of Shaula or a descendent."

Katz's words were translated for the kones, who whispered among themselves.

"Thank you, Captain," Runacres said, commanding silence. "That transmission," he continued, "haunted me during the hyperlight transit. So much so, I have decided to return to Pitcairn, but not to seek contact with the Ulaggi. This mission will be a covert effort to locate and, if possible, rescue these human beings. In my judgment the longer we delay this mission the more likely these prisoners will be relocated beyond our reach . . . or worse."

"Again, I volunteer the PDF fleet to assist in this endeavor," Tar Fell boomed.

"Again, I must decline," Runacres replied. "Until your ships and crews are trained to operate with humans, and until my government grants such latitude."

Tar Fell listened impassively.

"Commander Buccari," Runacres said, "what is the status of cliff dweller training?"

"Sir?" she replied.

"This mission seems suited to their talents," he said.

"I'm not qualified to judge, sir," Buccari said, a hint of truculence in her tone.

"The cliff dwellers have integrated well," Katz said, stepping in. "Major Buck reports excellent progress. The Commandant of Marines has cleared the first integrated hunter company for fleet duty."

"I want the dangers of this mission explained to them," Runacres said, "and then ask for volunteers."

"Admiral," Buccari protested, "their culture respects authority above all else. If asked, all will volunteer. Cliff dwellers do not question or temporize; they simply do, or die trying."

"Good. I want the best insertion team possible," Runacres ordered. "We may only get one chance to extract these people."

"Admiral, I don't think they're ready," Buccari said.

"Commander Buccari," Wooden barked, "it's not your call."

Buccari darkened but remained silent.

"The cliff dwellers proved their worth on Hornblower Three," Runacres continued. "Somehow, we must give these people hope. We must let them know that we're trying to rescue them. If the cliff dwellers are the best tool we have, then we'll use that tool."

Buccari stared Runacres in the eye and nodded.

"Very well," Runacres said. "We'll meet in one standard week for a tactical planning session. I'll want Major Buck and that science officer . . . Godonov."

"I would like to help, Admiral," Buccari said. "I can—"

"Captain Ito will coordinate," Runacres ordered. "Commander Buccari, it's been brought to my attention that you've been working too hard. I'm relieving you from duty until further notice."

"Sir?" she blurted.

"Go back to your ship, Commander," Runacres said impatiently. "Take your corvette to orbit for shore leave."

"Sir, I—"

"For heavens sake, Buccari, go to your son."

"Aye, Admiral," Buccari replied, green eyes flashing. She turned, brow furrowing, to Merriwether.

"We'll reschedule that dinner, Commander," Merriwether said. "I believe the admiral issued a direct order."

Buccari threw Carmichael a wistful glance and sailed for the hatch.

SECTION TWO

WORLDS APART

ELEVEN

KAR-ULAG

Ancient were the Ulaggi millennia before konish warlords mastered their gravity-wracked planet and declared themselves noble. Ancient was Ulaggi civilization eons before man walked upright. Ancient were the indomitable Ulaggi when their own womb-planet died, blasted by a star gone nova. Yet the virulent race perished not. The Ulaggi probed the infinite void, desperate beings seeking viable sanctuary. The racial spark burned dimly, the thread of life century upon century so near breaking. Mutating as it probed, the erratic germ sought beneficent planetfall, evolving to survive, survival the only end.

Ultimately, one foray did not fail; one strain, bifurcated genetically by centuries in space, callused by sterile frustration, at last made orbit around the fourth planet of an impossibly distant star-system. How those time-hardened creatures, reduced to a few dozen extant organisms, must have rejoiced, gliding on orbit over the white-spiraled atmosphere of a vibrant world. A treasure in time and space lay below them—a new home, at last within their grasp!

They named the planet Kar-Ulag.

Jakkuk surfaced from emotional chaos. She sorted the telepathic ambience—a sensory cacophony—and reestablished dendritic link with her ship-mistresses. All was well, or at least as well as could be. Jakkuk's interstellar cell had returned to Kar-Ulag, the capital planet of the Ulaggi Triad, the seat of the Ulaggi Empire.

Jakkuk governed unseemly thought waves.

"How obscenity long?" came Ship-Mistress y'Trig's insubordinate query; y'Trig was roon. When in the Kar System, roons, fearless and death-seeking in combat, did not leave their ships.

"Too long," lifted the course thoughts of a'Yerg, the attack commander. "Too obscenity long."

Jakkuk squelched the roonish sedition with an overwhelming dendritic surge—an emotional battering ram. To respond in any other way was to condone the whining. She concentrated on course adjustments, maneuvering her cruiser cell for holding orbit around Oracle, Kar-Ulag's largest satellite. Surprisingly, her ships were immediately cleared through the holding queues; the cell's ore-loaders were ordered directly to the moon's surface for off-loading.

Jakkuk sensed Kwanna's cell exiting hyperlight; her sister cell-controller's thought waves groped uncertainly for reference. Jakkuk provided a phased dendritic link which was gratefully accepted. The newly arrived cell stabilized. Kwanna's cell also received immediate docking orders. Most peculiar; Tir-Ulag ships rarely received direct routing.

Satisfied with her cell's vector, Jakkuk allowed her mind to probe the riot of communications, electronic and telepathic. Twenty cell-controllers, at least half of those battleship cells, operated within her mind's range. There were probably thrice that many in the Kar System, assuming an equal amount on the planet's far side and a like amount in refit. Sixty combat cells! Two full battlefleets. All held in defensive reserve against the rebel dreadnoughts.

Like frightened *kar* in a breeding pen.

Jakkuk's dendritic interface filtered the incoming hails. Most Imperial cell-controllers were hajil, but no few were lakk, especially the battleship cell-controllers. The links from the lakks were powerful and emotionally preemptive. Jakkuk was no lakk, but her emotional powers exceeded most hajil. Thus was she a cell-controller.

The unsanctioned telepathic intercourse of her cell's roons had dramatically quieted. Jakkuk could still sense the collective *g'ort* of her roonish officers, a caged beast pacing. She prevailed over the roons but only from the technological bastion of the dendritic interface. She, a hajil, could never dominate a roon brain-to-brain. Truly the one blessing of being in the Kar System was that roons were unnaturally submissive.

"We will have visitors," announced the political, her slithery voice beckoning all bridge officers to attend.

Jakkuk emerged from the interface, sensing the lakk's presence in her mind before hearing her voice. Karyai had been probing her thoughts, a cursory violation. The lakk frequently strolled the cell-controller's synaptic paths, linking to the dendritic interface through Jakkuk's mind.

"Of what nature, mother?" Dar inquired, black braid swirling. Dar was outwardly calm, but Jakkuk sensed the dominant's tension.

"Imperial Tribune Cappa honors our cell," Karyai pronounced, smiling cruelly.

Pokkuk der Cappa! Jakkuk started.

Cappa held the highest rank of any Tir-hajil, an Imperial tribune, inner-circle adviser to the Empress, but that was not the reason for Jakkuk's reflex action. Pokkuk der Cappa was also Pokkuk Merde der Jakkuk's egg-source. Jakkuk was the spawn of Tribune Cappa.

"Also, the Imperial lakk-mother," the political said softly, as if a whispering afterthought.

Blood of the lakk-throne! Jakkuk's *g'ort* tremored and grew febrile. The sensual fear raised by the specter of her own mother was dispelled by a far greater terror. Jakkuk drew deeply from within, relishing the kindled warmth of her emotions.

Jakkuk sensed the hyperlight arrival of the Imperial barge. Surrounding the lakk-mother's great ship was Tribune Cappa's security cluster, six heavy star-cruisers casting an aura of brooding belligerence. The telepathic ambience heightened precipitously, not in incidence of activity as much as in the intensity and bandwidth of the pulses. Jakkuk's maneuvering signals were eclipsed. Intership communication was preempted by the tribune's cell-controller—a supercilious lakk who deigned not to link with her hajil counterparts.

Jakkuk held course and speed. The Imperial flotilla matched her vector. Lakk-piloted destroyers spewed from the interstellars, melding into an escort screen. From her own ships Jakkuk sensed a surge of roonish *g'ort*, a stifled rage. Emboldened, the hajil cell-controller allowed her sensors to scan the Imperial dispositions.

"Mind your station, daughter," Karyai reprimanded, her barbed thought signals much harsher than her words.

Jakkuk surfaced from the interface. Dominant Dar cast her cell-controller a perfunctory glare. Karyai's black eyes remained focused beyond the walls of the ship. The chastised cell-controller relinked and busied herself with dendritic harmonics. Her telepathic unit was tuned perfectly, but Jakkuk needed occupation, anything to keep vagrant thoughts from formulating. An Imperial interrogation cadre had boarded all ships. She felt an insinuating lakkish presence in the interface, officious, sterile, powerful.

"Cell-Controller Jakkuk," Dominant Dar's dulcet voice intruded.

Jakkuk broke link and lifted from the interface, her vision resynching to her optic nerve. "Yes, mother," she said.

"To your post, daughter," Dar said evenly.

"Yes, mother," Jakkuk replied, floating to her ceremonial station at the dominant's side. Jakkuk had come to deeply admire her fleet commander. She suspected the respect to be mutual. It had not begun that way. The cell-controller had struggled to overcome Dar's disdain, for Jakkuk's initial access to her post was due to bald nepotism. Now Jakkuk's powerful benefactress was about to reenter Jakkuk's life.

Preceded by a retinue, Imperial Tribune Pokkuk der Cappa floated onto the cruiser's political bridge. Cappa, with swarthy gray skin and magnificently beaked nose, was of an advanced age. Yet the old hajil's frame remained straight and tall, almost as tall as a lakk. Except for swaths of jet at the temples, Tribune Cappa's waist-length silky hair was silver-white. Her mottled amber eyes still pierced; her wide jaw was long and firm, her scarlet mouth uncompromising.

A brace of immensely wide guardmales orbited Cappa. One

thick-necked cretin in particular wore elaborate finery and occupied space well within the tribune's inviolate sphere. That the tribune kept a stable of males was not a surprise; not doing so would have been a greater surprise. The tribune riveted Jakkuk with a muddy-eyed glare. The cell-controller sought desperately to suppress her thoughts.

"My ships are yours, Tribune," Dar announced, causing Cappa to shift her burning gaze. The dominant pushed from her command station, ceremoniously deferring to the tribune's rank. The tribune slipped easily into the vacated position.

"The lakk-mother comes. Attend," Cappa announced evenly. "All honor to the lakk-mother."

The gathered officers and males repeated the litany, the boisterous thundering of the guardmales drowning all others. The Empress's own political, with Dar's fleet political at her side, floated onto the bridge. Karyai, a Tir-lakk, was decades older than Jakkuk, older even than Dar, her liquid black eyes sinister above bruised bags of livid purple, but in juxtaposition with the lakk-mother, Karyai appeared vibrant and youthful. The lakk-mother was beyond ancient, her once tall frame humped and twisted with time; her few strands of cobweb hair were pulled tight above a haunted, dolorous death mask; her nacre-skin was gray-mottled and fungal.

The lakk-mother's family name came uninvited to Jakkuk's mind: Wawn ula Reta, blood sister to Empress Enod III, the fourteenth daughter of the Wawn Succession. Jakkuk immediately dispelled the thought image. To Jakkuk's horror, the lakk-mother pivoted to face her, an indigestive smile contorting her face. Because of the lakk-mother's diminished physique, her hard eyes were on a level with Jakkuk's. The cell-controller felt the harridan's presence in her mind, not gently.

"So this impudent Tir-hajil is of your blood, eh, Tribune Cappa?" the lakk-mother said, her voice astoundingly firm.

"One of many," Cappa replied sourly.

"Speak my name, Pokkuk Merde der Jakkuk," the lakk-mother slithered. "Do not insult me with your thoughts. Speak."

Jakkuk sucked a lungful of air, drawing on her training and discipline. She rose to full height and stared straight ahead.

"Mother Reta, mother to all, permit this unworthy officer to apologize," Jakkuk said, encasing all other thoughts in stone.

The lakk-mother had already moved away, leaving tall Karyai's scowling face as replacement. The political tromped about Jakkuk's mind.

"Lakk-mother, the inquiry," Tribune Cappa said, with little diffidence.

Reta gazed intently into Dominant Dar's stern visage. "Yes," she hissed. "Begin, Tribune."

"We are here to discuss the engagements," Cappa announced, her voice lowering in timbre. "Call Destroyer-Fist a'Yerg to the bridge."

Dar nodded. Jakkuk linked to the dendritic unit and transmitted the summons. The roon's response was immediate. Into the telepathic ether lifted a terrifying roonish battle scream. Other roons, emboldened by a'Yerg's wail, echoed the attack commander's bellicose challenge. The telepathic ether resonated with foul emotion.

Jakkuk surged dendritic power. The roonish yodels were blasted into silence, and the cell-controller repeated her command.

"As the lakk-mother commands," came a'Yerg's sullen reply, not a transmission but a defiant, first-order thought emission.

Karyai snarled at the impudence. The lakk-mother merely smiled.

"Commence your brief, Dar-hajil," Tribune Cappa demanded.

Dar nodded to her cell-controller. Jakkuk floated to a mapping station and moved her hands over the controls. A holo projection depicted the Triad. An icon representing the mining colony where they had met the humans appeared as a bright orange point. The star map zoomed inward, the point of light expanding into a tiny globe.

"This is Ore Source Two-ten," Jakkuk reported. "Our mission was to take on three million *roget* of smelted iron. Near the completion of this mission we detected the arrival—"

"Detected is misleading," Karyai interrupted. "The humans came into the system transmitting pleas for galactic cooperation over all frequencies."

"As they have in all previous encounters," Jakkuk said.

The cell-controller regretted her outburst. Karyai leaped once again into Jakkuk's mind, bludgeoning her emotions. Jakkuk reeled.

"Ore Source Two-ten is but ten *kokots* distant from the Imperial security perimeter," Dar offered.

"Dar-hajil, it is always your fleet that stumbles upon the aliens—these humans," Reta said. The lakk-mother's eyes were closed. Jakkuk wondered in whose mind she was wandering.

"My units but perform their assigned duties, mother," the dominant replied. "Tir-Ulag's fleet is stretched thin. Perhaps if an Imperial task group participated in the security—"

"Mind your inference, Dar-hajil," Tribune Cappa preempted.

Dar's translucent copper skin darkened. The I'rd-Ulag battle fleet, under Dominant i'Tant, was at large. The Empress feared roonish adventurism, and the much vaster Imperial fleet remained bottled up in the Kar-Ulag System, afraid to sortie. So it had been for near twenty sun-cycles, since i'Tant had twice punished the Imperial fleet in the I'rd-Ulag sector. Somehow the I'rd-roons had developed a mind screen—a bloodcurdling development. Now the tribunes were fearful of pulling even patrol forces from the Kar System.

Was the lakk-Empire at last tottering? Jakkuk shoved her seditious thought into a cerebral dark place, refusing her mind license to range, but she sensed a burgeoning hostility. Characteristic thought patterns emerged, palpable, like an odor in the brain—a'Yerg. The roon approached; subliminal tensions increased; Jakkuk's dermal filaments tingled with nervous static; her ears rang. Destroyer-Fist a'Yerg was an exceedingly powerful telepath, and an extremely angry one.

"Ah!" Reta breathed. "The roon."

The attack commander floated onto the command bridge,

robes flowing, her calm outward appearance belying the raging storm within. Jakkuk felt her own *g'ort* resonating with the roon's infinitely more powerful animal. Even with so many powerful lakk about to counter the roon, Jakkuk's mind wished desperately for the shelter of the dendritic interface.

Fist a'Yerg stopped before the lakk-mother. The forever tall roon captured the old lakk's unblinking black-eyed gaze and held it. The attack commander was a silver-eye, with pupils like knife slits. Karyai, mouth twisted in a sneer, moved protectively closer.

"Destroyer-Fist a'Yerg," Tribune Cappa said. "You honor us with your presence. Your battle record is legend."

"I serve Tir-Ulag," a'Yerg's mind emitted, her eyes not leaving the wizened lakk's. Karyai fumed, as if the roon's surly unspoken response were replete with obscenities.

"Tell us what happened, roon," Reta demanded.

"My destroyers never engaged," a'Yerg growled, using her voice. "Cell-Controller Jakkuk's perspective serves best."

"Your counsel then, fierce roon," Reta said.

"The aliens have come too far," a'Yerg snarled. "Pursue them and kill them, or they will be emboldened by their survival. We must run them to ground."

"Perhaps it was a trap," Karyai said.

"It was no trap," Jakkuk said. Tribune Cappa's slow-burning glare turned Jakkuk's blood cold.

"It was no trap," a'Yerg uttered, regathering everyone's attention. "The *humans* are weak and frightened, but they are no longer alone. There are now two races in union against us. To delay is foolhardy. If the Imperial Fleet will not sortie, permit the cells of Tir-Ulag the honor of savaging the intruders."

"The roon counsels well," Dar said. Jakkuk added her concurring thoughts.

There was no reply from Reta. The roon and the lakk-mother stood silently, their glares and their minds locked in deadly embrace.

"To where did the aliens run?" demanded Tribune Cappa.

"On the flux gradient leading to System 396, mother," Jakkuk replied, exhaling. "As they have in the past."

"I await your orders, Tribune," Dar announced.

The iron-hard glares of the roon and the lakk-mother remained locked in a telepathic trance. Cappa gazed at the emotional battle for several seconds before responding.

"Indeed, action is overdue," the tribune declared.

Jakkuk glanced up. Were the tribunes finally to relent?

"It is decided," the lakk-mother declared.

A'Yerg's silver-eyed stare broke from its trance, more defiant than ever, Jakkuk thought. Without speaking, the terrible roon arrowed from the bridge, iridescent robes swirling. The lakk-mother smiled, but Jakkuk thought her diminished, fatigued. Reta's pearled eyelids drooped improbably lower.

Tribune Cappa floated upward from the command station.

"Do we give chase?" Dar asked.

"Dar-hajil, great honor is yours," the lakk-mother growled.

"My orders, mother," Dar persisted, her emotions flickering.

"Dominant Dar," Reta's voice slithered, her Kar-Ulag accents exaggerated, "your fleet will return its ore-loaders to Ore Source Two-ten. From there you will trace the retreat of the human fleet."

"Our mission, Tribune?" Dar inquired.

"To find the human home planet," Tribune Cappa replied.

"And to punish." The lakk-mother smiled wickedly. "To kill."

TWELVE

KING OLLANT IV

The sky was of one piece, a uniform golden haze suffusing the atmosphere, not bright, not dim, but undeniably hot—a torrid, fuzzy glow. The colloidal ether did not arch over the Hegemonic capital, rather it lay like a blanket. A kone could throw a stone farther than he could clearly see, and shadows, when shadows were cast by natural light, had no edges, only shades of muted intensity.

King Ollant relished the absence of thought induced by arduous exertion. Disdaining both sedentary and prudish conventions, the king galloped naked through the maze of sinuous paths weaving about the Imperial gardens. The hegemon's huge hands and splayed feet grabbed the manicured ground; his gargantuan golden thews exploded against their purchase. His massive, rippling form hurtled forward, leaving behind rattling gouts of gravel. Ollant's lungs sucked in copious quantities of full-bodied, yellowish air and exhaled the exchanged gases in vaporous huffs of thundering resonance.

A network of scar tissue marbled the monarch's broad back and thick neck, horrific damage inflicted by the rapier claws and dagger teeth of a frenzied Genellan she-bear, a beast even more massive than a kone. That Ollant survived and came to be king of the Northern Hegemony was attributable to the quick and selfless actions of the human, Citizen Sharl. The green-eyed Earthling's image haunted Ollant's thoughts as he pounded through his gardens, around magnificent stands of flowering, orange-leafed *kotta* trees and over crimson glades of fragrant *wahocca*.

Ollant thundered past the golden waters of the reflecting

pool, his royal finish line, and slowed to a steamy, sweat-dripping canter. An attendant garbed in crimson livery marked the elapsed time. The *trod*, still with the mobility of youth, cantered in the king's wake. Other attendants crawled forward with robes and articles of sustenance. Ollant listened with satisfaction to his pace times, grabbed a silken robe, and waved the retinue away. Tossing the robe to the verdant lawn, Ollant splashed magnificently into the fountain pool, luxuriating in the buoyant relaxation of gravity's onerous pull. Trailing a stream of odiferous bubbles, the massive noblekone dog-paddled once around the gurgling fountains and returned to his starting point. He beached himself upon the grassy embankment and lay on his back, dripping but refreshed, an aura of steam rising from his supine carcass.

Niggling details of trade agreements and boundary negotiations, of government appointments and funding decisions, wormed their way into the hegemon's exertion-flushed consciousness. He forced away the bureaucratic cobwebs with thoughts of beautiful Genellan, of her unremitting cold, but also of her crystalline skies and aquamarine seas, and of snow-capped mountains, and of sunsets that stole one's breath. His thoughts dwelled once again upon the green-eyed human.

"Your Majesty," rumbled a voice. Ollant rose on an elbow to see his slug of a chamberlain. The old red-jacketed commoner, at attention on all fours, was significantly more massive than even the king; his distended midsection furrowed the grass. "Prime Minister Et Kalass and General Talsali."

Ollant grunted and rolled over onto callused forearms. From his knees he heaved majestically to his hinds and lumbered after the crawling servant. Spreading beyond the splashing fountains stood a particularly magnificent *kotta* tree, the centerpiece around which the Imperial gardens had been rebuilt. The orange-leafed tree was improbably twice the height of a mortal kone. Its ponderous, fruit-burdened canopy was supported against the inexorable pull of Kon's gravity by four gnarled primary trunks, each umber stem ten paces thick and buttressed with a knuckled webbing of roots. In the diffuse shade of the ancient *kotta*, breasting upon gravity lounges, awaited General Talsali, Commanding General of the Planetary Defense Force, and Et Kalass, Ollant's prime minister.

Talsali wore PDF khaki piped in yellow and red. The old commoner stood to attention on all fours and politely averted his eyes until Ollant pulled on his dazzling alabaster robe. Et Kalass, in billowing white trimmed in midnight-blue, rose to his hinds and bowed. Ollant's prime minister remained trembling on his hinds, determined not to accede to the demands of gravity.

"What transpires, General?" Ollant asked, waving both kones to their lounges. He remained standing. "I hear news of Admiral Runacres's return. And of alien conflict? What has Tar Fell to report?"

"Armada-Master Tar Fell sends his respects, Your Highness," Talsali reported. "Admiral Runacres was once again engaged by the Ulaggi, in a brief but deadly encounter at a star-system called Pitcairn, ninety parsecs into the Red Zone. One of the Legion motherships sustained significant damage, fortunately with minimal loss of life. Admiral Runacres feared pursuit, but your Scientist Dowornobb has evidently discovered—"

"Master Dowornobb has informed me of his discoveries," Ollant said, russet eye tufts dancing. "Dowornobb also indicates that we jump first to Sol System—to Earth."

"Dowornobb's information is correct, Your Majesty," Talsali confirmed. The old general's eye tufts likewise flickered upward. "The time and destination of our first hyperlight event have been established. We jump to Sol System with Admiral Chou's Second Fleet within the moon-cycle. Tar Fell signals his ships are ready."

"Gravity, I envy the Thullolian," Ollant sighed, eye tufts settling. "He makes history. To Earth . . ."

"Your duties, sire, are here," Et Kalass pontificated. "You must pilot this planet."

"Worry not, old worrier," Ollant grumbled, feeling the wound-shortened tendons in his shoulder stiffening. Or was it his age? "Worry not. I know my proper place."

"Admiral Runacres sends his respects, Your Highness," Et Kalass pronounced. "The admiral regrets he is unable to make an official state visit. Admiral Runacres hopes His Majesty would understand why and importunes the king's indulgence. The admiral indicated he had not yet recovered from his last visit. Something about gravity stress and a *kotta* hangover."

"Acknowledge in my name," Ollant replied. "As usual, extend to Admiral Runacres an invitation to our planet at his future convenience. He is welcomed as a friend to all kones."

"So ordered, Your Highness," Et Kalass replied.

"Your Majesty," Talsali said, "Admiral Runacres has notified me of plans to immediately return to Pitcairn System."

"So Dowornobb informs me," Ollant said. "That there is a likelihood of human prisoners. Runacres returns to the dragon's lair."

"Your Highness," Talsali continued, "Admiral Runacres proposes a konish interceptor accompany the human fleet, for training purposes. The armada-master concurs. Et Lorlyn has volunteered himself and his crew. Since Et Lorlyn is a northerner, I seek your endorsement."

"Granted," Ollant replied, sighing with envy.

"Also, Your Highness," Talsali said, "Admiral Runacres requests the services of Scientist Dowornobb on this dangerous mission. Admiral Runacres desires to learn more of Scientist Dowornobb's discoveries and to employ those technologies at once."

"Ah, this is news," Ollant replied. "What says Tar Fell?"

"He is opposed," Talsali answered. "Tar Fell is of the opinion that Dowornobb's technical advances should be closely held, to be exploited to our advantage. Tar Fell also suggests that putting Dowornobb in harm's way is foolhardy. With this opinion I concur, Your Highness."

"Much of me agrees," Ollant mused. "Prime Minister, what say you?"

"I would allow the scientist to decide for himself, My Hegemon," Et Kalass replied. "We gain either way. However, sire, you intended to designate your Earth envoy, did you not? That designation may have bearing on Dowornobb's decision, for that estimable kone has not seen his mate in many moon-cycles."

"Ah!" Ollant exclaimed. "Of course. Inform Tar Fell that Ambassador Kateos will accompany the konish fleet to Earth, as my representative. Prepare the ambassador's portfolio."

"That should tilt Scientist Dowornobb's decision, Your Highness," Et Kalass replied, bowing feebly.

"I for one," Ollant replied, raising his hand in dismissal, "will be surprised if Dowornobb does *not* choose harm's way. And with his mate's encouragement."

"Master Dowornobb and Ambassador Kateos have already sacrificed greatly, Your Majesty," Talsali said.

"Sacrifice is the essence of character, General."

THIRTEEN

CALL TO DUTY

"I miss your touch, my mate," Dowornobb said. His holo image reached for her. Kateos could not help herself; she put out a hand to meet his grasp and came up with a great emptiness. Her sorrow bladder discharged, its sweet emanations escaping her suit and permeating the considerable confines of her exploration vehicle. The exhaust system hummed into operation.

"You go into great danger," Kateos said.

"And you to great honor," Dowornobb replied. "And also to no little danger, my mate. Yours will be the first konish ships to leave our star-system."

"Why could we not go on great adventures together?" she said.

"It was not to be, my life," Dowornobb lamented, eye tufts sagging tragically. They stared silently for long moments.

"It will be difficult for you, my love, living on a human ship," Kateos said. "It will be cold. You must take care of yourself."

"A special environment is being constructed for my technical team in the habitation ring of Citizen Sharl's ship," Dowornobb replied. "We will be too busy to be cold. It is exciting. The humans are most helpful, and most flattering. We continue to learn from each other."

An alarm sounded.

"The download reentry has commenced," she moaned. "I must go."

"Citizen Sharl makes orbit soon," Dowornobb said. "Will you see her? Her time on Genellan will be brief."

"I have talked with her," Kateos said. "Citizen Hud-sawn and I will fly north today, after the download. We will have joyous times again, if only for a short time. Oh, I wish you were here."

"My mate," Dowornobb whispered.

"I must go now, my heart," Kateos said.

Ba-booom! The electric-blue skies above New Edmonton thundered with the Legion downloader's unseen hypermach passage.

"They're coming, Daddy!" Emerald shouted, her brilliant eyes a perfect match for the exquisite heavens. Hudson's daughter danced with excitement, her flaxen hair tossing back the sun's rays doublefold.

"Not long now," Hudson replied, rubbing the stubble on his head. He tore his eyes from the jewellike perfection of the skinny three-year-old and looked up, knowing the downloader would not yet be visible. The sky was a blue so deep as to seem artificial. No cloud marred the radiant dome from southern sea to northern snowcapped mountains. Genellan's moons, within five degrees of arc, were improbably distinct. Ocean tides would be strong on this day. A welcome breeze carried the scent and rustle of dry grass.

"Daddy, when are we going?"

"Real soon, Em," Hudson replied. His lanky body lay curled inside the massive rim of a low-pressure drive wheel, one of six supporting the konish all-terrain vehicle. He sensed movement within; the airlock hissed open and Kateos bounded to the ground, landing on all fours and pivoting like a 250 kilo cat to scoop up the squealing child. Hudson replaced his floppy-brimmed hat and pushed off.

"We must hurry," Kateos said. Her deep, liquid voice was strained, her huge brown eyes red-rimmed.

"You okay, Katie?" Hudson asked.

"Quite fine, Friend Hud-sawn, thank you," Kateos replied, setting Emerald on her back. "Hold on, Emmy. We must hurry."

Konish Genellan suits were covered with folds, pockets,

and lanyards. The girl was familiar with the terrain. The kone, with the laughing child clinging to her neck, leaped into a gallop. Hudson followed the bounding kone, his long legs breaking into a full sprint. Feeling the solid ground of Genellan pass easily under his rehabilitated body, Hudson could not imagine himself any happier. Technicians and ground crews heading for their bunkers whistled and cheered as Kateos pounded by. Hudson whooped with joy.

The sign on the site command bunker read: NEW EDMONTON EXPANSION SITE SIXTEEN-ALPHA. It was 6.5 kilometers from city center, on the southwest expansion radial. Four rectangular landing pads at precise five-hundred-meter intervals had been laser-scraped to geometric flatness. A wide boulevard, curving elegantly over rolling contours, led from the site toward the city center. Site Sixteen-Alpha was but one of ten new settlement nodes on NEd's perimeter. Each site was scheduled to receive from one to four downloaders; each downloader carried one hundred settlers and their allotted belongings. Two thousand new settlers were descending, bringing their hopes and dreams.

Kateos, holding Hudson's tiny child in her huge arms, waited for him at the bunker. Hudson hit the entrance bar, and the outer door slid from the entryway. He waved Kateos and Emerald through the lock and then followed the ambassador's generous rump down the bunker ramp and into the cool, darkened control environment. Et Silmarn's mountainous form was there to greet them. The planetary governor plodded forward and relieved Kateos of the child, nestling her like a doll in his titanic clutches.

"Ambassador Kateos," Art Mather hailed. The chargé and her entourage flowed toward the kones. "I was afraid you might not make it in time. I hope there is nothing wrong."

"Nothing is wrong," Kateos replied. "Thank you for your concern."

Kateos, her official demeanor firmly in place, politely received Mather's salutations. The representatives of their respective races began discussing things political. Hudson wisely moved away, looking for the mother of his daughter.

Quinn, sitting at an admin unit next to the download controller, was under siege from several underlings. Hudson walked into her field of vision and twisted his features into a funny face. The corners of her mouth only hinted at a smile, and she turned away, struggling to keep her demeanor intact.

"We have a priority one communiqué from the Thullolian delegation, Commander," one officer reported.

"Art," Quinn shouted, "can you take care of that?"

"I'll get someone right on it, Commander," Mather replied, coming over to check the message. She pointed at one of her assistants, who ran for a communication terminal.

"Manifests indicate we got another commissary pallet coming down, Commander," reported a uniformed aide with a digital clipboard. "Nonpriority, discretionary articles."

"Another one?" Quinn growled. "We're wasting cube dragging toys and designer clothes across the galaxy. The settlers don't need fashionable underwear; they need boot jigs and machine tools. I've half a mind to shut down the commissary."

"Now, Commander," Artemis Mather replied. "You would deprive our settlers of the little things that make being human enjoyable. The commissary is a communal meeting site and an exchange for Legion Monetary Units. It's imperative our settlers have a controlled currency."

"You really mean it's imperative the Legion have controlled settlers," Hudson said.

"Don't start, Nash," Quinn barked. "Not here. Not now."

"Sorry," Hudson said, not sorry at all. He impishly reached in his pocket and pulled out a metal disc. "Here, Art, check this out." He flipped the yellow coin through the air. It made a heavy *splat* in Mather's palm.

"Unauthorized coinage," Mather said. "Where'd you get it?"

"Pretty, ain't it?" Hudson asked. "The settlers sure like them."

"Nash," Quinn admonished, "you're lobbing hand grenades."

"Life is good," Hudson replied.

"What-ah purpose does that-ah medallion serve?" Et Silmarn rumbled.

"It is a barter medium," Kateos replied.

"It-ah is but a disc of gold," Et Silmarn said.

"On Earth, gold is an extremely rare metal," Hudson replied. "Its value on Genellan isn't clear, but the market will tell in the end, right, Art?"

"Here's your nickel back," Mather said, tossing the coin. Hudson caught it adroitly.

"He's right, Art," Quinn replied. "Doesn't matter how much gold there is; unbacked LMUs will soon be worthless, commissary trinkets or no. There's a free market taking charge. Pure exchange."

"Something humans haven't enjoyed for centuries," Hudson said. "The Legion won't be able to control supply and demand on Genellan; there's just too damn much of both. And you can't control the money supply when the exchange system is barter-based."

"That's what laws are for," Mather replied.

"That's the last damn thing laws are for," Hudson replied.

"Your language leaves something to be desired," Mather remarked.

"Five minutes," the landing controller announced.

"Quiet," Quinn ordered. "We're bringing settlers down."

"Downloader is at high key," a technician reported.

Hudson moved to an observation slit. Beyond the rolling grasslands he could make out the distant ocean, its perfect horizon balanced with a single towering cumulus. Mather moved next to him. Hudson detected her dusky scent. It was warm in the bunker.

"What's your point, Hudson?" Mather asked.

"My point?" he said.

"Why can't you get with the program?" Mather said. "The Legion's trying to make a home for humanity. Ingrates like you and St. Pierre just want your own world, your own paradise. So you can pull up the ladder and leave the others behind. You're selfish."

Hudson looked down at the stout lady's intense demeanor. Mather's blood was high; her dark complexion was tinted purple.

"Selfish?" Hudson pondered aloud. "Perhaps."

"What right do you have to play god?" she asked, nostrils twitching with anger.

"I would ask the same of you," Hudson replied.

"Optical!" the controller shouted. Hudson looked at the main display. An optical tracking repeater captured the downloader in high-power magnification. The double-delta planform of the habitation module arced to final, a massive cylinder, falling more than flying, a hundred souls inside its belly, men, women, and children, praying for their lives and their futures.

"Unlike you, I do not broker my own selfish feelings," Mather replied. "I am an advocate for the Tellurian Legion, the elected representatives of our government. *Your* government, Mr. Hudson. The same government that saved your life and put you back together. The same government that saw fit to return you to this planet. I work for the greater good, something you obviously do not understand."

"Whose greater good?" Hudson asked. "The powerful and privileged of Earth, maybe. You aren't working for this planet's greater good. Sharl Buccari doesn't want Genellan to be another Earth. Neither do I."

"Buccari has sensibly abjured her political interests," Mather said. "She is a fleet officer, loyally serving her government. You can learn from Commander Buccari, Hudson."

"Sharl always said I was a slow learner," Hudson said. "Genellan needs an advocate, so I guess that's me."

"It's an empty planet, for goodness sake," Mather said.

"Hardly empty," he retorted. "There are already too many people."

"You're joking," she scoffed, voice rising. "There are only twenty thousand people on this planet. Twenty thousand human beings on the whole frigging planet—"

"Now whose language needs work?" Hudson said.

Mather's jaw clamped shut; a vein in her temple throbbed. "Bite my ass, Hudson," she said, much too loudly.

The bunker went stone quiet. Hudson looked up to receive the full force of Quinn's furious glare.

"In the groove!" A controller broke the silence.

Hudson, chagrined, gave Mather a perfunctory bow and relinquished his spot at the viewing position. He joined Et Silmarn and Kateos at a safe distance from Quinn's wrath. Kateos held Emerald in her arms.

"Commander Quinn is not happy with you," Kateos said.

"Mama's mad!" Emerald added.

"No kidding," Hudson replied, taking Emerald into his arms. "How does Cassy put up with that? She doesn't like what's happening to this planet any more than I do."

"The answer is simple, Hud-sawn," Et Silmarn said. "It is her duty."

"Pad acquisition!" a technician shouted.

The atmosphere in the bunker was electric. The pitch and tenor of the technicians' voices changed, their movements quickened. The bunker's main video display imaged the descending ship from dead ahead. A framework of reticules defined glide slope and lineup excursions, constantly correcting. A matrix of numbers called out altitude and airspeed. The downloader was configuring for landing.

"All telemetry solid," the controller reported. "Positive glide slope, positive lineup. Go for gear. Go for pad. Go for retro."

The PHM's stabilizers sparkled, spraying out a shimmering halo of energy. Puffs of white sputtered into the slipstream. The huge vessel slid down the glide slope, its nose elevating. Laterals erupted—banks of flame angled from the habitation module's flanks. The concrete underfoot vibrated. A gout of flame shot from the ship's nose.

"Braking thrusters!" the controller shouted.

The PHM, discolored by reentry, was too big to be hanging in the sky. Perimeter thrusters engaged. Red flames defined the PHM's hull, projecting down and bending back in the diminishing force of the slipstream. The ship descended, its forward momentum easing to a crawl. The core internals boomed into life, blasting the ground with white-hot fury, their cacophonous report thundering into the heavily insulated bunker. The ship settled into the retro flames, perfectly aligned with the geometrical scar scraped into the ground. Vertical motion ceased. The last gouts of fire shot from the hull and disappeared, leaving the planetary habitation module sitting quiescent on the planet, a silent, solitary chunk of civilization, shimmering in its residual heat.

"We're down," the duty officer reported. "Ground crews to your stations."

"Okay, people," Quinn shouted. "Let's make 'em feel at home."

FOURTEEN

MACARTHUR'S VALLEY

Humanity's initial contact with the konish race had been bloody and one-sided. The Tellurian Legion fleet, with significant loss of life, was violently rejected from the konish system, leaving behind a single corvette, *Harrier One*. The settlement of Genellan was the legacy of that ship's crew, especially of the corvette's copilot, Sharl Buccari. That any of *Harrier One*'s crew survived the tragic first winter on Hudson's Plateau was a miracle—a miracle of persistence and communications and leadership. Cliff dwellers reluctantly accepted human beings into their care. The Earthlings survived, and the universe was forever changed.

While cliff dwellers may have delivered the fragile humans through their first winter, it was the settlement at MacArthur's Valley that gave Buccari's Survivors their first foothold on Genellan. In MacArthur's Valley the Earthlings were able to sustain themselves, hunting, fishing, and planting. And building. Beneath the valley's glacier-hung walls and crashing cascades, the humans built shelters to protect themselves from unrelenting elements. They built a palisade of stout tree trunks to protect themselves from predators. They built families to protect themselves from abiding loneliness. And most importantly, from MacArthur's Valley the human castaways built a relationship with the konish masters of the solar system.

The passing years brought change to MacArthur's Valley. Buccari's Survivors and the new settlers cleared patches of hardwood and pine from the valley slopes, erecting homesteads in mutually supportive four-unit clusters. These small neighborhoods were marked by water towers and stone silos lifting above a patchwork of terraced fields and thick forest. At the steep southern end of Lake Shannon nestled the bustling frontier town of Hydro. So different from the saffron plastic of New Edmonton, Hydro's buildings were constructed of wood and stone, with high-peaked roofs and heavy beams intricately carved and brightly painted. Two prominent exceptions bracketed the lake town like bookends: the Legion administration building on the west end, and the hydropower plant, a three-story cube, at the east end. These official structures were constructed of Legion-yellow composite extrusion.

Rivaling the power plant as MacArthur's Valley's most notable landmark, at least of those crafted by man, was Tookmanian's Church. Known more recently as Maggie's Chapel, the simple clapboard and stone structure stood high on a ridge, far, far above the valley floor. The remote chapel's graceful steeple, a brilliant white spire, protruded above the tree line, pointing to twin pinnacles of rock atop the ridge. Beneath those pinnacles, humans and cliff dwellers had died fighting kones.

Cliff dwellers, a branch of the species known as mountain flyers, also came to live in the Valley-of-the-lake. Population pressures drove thousands of the creatures from their plateau warrens on the cliffs above the Great River. Cliff dwellers followed the long-legs to Valley-of-the-lake in a grand and daring social experiment. They chose as their new home a steep ridge face to the north and east of the palisade, above the meadow where bear-people landing machines had once blasted away the thick forest, and where yellow long-leg flying machines now roosted.

Hunters swept the granite ridge clear of predators. A parlous task, for gigantic Genellan bears, the greatest of the forest gods, still inhabited the caves, and fierce giant eagles maintained aeries on the rugged escarpments. But hunters, once tasked, persevered. The crafty warriors flushed the towering bears from their rocky dens with thrown stones and sonic bedlam. No bears were slain, a good omen and great good fortune. The eagles of the valley, however, refused to give quarter and were exterminated. Hunter and eagle would forever struggle, for there could be but one ruler of the skies.

Cliff dweller guilders followed hunters to the valley. Stone carvers with chisel and hammer built stout fortifications and family abodes from the valley's granite ribs. The cliff dwellers' new habitation had flowing springs and runoff rills aplenty, but unlike the plateau, there were no magma chambers to manufacture steam. In the absence of that energy source, steam users employed long-leg magic—the magic of the glowing metal. Long-legs brought power overland through coated wires hung from poles. The long-legs also gave the cliff dwellers engines, with shafts that spun rapidly when connected to the metal strands. Powerful engines! The steam users soon learned their danger and potential, harnessing the flows and distributing fur-tingling power over their own networks of pure gold.

Cliff dwellers of the fisher guild constructed fish farms in the narrow lake shallows, creating enchanting patterns of rock and water. Gardeners cleared forest and tilled fields, improving on the long-leg methods, although the grains of the long-legs were wondrous and plump, far surpassing native grains in yield and variety. The cliff dwellers' new home in the valley was not as easily guarded as the plateau, but it commanded a deep lake full of fat fish, forests rustling with game, and bountiful soils to clear and plant.

Falling rain obscured lake, forest, and field. Ki, widow-of-Braan-the-hero, mother-of-Brappa-the-star-warrior, and great-mother to the whelp-of-Short-one-who-leads, finished banking her breakfast fire. It had deluged the night through; dampness penetrated Ki's thin bones. With the downpour's din and the rumble of waterfalls, the long-leg valley was not quiet. Still, Ki missed the constant thunder of the Great River.

The old huntress pulled an otter cloak about her narrow shoulders, sinking under its cowl. Ki stepped resolutely from under her abode's granite overhang and into a relentless downpour. Rain sluicing off her cloak, she crossed her narrow terrace and descended a steep path along the face of the cliff, her talons grinding and scratching wet stone. Ki entered a smooth-quarried crevice, awash with runoff. She soon arrived at a junction with a downward slanting tunnel, illuminated with the steady glare of long-leg magic. Runoff, confined in a bermed gutter, gurgled along the polished floor.

Her downhill march led past barracks, storage caves, and confluences with other tunnels. As the passageway flattened it converged with a wide, dimly lighted thoroughfare. This greater tunnel doglegged past deadfalls and portcullis drops, and finally emerged to the gray light and shifting breezes of the stormy day. Sentries, peering from shadowed recesses and murder-ports, monitored the huntress's progress.

Ki waddled out on the main terrace, a walled promenade overhung with polished quartz. The terrace wall was crenellated and bedecked with ceramic pots flourishing with spring blooms, scarlet and gold. Gushing runoff poured from the rocks behind her, channeling energetically into gargoyled scuppers and graceful gutters. In the darker niches of the cliff wall, sheltered by big-leafed river fern and thickweed, gardeners tended stone planters of mushrooms and herbs. Ki deviated from her course to inspect the medicinals. Huntresses and gardeners shared the lore of healing.

"Long life, Greatmother," a tall guilder chirped, bobbing his head. The begrimed and dripping gardener, wearing but a leather codpiece, dutifully ministered his plants, oblivious to weather. As with all gardeners, the guilder's atrophied flight membranes had been surgically removed.

"Abundance is thine, guilder," Ki chittered, nodding with approval at the gardener's turgid fungi. She did not dally but continued along the promenade, past the lift platform terminus, where she greeted more hunters and guilders, coming and going. All who met the old huntress saluted with generous deference.

Ki came to an external gate. Sentries with pike and bow, young countenances comically severe, patrolled the casement, talons clicking with martial precision on rock parapets. The novice hunters, fully exposed to the weather, smelled of wet fur and leather. They studiously ignored the huntress, maintaining their vigilance outward.

Rain drilling her cowl, Ki waddled through the gate and down the switchbacking cobbled road, her elevation sufficient to give view over the misty forest canopy. On the rainswept meadow, yellow, stiff-winged flight machines squatted in line. Hard-falling rains made flying improbable for long-leg and hunter alike.

Short of the long-leg road, Ki set off on a parallel path toward the palisade. Though softened by rain, the path was covered with needles and hardwood leaves, so it was not muddy. The rain fell less profusely through the boughs, but in larger drops. She covered the distance to the palisade in a steady pace. The wooden fort at last appeared through sodden spring foliage, and then as quickly disappeared in a gusting downpour.

Lightning flashed blue-white. Thunder detonated overhead, its rain-muffled peals rolling through the valley. Ki held her cowl with both hands and trotted faster. A sinister shape moved in the bushes. She drew up, startled. The slinking shadow melted into the downpour. She peered after it but detected only wind-gusted and rain-slickened foliage. She took a tentative step, when a precipitation-shrouded blur moved furtively on her right.

Ki filled her lungs and was about to blast forth a sonic signal, when the downpour relented. Her surroundings were revealed. Numerous forms moved stealthfully through the woods about her—hunters. She heard long-legs crashing through the forest. And smelled them.

From the palisade rose an alarm.

Battle cries lifted from the woods. Hunters, sentries, and green-garbed long-legs poured from underbrush on both sides of the forest path.

"Hast thou joined our attack, fierce huntress?" chirped a wonderfully familiar voice. "We sorely need thy help, for the palisade sentries have declared our presence."

"*Awrrk,*" Ki squeaked, whirling. Standing there, rain splattering crazily off his armor, was her brave son.

"Respected mother," Brappa trilled, bowing respectfully.

"My son," Ki chirped happily, returning the gesture. Standing erect, she observed Big-ears and Sharp-face by her son's side. Behind her, Giant-one exploded from the sodden undergrowth. Ki was ashamed long-legs could steal so close.

"I was not vigilant," she whispered.

"Wind and rain sweep clear the air, mother," Brappa chirped. "I beg thee, come with us. We form to march."

The clouds swept rapidly to the east, permitting teasing flashes of sunlight to illuminate their verdant surroundings. Glorious shafts of gold sparkled through raindrop-bejeweled leaves—a sign from the gods. Ki's warrior son chirped and hand-signed to Giant-one. The behemoth approached the old huntress, bowed stiffly in the cliff dweller manner, and knelt. Ki nodded regally and stepped with graceful dignity onto the giant's meaty forearm. The towering long-leg stood erect, his elevation as high as a tree limb. She leaned against his broad chest, like a shouldered weapon. Thus did they march triumphantly across the cleared area before the palisade. Ki, her legendary voice still strong and sweet, screeched the clan clarion of her valiant husband and son.

Godonov watched Chastain lead the march across the clearing, like some misbegotten falconer. Sentries on the palisades raised an ear-splitting accolade. A marine piper in Glengarry and kilt scaled the parapet and joined in, exuberantly priming his bagpipe. The warriors of Hunter Company, human and cliff dweller wearing nightmare skins over their armor, fell in behind the big sergeant. Lizard Lips's apprentices, no longer an independent platoon of guilders, waddled proudly with their fire teams. Lizard Lips, arms akimbo, stood at Major Buck's side, inspecting the troops as they marched in review.

Godonov walked from the forest into clear sunlight. With the front's passage, it had grown cooler. He found himself above the cemetery, its weathered mounds flattened and overgrown with spring flowers. Beyond the graves were the beginnings of the settlement vegetable fields, tender green shoots bursting from moist black soil. And beyond the fields was the dark green cove, moodily reflecting the spring foliage of the rocky peninsula. Godonov walked up the gentle slope, joining Buck and Lizard Lips.

"Got a lot closer than we should have," Buck said. "Someone wasn't watching the security outputs very closely."

"The heavy rain cooled down the IR, and the wind fouled up the background sensors," Godonov replied. "They probably turned off the motion alarms."

"I am going to chew butt," Buck snorted, yanking off his dripping helmet and spraying water from his lips. He shook like a big dog and then shivered.

"Never thought I'd be so happy to see these stinking wooden walls," Godonov said. "A hot shower and a real bed, the marine's definition of civilization."

"Hell," Buck laughed, "throw in hot chow and you have the meaning of life. Let's go. Admin says we got orders waiting."

Sergeant Gordon's fire team marched by. Buck and Godonov, with Lizard Lips in between, fell in at the rear of the column and marched through the gates. Godonov was gladdened. The wooden walls were home for Hunter Company, although the palisade itself was more symbolic than necessary. Defense against predators, the fortress's original purpose, was no longer an issue. A network of detection systems veined the valley and its perimeter, keeping humans and cliff dwellers aware of all animal movement. Bear had been pushed from the inhabited areas, and nightmare and rock-dog packs had been all but eliminated from the lower valley. Lake elk and toy deer populations had exploded.

As complement to the sensor network, hunter sentries patrolled the higher ridges, and human aircraft patrolled the distant slopes for dragon. The two-ton bladder-throated monsters, six meters from fanged maw to spiked tail, were intercepted long before they became a threat to the valley's population. Humans hunted them for sport.

The interior of the palisade roiled with good-natured excitement. The arriving warriors were greeted by fellow marines and hunters. Godonov, inhaling the rain-sweetened air, noticed a collection of Buccari's Survivors gathered on the lodge's steep porch. He recognized Sandy Tatum, Nancy Dawson, and Terry O'Toole. The settlement lodge, a two-story stone building with a steeply peaked roof, was the Survivors' unofficial headquarters. Another Survivor, Beppo Schmidt, his shock of tow hair reflecting the sun, walked away from the others. He led two golden Genellan horses up the gentle hill, toward the paddock in the palisade's southeastern corner. On each of the stubby-nosed beasts perched a hunter.

Tatum shouted across the common, hailing Chastain and Gordon. The tall redhead waved his single massive arm. Major Buck dismissed the sergeants, and they double-timed across the wooden bridge spanning the flower-margined brook. Chastain still carried the old huntress on his forearm. Godonov followed the marines. A cliff dweller sailed past him, pulling in its great, luffing wings to perch on the porch railing. It was Spitter, lead hunter of the horse-tending cliff dwellers and Sandy Tatum's constant companion.

"Sharl's entering orbit," Tatum shouted. "St. Pierre called from Hydro. He and Colonel Pak are taking the helo to pick her up."

Buccari! Sharl Buccari was coming home. Now Godonov was more anxious than ever to take a bath. The warm bed could wait. He debated hacking off his whiskers.

"Hey, Nes," Tatum hailed.

The one-armed Survivor was as tall as Chastain, a full two meters, and nearly as wide of shoulder, but thinner of hip and thigh.

"Hey, Sandy," Godonov shouted, his high spirits lifting euphorically. Buccari was coming home.

"Didn't recognize you in all that field gear," Tatum boomed. Despite the damp chill, Tatum wore only leather vest and breeches. The exposed biceps of his remaining arm was larger than Godonov's thigh. "You could pass for a grunt, sir, except for the face fungus."

Godonov laughed. "You should talk."

Tatum's face was a mass of freckles and peeling skin, framed with a mountain-man beard and an extravagant, leather-wrapped ponytail. Nancy Dawson, taller than most men and big-boned, stood with her arm around Tatum's waist. Where Tatum's hair was sun-washed orange, Dawson's uncontrolled explosion of curls was carrot-red. Where Tatum's eyes were deep brown, hers were pale blue. Dawson was profoundly pregnant—again. Toddling on the porch behind her, swaddled in leather, were a set of rusty-thatched twins.

"Ain't no marine no more," Tatum replied, a wistful smile softening his granite features. "Need two arms to be a marine."

"But only one gun," Dawson said, rubbing her great stomach.

"Once a marine, always a marine," Chief Wilson thundered, coming out of the lodge. "No way a man can learn to be that dumb. Being a marine's a genetic deficiency."

"Like being fat, bald, and ugly, Gunner?" Dawson snorted.

"Don't start with me, Dawson," Wilson growled, puffing up his barrel chest. "I'll chew your tall ass up and spit it out."

"Like hell," Dawson growled back, thrusting her nose into the shorter man's face and bumping him with her gravid belly. "You'll be using your butt for a porthole by the time I'm finished pounding on your head. If you weren't the cook, we'd a used you for lard long ago."

Wilson tucked in his multiple chins and opened his eyes wide, at least partially feigning fear. The portly man fell back, awkwardly raising his fists in burlesque belligerence. Dawson pressed forward.

"We're having fun now." Tatum chuckled, grabbing Dawson by her coat and reining her in.

"Golly, just like the old days," Chastain softly thundered. Everyone turned at the big man's resonant voice, so rarely offered. Chastain stood wide-eyed and innocent. "Everyone's happy because Commander Buccari's coming home."

"Golly, Jocko," Wilson mocked, "when didya start speaking in whole sentences?"

Chastain turned red and looked at his huge boots.

"Gunner's a nitwit, Jocko," Dawson said, taking charge. "Damn right we're happy, and we're going to celebrate.

O'Toole, pass the word. Sandy, you and Beppo get a firewood detail together. Bonfire tonight on the common. Gunner, get Tookmanian and Mendoza. Start planning chow—"

A happy shriek lifted into the air.

"News already hit the net," Dawson said.

Guilder stone carvers, with help from the Survivors and marines, had built the new schoolhouse against the palisade's southern wall. It was a fortress of a building, constructed of variegated rock, precisely chiseled. Lintels of alabaster capped all windows and doors, and stone planters flourished with colorful blossoms. Exploding down the school's steep steps came the settlement's children, the oldest first. Those over ten years of age carried rifles and self-importantly scanned the skies. Mrs. Jackson came last, ushering the children into a squirming double-line formation. When they were finally at some semblance of attention, the teacher dismissed the schoolchildren living within the palisade. These youngsters broke ranks and sprinted toward the lodge. Waving at the Survivors, Mrs. Jackson marched the rest of her charges toward the spring sally-gate, the older students with their rifles ready.

No sooner had the formation of children cleared the gate than Leslie Lee, with two gardeners waddling behind, burst through. She ran up the hill along the flower-shrouded brook.

"Winnie!" Leslie Lee shouted, short legs in full sprint, her blue-black hair trailing in her wake. "Is Winfried coming down?"

"Yeah, yeah, yeah. Fenstermacher, too," Wilson replied.

"Into every life a little rain must fall," Dawson said.

"Be nice," Lee chastised, huffing to catch her breath.

"That was nice," Wilson retorted. "For Dawson."

Dawson laughed. "Piss in your white hat, Gunner."

"I rest my case." He sighed, rolling his eyes.

Greatmother shrieked, halting the happy banter. The old huntress hand-signed: "Where Thunderhead?"

Dawson and Lee looked at each other.

"Where's Charlie?" Dawson asked.

"He wasn't in school," Tatum's leggy daughter said. Honey Goldberg. Ten standard years of age, the first human born on

Genellan wore morbidly scuffed horse chaps and carried a carbine, the badge of her age and training.

"He left the cabin this morning with Hope," Leslie Lee replied.

Lee and Fenstermacher's black-haired daughter nodded shyly.

"Charlie tol' the teacher he was working in the stables," burly little Adam Shannon said. Not as tall as Honey but also a year younger, Adam's face was an unfreckled replication of Nancy Dawson's, only his thick hair was jet-black, like that of his deceased father. "Charlie left straightaway. I watched him to the stables."

"Never showed," Tatum said. "I never saw him."

Moisture dripped heavily from the lodge's eaves.

Greatmother hand-signed again: "Where Thunderhead?"

The huntress's sharp snout moved in quick jerks. Suddenly she raised her tooth-filled maw and emitted a sharp series of chirps that turned ultrasonic.

"Not again," Lee cried.

"Sergeant," Godonov said, pivoting for the barracks, "send the hunters back out. Fire-teams One and Two take the west side of the lake. Three and Four the south and east. Team Five will search the river."

Chastain acknowledged on the run. Billy Gordon sprinted ahead, shouting.

FIFTEEN

MOTHER AND CHILD

Condor Three was established in Genellan orbit. Buccari, in silver EPL suit, pulled herself into the endoatmospheric lander's snug cockpit. She connected her single-point umbilical and engaged tethers.

"Computer! Systems status . . . initiate," she barked. "Pilot Buccari."

Ladder lights on the console sequenced. The EPL's op computer replied with a synthesized voice: "Pilot Buccari. Control authorizations check. Pilot has command."

"Launch sequence," Buccari ordered. The computer initiated system checks. Crew calls flashed.

"All systems checking good, sir," Thompson reported from the systems station.

"Cabin secure," Fenstermacher reported.

"Rog'," Buccari acknowledged. Her fingers and retinal cursor flew about her instruments. The prelaunch checklist scrolled down her command monitor as she satisfied each requirement.

"Checks complete," Buccari announced. "Stand by to jettison EPL!"

"Rog'," Flaherty responded from the corvette flight deck.

"Front's scooting through," Thompson reported. "Stink Tower reports breaks in the overcast. Visibility unlimited except in showers. Moderate turbulence in clouds."

"Copy," she replied. A few clouds were not going to stop her from getting on the ground.

"Apple cleared to launch," Flaherty transmitted. "Report clear."

EPL bay doors yawned. An overwhelming blackness crept through the widening aperture, a blackness richly relieved with pinpricks of unflickering white—an infinite multitude of heavenly bodies. Vibration hummed through metal; the lander moved outboard, pushed by a spidery gantry crane. Reflected light from the planet bathed the cockpit. Her visor darkened automatically. Buccari released the attachment fitting, fired a micropulse on the port maneuvering rockets, and reported "Clear."

Euphoric, she rolled the lander on its back and fired retros.

Eagles screamed beyond the ridge.

The boy, arms wrapped around the egg, bounded down the steep scree, his sandaled feet pushing avalanches of wet talus, his grimy toes stubbed raw and bloody. He glanced over his shoulder, gunmetal eyes flashing in bright sunlight.

Another noise echoed across the alpine valley, a double explosion sonic boom from an orbital lander penetrating the atmosphere. It barely registered. Concealment! The boy needed a place to hide. But for a few lustrous puffs, floating serenely indifferent below his lofty elevation, the rain-swirling clouds that had earlier provided cover were gone from the valley. The youth, lithe and sinewy, stared hopelessly at the distant tree line. An impatient gust lifted a sweat-matted, sun-bleached lock of brown thatch, revealing a filthy brow folded with concern.

Closer, less than a hunter's bowshot along the talus field, a stubby granite pinnacle jutted from the mountain. Altering course, the boy traversed the unstable face of the bowl, struggling to hold elevation. The screeching heightened, a cawing blood lust growing louder, closer. The boy looked to the ridge and was not surprised to see an eagle lift above the planet's profile. The raptor's stately black and tan body was silhouetted against blue skies, twelve-meter wingspan rigid against buffeting updrafts. Tail feathers splayed wide, the eagle hovered with predatory efficiency, its great head scanning the broad expanse of rock.

Knowing with fatal certainty that he had been discovered,

the boy cradled the egg in his elbows and placed two fingers of each hand against the tip of his tongue. He whistled a shrill, ululating signal. He paused, listened, then whistled again, desperately, his dirt-daubed cheeks turning crimson. Fingers dropping from mouth, the boy looked skyward to see a second giant eagle swoop across the ridge, followed by a third, and a fourth, all screaming with piercing, atavistic hate.

The urchin lurched to a sliding gallop, grimly measuring the distance to the escarpment. There were clefts and narrow defiles in the rocks, shelter from flesh-ripping talons and bone-crunching beaks. Another surge of adrenaline rushed down his neck, along with the hot chill of fear. Increasing his pace to a stumbling sprint, he shifted his burden to the crook of his right elbow and used his downhill arm for balance. His grip on the egg tightened.

Monstrous shadows raced down the steep slope and across his peripheral vision. He dared not risk a glance into the threat-filled skies. The screams were indication enough. Death was near. The boy's whole being focused on the tumble of rocks. Not far, but as he dodged around smaller boulders dotting the approach to the outcropping, the sun was extinguished by an intervening presence. Whistling air added to the exploding sensation of peril. The boy took an abrupt step uphill and moved his shoulders as if to turn in that direction, but then threw his body backward, down the precipitous slope, tumbling and somersaulting, protecting the egg with arms and stomach.

The feint worked. A huge pinion thrashed the boy's head, but the crushing talons missed. The great bird's headlong dive propelled it awkwardly against the flinty talus The thwarted predator sprang backward, pushing strongly into the air—directly into the paths of a second and third eagle, disrupting their attacks on the scrambling egg-stealer. The eagles screeched in riotous frustration, slapping at the air with monstrous wings, struggling to regain maneuvering speed.

Wing-thrusted air exploded against the mountainside, lifting dust and fluttering the boy's scuffed leather garments. The tumbling youth had eyes only for the warrens and boulders sliding uselessly past. Stiffening his legs and digging into sharp rocks with his bruised and abraded knees, the boy stabilized his flailing trajectory. Still sliding downward in an avalanche of talus, he crabbed toward the haven of heavy stones. He glanced upslope. A gigantic raptor skidded to ground only paces away. The yellow-eyed killer, steadying itself with extended wings that blotted out the mountainside, lunged, thrusting viciously with its great hooked beak. The boy, wide-eyed with horror, evaded the death stroke by twisting sideways, falling hard on his shoulder and back, again sliding uncontrollably down the mountainside. The eagle gathered its wings and stuttered closer. A second infuriated raptor, its wing gusts moving pebbles, crunched onto the rocky slope, cutting off escape. Both landed eagles darted forward to seize the egg-stealing vermin.

Panic welled in the boy's gut. His slide had carried him nearly past the tumbled granite. A protrusion jutting through the rock litter painfully halted his slide, but it also provided solid purchase from which to launch a dive to safety. The death shadow of a third screaming eagle darkened the rocks, and cold currents of air swirled crazily as the boy lunged toward the rock shadows, the shadows of hope.

A mighty force wrenched at his sandaled foot.

Buccari yawned to equalize her inner ears. She grabbed the EPL's side stick and blinked off the autopilot. The endoatmospheric planetary lander plunged deeper into the atmosphere, rolling slowly onto a wing. Buccari reversed bank and pulled the nose of the apple into a hard turn, losing altitude. Luxuriating in building gee forces, she relaxed bank angle and carved a continent-sweeping turn. Far below, etching the planet, the Great River snaked out from under clouds brilliantly white.

"Engines hot," Thompson reported. "Fuel pressure's in the green."

"Roger," Buccari replied, pulling the lander across a horizon no longer purple. Planet textures took definition, expanding into geographic relief. Gee-loading climbed. On her headup the descent funnel warped and twisted, responding to her maneuvers. A caution light illuminated.

"Compute . . . command. Autoconnect," she announced, restoring control to the computer. The lander banked smoothly to port. The tracking bug on the course indicator drifted smartly onto the approach course. The descent funnel straightened. The signal from the MacArthur's Valley navigation beacon was strong and steady.

The sandal ripped from the boy's foot, but his dive for cover was not halted. He landed again on bruised shoulders and twisted his body, crawling on stone-slashed knees into a cramped alcove. His mouth and throat were caked with dust; his lungs gasped for sustenance in the thin air, but the precious egg still lay nestled in the crook of his arm. In mindless fury, the great eagles scrambled over the rocks, talons scraping granite, screams rending the heavens. The crawl space narrowed. The boy needed to get farther in; the eagles could still reach him with their leg-length beaks. He turned on his side to fit through a pinching crevice, pushing the egg before him. The boy gouged desperately at the pebbly wrack, burrowing and scraping with bloodied fingers, pushing with his toes. With agonizing effort he rounded a boulder and pushed himself into an angle in the rocks.

The boulder behind which the boy squirmed was shouldered closely by larger stones, with other great rocks tumbled above. There was room to draw up his knees, but he was not yet safe; too much monochromatic sky was visible. The boy inched his way, digging furiously. At last his way was blocked by solid, unyielding rock.

An eagle screeched insanely. The boulder behind which the boy had taken refuge trembled. The patch of hard blue sky was blotted out by an assault from the top; a gaudy fire-orange beak probed violently. A second hooked beak thrashed its way between another opening in the nested boulders. The boy cringed into the deepest pocket of his sanctuary and feebly wristed handfuls of pebbles into the thrashing maws. Rising dust clogged his throat. He coughed uncontrollably.

The boulder lurched and thumped like a molar being worried from the jaws of the earth. A taloned claw worked its way between the protective stones. Thickly feathered muscles contracted, and the narrow opening between the stones slowly, inexorably, widened. As one eagle screamed maniacally, a second huge talon took purchase. The boulder twisted from their grasp; but it had been moved. Rocks shifted and settled; the patch of sky was doubled. A malevolent yellow eye glared down. The boy, overcome by coughing, set the egg between his bleeding legs and leaned against unyielding rock. He bowed his head.

An eternity dragged by—too much time. The fierce raptors did not torment their food. The boy glanced up, wondering why he still breathed. A desultory blizzard of small rocks plinked against the boulders and thudded against feathered muscle. A stone ricocheted from the boulder just over his head. Screams rose from the eagles, but different—cries of anger, cries of warning. The hulking eagle jerked upward. A feathered dart flitted into the bird's shoulder, driving the eagle backward. Another arrow struck a glancing blow off the eagle's beak. The eagle hopped away, screeching and limbering its wings. Over the eagle cries the boy heard familiar clarions. Cliff dwellers! He was rescued!

Rocks rained down. Covering his head against the stinging missiles, the boy wiggled from between the boulders, retrieving his sandal. One eagle skimmed downslope, distancing itself from painful darts and bruising stones. A small hunter, a sentry, gliding fast and low over the outcropping's blunted pinnacle, flew directly at the remaining eagles, inciting their predatory fury. It was One-son. The small black form wheeled like a bat, violently reversing course. The magnificent raptors lifted from the rocks, lumbering upward with mighty downthrusts of their wings.

One-son's membranes thrashed desperately. The sentry struggled to make the craggy prominence. The eagles gained altitude and velocity with unnerving ease, closing the distance between hound and hare with alarming speed. As the eagles neared the pinnacle's peak, two sentries sprang against the blue sky, short bows nocked with arrows. The hunters-to-be squawked their battle clarions. Bowstrings strummed.

"Mach one point two, altitude on schedule," Thompson reported. "In the groove. Checking good, Skipper."

Buccari responded with a double-click of her eye cursor. They were on final; the autopilot held altitude while airspeed decayed. The glide slope indicator settled on center, precisely bisecting the course indicator. The unpowered lander started resolutely down the glide slope. Buccari peered outward; far ahead, the gray gash that was the rollout runway lined up perfectly with her nose. In the distance, impossibly vertical mountains climbed, snowcapped, above the clouds.

"Landing checks complete, Commander," Thompson reported.

"Checking good," Buccari acknowledged. The river valley came out from under the left wing, the Great River flowing silty and powerful. The endless sweeping plains to the north swirled with browns and irregular patches of gold—grazing musk-buffalo and Genellan horses beyond count.

The vibration of the slipstream dampened to silence. Terrain features sharpened; lesser peaks passed down the left side. Wing-tip fences snapped erect; the flaps growled as they warped out from the trailing edges of the delta wings. The lander flared, its nose elevating until the angle-of-attack indexer centered. Airspeed held steady. The runway flowed at them, flattening and growing wider. She ached to take control. The computer flew a masterful approach, radar altimeters and laser range finders feeding back distances and vertical speeds precisely. The touchdown was signaled only by the vibrations of the landing gear suddenly rotating against the hard surface of the runway.

"Apple's on the ground," Fenstermacher celebrated from the cargo hold. "Papa's home! Hot damn!"

Buccari grunted. One gee tugged at her heart.

Pointy-head and Two-son fired their arrows at the climbing eagles. A pincushioned eagle broke away, flying erratically downhill, but the remaining pair of enraged eagles closed in on the cliff dwellers, intent on mayhem. One-son luffed up and grounded on a lower peak, an arrow nocked. Pointy-head and Two-son scattered before the unrelenting fury of the great birds, their small dark forms swooping close to the rock tumble, seeking shelter in the crevices. One-son, screeching madly, fired one last arrow and dove into the rocks a fraction of a second before a giant set of talons sliced the air in his place.

The boy emerged into sunlight and crept along the escarpment, his mind racing. Now they were all trapped. One of the eagles jerked its great black-crowned visage directly his way, its yellow eyes homing like lasers. The eagle screeched. The boy, frustrated with helplessness, screamed back. The eagles, one after the other, pushed from their rocky perches, swinging their cruel talons. The boy dove for a hole, praying the diversion would give the sentries time to make their escape. He slipped into a narrow crevice that ended too abruptly; the eagles would rip him out.

A screaming feathered giant grounded against the opening, its yawning wingspan shutting out the day. An orange beak hooked at him violently. Just missing. The talons would be next, and they would reach. The boy shut his eyes. The sentries were screaming, but he also heard something else. To his ears came a full-throated battle clarion, the screams of mature hunters. The attacking eagle fell back.

Lifting over the ridge beyond the eagle's noble profile appeared a flight of warriors. The eagle rejected the rock-bound quarry and pounded air, lifting to meet the brazen challenge. There was no contest; the phalanx of cliff dwellers, firing deathsticks on full automatic, blasted the giants from the sky. The intrepid hunters swooped past the tumbling behemoths, vortices from their membranes stirring up a blizzard of shattered feathers. Lifeless eagles crashed to the rocky slopes, twelve-meter wingspans carpeting the flinty talus with soft brown pinions.

The warriors floated to the stony ground, holstering their weapons and stowing their flight membranes with casual ease. Their demeanors were uniformly stern and slit-eyed. At their head was Captain Two, the leader of all hunters, armored in sweat-stained leather, fierce and battle-scarred. Tonto, his mother's staunch protector, strutted at Captain Two's side. The father of One-son and Two-son wore Legion armor. He screeched for the young sentries and for the human to descend from the rocks.

The boy eyed the dead eagles, for an instant debating which fate was the more intolerable—death or reprimand. He un-wedged himself and stumbled forward. One-son, Two-son, and Pointy-head, black eyes downcast, floated breezily to the ground at the boy's side, their talons dislodging small avalanches of dull-ringing shale. The sentries were a half head shorter than the human, the human child a half head shorter than the full-grown hunters. The boy, still holding the eagle egg, bowed low to the warrior leader. The three sentries, with comical imprecision, followed the human's example.

Tonto exploded into a chittering frenzy, his tone rising with ear-shattering volume and intensity. The boy understood the essence of the hunter's tirade, even if most of it was delivered in frequencies beyond his ken. He dared to lift his head; blood trickled down his abraded elbows and calves. Tonto screeched; the other hunters glared.

Not knowing what else to do, the boy held out the eagle egg.

"Stupid! Stupid!" Tonto gesticulated emphatically.

Captain Two chittered gently and Tonto paused. The hunter leader, his red-rimmed, double-lidded onyx eyes inscrutable as stone, stared down at the boy. Tonto resumed his animated screeching, focusing on the sentries. Captain Two silenced his lieutenant with a less gentle chirp.

"Thunderhead!" Captain Two screeched the boy's cliff dweller name.

The boy understood many cliff dweller words. His name, especially when spoken in such commanding tone, he knew well. The boy stood erect and faced the scarred warrior.

"Perform the ceremony," Captain Two's gnarled, four-digit hands signed with graceful clarity.

The boy struggled with a communication he could not possibly have perceived. Captain Two repeated the signs and added: "Quickly. Thy mother soon arrives."

The boy, astounded, watched the hunter leader's sign language carefully. His mother was back! Wonderful news, but even more wonderful, Captain Two had ordered him to perform the egg-sharing ceremony, a ritual for warriors, by warriors. The boy looked to Tonto, his mother's old friend. That warrior impatiently repeated the commands.

The boy whistled a hunter's acknowledgment and knelt on the hard rocks. He placed the orange-mottled egg between his bloody knees and picked up a stone. Captain Two chirped. The boy looked up. The hunter leader thrust at him a worn Legion survival knife, handle first. Tonto screeched into the skies. The boy, wide-eyed, reached up and accepted the heavy knife. On its hilt were carved the initials: C.M.

"Yours now," Captain Two signed.

Charlie was stunned.

"Keep," the hunter leader commanded.

"Cohorts forever," the boy whistled crudely, a timeless cliff dweller response.

"Proceed," Captain Two shrieked. The other hunters cheered shrilly, displaying an unseemly impatience.

The hefty knife balanced in his grimy hand, the boy gently tapped the egg's tapered end until it was fractured completely around its crown. He stuck the tip of the knife into the crack and, with a flourish, flipped the shell cap to the ground. Hunters chittered their approval. The boy stood erect and made his best effort at shrieking the hunter ritual song of death. His efforts were immensely enjoyed by the hunters. The warriors pointed their pickax snouts skyward and screeched, going in and out of audible range, joining in bizarre harmony.

The boy held up the decapitated egg. Captain Two accepted the trophy and lifted it to his sharply pointed snout. Viscous albumin and garish orange yolk flowed from the corners of his tooth-lined jaws, dripping down his leather armor. Captain Two sighed contentedly and handed the egg to the boy, who took it in both hands and repeated the process, tilting the egg until its contents overflowed onto neck and shoulders. The boy passed it to Tonto, who took his turn. Around the egg went, the draughts getting smaller, more ceremonial than real. The last one to drink hurled the empty shell into the void, and the death song was screamed by all.

SIXTEEN

HOME AGAIN

Reggie St. Pierre watched Buccari's apple kiss the runway atop two white puffs. The tower's observation deck had enough elevation to view the entire length of the runway, a four-kilometer black gash on the planet bordered by bulldozed mounds of tortured tundra and red topsoil. It stretched westward, pointing to the twin volcanoes, and to the plateau beyond. Backdrop to all were the towering peaks of the continental spine, their hoary, jagged spires tinged blue by distance.

St. Pierre breathed deeply, enjoying the symphony of his senses. The acrid taint of buffalo musk stalked the fringes of his awareness.

"Wind's shifted," Colonel Han Pak remarked, cutting the silence.

"Yeah," St. Pierre replied, flipping back his parka hood. The sun's warm rays mixed with a chill breeze. St. Pierre stared into the distance. The EPL cleared the runway. A bright yellow ground tractor took the lander in tow, bringing Buccari ever closer. His insides were in turmoil. A soft groan escaped his lips.

"Something wrong, Reg?" Pak asked.

"Nothing," St. Pierre exhaled, affecting a smile.

"When you worked for me, you were a much better liar," Pak said.

"Get off my back, Colonel," St. Pierre snapped. The old assassin could read him too well. "You're not my boss anymore. You're not my father. You're the mayor of a dinkass, jerkwater settlement in the middle of nowhere, going nowhere, hibernating your frigging life away."

145

A pause, maybe a heartbeat.

"Fishing's mighty good," Pak mused, staring into the eastern sky.

St. Pierre laughed. He followed Pak's squinty gaze. A konish utility airplane, an *abat*, turned on a long final, its thick white fuselage and long wings reflecting the bright sun. It was Ambassador Kateos's plane with Nash Hudson on board. Hudson and Buccari both coming home. A momentous day for MacArthur's Valley.

"Ask her," Pak asked, slapping him on the back. "She might—"

"You make a pathetic cupid, old man," St. Pierre snarled, spinning for the ladder. He descended athletically from the tower's observation deck. Pak, moving like an old panther, followed.

St. Pierre, forcing his mind off Buccari, took inventory of his surroundings. On the concrete mat squatted three light helicopters, a heavy sky-crane, and two utility fixed wings. An assortment of construction equipment, yellow ground tractors, and emergency vehicles dotted the pavement, some parked, some grinding about their business. In the distance a tracked land rover paralleled the runway, sirens howling and dome lights flashing in a never-ending effort to keep the great eagles and other flying fauna from obstructing the landing surface.

Parading across the tundra like red channel buoys in a rolling sea, the stanchions of the security barrier glinted in the late morning sun. Easterly breezes occasionally swamped the spaceport with the fetid musk of buffalo, but the prevailing westerlies usually purged the region of nature's miasma. Rarely, however, was the odor totally absent, as the crudely painted sign welcoming newcomers attested:

WELCOME TO PLANET GENELLAN
CONTINENT OF CORLIA
MACARTHUR'S VALLEY SETTLEMENT
MALODOR MEADOWS SPACEPORT—SMELLIEST
PLACE IN THE UNIVERSE

STINKMETER

⇒ 1. REAL BAD (AS GOOD AS IT EVER GETS)
2. HEADACHES
3. NOSEBLEEDS
4. DEATH

Buccari's EPL was deposited on a support pad and surrounded by service vehicles and ground crew. St. Pierre walked faster. Pak trotted to keep up. The day was cool; the lander's skin temperature would stabilize quickly. Cargo hatches and access ports slid open and members of the crew appeared in the openings. St. Pierre recognized Fenstermacher's wiry form. He stopped, unsure. Pak kept walking.

"Hey, Colonel Pak!" the boatswain shouted, looking up from his postlanding duties. "How's the fishing? The damn cliff dwellers take all the frigging fish yet?"

Sharl Buccari, in dun fatigues, stepped from the EPL with the cautious gait of a spacer too long removed from gravity. Stress-bruised eyes flashed green in the rain-freshened sunlight; her egg-shiny bald head glistened like a pearl. Buccari squinted at the sun and donned a soft gold beret. She was beautiful. St. Pierre knew his dreams had not done reality justice. They could not.

Buccari took a deep breath. Unmistakable odors assaulted her sinuses. After six months away, her olfactories had resensitized. She hocked and spat, clearing some of the incipient irritation. Reflexively, she scanned the skies, searching for eagles and hoping to see hunters. Hunters always knew when she was back. She saw only a gauzy rainbow backdropped by soaring, snowcapped mountains, a rearguard for retreating battalions of blue-bottomed cumulus. No hunters.

Disappointed, Buccari brought her gaze back to the surface. She saw Colonel Pak jawboning with Fenstermacher, and then she noticed St. Pierre, standing alone, staring at her. Blood pulsed warmly in her cheeks. St. Pierre's countenance was powerful. His black eyes were not lusting, she told herself, at least not overmuch; instead they measured her, poetically. Buccari walked up to the very tall, very handsome man.

"Welcome home," St. Pierre said, taking her in his strong arms. She returned his pressure. The widower's embrace was warm and encompassing; his heart pounded against her cheek. Buccari reluctantly pushed away.

"Reggie," she said, trying not to smile too much. "Why aren't you at NEd, covering the downloads?"

St. Pierre's smooth complexion was still pale from the deprivation of Genellan's long winter. By early summer his symmetrical features would sensually darken, and by autumn he would be abjectly swarthy, an intriguing metamorphosis. St. Pierre, a member of Genellan's initial settler complement, had intrigued Buccari from the first moment she had met him.

"I knew you would come here first," St. Pierre said. His eyes bored gently into her soul.

"I'm glad, Reg," she said. "I scan your service every day. Great stuff. It's like you're reading my mind."

The *abat* taxiing nearby suddenly made it hard to hear. She donned glare goggles and squinted, trying to see into the cockpit. The airplane pivoted into a parking spot and its engine shut down.

"I'm leaving, Sharl," St. Pierre said in the sudden quiet. "I'm moving to NEd . . . to live."

"To live, Reg?" Buccari asked, tilting her chin.

"That's where the politics are," St. Pierre replied. "If I'm going to run a news agency for the settlements—like you ordered me to," he emphasized, "I need to be where the issues are. All the decision-makers are in NEd. That's where I should be."

"You mean so much to MacArthur's Valley. You're a part of—"

"There's nothing here for me except bad memories," St. Pierre mumbled. "Except . . . I mean, if you . . . if there was a chance you—"

"Oh, Reg," Buccari moaned, taking his hands.

"I've had enough pity," the widower replied.

Buccari remained silent, her head bowed.

"I'm sorry," St. Pierre apologized, after the silence had grown too long. "You're home for such a short time, and what do I do but get maudlin. I am sorry, Sharl."

"Don't be sorry, Reggie," Buccari said, taking off her goggles. "From that first day you and Maggie arrived, I thought you were special. It's just . . ."

"You're in love with someone else," St. Pierre whispered.

Buccari looked at him and tried to smile, but a tear broke loose instead. She returned the IR goggles to her eyes.

"Citizen Sharl!" thundered a familiar voice.

Buccari pivoted to see Et Silmarn's immense form descending from the parked *abat*. The governor turned to the crew hatch. Emerging into the sunlight behind him came Kateos, her bovine features bursting with joy. The ambassador leapt from the high hatch and landed softly on all fours, breaking into a ground-quaking sprint.

"Katy!" Buccari shouted. She should have been disconcerted by the hurtling mass of muscle bearing down on her, but she had borne the brunt of the kone's affections before. She was scooped bodily into the air and surrounded by stiff-garbed muscle. Kateos's tawny eye tufts were rigid, her huge cow eyes brimming with joy. Buccari's eyes were also suddenly flooded with tears, both from her happiness and from the overwhelmingly bitter stench emanating from her bosom friend's rampantly discharging emotion bladders.

"Sharl, my sister, look at whom we have brought with us," Kateos rumbled silkily, placing Buccari gently on the ground. Buccari peeked around Kateos's broad person. At the foot of the *abat*'s boarding ladder, holding his daughter's hand, stood Nash Hudson. Buccari's breath left her body. She had talked with him on vid-comm; she had seen his repaired face, but seeing her old shipmate in person again, whole and unscarred, was breathtaking. She stumbled into a trot. Hudson lifted his daughter and ran forward. They collided in a three-way hug.

"Auntie Sharl!" Emerald shouted.

"Oh, Nash!" Buccari said, laughing. "You're beautiful." She reached up with both hands and felt the tall man's reconstructed face. A remarkable job, his skin perhaps smoother than natural, his features a little more regular than she remembered, but Hudson's radiant, tear-brimming eyes were a lovely constant. She kissed him flush on his rebuilt lips.

"God, I missed you, Sharl," Hudson said, blushing spectacularly.

"And I missed you, Brown Bar," she said.

"Auntie Sharl," Emerald persisted. "Where's Charlie?"

"We're going to see him now," Sharl replied, lifting the little girl from Hudson's arms, forcing her gaze from Hudson's perfect new face. "Oof, Emmy, you've gotten so big since I saw you last."

As Buccari stepped away with Emerald in her arms, Hudson was attacked by St. Pierre, Pak, and Fenstermacher in an orgy of backslapping and shoulder punching.

"Hey, Winnie, feel my thigh!" Hudson shouted. "It's real muscle and fully rehabilitated. I—"

"I'll give you something to feel!" Fenstermacher roared.

Buccari turned joyfully to Kateos. The kone had fallen to all fours, her huge face at eye level with Buccari's.

"I am going to Earth," Kateos said.

"King Ollant communicated that to me," Buccari said, speaking konish. "He asked if it was the right thing to do. I told him there never was a decision better made."

"Hud-sawn tells me many things about your planet," Kateos said. "It is an exciting and frightening place. Your history is tumultuous."

"You must make your own judgments," Buccari said. "You are King Ollant's envoy, not mine, not Nash Hudson's."

"Of course, my sister," Kateos said.

"Commander Buccari," Pak prompted, "your gear is loaded. The entire population of MacArthur's Valley is waiting for you."

"I'm ready, Colonel," she said, looking vainly one last time into the skies. Something was wrong. Hunters always knew.

Pak led the landing party to the helo pads, ushering everyone into a big Legion utility chopper. The helo lifted off and immediately plunged over tall cliffs into the Great River's immense riparian valley. Buccari, as always, was filled with wonder at the wide river, its powerful course green-gray with silt. Upstream thundered the foamy explosions of the cataracts.

"The cargo tram's finally finished," Colonel Pak said, pointing downstream. "We tested a two-ton load yesterday. Went like a charm. Cargo transfer from the spaceport only takes a few hours now."

She looked downstream. Thick cables fell like gossamer threads from the river cliffs to an immense tower on a riverine island. From there the tram catenary curved across the river, supported on progressively shorter towers rising from concrete piers embedded in the river. Near its low terminus the new breakwater slanted from the shore, harboring the river ferries.

The helo arrowed across the ever-wide river, aiming for a gash in the glacier-hung mountains. Buccari's heart expanded with each familiar landmark. MacArthur's Valley's precipitate western wall was rife with sun-washed silvery cascades and hanging glaciers, but it was the surreal, alpine-blue expanse of Lake Shannon lifting into view from behind forested moraines that shivered her backbone. She was home again, if only for a short visit. She imprinted the vision on her mind, wondering when, if ever again, would she have the bittersweet pleasure of returning home.

The boy, heavy knife in hand, descended the valley's western wall, traversing its precipitous slopes in a downhill slalom around stately pine boles. An escort of screaming hunters soared high overhead. Below him the lake flashed neon-blue through shadowed boughs. At the elk run his pace increased from a sliding, side-hill lope to a headlong sprint. The floor of the valley rose to meet him. Hardwoods replaced pine, and underbrush thickened. He vaulted a white-splashing rill, and suddenly the lake trail was under his thudding foot-falls. Lake Shannon on his left hand shimmered in the late morning sun. Hunters swooped over its surface in ground-effect, membrane tips shearing its silken surface.

Charlie Buccari, sweat-soaked and grimy, begrudged the

hunters their effortless flight. He pounded across a trio of heavy-timbered bridges marking the misty confluence of mountain streams. The dirt trail paralleled another crashing watercourse as it passed under the looming yellow edifice of the hydropower plant. There the rutted trail suddenly transformed into a road paved with water-smoothed rocks. Its softly variegated surface of white, dun, and russet cobbles curved around the lakeshore and passed through an unguarded gate in Hydro's wooden palisade. A reception committee of chirping hunters waited, perching on walls and tree snags. Charlie did not slow, running full pace through the gate. Cliff dwellers exploded into the air, pounding upward to join other hunters swirling overhead on the strengthening thermals.

Hydro's cobbled main street was crowded. Faces turned as the boy ran by. People pointed and shouted his name. He jogged onto the boardwalk, his footfalls slapping the wooden planks. A settler's cart pulled by a golden Genellan horse rattled along the gently curving waterfront road. There were no structures on the lake side of the road except for the yellow two-story Legion admin building at the far end of town. The roadside opposite the lake was lined with a boardwalk and an uneven assortment of painted wooden storefronts, settler hostels, taverns, and a laborer barracks. On the lake side the road was bordered with a low rock wall, interrupted with shallow stairs leading to a wharf. Wooden piers with davit gantries protruded from the wharf at right angles. A crane squeaked under the load of a boat being lowered into the water.

As the boy went under the carved beams of Citizen O'Toole's tavern, a cluster of laborers disgorged through the weather doors, overflowing onto the boot-worn boardwalk. Rank odors of perspiration and ale drifted with them, blending with hewn pine, horse manure, drying fish, and a vague hint of buffalo musk.

"Look, a kid! Where ya going, little babe?" roared a threatening voice, deep and resonant.

The boy tried to dodge away. Someone grabbed his collar and yanked him to a halt, twisting him roughly around and slamming him against a hitching post. A golden horse whinnied at his back, startled by the abrupt motion. Charlie was suddenly cheek-to-jowl with a fat, bearded brute. Foul breath flushed warmly against his face.

"A tender young . . ." snarled the drunk. "Damn, kid, ya stink worse'n I do."

"Let him go, Hanjk!" shouted another man coming through the door, a gruff older tradesman the boy recognized. "That's Buccari's kid."

"Well-l-l," Hanjk exclaimed, squeezing the boy's clothing tighter in his meaty fist. "Queen Scarface's minnow, eh?"

"Let 'em go," a voice, deep and powerful, commanded.

Hanjk released Charlie's shirt so quickly the boy almost fell. Charlie recognized Tatum's voice. He turned to see the one-armed man sitting astride a thick-chested golden horse. The horse was Charlie's favorite; its name was Tank. On Tank's broad rump perched the hunter Spitter, his long razor-toothed maw hissing open. Two more displeased hunters landed on the hitching post, their membranes gusting. The laborer, hands up in a pleading gesture, slid along the tavern wall until he disappeared into the crowd.

Tatum dropped to the ground and deftly hitched Tank to the railing. Charlie looked out on the street. Half the settlement was approaching, some on horses, most walking. Jocko Chastain and Billy Gordon double-timed in the forefront. More cliff dwellers swished by; Captain Two and Tonto landed on the hitching rail, their huge wings stirring dust. Nestor Godonov and Lizard Lips also appeared. The guilder screeched and chittered his annoyance.

"Your mother's coming down," Tatum said gently.

"I know," Charlie replied, reaching up to pat Tank's stubby nose. The muscular horse acknowledged the boy's attentions, snorting and pushing against the pressure of his dirty hand. Leslie Lee burst through the crowd, her long hair swirling blue-black in the late morning sun.

"There you are," Lee huffed, grabbing his arm and inspecting his bones. "You're bleeding. Are you okay?"

"Yes'm," Charlie answered.

"Good, because I'm going to beat the crap out of you."

"Careful, Les. Charlie's damn near as tall as you are," Tatum said, laughing and taking the boy by the shoulders. The one-armed man squatted close. "What's that you got?"

"A knife," Charlie said. "Captain Two gave it to me."

The red-bearded giant stared at the weapon for several long seconds, not touching, just looking. "Take good care of it, Charlie," Tatum said, putting his big hand on the boy's shoulder. "Belonged to your old man."

Charlie stared down at the treasure. The sound of a helicopter lifted into his awareness. He looked up and saw the helo far up the lake, heading for the cove.

"She's coming!" someone shouted.

Tatum recoiled to his full height, sniffing the air. *"Pshew!"* he exhaled. "You stink bad. Let Jocko hold the knife."

The helicopter flew down the long lake, past Longo's Meadow. The cove and the settlement palisade came into view.

"They found your son, Commander," the helicopter copilot reported.

"What?" Buccari shouted, suddenly anxious.

"Your son! They found your son."

"I didn't know he was missing," she said.

"Sorry, sir," the copilot continued. "I thought you knew. Radios are burning up with search activity. Cliff dwellers found him on the west face. They've got him in Hydro. You want me to take you there?"

"Please," she said.

The pilot waved off his approach. Except for the new school, the settlement looked the same. The marine barracks squatted at the palisade's main gate. The wildflower-bordered spring lifted from above the high-peaked lodge in the palisade's center and flowed in a gentle curve to the lake cove. Beyond the lodge rose the stone silos, the kilns, and the family cabins. Against the eastern wall rose the water tower. The stable and paddock nestled in the southeastern corner.

Marines on guard waved; she waved back. Other marines and hunters emptied from the barracks. The pilot flew down the shore, past homesteads and fields cut from hardwood forest. Settlers ran from their cabins. Buccari sat in the open door, returning their exuberant waves. The helo paralleled the lakeshore. A rock wall bedecked with crimson flowers ran along the puddled gravel road, and piles of stumps served as distance markers. A steady trickle of settlers, some on foot, some on horseback, moved below. In the bed of an electric lorry she recognized Nancy Dawson's carrot-red hair.

"I see your son, Commander," the pilot reported as they approached Hydro. "Check the pier."

Buccari looked down at the lakeside village. The roof peaks, the rock walls bordering the wharf, the davit gantries on the piers, all were thick with perching cliff dwellers. And in the skies, staying clear of the helo, hunters swooped and wheeled. Her gaze stopped on the pier nearest the helo pads. Sandy Tatum's wide-shouldered form was unmistakable, his red hair like a beacon on the water. With Tatum, made small in comparison, was her brown-thatched son. Charlie waved as the helo crossed the shoreline. She waved back and wondered why Tatum had him on the pier.

The helo settled onto a Legion landing pad. Well-wishers pressed forward. Marines formed a cordon against the settlers' exuberance. A chant rose over the winding turbines: "Booch! Booch!"

Buccari jumped to the ground with the blades still spinning. Leslie Lee ran forward and they hugged. Chief Wilson, Terry O'Toole, and Beppo Schmidt were on Lee's heels, along with Mrs. Jackson, Sam Cody, and Nestor Godonov. Tookmanian, a huge smile lifting his black mustaches, slipped from the crowd with Mendoza and Mendoza's new wife close behind; Billy Gordon and Jocko Chastain, both grinning, remained in ranks. Buccari's heart swelled magnificently; these were her friends. Buccari's Survivors, the settlers of MacArthur's Valley, and the children of both, pressed forward to see her, to touch her.

A joyful roar went up when Hudson appeared. Survivors and settlers pushed past Buccari to mob the tall man, so long absent from their ranks. Kateos and Et Silman appeared in the helo's hatch. Their presence quieted the crowd, if only momentarily. Buccari, thankful for the diversion, pushed through the happy gathering, shaking hands and hugging old friends.

With Godonov running interference, she came to the headland defining the limits of the town's shoreline. She stepped on rocks above crystalline Lake Shannon. The closest pier, thirty meters away, floated on the fluid facets of a sparkling blue-green jewel. Tatum and her son stood on the pier, Captain Two and Tonto roosted on a davit behind them, their reflections dancing on the waters. On the shoreline, settlers stood shoulder-to-shoulder. Their excitement stilled in anticipation. It grew quiet. Moaning glories coming into sunlight at the water's edge foghorned softly, a gentle accompaniment to the distant roar of the valley's waterfalls.

"That's as close as you want to get," Tatum shouted.

"What's going on?" she asked.

"Charlie was, ah . . . pretty dirty," Godonov said. "Tatum thought he would give Charlie a bath."

"He stunk to high heaven, Sharl," Tatum shouted. "He's got eagle egg all over him."

Buccari moaned.

Her son, his peeling, freckled face broken with a huge grin, waved exhuberantly. Tatum shook the boy, stifling both grin and wave. The redhead hoisted Charlie effortlessly over the lake. The hunters screamed, their sonic blasts rippling the water.

"With your permission, Commander," Tatum shouted.

"Use your best judgment, Sandy," Buccari shouted back, standing erect and taking in the panorama of the spectacular mountain valley. Waterfalls tumbled from the western walls. Hanging glaciers pouring through high mountain valleys reflected the late morning sun with blue-green splendor.

"Well, then . . ." Tatum shouted. Half turning, like a discus thrower, the one-armed giant heaved Charlie out over the lake. The boy screamed with glee, twisted like a cat, and cleaved the water in a tight dive. Before the splash had settled, Captain Two and Tonto had speared cleanly into the boy's bubbling wake. In seconds the lake boiled with hunters diving from the water's edge. From high overhead hunters pulled in their membranes and plummeted downward, raising geysers of white. Buccari clapped with delight. Impetuously she ripped at the quick disconnects on her boots and kicked them off. To the cheers of the multitude, she dove from the rocky headland, hands outstretched, reaching for the heart of Genellan. Lake Shannon parted like icy silk.

Her eyes opened easily in the crystalline waters. Torpedoing hunters streaked everywhere, trailing cavitation bubbles that formed gyrating strings of wobbly pearls. There was her son, tawny hair drifting like smoke. She frog-kicked toward him. Charlie, feet and hands flashing like a river otter, met her halfway. Submerged in sun-shafted silence, mother and son embraced, his thin, hard-muscled arms wrapping gloriously around her neck. The boy had grown so much longer and stronger. Together, with the mother's hot lips pressed against her son's cold cheek, they burst from sparkling lake waters into sun-fired air.

SEVENTEEN

THE GREATER NEED

"Philippe Belanch does not do *work*," a deep voice shouted from the elevator landing. "Philippe Belanch dances the ballet."

Quinn was absorbed in a vid-conference with her engineering department heads; a major water project was about to commence, and critical decisions needed to be made concerning locations and capacities of reservoirs. The settlement administrator looked up to see Artemis Mather and a male settler storming into her office. The man, of below medium height and lithe build, was vaguely familiar.

"Excuse me," Quinn said to her vid-conferees. "Please continue. I'm recording, and I'll rejoin in a moment." She suspended her connection and turned to the unannounced visitors.

"May I help you?" she said, forcing patience.

The little man, hands on hips, looked to Mather.

"Commander Quinn," Mather said, "allow me to introduce Monsieur Philippe Belanch, principal artist of the Montreal Ballet Company."

"Montreal is on Earth," Quinn said.

Belanch stared at her as if she were retarded. "Belanch is here," he said. "Belanch is an *artiste*. A mistake has been made. I have been told to work as a common laborer. I am not a common laborer; I dance the ballet."

"Ah, of course," Quinn said, recognition dawning. She had seen Philippe Belanch perform on Earth. Never in person, of course; tickets to his performances were too dear.

"Ah, you agree there has been a mistake," Belanch said.

"Ah . . . no," Quinn replied, trying desperately to smile. Her work schedule weighed on her shoulders.

"This is insanity!" he exclaimed, stomping his foot.

"It is necessity," Quinn replied, her smile fading. Belanch was not the first settler to arrive expecting civilization as usual.

"Monsieur is a special case, Commander," Mather said. "He is—"

"All settlers are special cases," Quinn said, trying to keep her voice even. "But all settlers are obligated to perform a colonial internship for their first two years. When that obligation is satisfied, they may do whatever the economy and their skills allow them to do, within the bounds of our constitution and laws, of course."

"That is slavery," the man said.

"Mr. Belanch, you signed an agreement before you left Earth," Quinn said, reining in her exasperation. "An oath of allegiance, in fact. Your skills and talents were carefully reviewed, and you were assigned a function suitable to your practical value."

"Preposterous!"

"We are an outpost settlement far from civilization," Quinn continued, temper flickering. "Every settler's welfare depends upon the efficiency of our colony. This society does not yet support noncontributing segments."

"You affront me!" Belanch spewed. "My talents are an invaluable contribution to any society. You do not value the arts."

"The arts are vital to this colony, Mr. Belanch," Quinn said. "If you attend our weekend concerts and art exhibitions, that will be apparent. Our settlers are extremely talented. However, unlike Earth, our artists, our journalists, our athletes, our entertainers, even our legislators, must first be material contributors—workers. We cannot afford a parasitic elite; there is simply too much real work to do."

"Parasitic, indeed!"

"Perhaps a poor choice of words," Quinn said. "Professions such as yours are important, but they do not put food on the table or roofs over our heads. Our needs are more basic."

"NEd has reached a significant population, Commander," Mather said. "Perhaps it is time we gave more weight to the arts. I would agree with Monsieur Belanch—"

"Of course you would," Quinn snapped. She turned to the dancer and stared at him eye-to-eye.

"Mr. Belanch," she said. "I've seen you dance. You're extremely talented, but regardless of how much talent you have, if you were to perform with the dancers of NEd's ballet company, you would severely diminish its quality. Our dancers make no money and get no privileges. They dance for the love of dancing, and to make their fellow colonists happy. That makes them true artists. You will love dancing more, and yourself less, if you can learn to pull your weight for the good of your fellow settlers."

"You would sacrifice art for—"

"We don't sacrifice art. We sacrifice ourselves. There is a difference. See if you can figure it out. Now report to your assigned work detail, or I'll throw your skinny ass in the brig."

Belanch sucked in a huge breath and held it. Face turning red, he spun on his heel. Mather, a quirky little smile plastered to her face, turned to follow.

"Mather!" Quinn barked.

The Legion official turned slowly.

"That self-centered moron does not deserve to be on this planet. If you can't intelligently screen out these meat hooks, then I'm sending you back to Earth."

"That sounded like a threat," Mather said quietly.

"Yes," Quinn replied, turning back to her responsibilities.

Wrapped in silky rock-dog furs, Buccari leaned against the smooth-worn log and stared squint-eyed at the flickering tendrils of flame. Genellan's full planetary gravity embraced her. Her child, no longer small, curled next to her, angelic in slumber.

"Complaining about Legion politics isn't going to make it better," Godonov said softly, adding a log to the dying fire.

"I'm not complaining, Nes," Hudson said. "I'm evaluating."

Hudson, his handsome face bottom-lit, threw on two more logs, stirring up an ephemeral constellation of floating embers.

The watch on the palisade was changing; the night's reign had only a few hours to run. The homecoming was over, the revelers surrendered to the surfeit of food and drink. Survivors and settlers were retired to their cabins, the marines to their barracks, and the kones to their tropically heated tent. Life in MacArthur's Valley was not easy; work started early.

Godonov sat down on a log next to Colonel Pak. Hudson poked at the burning logs, stoking the flames. A scattering of hunters lurked about the ebbing fire, their eyes glinting like orange-fired diamonds. Greatmother perched on the log behind Buccari, snoring softly.

"I agree with Nash," St. Pierre said. He lay on his back, hands behind his head, a buffalo hide partially covering his long body. "We need to establish our principles, or the Legion will fill the vacuum."

"I second the emotion," Colonel Pak said, pulling a pipe from his mouth. "Reggie and I were part of that security apparatus for too many years. The Legion's main concern is to perpetuate itself."

"The Legion doesn't have a choice," Buccari said, staring at the rekindled flames. She was home, under the rich and lustrous constellations of Genellan, with her son at her side and surrounded by friends. She wished the night would never end.

"What happened, Sharl?" Hudson said. "You used to—"

"I'm not getting involved in planetary politics, Nash," Buccari said. "And neither should Nes."

"Aye aye," Godonov said, yawning.

"Why does wearing a uniform make people so stupid?" Hudson grumbled.

"At least we have an excuse. What's yours?"

"Depilatories sucked out your brains," Hudson retorted, punctuating his sentiments with an obnoxious snort.

"If I wasn't so happy, Nash, I'd shoot you," Buccari growled.

"Aw, go ahead," Godonov said.

St. Pierre laughed, a rich full laugh.

"Back off, Nash," Pak said. "Sharl can only serve one master."

"I want to preserve the freedom of this planet," Hudson said. "And so do you, Reg, and so does Sharl, probably more than any of us."

"And so will the settlers," St. Pierre said. "Especially after they've lived here a few years and built families. We all speak the same language; we're all educated. There's no history of tribalism or nationalism on this planet. There's no destructive history."

"History's a function of time," Hudson said. "In a few generations it will be too late to break habits."

"Then we have to rise above human nature," St. Pierre said. "That's a function of leadership. It's up to us."

Buccari glanced at his supine form, marveling at the man's emotional and philosophical resilience. St. Pierre had lost his beloved wife to senseless human rage. His professional life before Genellan had been dedicated to subversion and secrecy.

"I hope you're right, Reggie," Buccari said.

"Just watch," Hudson said. "Take the long view. Watch what happens when different religions start competing for men's souls, when cities and regions start competing for people and resources."

"Free men will always compete," Pak said, blowing a smoke ring.

"Bless their brave hearts and damn their greedy souls," St. Pierre said.

"And sheep will be led," Hudson growled.

"Universe without end, amen," Pak muttered, standing and banging his pipe on a log. "On that profound note, I bid you all good night—er, good morning."

"Good night, Han," Buccari replied. The others seconded her words.

Pak stepped from the fire's illumination and was gone. Logs crackled in the silence.

"Why do you say the Legion has no choice, Sharl?" St. Pierre asked, leaning on his elbow and turning to face her. His face was masked with shadow.

"In the final analysis, societies exist for only one reason," Buccari said. "For self-protection. People submit to government rule for security. To protect the governed, the government must first protect itself."

Godonov yawned hugely.

"Sorry," Buccari said. "It's too late for philosophy, isn't it?"

"People revolt against government," Hudson persisted.

"Only if enough rebels can unite in a metagovernment powerful enough to prevail," she replied. "It's like a snake shedding its skin. Revolutionaries don't end government, they just reinvent it, almost invariably for the worse. Government is power; rebels rarely understand justice, but they certainly understand power."

"What has that to do with the Legion?" St. Pierre asked.

"The Legion, actually all of Earth, has been reduced to a tiny galactic village. That village is threatened by an alien race. To protect itself the Legion must exploit its resources, and that includes this planet, this outpost in space. Principles don't count for much when your village is under attack."

"So what should Nash and I do?"

"Like I said," Buccari said, staring into the mesmerizing flames, "I refuse to talk planetary politics."

St. Pierre laughed. The fire popped and hissed.

Someone coming up behind her broke the trance. It was Chastain, his features bloated and wrinkled by hard sleep cut short.

"Excuse me, Sharl, er . . . Commander." Chastain tried to whisper, but his voice was incapable of moderation. "We got a hunting pair inside the perimeter."

Superdragons! Buccari was suddenly wide awake.

"Tatum's taking a patrol out to intercept," Chastain continued.

"I'm coming," Hudson said.

"Me, too," Godonov said.

"Not me," St. Pierre said, yawning. "I'm hitting the sack. Welcome home, Sharl." The widower gave her a gentle hug. His soft gaze lingered. She felt a deeper urge taking hold, a compelling want.

"Good night, Reggie," she said, her voice husky.

"Do you want to come, Commander?" Chastain asked. "Tatum thinks they're sleeping. Wants to hit 'em before sunrise, before they start moving. We gotta get on the road."

"Ah . . . yeah, Jocko," Buccari said, turning from St. Pierre and flashing hand-sign at Greatmother. The old huntress took Charlie by the hand and led the sleepy child away. Buccari turned back to St. Pierre, but the tall man was gone into the shadows, back to his cabin. His cabin was next to hers. Buccari exhaled and turned to see Hudson staring at her. Godonov and Chastain trotted down the slope toward the palisade gate, leaving them alone at the fire.

"Reggie likes you," Hudson said. "A lot."

"Mind your own business," she replied.

"Aye, Skip," Hudson said. "Damn, I missed you chewing on my butt."

"Yeah," she snarled, putting her arm around his waist. "Let's see if your new legs work better than your dumbass brains."

"Am I pushing too hard, Sharl?" Hudson asked as they walked across the settlement common.

"Welcome home, Nash," she said. "We're a team again."

Red lamps flooded the marshaling area in front of the marine barracks, where a pair of all-terrains idled in the cones of muted light. Chastain had field vests, rifles, and helmets waiting. They loaded up. The tracked vehicles rumbled through the palisade gate and turned uphill. They entered the dark forest and started climbing the steep flanks of the valley. Headlamps, casting hard shadows, tracked the pasture trail as they traversed the switchbacks. Insects and dust motes danced in the yellow beams. Eyes glowed in the underbrush, toy deer and bat-rats and other creatures of the night.

The pasture trail at last rose above the tree line. Stars shone brightly overhead. The small moon was near full, the large moon set. A herd of golden horses, knee-deep in tall grass, appeared in the headlights, stirring nervously at their approach. The shepherds' compound came into view, a low adobe bunkhouse and kitchen with sod roofs supporting photocell arrays. An adjacent paddock held mares ready to foal. A troop of black-eyed hunters perched on the fence rails. Beppo Schmidt came out to meet them.

Each truck was data-linked to the settlement intruder net. In addition Godonov and Tatum carried field units with sensor grids. The fix on the dragons was refined, and the two-truck safari drove down the backside of the ridge, into the next valley. The forest on the ridge's eastern slope was thinner, and the terrain steeper. There were no trails. After an hour of teeth-rattling overland driving, they left the trucks and started hiking, so as not to alert the sleeping dragons. Dawn's first hints tinted the eastern sky.

Gradually the steep valley flank grew less precipitate. In the damp gloaming they trooped past a series of descending kettle lakes hollowed from granite. Tall pines grew in sparse clusters. Somewhere below, a jolly river gurgled and splashed.

"I have them at three hundred meters," Godonov said, studying his field unit. "Azimuth zero one five. No movement. Got what looks like a bear to the north, heading away."

"Concur," Tatum replied, checking the dawn-silhouetted treetops for a breeze. A large bird pounded noiselessly overhead, a night raptor returning to its aerie. Somewhere far away another bird heralded the coming day. The sky had lightened. Buccari secured her night vision optics and raised her visor.

"Point has visual contact," Chastain reported.

They clambered along a line of boulders to where the point man was standing, staring across the river defile with night glasses.

"Check the small stand of scrub pine just below the darker rocks," the scout directed. "Looks like a pair of smooth boulders."

The marine handed his glasses to Buccari. She scanned the designated area, first without the field optics, and found them. Raising the glasses to her eyes revealed their distinctive thermal auras. She steadied her stance and stared. The creatures' inanimate state was belied by the gentle rise and fall of their flanks. As Buccari watched, one of the dragons jerked its head upward to sniff the air.

"They're stirring," someone whispered.

The abrupt movement startled the other dragon awake, a male, obvious due to its much larger profile. The giant creature leapt to its clawed feet with breathtaking agility, its short, thick tail twitching in counterbalance. The female was on her feet a heartbeat later, back-to-back with the male.

"They've got our scent," Chastain said.

"I wish we could scare them away," Buccari said.

"Too stupid," Hudson said.

"Not stupid," Tatum said. "Fearless. They're the top of the food chain. They see food, they kill."

The male leaped atop a fallen log, huge head pivoting, thick tail flicking in counterbeat. Audible even at this distance, the reptile's air sampling inhalations surged in and out of his olfactory cavities like a steam locomotive; his throat swelled, the yellow and green fluting expanding with each intake. He roared, a blast of primal ferocity erupting from his fanged maw and increasing to ear-shattering intensity. Reverberations of the reptilian challenge echoed in the stillness of morning for interminable minutes.

"Damn," a marine whispered.

"Hey, look!" another marine said. "They got a baby."

With both saurians on their feet, a smaller one was revealed. It was greenish-gold in color compared to the mature dragons' darker hue.

"Spread out," Tatum ordered. "Jocko, deploy your team along this high ground. I'll cover the low end. Get clear firing lanes. Make sure you know where everyone is before you start firing."

The dragons were fully alert, all with snouts high. They started moving, the female first, hopping out of sight into the intervening river gorge. The fall of the land blocked any view of their advance, but there was no doubt the dragons were coming. Buccari hefted her assault rifle and checked the magazine. It was suddenly very quiet. Birds sang and fluttered overhead. Somewhere, a giant eagle screeched. Buccari took position behind a deadfall and flipped off the rifle's safety. She stared through the weapon's homing sight and set her laser range detector. And then she waited.

"They're coming!" someone shouted.

Crunching footfalls grew louder. Huffing intakes seemed to heat the air.

"Visual!" another marine shouted.

The male dragon bounded over the rocky rise, less than fifty meters away; the female and child followed closely. The monster screamed horribly, but its yellow eyes were locked onto a target. Buccari looked to her left. Tatum stood in plain sight atop a boulder, an antiarmor cannon raised to his shoulder, his single great arm supporting the heavy weapon. Advancing at an alarming pace, the dragon roared again. Tatum fired a single shot. The weapon's hollow report was harshly incongruent with the monster's scream. The projectile detonated under the giant's jaw, nearly decapitating the massive skull from the sprinting engine of mayhem. The creature's horrible hind claws ran out from under its torso, and the dead monster collapsed to the ground with a scaly, sliding *thud*.

"Never had a chance," Hudson gasped.

"This isn't sport," Tatum said, training his weapon on the slain dragon's mate.

At the explosion, the female dragon leaped high into the air. She roared and skittered sideways to avoid her fallen mate, but she did not slow down her menacing advance. Buccari pulled the cold rifle stock to her cheek. All along the firing line marines raised their assault rifles. Tatum fired again, hitting the female dragon in mid-leap and nearly cutting her in two with armor-piercing ferocity. The horrible monster's leap and her ferocious scream were cut off with merciless finality. She was blasted backward into oblivion.

"It's self-protection," Tatum said, reloading.

The immature dragon bounded up over the rise and halted. It was small but only in relative terms, for it was still taller than a man. The confused juvenile looked down at its sundered parents and then at the humans. It bared its yellow teeth and screamed, a high-pitched yodel. It took an uncertain step forward, its claws scraping stone.

The tall redhead fired a third round. Buccari turned from the slaughter.

Where really, she wondered, was the top of the food chain?

EIGHTEEN

THE GREATER DANGER

The PDF orbiting defense station, a bronze and silver moon, filled the flight deck viewscreen. Massive gauge optics shields bulged from its surface like a crown of opal-cut diamonds. Carmichael piloted the admiral's barge on a cautious approach to docking bays at the satellite's south pole.

The settler downloads were complete. Carmichael, firmly entrenched in his new duties as group-leader, was ready to get under way. Everyone in the fleet was anxious to jump. Despite efforts to maintain secrecy, rumor of humans imprisoned on Pitcairn Two had spread throughout the fleet, the story growing more fantastic and more gruesome with each telling. To kill the rumors, Runacres had at last conducted an all-hands vid-cast, defining the reality of the mission and the low probability of success. The news had been sobering, but the old man had given one hell of a briefing. Throughout the fleet, ships' crews had reacted with uniform resolve and unfettered spirit. Angry shouts and determined cheers had reverberated all motherships, continuing unabated until duty officers restored order to the watch. Everyone was ready to jump.

The PDF defense station was immense, with a measurable gravity well. The surface of the weapons-festooned hemisphere glided overhead, a seemingly endless expanse of unnatural terrain. Carmichael checked distance readouts on his HUD. He concentrated on his lineup. The landing bays were large, designed for konish interceptors, but Carmichael had to be wary of his craft's endoatmospheric control foils. He brought the barge into the slip on its side, easing the craft into a hard lock like a toy boat in a bathtub. Docking locks secured the Legion ship with resonant hull impacts.

"Damned impressive, Group-Leader," the barge's assigned pilot said, deferentially acting as copilot. The young lieutenant commander busily completed shutdown checks. The ship's computer verified secured status, but Carmichael was reluctant to leave the controls.

"Stow the brown-nosing," Carmichael muttered.

"Aye, sir," the chagrined pilot replied.

"Admiral's waiting, Jake." Captain Ito's voice came over the secure circuit.

"On my way, Sam," Carmichael acknowledged, breaking loose from his tethers. The group-leader slapped the barge pilot on the helmet and pushed from the flight deck. The primary docking hatch was topside amidships. Carmichael pulled himself upward through a mating trunk. He elevated into a wide concourse. The admiral and the rest of his staff had gone ahead. A single, unhelmeted kone floated in the center of the passageway; a flight officer by uniform, but the gold-complexioned giant wore unfamiliar insignia. Carmichael approached the behemoth.

"Captain Carmichael," the giant thundered in proficient Legion, "I am-ah Colonel Et Lorlyn of the Hegemonic Rocket Force. I am-ah reporting to you for duty, with my interceptor and-ah my crew."

Hegemonic Rocket Force, that explained the insignia. Et Lorlyn was not a PDF pilot; he reported to King Ollant. The noblekone's blue-black eye tufts were firmly erect.

"At last we meet in person," Carmichael said, sticking out his hand. "Commander Buccari claims you will be the best pilot in my group."

"But-ah for her," Et Lorlyn replied, tentatively extending his massive hand and gently encompassing Carmichael's. The giant's eye tufts softened as a smile captured the wide, flat-lipped slash that was his mouth. Et Lorlyn's great brown cow eyes sparkled good-naturedly; his features were mountains of pebbly skin bunched with expression. Carmichael was taken with the noblekone.

"When do you come aboard?" Carmichael asked.

"I have just-ah this day been informed my crew-ah quarters are ready and-ah docking accommodations on *Novaya Zemlya* have been completed," Et Lorlyn replied. "My ship-ah will join Condor Squadron immediately after Tar Fell's hyperlight departure."

"Excellent," Carmichael replied.

"I am honored to be one of your pilots, Captain. You are held in high regard by all konish pilots for your bravery during our conflict. Your combat record is the standard by which all are measured. I hope I will earn-ah your respect."

Carmichael stared at the giant for several seconds. "How many Legion corvettes did you destroy, Colonel?"

"Four-ah," the noblekone replied. "And then I ran out of fuel."

"You also have my respect, sir."

"I am-ah to escort you to-ah the meeting chamber," Et Lorlyn said, pushing off and gliding down the wide passageway. After a short distance they entered an octagonal room with doors color-coded red, blue, and yellow. They moved through a red door into a smaller cylindrical space. Et Lorlyn slipped massive feet and arms through restraints and indicated Carmichael should do the same. Satisfied with the human's readiness, the kone touched a series of panels; the cylinder accelerated, stabilized, and then commenced a startlingly firm deceleration. The persistent force on Carmichael's body decreased but did not go away. The door slid open. They were in a realm of induced gravity, nearly a full gee.

"This-ah way, Captain." Et Lorlyn waved a tree-trunk arm. Carmichael walked, knee joints awakening, from the elevator into a dimly lighted operations center. Status plots and colorful arrays of tactical icons and angular konish script greeted him. Carmichael recognized the dispositions of the combined fleets. One screen was illuminated with Genellan's crescent limb.

"This-ah is weapons control," Et Lorlyn boomed. With a floor established, the kone's towering bulk was all the more apparent. Et Lorlyn politely dropped to all fours, putting his eyes even with Carmichael's.

"Et Lorlyn, how many energy weapons does a defense station have?"

"This is-ah *Kreta*-class, a medium station. It-ah has thirty-two main-ah battery ports and twice that-ah many light batteries."

Carmichael stared at the activity, appreciating the scale of firepower by which he was surrounded. The kones had developed defensive warfare to a monumental scale. It was comforting, and intimidating.

"The command center is this way, Captain." Et Lorlyn towered to his hinds and paraded along the command center's perimeter. Konish crewmen leaped from the noblekone's path, some hitting their foreheads on the deck with audible force.

They passed through a hatch and entered an ovate conference arena divided by a transparent partition. At the focus of the compact arena, split by the pane of carbon glass, was a long conference station with embedded consoles and translation devices. Surrounding the primary conference table and raised slightly was an annular row of observer seats. Armada-Master Tar Fell, Flotilla-General Magoon, and Scientist Dowornobb conversed on the konish side of the partition. Seated beyond the environmental barrier was the human contingent, their helmets removed: Admirals Runacres and Chou, Commodore Wells, Captain Ito, and a raft of high-ranking science officers. Carmichael was ushered through an environmental lock to join the members of his race. He removed his helmet; the air was warm but tolerable. Ito motioned to a seat at the primary table. Opposite him, beyond the environmental barrier, sat Et Lorlyn, all expression carefully absent.

Carmichael slipped on a lightweight headset and connected to the conference circuit.

"—take at least six moon cycles to maneuver the defense station into geosynchronous position over Ocean Station," Magoon reported, his thundering voice moderated only slightly by the translation program.

"*Madagascar* will remain in Genellan orbit in a colony support capacity," Runacres said. "She's not a PDF defense station, but she will provide communications support and some defensive capability."

"Very little," Admiral Chou said.

"There is no alternative," Runacres said. "We must return to Pitcairn. This opportunity may never occur again."

"I am not yet reconciled to my diplomatic mission," Tar Fell said.

"Yours is the greater danger," Runacres said.

"You humor me," the translation thundered.

"Armada-Master Tar Fell," Runacres said, "the enemy I face is vicious, but predictably so. There is nothing predictable about diplomacy. In meeting the leaders of my planet, you must operate on a battlefield strewn with innuendo and misdirection."

Tar Fell listened to the translation. Uncertain, the armada-master disabled his translator and asked a question of Dowornobb. Captain Ito said something in konish. The translator failed to convert his words, but Dowornobb and Tar Fell laughed.

"Captain Ito's idiomatic konish is quite good," Dowornobb said. "He reminds us of an old-ah konish *kotta* toast, roughly translated: 'Tis-ah better to die, than to-ah live by the lie.' "

"Hardly diplomatic," Runacres said.

There was a stirring on the konish side of the barrier. Dowornobb rose suddenly to his feet, eye tufts like quills.

"On the matter of diplomacy," Tar Fell announced. "Ambassador Kateos's shuttle arrives momentarily."

"Ah, the blessed voice of mercy," Runacres exclaimed. "Excellent."

"Scientist Dowornobb," Tar Fell boomed, "would you be so kind as to escort the ambassador to this conference?"

"It would be my pleasure," Dowornobb replied. The huge kone bounded to the compartment's exit hatch.

Kateos was reminded how much she hated space travel. Pressurization changes caused her gas bladders to flutter with spontaneous discharge. Her sinuses throbbed; her stomachs churned. Compounding her discomfort, induced gravity was secured for the approach to the defense platform. Kateos activated her magnetic flux field, dialing just enough force to keep her feet in contact with the deck. The ambassador moved into a docking station near the exit hatch and waited. Impatiently.

The thunking of docking grapples and the grinding of berthing lock-downs sliding home were music to Kateos's ears. More pressurization changes tormented her as the interceptor's environment equalized with the defense station, but Kateos was too excited to suffer. Her only thoughts were for her mate. She knew Dowornobb would be waiting. Her life mate, her love. She knew. Her emotion bladders blasted away the exquisite pressure of her joy as fast as it accumulated. She cared not.

Warning tones sounded. Kateos pulled off her helmet and pressed even closer to the airlock threshold. She closed her eyes and held her breath. The airlock doors slide back. A gush of robust air, hot and heavy with particulate, caressed her face. Borne on that wonderful zephyr she detected the bitter aroma of her lover's joy.

Kateos opened her eyes. He was there. Her joy bladder discharged with a clap of thunder. Dowornobb's physiology answered in a lower register but with greater duration, spewing acrid fumes.

"My life," Dowornobb gasped, pouncing.

"My love," she coughed, leaping forward. The giants collided in Olympian embrace. Kateos's lungs heaved; Dowornobb's musk was overpowering. Their love was total.

A hatch slammed shut. A ventilator roared into high volume air transfer, flushing the airlock with positive pressure turbulence. The PDF docking bay crew, with good-natured protest, retreated from their posts, returning with breathing units in place.

"How long do we have?" she whispered, clinging tightly. Her joy transformed to sorrow; the oleo of odor grew heavier, sweeter.

"Admiral Chou jumps this time tomorrow, my mate," he replied.

"One day," she moaned, reluctantly separating from her

mate. Kateos pushed from the airlock and floated onto the defense platform. She stopped a senior PDF officer.

"You know who I am?" she asked.

"Of course, Ambassador Kateos," the officer replied, pulling his head to the deck.

"Extend my apologies to Armada-Master Tar Fell and to Admiral Runacres," Kateos said firmly. "Inform them the ambassador will be detained one hour."

NINETEEN

THE HURDLE OF TIME

"Behold the king!" thundered loudspeakers.

King Ollant IV marched onto the grand promenade. The multitudes roared triumphantly. *Trods,* soldiers, technicians, merchants, scholars, even noblekones, had been assembling for days. They crowded into the Imperial Plaza, their upturned faces and their joyful bodily discharges blending into the low, golden haze. A thick and humid day, the Victory Spire in the plaza's center climbed dimly into yellow miasma, a pair of converging vertical lines that never quite joined.

Behind the king, a holo-vid spanning the palace facade displayed silver images of PDF and Legion ships hanging in ebony space. The planet Genellan provided dramatic backdrop. As the king arrived at the balcony's brazenly cantilevered pulpit, his image materialized on the giant holo, replacing the scenes of space. Ollant towered on his hinds and raised ponderous arms. The rumbling crowd fell silent, except for the muted rippling of glandular discharges. The dusky amalgam of odor, inescapable and thick enough to cut, was at the same time intoxicating.

"Citizens of the Hegemony! Citizens of planet Kon!" Ollant thundered, his voice and image echoing from gigantic holos interspersed throughout the vast throng. "On this day interstellar ships of the Konish Planetary Defense Force travel the stars."

The crowd's roar vibrated stone. The thick odors grew impossibly stronger. Ollant sucked in the full-bodied essence, the palpable emotions of his subjects. He pumped his fists. The bedlam continued unabated, and Ollant made no effort to quell the crowd. The king's image faded from the screens and was replaced once again with sparkling scenes of interstellar ships. Words were of little value on a day such as this.

Ollant monitored the chronometer. Flashing lights on his lectern signaled a cue, and once again the king's image was everywhere. He raised his arms, beseeching the crowd to silence. Slowly the multitude came to order.

"This is a moment for all time," Ollant boomed. "It is not my moment. This moment belongs to our intrepid space-farers. Citizens of Kon, I give you Armada-Master Tar Fell."

The king's image dissolved and was replaced by the interior of a spaceship, its crew members moving intently about their business. Tar Fell's massive form moved into the holo field. Floating alongside the Thullolian was Ambassador Kateos. Both wore full battle armor. They slipped into adjacent acceleration stations and strapped in. The crowd quieted to enraptured silence. Tar Fell did not face the holo; rather, he remained busy issuing orders and scanning his bridge.

"Tar Fell! Tar Fell!" the exuberant crowd chanted.

No longer the focus of the crowd, King Ollant walked from the balcony into the royal staff chambers. An array of holo-vids and status boards lined the walls of the oval room. Dynamic projections of Kon and Genellan each filled an entire holographic bank.

"If they have jumped on time," General Talsali said, "then they are already departed."

"We are watching electronic ghosts," Et Kalass added.

Ollant checked the time. It was true. The jump hour had passed.

"We take miracles for granted, do we not," he commented.

The crowd noises subsided. Tar Fell was facing the holo, hand raised in greeting. The Thullolian looked tired, and more uncertain than Ollant could ever recall seeing the truculent warrior. Ollant took pity. Tar Fell's responsibilities held no margin for error.

"To King Ollant. To all rulers of Kon. To all konish citizens," Tar Fell intoned. "It is my honor to preside over this momentous occasion—the very moment of our freedom. No longer are we held hostage by ignorance."

He paused and glanced at the konish female at his side.

"But such a moment must have a purpose, a mission. I have asked Ambassador Kateos to define that mission. I present our planet's ambassador to Earth, the esteemed Teos Tios Kateos."

"He declares her ambassador for the entire planet," Et Kalass exclaimed. "Kateos has bewitched even Tar Fell."

"Kateos bewitches us all," Ollant said.

"This is a first," Et Kalass said. "Never in our history has a female employing her own words addressed so much as a single city. Ambassador Kateos addresses our entire world."

"Today, everything is a first," General Talsali said.

"Four centuries ago," Kateos began, her voice commanding, "Kon was violated. By a race of monsters. They invaded, spewing terror and death, leaving behind anarchy and despotism, and a fortress mentality. A decade ago we were again invaded, or so we thought. We reacted violently, attacking the attackers. As we know now, we attacked friends, our galactic neighbors from Earth, with tragic loss of life on both sides. From these aliens, these humans, we gained a valuable lesson: We learned that the universe is not always hostile. We learned that different races, different worlds, are capable of trust—and mutual gain.

"With that difficult lesson learned, we travel to the stars. Our mission is to journey to Earth, to work with the human race, to understand them, and to help them understand us. It is a good mission. We go to Earth."

The plaza erupted with jubilation.

"We go to Earth," Et Kalass mumbled. Ollant glanced at his prime minister. The hard old noblekone's eyes were moist, and his emotion bladders had taken control, also a first in Ollant's memory.

Tar Fell took center screen. The crowd noise clipped to silence.

"It is time," Tar Fell announced. "Ship captains, respond to orders. Make ready to get under way. Flotilla-General

Magoon, signal Admiral Chou. The konish fleet is ready to jump."

Tar Fell saluted the holo, and the crowd noise rose to an impossible crescendo. The armada-master's image faded to black and was replaced by a highly magnified scan of human and konish ships at varying distances. The main image split into multiple views of fleet ships; the delicate shaft and torroid configuration of Admiral Chou's ships was markedly distinct from the heavy cylindrical lines of the konish vessels. King Ollant stared, fascinated, wishing with all his soul that he were not king. Would that he were instead a star-ship captain.

And then the ships were gone.

Tar Fell reeled with incapacitating nausea. Would the jump never end? He forced open his eyes. Ambassador Kateos, eyes clamped shut, her body near catatonic, gripped the armrests of her acceleration station. Kateos opened her eyes and attempted a smile, unsuccessfully. Tar Fell pushed from his tethers and glanced at the human section of the technology bridge. Captain Ito observed them. The human nodded and returned to supervise his gravitronic technicians. Tar Fell concentrated on his own instruments. Without knowing exactly when, Tar Fell realized that the gut-twisting vibrations had ceased.

"We are in hyperlight," Ito broadcast calmly.

An alarm sounded.

"There is a problem," Magoon announced.

"What?" Tar Fell demanded.

"A gravitronic grid tolerance had been exceeded," Ito replied through the translator. "*Mountain Flyer*'s grid-link is intermittent. My technicians have a solution, but it is imperative for your hyperlight crews to resolve it on their own."

The konish technicians, uncertain at first, released their fittings and clustered together. Within seconds they developed a remedy. Magoon, bellowing orders, repositioned his ships. Grid generators were boosted. The emergency was over.

"Was it serious?" Tar Fell asked.

"Not this time," Ito relied. "Your ships are redundantly

linked within Admiral Chou's grid. Even if your grid generators had failed, you would have been carried along in the
matrix, although the ride would have been much rougher.
Much, much rougher."

"My ships did not jump on their own?" Tar Fell thundered.
"Gravity, why was I not informed?"

"Your ships jumped on their own, Armada-Master," Ito
protested. "Admiral Chou's fleet link overrode—"

"Pah," Tar Fell growled. He wished that Scientist Dowornobb were here to explain how this could be. Dowornobb
would have perceived the technical treachery. The konish
bridge crew stirred nervously at the armada-master's outburst.
Ito spoke rapidly in his own language.

"I assure you," the translation program related, "the konish
ships jumped within their own gravitronic matrix."

"But with a safety net, yes?"

"Yes," Ito replied. "President Duffy insisted you survive."

"I will be told of—"

"Armada-Master Tar Fell!" Kateos exclaimed. "We are in
hyperlight!"

"Hyperlight!" Magoon shouted, eye tufts springing erect.

Tar Fell swallowed his anger. The kone checked the status
plots. The vid images of the heavens were uniformly gray, the
darkest, deepest of grays, a blackness that glowed. Optical
sweeps revealed only the other ships of Admiral Chou's grid
matrix. Tar Fell closed his eyes.

Konish ships had leaped the hurdle of time.

TWENTY

OLD BATTLES

"People call you Queen of the World, Mom," Charlie said.

Buccari grunted her displeasure and dropped from her horse. Her son leaped from his, leaving Spitter with the reins. She handed her reins to the hunter and turned to follow her son up the ridge. They always left the horses at Tookmanian's Church. Once above the tree line the boy stopped to pick blackberries growing in thick mats. He shoved them in his mouth.

"Your world is the only world that concerns me, dirty-face," she replied, grabbing his neck, his sun-bleached brown hair like silk on the back of her hand.

"But that's what they call you," the boy persisted, his brow furrowed. His lips were stained purple.

"I get called a lot of things. So will you," Buccari said, taking his dirty hand. The boy's strong fingers intertwined with hers.

"Why, Mom?"

"Don't know, Charlie. Just remember, names mean nothing, no matter how mean and ugly they are, unless you answer to them. Unless you're afraid they're true."

Charlie said nothing.

"So what do you call me?" Buccari asked her son. They were almost to the ridgetop. Twin pinnacles, like the bones of the planet, loomed hard and white against a perfect sky.

"Huh?" Charlie asked.

"What do you call me?"

"You're my mom!"

She dropped her son's hand and cupped her mouth. "I . . . am," Buccari shouted, ". . . Charlie's mom!"

Her words echoed from the near ridges and again from the valley's farther reaches, reverberating into distant whispers. Hunters shrieked.

"Aw, Mom," the boy said, hard blue eyes softening with laughter.

"That's all I need," she said, pulling him into a hug. "Much better than Queen of the World."

They breasted the ridge and climbed along the mountain hogback. Charlie trotted easily ahead, his bare, muscular legs plowing a furrow through blossoms of crimson and blue, stirring their scent into the gentle breeze. Buccari tilted her head, opened her mouth and filled her lungs with perfumed air. Low overhead, hunters wheeled in easy figure eights, their great wingspans hissing the air.

She trudged up the slope, perspiration tickling the small of her back. It was a good feeling, the reward of exertion against honest gravity. Her body felt strong, alive. She lifted her floppy canvas cap, allowing the breeze to cool her brow. The sky was dark and clear; she could see day-stars. To the northeast a distant squall dragged its hem over the infinite flatness of the taiga plain. To the west the granite walls of the continental spine marched to northern and southern horizons in stolid grandeur, glacier-draped and snowcapped, a vista rich beyond comprehension. A new world. A world no longer hers—as it might have been. To be possessed, it was a treasure that needed to be shared.

Almost there. She lifted her canteen and drank deeply. She collected her thoughts, concentrated her feelings, and savored bittersweet memories. Charlie sprinted ahead, to join the hunters. She walked forward, pushing herself, but her pace grew slower while her heart quickened. Tears welled warmly, the first seeping elements of the inevitable catharsis. She brushed them away. It worried Charlie to see her cry.

A meandering wall defined the battlefield's perimeter, and mounded cairns marked the fallen—large heaps for kones, more numerous and smaller stone stacks for hunters. Blue blossoms grew thick across the field. White heliotropes climbed rock walls and cairns. As she stepped over the perimeter barrier she added a flat rock to its elevation, a tradition, a duty. Cliff dwellers made frequent pilgrimage to the site, cementing the stones in place, countering the effects of weather and gravity. Eventually the wall would be too high to step over. An entrance would have to be constructed. She wondered where the stone carvers would break the wall.

The density of cairns thinned as Buccari moved from the main battle site. She trailed behind her son, who, with the hunters, had assembled beyond the top of the ridge, toward the precipitous descent of the mountain's eastern slope. An isolated cairn stood at the cliff's brink, so near the tumbling shelter of boulders littering the base of the pinnacles. So near to safety, yet so far away. Grief stricken, not because she could no longer hold back the shattering memory of the day Mac-Arthur died, but because that precious memory was slipping away. Tears overcame her. She fell to her knees, holding her face. She could go no closer, at least not yet. The mournful screeching of hunters, keening over the death of great warriors, human and hunter interred together, drifted fitfully against the breeze.

"Mom, you all right?" Charlie asked, touching her shoulder. "Don't cry. You shouldn't come if it's going to make you cry."

Her son stood before her, his sweet face twisted with concern. She pulled him to her.

"I'm okay, Charlie. Really, I am. It makes me smile, too. The memories make me smile. It's important to be here . . . and it's going to be a long time before I come back."

"Why do you have to go, Mom?" he asked.

She fell backward, cross-legged in the wildflowers, and looked at her child, his skin and hair burnished to shades of copper and gold, a disconcerting and yet comforting image of his father.

"It's my job." She smiled, wiping away tears. She looked into his eyes and wished she could explain away the inevitable.

" 'Cuz of the damn Ulaggi," he said.

"Don't say, 'damn,' " she admonished.

"We could stay with the hunters," he pleaded, his expression so assured, so innocent. "No one can hurt us then."

"Someone has to protect the hunters," she said. "Someone has to protect this planet, and Earth . . . That's my job. Someday it will be your job, too, but you have a lot to learn."

"I learn a lot from the hunters," he said.

"Too much," she said. "But they'll never teach you how to be a corvette pilot. I thought you wanted to be a spacer, like me."

"Yeah," he said, his eyes growing big. "Can I really be a pilot?"

"If you're good enough . . . and smart enough," she said, lunging forward and wrestling the boy into the flowers.

"I'm smart," Charlie shouted, giggling.

"Not smart enough," she growled, pinning him. "You have to learn math and engineering and science. You'll have to go to school all day long."

"All day long?" he groaned.

"Yes," she said. "On Earth."

"I get to go to Earth?" he shouted.

"Yeah, to Earth," she said. "No sneaking off to steal eagle eggs."

"Don't they have eagles on Earth?" he asked.

"Not like Genellan eagles."

"When, Mom?"

"A couple years, maybe," she replied. "We'll see."

Hugging her squirming son, she rolled onto her knees and tickled him. The hunters moved closer, young sentries mostly, except for Spitter and Bottlenose. The ugly creatures stood in a row, watching mother and son frolic in the grass. All displayed razor-toothed smiles.

Buccari looked up and was saddened because Tonto was not present among the hunters, as he usually was, on this her last day on the planet. The cliff dweller had duties, too. Hunter Company was going to space. Cliff dwellers had joined the space battles, and this bothered her greatly. Buccari checked the sun-star; she, too, must leave soon.

"Can hunters come with me, Mom?" Charlie asked. "To Earth?"

"Maybe," she grunted as she stood and pulled him to his feet. She continued walking over the ridge. Hunters hop-waddled in column behind the humans. The tall isolated cairn lifted completely into view.

"Yeah?" Charlie exclaimed.

"It's not up to me," she said, emptying her mind of thought. She stared at the rocks. "We'll have to ask Captain Two, and the elders."

The cairn was before her, rising from the flowered ground. She stopped and breathed deeply. A vine of white blossoms intertwined the stones. Closing her eyes, she reached out and placed both hands on sun-warmed rock, and tried to re-member. The memories were strong. Again the tears came. As she wiped them away, her fingers lingered on her cheek, stroking the pearly hardness of her long scar. Her heart was leaden.

"Aw, Mom," Charlie pleaded softly. "Don't cry."

Charlie grabbed her fingers. His hand was warm and vital, his grip strong. She looked down at the dark blue eyes shared by father and son, and the pall of bereavement was buoyed by the spark of life.

"Come on, Charlie," she said. "Time to go."

Without looking back, mother and son, hand in hand, strode away from the tall cairn by the cliffs.

TWENTY-ONE

EMBARKATION

The Thor-class heavy-lifter came to ground on hissing wings, its landing gear chirping against the runway. Nestor Godonov watched the ponderous endoatmospheric vehicle coast onto the taxiway, its anticollision beacons twirling. A yellow ground tractor took it in tow and hauled it slowly to a loading station, joining the other heavy-lifters on the ramp. Two corvette EPLs, like baby bullets, squatted alongside the larger landers. An oleo of diesel exhaust, burnt rubber, hydraulic fluid, scorched metal, and buffalo musk wafted on the afternoon breeze. Aircraft and helos buzzed and clattered overhead in their landing patterns, maintaining continuous shuttles to the valley. Ground tractors moved equipment pallets from staging areas to loading queues. Equipment loaders reordered the cargo and stuffed it into gaping lifter holds.

Soon he would be back in space. On an intellectual level, Godonov was pleased to leave the planet, to once again abide in the civilized environs of a Legion mothership. Clean body, clean clothes, clean bed; warm body, warm depilatories, warm food. Yet viscerally, Godonov regretted his departure; he would miss the palette of the sun rising and setting; he would miss the tempestuous variations of weather and the clear mountain waters; he would miss nature's immensity and even her cruel demand for unending competition.

"Sure wish we were goin' with you, Commander," Gordon shouted.

Godonov returned his attention to the company of humans and cliff dwellers in loose formation on the parking ramp. Only one of Hunter Company's platoon was deploying, winnowed down to a cadre of cliff dwellers and humans most highly trained. Sergeant Chastain, awaiting orders to load, stood over his marshaled platoon like a brood hen. Tonto and Bottlenose shadowed the massive human. The hunters screeched and hand-signed at each other with manic intensity.

"Someone has to keep the training going, Sergeant," Godonov said. "It'll be your turn next time."

"Yes, sir," Gordon replied. "I hate missing the action."

"We'll probably stay bottled up in the ships for the whole cruise," Godonov said. "You know how it is—hurry up and wait."

"Yes, sir," Gordon replied.

It was a warm, clear day; the concrete matting beneath Godonov's field boots radiated heat. He departed the marshaling area and walked under a flapping field awning where Major Buck and his platoon leaders were in conference. Lizard Lips sat at a portable field station monitoring loading manifests and checking real-time container locators. Fenstermacher, in his EPL crew suit, leaned against an awning support, taking advantage of the shade.

"Hunter Company, Fleet Logistics. Over," the radio crackled.

Lizard Lips acknowledged the radio call electronically.

"Heavy Six has a 1900 orbital slot, Hunter," the fleet loadmaster, a gravelly throated female, announced. "Crank up your loaders."

The guilder screeched for Godonov, waving hand-sign.

"Put someone on that speaks Legion," the loadmaster demanded.

"Hunter, roger," Godonov replied, moving into vid-cam view. "I copy your request."

"Not a request, Hunter. We're running a schedule."

"Loosen your skivvies," Godonov replied. "We'll make our orbit window. Hunter out."

The loadmaster signed off mumbling, "Goddamn marines."

"She called you a marine, Mr. Godonov," Fenstermacher said. "What an asshole."

"You didn't even thank her," Buck said, coming near.

"My IQ will never recover," Godonov said. Lizard Lips chittered and flashed hand-sign; the last equipment load was moving on board.

"But you'll be a hit with the ladies," Buck said.

"Yeah, like Mr. Godonov really charmed that one," Fenstermacher said. "I'm sure it woulda friggin' been diff'rent if she coulda smelled him. Can't tell a marine from a friggin' shitheap without being able to sniff it up, and then it's friggin' fifty-fifty."

"Last I checked, I outranked you by at least a frigging shitheap, Boats," Godonov snarled. "Do something useful, or go jump off a cliff. That's a frigging order."

"It's also friggin' redundant."

Godonov turned abruptly at the commanding voice. Captain Carmichael strode under the shade of the field awning. The newly appointed group-leader wore a buff-colored flight suit and a gold beret.

"Hey, Cap'n Carmichael!" Fenstermacher shouted.

"Attention on deck," Major Buck barked.

"As you were, gentlemen," the group-leader said. "You, too, Fenstermacher."

Fenstermacher immediately put a finger up his nose.

"How much longer, Major?" Carmichael asked.

"Afternoon, Captain," Buck responded. "Equipment load's almost complete. Troops embark in fifteen minutes."

Carmichael looked around. The cliff dwellers suddenly exploded into a rallying song; their sonic cacophony vibrated the awning's tie-downs. Lizard Lips chittered in piercing harmony.

"Fenstermacher, is that *Condor One*'s apple?" Carmichael shouted.

"Yes, sir," Fenstermacher replied. "Just finished maintenance preflight. She's go for orbit."

"Where's Commander Buccari?"

"Skipper's on her way up from the valley, Captain," Fenstermacher replied, tossing a ragged salute. "I expect that's her helo coming in now. By your leave, Captain, I best be getting to my duties."

Carmichael grunted. The group-leader's eyes remained fixed on the approaching helicopter.

Railings on the control tower's observation deck bristled with knobby heads of black and gray, toothed maws screeching and shrieking in and out of audible range. Cliff dwellers perched everywhere, spectators to the noisy bustle. Even guilders had arrived in abundance, availing themselves of the long-leg cable conveyance from the valley. Groups of the curious creatures waddled through long-leg operations areas and along flight lines, inspecting and chittering officiously. Only cliff dweller males were in evidence. Females and children remained on the cliffs or in the valley. Those most difficult and most intimate farewells had already been taken.

Brappa was indeed sad. Visions of his beautiful mate yet tormented him. Throughout time huntresses had endured the absence of their mates, too often suffering their injury or death; but going to the stars was living death, for the time away from home was longer than any salt mission or scouting expedition. A mission to the stars lasted entire cycles of the sun—an eternity of time, precious and irretrievable. When Brappa next saw his family, his youngest would be near fledged, and his two oldest sons would themselves be warriors of their clan. His sons would also become star-warriors, of that Brappa was certain, and for that reason was doubly forlorn. Only young warriors, those without mates, were chosen to be star-warriors. There were some exceptions, but not many. Brappa had no choice; Brappa-the-warrior, clan of Braan, son-of-Braan-the-hero, was leader of the star-warriors.

Brappa's melancholy was softened by his pride. His green-armored warriors were ready, ready to blast off to the stars, to do battle. Feisty and spirited, his young hunters puffed their chests and spouted braggadocio, kidding good-naturedly with each other and with their fellow long-leg warriors. They used a hybrid sign language. Some long-leg warriors communicated with proficiency, but none so well as Giant-one. Not even Big-ears could match Giant-one's skill with hunter sign.

Brappa glanced up at the giant creature, of a size to rival the bear-people, but gentle and fiercely loyal.

"Our time is near," Giant-one signed, his enormous, five-fingered hands moving with graceful efficiency. "How fare thee, cohort?"

"In thy presence, I am calm," Brappa signed, replying with an ancient wisdom. Brappa was proud to be a cohort of Giant-one.

"Hold, Craag comes," a warrior shrieked.

Craag's distinctive flight profile, wide of span and strong of stroke, appeared to the south, rising above the river cliffs on vigorous thermals. On his right wing was the warrior Bott'a, son-of-Botto. On Craag's left wing, Brappa's previous station, flew Tokko of clan Kutto.

Kraal, son-of-Craag, lifted the battle cry of his father's clan, clan Veera, also clan of Brappa's mate. Hunters all around joined in with resounding tenor, paying tribute to the hero and leader. The sonic clamor rose to higher and higher levels, with Brappa enthusiastically adding his strong voice.

Craag screeched in acknowledgment. The magnificent creature, muscles rippling and black eyes darting, wheeled into the wind, his skilled wingmen maintaining tight interval. The formation dropped gracefully to ground. The multitude of hunters fell respectfully silent. Great membranes, hissing like rustling silk, were stowed quickly into double folds behind powerful backs. The old warriors wore traditional leather armor, stained dark with sweat and blood, but each hunter also wore a long-leg deathstick. Their cruel countenances, especially that of Craag, bore the scars of the old ways, vestiges of the days when hunters fended off growlers, rock-dogs, and eagles with naught but arrows and pikes. Life had changed. Indeed! Hunters went to the stars.

"Hail, Brappa, leader of the star-warriors," Craag chittered.

"Rising winds, leader of all hunters," Brappa replied.

"Son-of-Braan, thy father's spirit smiles upon thee," Craag shrieked. "Go to glory, young cousin. Come home to happiness. May the gods be with thee."

Bott'a shrieked the clarion of the clan of Braan, the most

renowned of all battle cries. The hunters exploded with sonic exhilaration, screaming Brappa's name as legend. Brappa was proud.

Sherrip's head jerked to the breeze. Brappa and Craag also detected the signal drifting on the air.

"Harken!" Craag chirruped, silencing the bedlam.

Closer, near overhead, a circling scout relayed the signal, his screech triumphant, a harbinger of joyful tidings.

"She comes," Sherrip screeched.

It was the signal for which they were all waiting. Word spread with ultrasonic efficiency. To the south a long-leg hovering machine elevated above the river cliffs, its trajectory skimming the terrain. The flying machine bore down on the bivouac. At the last moment it skidded into a steep bank and halted its headlong progress over the taiga. The machine descended, its whirling blades flashing black and silver in the sun. Short-one-who-leads jumped from its belly. She turned, and a battered duffel tumbled after her. Its mission accomplished, the machine thundered away.

Holding her beret to her head, Short-one-who-leads shouldered her bag. Hunter Company, hunter and long-leg, thundered their welcome and shifted to receive her. Toon-the-speaker broke into a waddling sprint. Behind the guilder came Big-ears and Sharp-face. Behind those long-legs trailed a familiar officer, a large and powerful warrior, shorter than Giant-one, but built on the same broad, strong lines. Brappa recognized the Consort-of-Short-one-who-leads.

Short-one-who-leads halted when she caught sight of that warrior, her pale complexion flushing radiantly. Recovering her composure, the green-eyed long-leg dropped her bag and bowed to Craag and Brappa in the cliff dweller manner. The hunter leaders returned the bow and screeched salutations.

Big-ears and Sharp-face began issuing orders. Giant-one flashed hand-sign to Toon.

"Attention!" Toon-the-speaker screeched. "Commence the load!"

Sherrip issued orders to the embarking hunters. Giant-one shouted commands, and the long-leg warriors marched forward.

Sherrip and the hunter column followed. Short-one-who-leads stood transfixed in the shifting crowd of warriors, her gaze locked on that of her consort. The tall long-leg stared back, both beings oblivious to their surroundings.

Brappa turned politely from the lovers and stepped into the formation of departing hunters. Sherrip commenced the death song. Brappa added his strong voice. The attending legions of cliff dwellers joined in, celebrating the nearness of death and of the star-warriors bravely marching to meet the specter of doom. In ever-increasing numbers they elevated into the air, rising in swirling clouds like black smoke.

The star-warriors marched aboard the heavy-lifter. Loading crews directed them to their acceleration stations, helping them into their tethers and securing loose equipment. Brappa took a last look out the loading hatch at his home planet. Short-one-who-leads and her consort still stood facing each other, but then the outer doors eased shut with taunting deliberation. The inner hatch locks slammed home with daunting finality.

Carmichael stood there, a small boy expression holding his features hostage. Buccari smiled, lifted her flight duffel onto her shoulder and stepped forward. The group-leader met her halfway, but they did not touch. Together they walked toward the flight line.

"I didn't expect you, Jake," Buccari said.

"I should have come down a week ago," he replied. "And done this right."

Buccari colored slightly. She pulled off her beret and rubbed her auburn burr. Stubby eyebrows highlighted her bright green eyes. Takeoff alert Klaxons sounded. The first heavy-lifter on the line moved ponderously under tow toward the departure zone, an area designed to withstand the vulcanizing temperatures of blast-off. As the first lander cleared the loading ramp the second heavy-lifter was pulled into motion.

"You're a long way from the flag bridge, group-leader," Buccari said at last. Loading trucks and ground tractors started pulling back.

"These heavy-lifters are mine. I came down to watch the operation," Carmichael replied.

"Yes, sir," she said.

"Sharl," Carmichael said, exasperated.

"It's okay, Jake," she said. "I'm happy to see you."

"Good," he said, his rugged face brightening. "You're the only reason I came down."

She laughed. "That makes me even happier," she said.

He grabbed her arm. The man and the woman faced each other, two people standing under an improbably blue sky. A line of atmosphere-battered heavy-lifters and landers provided backdrop; loading trucks and ground tractors trundled around them, but they were alone on the vast emptiness of the spaceport.

"Marry me, Sharl," Carmichael said.

"Jake," she said, "you wouldn't be able to do your job, and I wouldn't be able to do mine."

"I love you, Sharl," Carmichael said. "I can still do my job."

"Can you send me to die, Jake?"

He stared at her, his rugged features struggling. His grip strangled her fingers.

"Will you send me to die, Captain?"

"Yeah," he said, almost choking. And then louder, "Yes, I'll send you to die, Commander."

She pulled her hands loose. "I love you, Jake."

Carmichael closed his eyes. A moan escaped his lips.

"I always have, Jake."

A gust of wind swept the spaceport.

"Then you'll marry me?"

Buccari looked down at her boots, not answering.

"I want to kiss you, Sharl."

"Yeah," Buccari said, lifting her eyes. "I'd like that."

Takeoff sirens wailed into being.

Carmichael wrenched his gaze from Buccari's. Fenstermacher fidgeted at the loading hatch of *Condor*'s EPL. Crew trucks hustled along the taxiways, retrieving ground crews and equipment. The cliff dwellers were gone from the tower structure and rooftops. The cloud of hunters had drifted safely to the south, and the guilders were moving en masse toward the river cliffs, opening up distance between them and the heavy-lifters about to blast into the heavens.

"Board your ship, Commander," Carmichael ordered. "We'll finish this discussion . . . at a more convenient time and place."

"Aye aye, Captain," she said, saluting smartly and pivoting for her EPL. She turned completely around and, running backward, shouted, "See you in hyperlight, Jake."

"I love you, Sharl," he shouted. The distinctive sounds of heavy-lifter secondaries surging to military power captured Carmichael's full attention. Hands over his ears, the group-leader sprinted for his own apple.

TWENTY-TWO

RETURN TO SPACE

Buccari pounded up the EPL loading ramp, her battered boots grabbing the metallized nonskid. Like the victim of some mechanized Venus's-flytrap, she was pulled into the ship's cramped hold, leaving her planet and her son behind. Nothing but danger lay ahead, but there was no turning back. She was not sorry. The lure of space was strong. And she was in love.

Fenstermacher secured the loading hatch behind her. "Back to work, eh, Skip?" the petty officer said.

"It's like we never left, Boats," Buccari answered as she moved forward through the cargo compartment. Petty Officer Nakajima's helmeted head leaned from the systems operator station. The boatswain moved aside as Buccari slipped past her into the crew locker. At that moment the first heavy-lifter ignited primaries. A split second later the shock wave slapped the EPL. The big ship's takeoff rumble rapidly dissipated.

"Nakajima, tell Mr. Flaherty to hold checks," she ordered, pulling off her boots. "I'll be taking her up."

"Aye aye, Skipper," Flaherty replied. Her copilot peeked into the locker. Flaherty's nose was sunburned and his space pallor replaced with a nut-brown tan. "Figured you would. I'll ride systems, Nakajima."

"Aye, sir," Nakajima replied, moving aft to join Fenstermacher in the cargo hold. The ground-trembling rumble of a second heavy-lifter initiating takeoff vibrated the apple. Big-iron primaries engaged with throaty imperative. Another shock wave. Buccari pulled on her pressure suit and flight boots, slamming shut the quick-action couplings. Flaherty strapped himself into the systems station.

"You look like you had a good time on the beach, Flack. Are you ready for work?" she asked, twisting on her helmet and engaging pressure seals. Oxygen flowed from her suit reservoir. She initiated suit system diagnostics. Status symbols flowed across her helmet headup.

"As ready as a Selenian hooker at liberty call, Skipper," Flaherty replied, busy at his station.

"Ship status?" Buccari demanded as she moved forward.

"Checking good," Flaherty reported. "Tertiaries are spinning. Pressure's up. Gun barrels are hot. Nakajima, you and Fenstermacher secure back there?"

"Cabin secure, sir," Nakajima replied.

Buccari pulled herself into the cramped cockpit. Against rugged mountains and pure blue sky, two burgeoning columns of cotton blossomed heavenward, overlapping and melding. Ground winds herded the pillars of white to the east, dissipating their ephemeral majesty. The first heavy-lifter had already pushed over for orbit; the second lifter's plume was bending to follow. Buccari ripped her eyes from the horizon-leaping arcs and plugged in her umbilicals; the voice of the launch controller filled her auditory sensors. She blinked down the volume.

"*Heavy Six* cleared to orbit," the controller announced. "*Eagle One* Alpha is cleared to pad six."

Carmichael's EPL was taken in tow by a robot tractor.

"Compute! Systems status . . . initiate. Pilot Buccari," she barked.

"Pilot Buccari," the synthesized voice responded. "Control authorizations check. Pilot has command."

The remaining heavy-lifter on deck fired its secondaries, blanketing its thermal pad with rigid petals of incandescence. The ground shook as the monstrous lander elevated slowly atop its pillar of white heat. The big lander slid forward, its nose rotating smoothly to vertical. The heavy-lifter's primaries engaged; in the blink of an eye its shock wave rolled across the expanse of spaceport, kissing her canopy with a ringing hiss. *Heavy Six* leapt to the heavens on a sword of fire, pulling after it a third column of blossoming alabaster.

Buccari's attention was captured by a ground tractor taking position on her nose. The tow robot scanned her from under a dome of transparent carbon armor. Buccari passed an authorization code. The operating appendage engaged the tow fixture, and ladder lights on her auxiliary console sequenced, indicating positive ground control.

"*Condor One* Alpha cleared to pad eight," the controller announced. "*Eagle One* Alpha cleared to orbit."

As Buccari's apple commenced rolling along the main taxiway, Carmichael's EPL launched, its thundering primaries demure in comparison to the tumultuous departures of the heavy-lifters. Exulting in the smaller ship's lancing flight, Buccari watched Carmichael streak heavenward. She brought her gaze down to the planet. Hers was the only spaceship remaining unlaunched.

The tow robot positioned her ship on the thermal tiles and disengaged, accelerating smartly away, crash beacons and strobes firing maniacally. When the tractor cleared the primary launch radius, blast deflectors elevated from the surface.

"Gear up," Buccari ordered.

"Gear up," Flaherty responded.

As the gear retracted the apple squatted into launch position on its stabilizer skids, the nose jacked high in the air.

"Skids," Flaherty reported.

"Launch sequence," Buccari announced, settling into her acceleration harness and checking her ladder lights. "Systems?"

"Checking good," Flaherty replied. "All temps in the green. Pressures are up. Barrels hot."

Buccari put her forearms into the acceleration restraints. She gripped the throttle with her left hand and the control stick with her right. The thick, button-festooned controls welcomed her fingers and palms. They promised unchecked power and absolute control. She shoved the throttle past the takeoff detent. Caution lights winked.

"Throttle set. Ignition count on my mark," she said. It was a light load; she could take it easy through the pressure curves.

"*Condor One* Alpha cleared for orbit," the controller announced.

"Four . . . three . . . two . . . one . . . ignition," she announced, hitting the ignitors. Fuel pressures surged into actuator ranges. The tertiaries engaged, generating power and superheat. The apple trembled like a horse at the starting gate. At ignition-plus-two seconds, main ignitors commenced detonating in stages; a low-level static rasped in Buccari's helmet; hover-blasters screamed their high-pitched screech, establishing launch attitude as the secondaries fired from the tail.

The EPL surged forward and leapt into the air. The annunciator panel indicated the stabilizer skids had stowed. The nose rotated rapidly, searching for vertical, the main engines gimboling to line up with the lander's arcing center of gravity. Buccari had little to do but monitor the instruments, the computer controls balancing the craft on a column of fire. At ignition-plus-five the lander's main engines exploded into life with a monstrous kick of power, and Buccari was pressed into her seat. Her brain compressed; her vision tunneled; her eyeballs rattled in her skull.

The EPL knifed into the deepening purple heavens. Buccari looked over her shoulder to see the planet plummeting away, the grand mountains reduced to a wrinkle in the terrain, the Great River just a wiggle. With the planet's horizon curving away, the acceleration schedule altered dramatically. Buccari reached to disengage the autopilot; she would fly it the rest of the way. She nudged the stick, but the lander was no longer a creature of the atmosphere; the apple had gone fully ballistic, a rocket accelerating to orbital velocity. At five minutes past the stratosphere Buccari picked up a transponding corvette on radar.

"*Condor One,*" she radioed, "*Condor One* Alpha is up."

"Morning, Skipper. Welcome back," Thompson acknowledged. The watch day had only just started in space; Buccari's body had some adjusting to do.

"Our Charlie time's been moved up, Skipper," Thompson said. "Fleet rendezvous is 0945 hours. We'll have to hump it out of orbit. Chief Silva has the plant cranked up and spinning."

"Roger," Buccari answered. "On board in ten minutes."

She adjusted her vector with a generous squirt of maneuvering thruster and a blast of primaries. All the stars of the universe twinkled in their places, an explosion of white pinpoints against the infinite ebony depths. The silver star that was her corvette grew larger on the windscreen.

Planetbound no longer, Buccari was once again a space pilot.

TWENTY-THREE

BATTLE FLEET UNDER WAY

The ships of the human fleet, like the planet, were illuminated at quarter phase. The orbiting motherships, diminishing in size with the perspective of distance, were silhouetted against the profound darkness of Genellan's night half, gleaming white scepters encircled by silver rings. *Novaya Zemlya,* the nearest ship, lay 2,400 *kroits* off Et Lorlyn's nose; about 1.5 human kilometers. The noblekone was angry, too angry to enjoy the stark beauty.

"Manual-ah approach," Et Lorlyn growled in Legion over the traffic frequency, his fury welling magnificently. "Guidance systems disabled."

"It is my fault," Scientist Dowornobb said.

"*Abat One* cleared for manual approach," announced the approach controller. "Bay number two, starboard side. Tugs are standing by. Turn final now."

Tugs! Et Lorlyn's ignominy was sufficient to discharge his anger bladders, further fueling his disgust and pounding his severely dented pride. His suit's circulation system struggled unsuccessfully to vent his ire. Concentrating upon the task at hand, the noblekone pulsed a retro to slow his tangential overshoot, and twisted his ship onto final approach course. His vector set, he initiated an acceleration to bring his interceptor down the orbital radial.

"*Abat One* turning final," rumbled his copilot in heavily accented Legion.

"It is my fault," Dowornobb said again. "I did not think my programming changes would have this effect."

Et Lorlyn contained his rage. Now was not the time for emotion. The noblekone had logged many approaches to human motherships, but this approach was special. On this approach he, his crew, and Scientist Dowornobb's technical team would remain on board, permanent additions to *Novaya Zemlya*'s crew. They would leap with the humans into hyperlight, perhaps to do battle. Nay, not perhaps; battle was likely. And on this momentous approach his ship was experiencing a full guidance system casualty. It did not reflect well upon his leadership.

"On final," his copilot reported.

"The gravitronic detection program is functioning," Scientist Dowornobb muttered over the intercom. "I will find the problem."

Et Lorlyn fired axial thrusters to commence a positive approach vector, adjusting with cross-dimensional squirts of lateral impulse to hold lineup. Alignment and glide-slope cross hairs on the main digital reticule were dead-centered. The konish interceptor's attitude was oriented within limits to mothership vertical, but velocity readouts indicated a slower than standard approach. So it must be; he would come aboard like some underpowered ore-loader.

"It is definitely a software problem," Dowornobb muttered. The scientist pummeled the control panel at his station behind the pilots. "I will locate it. It is my fault."

Novaya Zemlya filled the viewscreens, gleaming hoary silver and white against the infinite blackness of space, a blackness beyond description, an emptiness beyond meaning. No longer backdropped by the shadowed planet, the mothership was contrasted against the starry heavens. The majestic sweep of brilliant stars only served to enhance the totality of the void. Space was forever and unforgiving.

A bright constellation of red, amber, and green dominated the pilot's senses. Et Lorlyn's gaze was captured by a scintillating pattern of laser beams lancing upward from the mothership's landing dock. The pattern changed with his ship's position on the glide slope. The pilot steadied up his heading, firming the oscillating laser pattern into a steady framework, with an amber circle squarely centered.

"Glide-slope lasers are calibrating," the copilot reported. "Calibration cross-check-ah complete."

"Very well," the pilot replied, easing his closing velocity.

"Abat One," called the mothership controller. "Confirm you have optical indicators. I show you on glide slope, on centerline. Will you require tug assistance?"

Three orbital maneuvering tugs hovered at emergency stations. One of the stubby OMTs broke formation and commenced an approach to the konish interceptor.

"Roger ball," Et Lorlyn thundered. "Negative tugs."

The konish interceptor tracked toward its rendezvous, sliding down the calibrated pattern of glide-slope and centerline projection beams. The mothership grew larger and larger, finally expanding past the frame of the viewscreens. The near curve of the silver habitation ring revolved overhead, while the operations core, a vertical column of bruised ivory, grew wider, fatter, and more detailed before them. Strobes and position lights blinked with methodical insanity. Alignment references for triangulation and parallax measurement became apparent. The skin of the mothership, so clean and smooth from afar, grew seams and angles. Ledges and grooves materialized, maintenance platforms and minor antenna arrays appeared. Caution placards, smudges, and a multitude of blemishes grew apparent. The yawning caverns of the docking bays grew closer.

"Abat One in the groove," the controller reported, talking them down the glide slope. "Tracking sweet. Verify engagement gear deployed."

The copilot reported: "Hooks out-ah. Braking thrusters armed."

"Roger, *Abat One.* Cleared to dock."

The operation core expanded past the viewscreen windows, and then the mothership bay was around them, the big konish ship easing into a fleet-fueler berth. The interceptor made a barely discernible jolt as it oscillated into its mooring. The clanging impacts of securing booms were far more pronounced.

"I have found the problem," Dowornobb said, looking up. "Oh, we are here. Excellent landing, Colonel."

Condor One was the last corvette into the stacks. The safety tug came aboard on Buccari's heels, and for the first time since the fleet's arrival in Kon System, all combatants and fleet auxiliaries were in their berths. Fueling and maintenance crews swarmed their hulls, taking advantage of the downtime afforded by the impending hyperlight cruise.

In Hangar Bay Two, beyond the mothership's keel truss, Buccari noted the sinister shape of the single konish interceptor docked among the fleet fuelers, Et Lorlyn's ship. The noblekone would report to her. She laughed without humor; Et Lorlyn had almost five times the null-grav throttle hours that she had.

As her crew worked through the shutdown checklists, Klaxons erupted and rotating yellow beacons began flashing. Blaring horns pulsed repeatedly as the mothership's ponderous doors in first one hangar bay and then the other were brought together with breathtaking speed, settling precisely into their armored seals. Green and blue integrity lights illuminated; horns and Klaxons ceased. At last the strobing beacons were extinguished. Hangar-bay pressurization commenced.

Her ship secured, Buccari floated through the corvette's top hatch and into the crew manifolds, taking pressure tubes to level nine. She emerged into the familiar navy-blue passageway. The hatch into Condor Squadron's ready room loomed directly before her. On the bulkhead was a stylized depiction of a condor rending carrion. Beneath the gory emblem, on the squadron command plaque, was her name, freshly engraved: Commander Sharl F. Buccari, TLSF. *Commanding Officer!*

"Looks pretty good, huh, Skipper?" Thompson gushed.

"I'll have to get new flightsuit insignia," Buccari muttered, feeling dizzy. She attributed her uneasiness to being planet-bound for so long. She removed her docking hood and rubbed the stubble on her head.

"I need a depilatory," she said, backing away from the hatch.

"Your squadron's waiting, Commander," Flaherty said, grabbing her elbow.

She stared down at his hand.

"Sorry, sir," Flaherty said, releasing Buccari as if she were radioactive. "They're waiting for you, Skipper."

Buccari looked into Flaherty's laughing brown eyes. For once they were serious. Smiling, she pushed off from her copilot's shoulder, twisting for the hatch. She floated resolutely through the squadron equipment locker and into the ready room. Into her ready room.

Et Lorlyn, his copilot, and his second pilot, in environmental suits and helmets, dominated the low-ceilinged compartment. The immense kones, floating horizontally, were surrounded by Buccari's officers, both races gesticulating with timeless hand motions common to all pilots.

"Condor on deck!" shouted Trash Murphy, the beefy pilot of *Condor Four*.

Her flight crews oriented to vertical and assumed easy positions of attention. Deirdre O'Shay, squadron ops, began hooting like a foghorn. The others joined in; the ready room resounded with a rising syncopation, a silly simulation of what a genuine condor might have sounded like, had any living human ever heard one. The kones were bemused.

Buccari lifted her arms, trying to bring order. The hooting had changed to a chant: "Booch! Booch!"

Thompson and Flaherty, floating behind her, added to the bedlam. Et Lorlyn, with just enough room to fit within the room's vertical dimension, saluted her in the human style. The giant pressed with one hand against the overhead as he did so, holding his boots firmly to the deck. Et Lorlyn was easily four times her size.

"Reporting for-ah duty, Commander," the noblekone said.

The alien's booming voice halted the raucous shouting in mid-hoot.

Buccari floated to the kone's eye level and returned the salute, also using the overhead to counteract her inertia. "Welcome aboard, Colonel," she replied, putting out her hand. "I have been looking forward to flying with you again."

"The honor is-ah mine, Commander," Et Lorlyn said, engulfing her hand in his. She shook the huge hands of all three kones.

The hooting resumed.

"Okay, Condors, tie yourselves down," she shouted.

Buccari drifted to the front of the ready room, stopping herself before the vid display and the variegated ship/crew status boards. She noted with satisfaction that Et Lorlyn's crew was posted on the flight crew listing. Next to their names were four icons representing their combat kills. The icon designer had done an excellent job; each miniature symbol clearly represented a Legion corvette.

The room quieted. The pilots crawled into their tethers, providing order to the previously free-floating crowd. She looked around the ready room, staring into the eyes of each of her pilots. She sensed their confidence in her, their respect. But she also looked past their apparent good cheer. There was something else in their eyes, even in the dark brown eyes of the kones. They were going off to do battle, and they were afraid.

Buccari was afraid, too, for just as Jake Carmichael would have to send her into battle, so would she have to send her own pilots. Some would surely die.

Runacres had no right to feel lighthearted. And yet his mood was full and strong. Sarah Merriwether was still with him. He stole a glance at his command console. The images of his ship captains were arrayed before him, but it was Merriwether's sun-reddened visage that captured his attention. His flagship skipper was intently focused on her ship's under-way preparations.

Runacres's new group-leader floated onto the flag bridge.

Carmichael, in full battle armor for the jump to hyperlight, pushed up the companionway to his command chair, signaling the group duty officer to remain at the watch console.

"Ah, Captain Carmichael," Runacres said, "you're back with us. Didn't know you were such a planet hound."

"Good day, Admiral," Carmichael replied, eyes smiling.

"Flight group status," Runacres demanded.

"All corvettes and heavy-lifters are in and locked down," Carmichael said, all business. "All cargoes are stowed. Sir, the flight group is ready for hyperlight operations."

"Very well, Captain," Runacres replied.

"All unit commanders have reported in and ready," Commodore Wells reported. "All positions are linked. All systems are ready. Waiting for optimum flux flow."

"Science," Runacres demanded. "Flux status."

Captain Katz appeared on the comm-vid. "Gravitronic flux is on the flow. Estimate peak in two hours," he intoned. "We have an improving vector. Tack angle is down to six microradians."

"Updated transmit time?" Runacres inquired.

"Forty-six standard days, Admiral," Katz replied. "U-radials are lining up nicely."

"You have permission to get under way, Commodore," Runacres said.

"Aye aye, Admiral," Wells replied, issuing fleet orders to break loose from orbit. A shrill pipe sounded "Attention."

"Stand by for departure maneuvers," the boatswain of the watch droned. "Tether down or take hold. Now maneuvering."

Alarms sounded. Seconds later the big ship commenced its orbital departure acceleration, imperceptibly at first, and then with increasing authority. From his flag bridge Runacres watched and listened to the measured commands on Captain Merriwether's operations bridge. Her under-way watch performed with that timeless intensity so characteristic of big-iron crews. The intensity was necessary; things could go very wrong very fast.

When the fleet had steadied up on its de-orbit vector, Runacres signaled his flagship captain.

"Still glad you're with us, Captain?"

"Helluva time to be changing my mind, Admiral," Merriwether drawled. "Ask me later."

"Angular momentum is null within tolerance, Admiral," Wells reported. "All ships alpha-alpha."

Runacres took a last look at the jewel called Genellan.

"Jump the fleet, Franklin," he ordered.

SECTION THREE

THE BATTLES BEGIN

TWENTY-FOUR

PLANET EARTH

Over the long months of his maiden interstellar voyage, Tar Fell fretted upon the debilitating effects of entering hyperlight. Captain Ito asserted the kones would grow accustomed to the unsettling transition. Not assured, Tar Fell steeled himself for his second hyperlight event.

The exit into Sol System proved even more disconcerting than the jump into hyperlight. Stomach-churning vibrations wracked the armada-master; vertigo disconnected mind from body. After an eternity, the internal oscillations dampened out. Tar Fell opened his eyes and struggled to regain a reference to physical dimension. A concerned Captain Ito scrutinized him from the human technical bridge. Tar Fell managed a weak smile. The human returned to his instruments.

"All systems are performing," Flotilla-General Magoon gasped, breaking the shipwide silence. "All grid links are stable."

"Very well," Tar Fell acknowledged, his nausea ebbing only begrudgingly.

They had done it. They had jumped from hyperspace. Kones had traveled the stars. Other stations reported; the swelling operational babble resonated with near delirious excitement. Tar Fell shook off the persistent, cloying aftereffects. His joy bladders discharged wantonly. His suit-environment filters ran at high power. They had done it.

All about him bridge crew stared at the vid images and navigation screens. Tar Fell was compelled to move to the observation blister, to see with his own eyes the wonders of an

211

alien star-system. There he found Ambassador Kateos, her eye tufts like spring steel.

"It is beautiful," she said.

"As are all destinations after a long and dangerous voyage," Tar Fell replied, yet his excitement was near uncontained. A bejeweled crescent dazzled his eyes. Earth, the human home planet, afforded bright contrast to the infinite blackness of deep space. It was no wonder the humans were so obsessed with Genellan. Hanging before him was that planet's sublime twin.

"Constellations we have never seen," Kateos uttered.

"How feel you?" Ito asked in improving konish. The helmeted human floated alongside the kones.

Tar Fell tore his gaze from the blue-streaked pearl.

"It-ah is . . . beyond words," Kateos replied for both of them.

"How soon before we descend?" Tar Fell asked.

"Admiral Chou has-ah established contact with the Legion Assembly," Ito replied. "An orbital lander is being prepared for your—"

"We will use our own ships, Captain," Kateos replied, swelling her mountainous diaphragm. "Armada-Master Tar Fell, you will prepare a lander to transport me to Earth."

"As the ambassador desires," Tar Fell replied. He pulled himself to the deck and executed a formal bow.

"Captain Ito," Kateos continued, "I wish to make an announcement to the people of your planet. To *all* people of Earth. Would you make arrangements for that to happen?"

"I-ah will inform the authorities," Ito said. The human started to turn away but checked his motion. "Ambassador Kateos, may I have-ah the privilege of accompanying your landing party?"

"Regretfully not, Captain," Kateos replied.

Ito's eyes widened, belying his otherwise impassive features. "I will-ah attend to your request," he said, bowing. The human pushed off and floated from the observation blister.

"You surprise me," Tar Fell said, watching the human

depart. "Captain Ito has been of great assistance. He is worthy of our trust."

"Captain Ito has my unending trust," Kateos replied. "But I am ambassador to the planet Earth, not just to a single human government."

"Ah!" Tar Fell rumbled. "I detect Citizen Sharl's handiwork."

"Actually," Kateos replied, "Citizen Hud-sawn."

The day of the konish landing was declared a global holiday by all governments of the human home planet. On this day the community of man was host to a race of beings from another world. Denizens from planet Kon, kones of the Genellan legends, Titans from space, were to walk upon planet Earth.

Word of the impending event flew around the world, faster than rumor, spreading to the dimmest reaches of human existence. Riots and mass demonstrations became hushed assemblies of the curious, crowding about vid screens and shortwave sets. Crime stopped. Wars ceased in place; armies deserted the field, abandoning their weapons. Where people were not fleeing storm or fire, they huddled in their hovels, listening, watching . . . hoping.

Billions observed the actual landing on holo-vids and ancient televisions, three black cylinders from space on thundering columns of fire, majestic against the smog-shrouded Canadian Rockies. Touchdown was in a remote corner of the Alberta Military Test Grounds, under a mantle of Legion security. The event had been long anticipated; the konish enclave, a special environmental facility, awaited its extraterrestrial tenants.

Upon landing, the kones summarily evicted all humans from their embassy and grounds, rejecting all audio and video communications. Konish work crews set about remedying construction deficiencies necessary to support their stay, and konish security teams patrolled the two-hundred-square kilometers buffering their embassy. All humans were restricted from the environs, but two divisions of Tellurian Legion paratroopers guarded its perimeters, keeping the curious and adventurous at bay.

All delegations were refused access to the konish legation; not even President Socrates Duffy and the Legion Council were excepted. Thus it was that Captain Ito, on the day of Ambassador Kateos's address to Earth's population, occupied an uncomfortable chair in the richly paneled Legion Council chambers. President Duffy and the council, nursing their relegation, were enthroned on the rosewood and mahogany bench symbolic of their office, impatiently waiting for the ambassador's speech to commence. President Duffy exhibited little energy. He seemed distant from the proceedings. There were rumors of degenerative illness, maladies beyond medical science's ability to repair. The burly politician was not yet eighty years old.

Ito was surrounded by senior fleet staff, including Admiral Chou and Vice Admiral Klein, Commander of Fleet Science and Intelligence. On the vid screens was displayed the sigil of the konish Planetary Defense Force. A countdown clock displayed the minutes remaining until the ambassadorial address commenced. The time remaining indicated mere minutes, but the countdown was on hold while a balky communication satellite hookup over the Indian subcontinent was remedied.

Business was conducted while the august body waited. The main holo-vid displayed the galactic region where the Ulaggi were most likely to be encountered—the Red Zone. That area of highest contact probability loomed nearer to Earth, inexorably reaching out as the universal gravitronic radials realigned. Dr. Jean-Marie Thoreau, the chief architect of Legion hyperlight technologies, and Admiral Klein briefed the President. Brightly colored data points marked the relative positions of Earth and Kon. Also garishly delineated were the Ulaggi contacts at Shaula, Oldfather, Scorpio Minor, Hornblower, and Pitcairn.

Admiral Klein, tall and elegant, summarized the recent technical advances in hyperlight technology. Ito remembered the senior fleet intelligence officer as having raven hair elegantly streaked with a snowy ribbon. No longer; Vice Admiral

Klein's long hair had gone uniformly white in the last year. Dark shadows haunted her dark eyes. Here was a human being who understood her plight.

"Marvelous work. I must meet Scientist Dowornobb," Dr. Thoreau muttered. The thin old man distractedly rubbed his snow-white crew cut. "Superb thinking."

"Will you be jumping to Genellan, Doctor?" Admiral Chou asked.

Dr. Thoreau, the human expert on hyperlight travel, had never once left his native planet. Several members of the council cleared their throats with poorly concealed amusement.

"Tempting," Dr. Thoreau replied, nonplussed. "I should like to see Commander Buccari again, but no, we have too many changes to make in the *Avenger* battleships. Gravitronic arrays must be designed and outfitted. I dare say I can improve on Dowornobb's design. His work inspires me."

"We must work fast, Doctor," Vice Admiral Klein said. "Admiral Runacres's mission into the Red Zone is likely to raise the ante."

"Ah, Admiral Klein, you also disapprove of Admiral Runacres's cavalier foray?" a deep, smoothly modulated voice inquired. Secretary of State Stark rose from his prominent position in the cabinet well. Up to that point the Tellurian Legion Secretary of State had been uncharacteristically quiet. Long of face and heavy-featured, the secretary's presence dominated the room. His glistening, jet-black hair and improbably smooth skin belied his years, as did his erect posture.

"On the contrary, Mr. Secretary," Vice Admiral Klein replied.

"I am confused," Stark said. Obscenely large jewels studding his earlobes sparkled like beacons in the chamber's diffuse light. "You implied that, on balance, Runacres's penetration will cause problems."

"*Admiral* Runacres's purpose is clear," Klein replied, too sharply. "It is the secretary's thinking that is confused."

"You are insulting!" a council member thundered, a heavy-set general in the gold and red service dress of the Alberta

Brigade. The tension in the room blossomed. For reasons Ito failed to understand, Stark was rabidly supported by the army general staffs. For reasons that were more clear, Stark was also the favorite of the privileged electorate.

"Admiral Runacres takes a calculated risk," Klein continued.

"A calculated risk?" Stark replied.

"There will never be a better opportunity to rescue hostages—"

"What proof of hostages?" Stark demanded. "Runacres seeks to rescue something that may not exist, all the while putting twelve billion living humans at risk."

"Those billions are already at risk, Mr. Secretary," Admiral Chou preempted. "Sir, our crews face certain death as a matter of routine. We buttress their loyalty by demonstrating our willingness to retrieve them from the most hopeless situations. Knowing with confidence that we will fight for them, our spacers will fight to the death for us."

"Nobly spoken, Admiral," Stark replied. "But sir, assuming these hostages are still alive, your own intelligence indicates they are descendants of the AC fleet destroyed at Shaula. These are not crews from a Tellurian Legion Fleet, Admiral."

"They are human beings, Mr. Secretary," Chou replied. "We should all claim membership to that fleet, sir . . . even you."

"Outrageous!" the Alberta Brigade general shouted. Other council members joined in the protest.

"Enough," President Duffy said, his deep voice retaining sufficient power to halt all discussion. "It is time."

The address countdown had resumed. The vid image of the PDF emblem dissolved to reveal a lectern backdropped by midnight-blue drapery. Kateos's gargantuan form moved gracefully before the konish embassy vid-cams. Ito straightened uneasily in his chair. The full gravity of Earth rested on his shoulders, but he realized his burden was vastly increased by morbid depression. The government of the Tellurian Legion, nay of all Earth, was hopelessly ineffective. All mankind was threatened, and human leadership remained immersed in petty squabble.

That Stark's political star continued to rise was astounding. This was the human responsible for Legion diplomacy. The disconnect was overwhelming. King Ollant would have no part of the man, and even the most opportunistic of the southern konish governments refused his gratuitous overtures. Stark was powerful because he was rich, and because he promised his powerful constituency whatever they wanted. That he rarely delivered was moot. He had innumerable and convincing excuses; it was not his fault that Earth was falling apart. He had convinced his following that if it were not for him, the world would disintegrate all the more faster. Even faced with the end of humanity, Stark's only concern was to improve his own lot, to gain more power, power for its own sake. Stark was a predatory insect seeking dominion over an anthill before the advance of a thousand year flood.

"Citizens of Earth," the konish ambassador announced, yanking Ito from his ennui. Kateos's voice was deep, clear, and strong. "I bring you greetings from the planet Kon."

Kateos's demeanor was self-assured, quietly powerful. Its effect on Ito was narcotic. Her speech, by human political standards, was appallingly brief. She politely disavowed any obligation or allegiance to the Legion. Next she invited delegations from all nations to visit the konish embassy, apologizing gracefully for making them come to her.

As Kateos spoke, an awareness overcame Ito. The konish female possessed those qualities of leadership so desperately lacking in his own government. Earth's government was in the hands of dangerously ineffectual and self-absorbed bureaucrats. There was no one in charge, no one responsible. Kateos, if only for the moment, had taken command of his entire planet, a feat no human could duplicate.

Ito's brain flashed with hot revelation. He was no longer conscious of Kateos's comforting words. There was a person, one human being, who could take command of Earth.

Buccari!

Sharl Buccari could be the leader of humanity. Buccari's standing among the people of the Earth had already attained international cult status. Even the government of Kon, northern and southern, deferred to her intangible powers, her charisma. Ito realized with the force of gravity and light—Buccari was humanity's best hope, against the Ulaggi peril and against humanity's own shortsighted selfishness.

Ito's veins coursed with a peculiar energy, an evangelical fervor. He would be her first apostle. His mind roiled with implication.

"She speaks Legion better than I do," President Duffy remarked.

Kateos's address had ended. The vid image changed to a functionary familiar to Ito. The kone detailed the order and timing of state visits. Kateos would be extremely busy over the ensuing months.

"Louder, too," Stark said, drawing a laugh.

"She seemed without guile," a council member remarked.

"Do not be fooled," Stark replied. "Ambassador Kateos is an extremely competent negotiator. She will lull you to sleep and then steal the pillow from under your head."

Stark's scurrilous words penetrated Ito's grand thoughts. The officer jumped to his feet, feeling an urge to rush the cabinet well and throttle the man. Grabbing the lacquered railing before him, Ito restrained himself, trying to remove the rage from his face. Everyone in the room glanced up at his sudden movement, Stark among them. At that moment an assistant handed Stark a communication. The secretary glanced down, giving it cursory notice, but then its contents captured his full attention.

"Captain Ito," Stark announced, looking up, "the konish ambassador desires your presence. She requests that you attend to her emissary in the capacity of official representative of the Tellurian Legion. May I welcome you to the State Department, sir."

For Kateos, the days on Earth swirled past in an endless fog of ambassadorial receptions. Heads of state came visiting, some repeatedly, pleading for dispensation, uniformly beseeching her sympathy. The national rulers and their emissaries brought gifts: jewels and works of art, some of obvious value in any culture, some gifts of inane impracticality and little aesthetic interest. They also brought bright, healthy children dressed in traditional mufti; they brought starving, crippled children garbed in rags. Kateos's instincts did not permit her to trust the human leaders; they spoke empty words and made selfish pleas. The children, however, cried real tears.

Across Earth's tortured surface, riot and battle inexorably resumed. Famine and pestilence had never ceased. The moratorium on man-made disaster created by the arrival of the kones had been but an illusion. The Asian Cooperative and the TGSR announced plans to reconstitute their interstellar fleets, and immediately declared war on one another.

Finally the day came when Kateos granted her last primary audience. She had talked, at least once, to the representatives of all recognized governments, and with many that were not recognized. She was little enlightened by this parade of want and anger, and immensely frustrated. The overwhelming common denominator, either directly stated or bluntly implied, was a desire to emigrate to Genellan. The leaders of Earth wished to flee their middens.

"My fleet jumps at the end of the month," Admiral Chou informed them. The Second Fleet commander had requested an audience, immediately granted. The Tellurian Legion flag officer was given full military honors. Captain Ito and Armada-Master Tar Fell were in attendance.

"Your timing is impeccable," Kateos replied. "We are ready to return to our own system. Tar Fell has not given me a moment's peace."

"Gravity, it is time to return to a world with weight!" Tar Fell roared. The giant's command of the Legion language had improved, thanks to Ito's tutoring.

"I will notify Secretary Stark," Ito said quietly.

Kateos thought the diminutive human's reaction subdued. Ito had been of invaluable assistance during the mission, coordinating the order and priority of state visits and briefing the ambassador on the stunning complexity of Earth's cultures and religions. She appreciated most of all his objectivity and his refusal to advocate for his own government.

"You are sorry to see us leave, Sam?" she asked. "Then you will return with us . . . unless you prefer to work for Secretary Stark."

Ito's moon face was overwhelmed with uncharacteristic emotion.

"Of course!" Tar Fell thundered. "Captain Ito is-ah member of my crew. You will return with-ah me. There will be no discussion."

"As you direct, Armada-Master," Ito replied.

"My commodore will issue grid rendezvous positions," Admiral Chou said. "Our prejump inspections will take place—"

Tar Fell held up his big hand. "I-ah grow tired of-ah escorts."

"It would be prudent if—" Chou protested.

"Thank you, but no, Admiral," Tar Fell rumbled. "Please return to Genellan without us. My hyperlight cell will proceed independently."

TWENTY-FIVE

RETURN TO PITCAIRN

A telescopy image of the planet projected from the main status board, a dun sphere marbled in dull emerald and dingy white. Runacres shook his mind clear of hyperlight's effects. He concentrated on the planet's image and waited, his breathing loud in his battle helmet.

"Jump exit complete," Wells reported quietly. "All ships alpha-alpha. Emission control status one. Defensive condition status one."

The Tellurian Legion fleet was returned to Pitcairn System, deep in the Red Zone. Synthesized computer outputs, designed to be soothing and nonintrusive, were loud and harsh compared to the muted tones of human circuit-talkers.

"Just another walk in the park." The familiar drawl came over the command circuit.

Runacres glanced at his comm-vid. Captain Merriwether's image stared back; her stolid countenance, lined and space-worn, buttressed his courage. She smiled and he was whole.

"Maintain senior battle watch," Runacres replied, shifting his gaze back to the status boards. There was nothing at which to stare; all active sensors were choked off. The screens were blank. His ships emitted no radars, no broad-band lasers, no electromagnetics of any kind. The fleet was not emitting, but it was listening; powerful telescopes scanned all objects in their detection range; motion detectors and full-spectrum analyzers passively processed the ethers of Pitcairn System. Every ear in the fleet listened, every nerve tensed, waiting for threat alarms to sound.

"Transmission delay to Pitcairn Two calculated by parallax at two point five seconds," reported the science duty officer.

"Very well," Runacres replied.

"Scientist Dowornobb," Runacres demanded, "are you reading anything?" The transmission to the konish scientist aboard *Novaya Zemlya* was by low-power laser.

"No-ah, Admiral." Dowornobb's grainy visage filled Runacres's comm-vid. "I detect-ah no hyperlight flux."

Seconds blinked off the digital chronometers. Navigation displays revealed incipient motion vectors as Runacres's motherships began slowly to accelerate into the gravity well, minding the irrefutable attraction of heavenly bodies.

"Science," Runacres barked, "what are we seeing?"

"Planets and moons, Admiral," Captain Katz reported, appearing on comm-vid. "Emissions are extremely light. A tittering of microwave intercepts and some on-planet LF hits. Meteorological and tectonic static. P-Two has a satellite constellation, but it's not painting outward—probably communication or resource imaging. Navigation radar, but no search or targeting lobes. It's real quiet, Admiral. I don't believe there are any other ships in the neighborhood."

"Perhaps they're all on the other side," Carmichael offered.

"Statistically unlikely," Katz replied.

"Time will tell," Merriwether drawled.

Runacres glanced down at his comm-vid. His mothership captain was busy supervising her bridge watch.

"Close enough, Franklin," Runacres declared. "Put us on orbit."

"Aye, Admiral," Wells replied, punching in the fleet vector. On *Eire*'s peak, from a mast above the antennae farm, a gang of laser beacons flashed a closed pattern of microbursts.

"Signal's in the air," the tactical officer reported.

The pipe of *Eire*'s watch boatswain sounded sonorously. Runacres shifted uneasily in his tethers. Firing impulse drives would generate an active signal, and a loud one. He prayed his fleet was far enough removed from Ulaggi sensors that the maneuvers would not be detected.

"Make ship ready for fleet maneuver," droned the boatswain. "Tether down. Secure all loose gear. Now impulse maneuvers."

"All ships are answering," reported the tactical officer.

The flagship's maneuvering alarm sounded.

"Executing," Wells announced.

Imperceptibly at first, and then with increasing sensory evidence, the spacer's faithful frame of reference shifted. Runacres's tethers activated, snugging him gently to his station. Small articles, not properly stowed prior to course change, became softly drifting missiles. A robotic claw, pushed about by a gimbaled air jet, doggedly retrieved the space flotsam.

"My pilots are ready, Admiral," Carmichael advised.

"Launch the penetration mission, Jake," Runacres said.

Buccari's crew performed their duties with a quiet focus born of fear. In efforts to dispel tension, Fenstermacher and Gunner Tyler rendered an off-key melody on the crew circuit, a ribald old spacer ditty. Warrant Officer Silva and Lieutenant Flaherty joined in lustily on the most degenerate refrains. Buccari deselected the crew channel and returned her attentions to corvette status telemetry. All Condor ships were full systems up. She had six crews to look after now, not just the crew of a single ship. Was she ready to lead six crews into combat?

"Burl, how are the passengers?" Buccari asked.

"Real quiet, Skipper," the medical petty officer answered from the crew decks. "Most of 'em are tethered down in sleep cells."

Marine insertion teams, each team comprising five humans and two cliff dwellers, were embarked on *Condor One* and *Condor Four*. Those corvettes would descend to planetary support orbit, launching their respective EPLs into the atmosphere. Assuming no enemy countermeasures, the landing teams would be jettisoned in penetrators. As soon as the landing team cleared a base, the rest of the reconnaissance force and their supplies would be delivered to the planet's surface by EPL. The reconnaissance team would be left on the planet for a minimum of four standard months.

A Klaxon sounded. Horns blared.

"It's happening," Flaherty announced.

Rotating beacons oscillated into life. Hangar-bay depressurization commenced. A ringing alarm sounded, and the huge hangar-bay doors were sucked aside. Stars exploded into view, the star-system's brilliant rays flooding into Hangar-Bay Two, overwhelming the mothership's muted operational lighting and casting stark shadows. Pitcairn Two, the size of a pea held at arm's length, lay dead off *Condor One*'s nose.

"Screen's launching," Thompson reported. "Eagle Squadron's screen commander. Raven and Kite on the flanks."

Buccari punched up the screen frequency. Nothing—the screen was deploying in radio silence. She laughed at herself, and at the irony. Out of habit she had dialed in the screen frequency, on the chance she would hear Carmichael's voice, but Carmichael was group-leader now; his tight, tall fanny was not going anywhere. Condor Squadron, on the other hand, was going in harm's way.

A launch signal sounded. The rumble of launch pistons discharging vibrated the metal under her feet.

"There go the tankers," Flaherty said. "We're next."

She was ready. Her anxiety transformed into excitement.

"Condor, this is group." The voice she wanted to hear came over a secure channel. Buccari synched into encryption mode.

"Condor's up," she replied.

"Good luck, Booch."

"Thanks, Boss," she replied.

"Come back to me," Carmichael said. "Well . . . eh, good luck again, Condor. Launch signal's in the air."

"Jake," she almost shouted.

"Yeah, Sharl?"

"Thanks for checking," she said.

A pause.

"Wish I were going with you, Booch," Carmichael said.

"I know you do," she replied. "I'm glad you're not. Condor out."

Carmichael signed off with a slow double-click.

"Tankers are fifty klicks out, Skipper," Thompson reported. "Velocity point six."

"Very well," Buccari barked. She exhaled hugely and grabbed the big throttles, snugging her wrists into the launch grips. Launch authorization sounded.

"Here we go," Flaherty shouted.

The operational release flashed on their annunciator; a steady green light flickered from the flight ops tower. Buccari hit the kick switch, and *Condor One* was abruptly trundling down the launch slides, being ejected into the starry abyss. The structural frame of the mothership disappeared behind them.

"Corvette away," Flaherty announced. "Hooty-hoot hoot!"

As always, once clear of the static reference of the mothership all sense of motion abruptly ceased. The majestic depths of ebony, star-shot infinity surrounded them. Buccari smoothly applied a power coupling, twisting the corvette's nose.

"Clear angle," Flaherty announced.

They drifted from the larger ship's shadow. The sunstar's direct rays flooded *Condor One*'s crew-worn flight deck with harsh light. Buccari's visor sensors activated, filtering the radiation.

"Four gees," Buccari broadcast. "Buster."

She hit the ignitors. *Condor One* leaped forward.

"Hoot . . . h-hoot," Flaherty grunted.

"T-Two's out. Three, f-four, five, and six," Thompson reported, laboring under the acceleration. "C-Condor flights away."

Buccari checked tactical. All corvettes were laser-linked. She signaled for cruise formation, and her skippers acknowledged smartly. Their ships maneuvered for position.

"Tanker rendezvous in ten hours," Thompson reported.

"Now for the waiting," Runacres said. "I'm going below."

"Admiral's leaving the bridge," the watch officer barked.

The oncoming and off-going watchstanders assumed a respectful position of attention until Runacres disappeared through the staff hatch. Carmichael finished his battle-stations briefing and floated up from the group operations watch console, giving way to one of his watch officers. He felt at once angry, worried, and useless. He was anxious for Buccari, and for all of his pilots, but he also felt a deeper melancholy.

"You'll survive Jake," Wells said. "First launch after you've been left on the deck is the toughest."

Carmichael looked up at the fleet commodore. The big, Sphinx-faced officer had been relieved at the flag ops console. Wells's ebony countenance was broken with a sleepy-eyed smile.

"Shows, eh?" Carmichael replied.

"Like your dog died," the barrel-chested commodore rumbled.

"I guess I thought I'd be a corvette pilot forever," Carmichael said, floating toward the bridge egress.

"Well, you're a big-iron driver now," Wells replied, grabbing Carmichael's battle armor. "Like the rest of us. Get used to it, son."

"That's not all that's bothering him," came Merriwether's familiar drawl. "Jake's worried for his flight crews, one feisty little green-eyed squadron commander in particular."

Wells laughed and Carmichael groaned, realizing that he was about to get mothered, whether he needed it or not. He peered over the flag bridge counter. One level below, the flagship's skipper pushed off from the command bridge and floated directly up to the flag mezzanine, flagrantly ignoring bridge protocol. But then, it was her ship.

"We are on orbit," Merriwether said as Wells pulled her to the deck. "The enemy is not in sight. Let us take advantage of this moment to celebrate Captain Jake's miserable change of status. I believe a touch of the amber is in order. Gentlemen, shall we adjourn to my cabin?"

"The admiral might care to participate," Wells said.

"He's waiting in my cabin," Merriwether replied.

Carmichael was grateful for the company.

TWENTY-SIX

PITCAIRN TWO ORBIT

Condor Squadron, five Legion corvettes and a konish interceptor, rendezvoused with a pod of fleet-fuelers, call-sign Atlas. Buccari drove *Condor One* under the ponderous fuel bladder of *Atlas One*, docking smoothly into the port fueling station. Et Lorlyn's interceptor plugged into the fueler's starboard station mere seconds later. The konish pilot's skills were of the first order. The other corvettes of Condor Squadron mated with the their assigned fleet-fuelers, two corvettes nestling under the fuel bladder of each tanker. All Condor ships topped off but remained mated. Conjoined to the tankers, the reconnaissance mission streaked planetward, the smaller ships consuming fuel directly from the fueler's bladder, conserving their internal loads.

Hours passed slowly, Nestor Godonov, reporting from *Condor One*'s survey laboratory, transmitted an updated planet survey. Buccari studied the briefing screen; it displayed a telescopy image overlaid with magnetic field and meteorological models. Pitcairn Two gave little hint of its secrets.

"Have you resolved the landing site, Nes?" Buccari asked.

"Negative, Skipper," Godonov replied over the intercom. "Still exploring the options. I'm trying to get as close to the intercept site as possible and still have covering terrain."

"How about a beach?" Flaherty added, floating into his copilot station. "This rock have any beaches? My tan's faded."

"The only tan you'll get in this system is from a bug laser blaster," Buccari said. "Maybe Thompson should be apple pilot."

"I'm ready," Thompson replied quickly.

227

"Cool your jets, Slim," Flaherty said. "This drop is mine. So, any beaches, Nes?"

"A few," Godonov replied. "P-Two's about forty percent ocean. High salinity ocean. Tremendous mineral runoff. Lots of desert. Lots of wind erosion. Fair amount of weather. Feast or famine stuff. Drought patterns and flood plains. Strong prevailing winds. Monsoons and typhoons."

"My kind of place," Buck replied from the crew deck. "Any signs of life? Besides the bugs? Any plant life?"

"Quite a bit," Godonov said, slewing the terrain model. "Some vegetation in marine wetlands and all along the coastal littoral, where you would expect rainfall from frontal uplifts. Also in midlatitude highland watersheds. Some serious mountain ranges, five thousand meters or higher. I can see plant life and freshwater lakes here . . . here, and here." He maneuvered a cursor, marking regions for his networked audience.

"You come down off the mountains, you get into arid terrain real quick," he continued.

"Deserts?" someone asked.

"Definitely deserts," he replied.

"Time to change the watch," Buccari ordered over the command circuit. She jettisoned her tethers. "Flack, you've got the ship."

"Rog'," Flaherty responded. "I've got the ship."

Buccari floated off the flight deck and headed for the crew deck. She would get some sleep.

Four watch cycles later the fleet-fueler's grapples released *Condor One* with a thumping vibration. Buccari pulsed number three and six contraverniers, initiating a symmetrical drift aft and downward. Through her forward viewscreen the parallax vanes in the orange-lighted fueling well smoothly receded.

"Clear tanker," Flaherty reported.

With increasing velocity, *Condor One* fell away. The fleet-fueler's bulbous bosom, a strobe-lit blackness occulting the pure light of the stars, grew smaller. Ahead, Pitcairn Two hove brightly into view, three-quarters full and filling Buccari's viewscreen.

"*Condor Two*'s coming out," Flaherty reported.

Above them Et Lorlyn's massive interceptor pulled clear from the fueler's grasp. Buccari fired a lateral, increasing her separation rate. *Condor Two* made an adjustment, dropping off the tanker smartly and maneuvering for position on Buccari's flank. Aft and to port, the running lights of two more corvettes became visible, separating from another tanker.

"Three and Four out and linked," Thompson reported. "Here come Five and Six. All 'vettes fueled and ready."

"Rog'," Buccari replied. She transmitted a burst signal to the tankers, authorizing them to return to fleet. Atlas lead acknowledged. An electric-blue bloom flowered from the tanker's stern; the ungainly ship jumped forward. Seconds later the other tankers shot past *Condor One*, one to each side. The fuelers accelerated out of sight, straight for the planet's brilliant limb and a gravity whip that would return them to the relative safety of the fleet.

Buccari brought her head back onto the flight deck. She checked tactical. Nothing painted them; there were no search strobes, no unusual communications. It was too quiet.

"How about some orbital parameters, Nes," she ordered.

"Fifty degree trace," Godonov replied. "I'm establishing final grid coordinates."

"Fifty degrees it is," she said. "Got a landing site yet?"

"I've narrowed it down to two," Godonov replied. "Still building terrain models. We're talking rough country."

"Orbital burn in ten minutes," Thompson reported.

"You've got one orbit to make up your mind, Nes," Buccari said, activating the maneuvering alarm with her optical cursor. She fired a coupled moment, twisting the big corvette to line up her main engines with the retro-axis. She stopped the twist with a deft counterpulse, tweaked the heading with a vernier, and tried to relax. All Condors verified retro-burn alignment.

Ten minutes later she fired main engines, establishing Condor flight in orbit around Pitcairn Two.

"Don't need the extra orbit, Skipper," Godonov said,

coming up on the science circuit. "Landing Site Alpha coordinates are dialed in. I'm ready when you are."

"Load insertion teams," she ordered.

"Aye, Skipper," Godonov replied. "Wish us luck."

Brappa, his knobby head confined in a helmet and his body shrouded in dark metal, felt his heart beating against his ribs. The dim red glow of his instrument dials provided the only illumination. The hunter monitored signals and numbers as he had been trained, ignoring the suffocating closeness. The instrument readings were in correct ranges. For this Brappa was glad.

"Report by number," Toon-the-speaker's voice chittered in his ear. The guilder would not descend with the hunters; a penetration was too dangerous for the nonflying cliff dwellers. Toon's guilders and the rest of the reconnaissance team would come down with the equipment, when a safe landing zone for the long-leg star-ferry had been reconnoitered.

"One," Brappa replied.

"Two," Sherrip chirped softly.

They had trained many hours for the penetration, undergoing punishing physical tests and performing countless disorienting simulations. Brappa felt prepared. And frightened.

"Our star-ferry leaves its womb," Toon announced.

A *thump* vibrated Brappa's shell, and then came a sustained racheting. Brappa's sonic and aural receptors detected motors whirring, gases flowing. There was gentle lateral movement; the star-ferry was moving. There came a quick rolling motion and then an interminable stillness, a floating.

"We are falling to the planet," Toon reported.

Many minutes later Brappa perceived a vibration. Metal hummed. The noise grew louder, the vibrations more violent. Brappa's cocoon twisted about him, buffeting the hunter against his restraining harness. Acceleration drove blood from the hunter's head as they entered the planet's ocean of air. To his shame, Brappa felt the hot flush of panic.

"Hold firm." Toon's uncertain chirp broke through the rising bedlam.

Brappa's cocoon bucked and shook, rattling the hunter's helmet with increasing violence. The warrior rechecked his bouncing numbers. All was in order. Brappa sensed the welcomed press of gravity, light and tenuous but growing ever stronger. He waited. The vibrations slowly dampened to hissing smoothness. It grew uncomfortably warm.

"Final report," Toon demanded. Brappa responded and then Sherrip. Brappa was pressed into his harness as the star-ferry sliced across the skies of a new planet, losing velocity. More turns; greater gee-forces.

"Rising winds, brave warriors. It is time," Toon reported.

Brappa's eyes darted to a number gauge, the one that counted time pulses backward to null. He made a final check of his harness and breathing apparatus, pulling all straps tight. The time-counter retreated toward zero, but Brappa's eyes never registered the cipher; with horrible imperative his cocoon was rocketed from rest. His sensory functions were annihilated by overwhelming acceleration; unconsciousness reigned, for how long, he knew not. The hunter's first sensation was nausea; his second was blurred sight. The thin atmosphere rushed past the rigid walls of his container. It grew hotter.

It was dark when Pake slipped from beneath her hides. She padded across the cold dirt floor to use the chamber pot. Her bladder relieved, Pake cracked a shutter to check the weather. Sparkling stars dotted a midnight-blue sky, a rare sight. Dawn's first brush tinted the jagged horizon. The wind was still. The huffing of the smelter echoed from the valley floor.

"Wake up," Pake said, not loudly, her voice husky with sleep. She stirred the banked ashes, finding red-glowing embers, all the while mixing in straw and dung. Flames caught. She added a precious cactus-wood faggot. Pake's daughters stirred under their leather blankets. Little One groaned like a wanton animal and pushed from her pallet. The girl got no farther than a squat. Her swollen abdomen, half hidden by a fall of black hair, glowed with gold light in the dim flickering. Pake helped her daughter to her feet.

"I'll feed the animals," Pake said, taking mercy on the pregnant child. No, no longer a child—Little One was a woman, a
worker, a bearer of children. "Make breakfast."

Little One grunted unintelligibly, stumbling purposefully in
the direction of the chamber pot.

Pake pulled open the wooden door. Overnight, the wind-
whipped haze had sifted from the skies. She inhaled, luxuriating
in a breath of air drawn without grit. She smelled morning cook
fires. Other phantoms of the dawn stirred, softly padding specters performing chores. From down the hill drifted an old song.
Pake did not feel like singing.

Awakening packers drowned out the soft, sad notes with
bleats of hunger. Pake opened the feed bin and checked the
stock of saw grass. It was near time to harvest more. The long-
bladed grass was used for adobe bricks, for weaving baskets
and mats, for tinder, and for packer provender. She lifted out a
sheaf and dropped it into the feeding trough, spreading it with
her foot to keep the packers from jostling each other and from
destroying the fragile paddock fence.

Ba-booom! The jolting clap of double-thunder stopped
Pake's foot in mid-stir. *Ba-booom!*

The rolling echoes blended together, haunting the clear,
quiet morning. Packer snouts jerked from their feed. Pake
looked to the east, where the mountains were starting to glow.

Seconds passed with hot, agonizing slowness. Brappa was
weightless; he was falling, helpless. Reflexively, the hunter's
membranes tried to deploy, pressing the walls of his cylindrical cell. He concentrated on the glowing numbers defining
his altitude. A warning signal flashed. His harness went rigid,
forcing the hunter stiffly upright. He closed his eyes as the first
brain-stunning jolt straightened his spine. *Wooom!* The hunter
lost consciousness.

A warning tone brought Brappa groggily awake. Shaking
his head, he whistled shrilly, struggling against his harness as
it constricted even tighter. He was no longer afraid; his head
hurt too much. He was angry. *Wooom!* The second thruster
fired.

Brappa shrieked his rage, refusing to lose consciousness.

Separation altitude approached; for this, Brappa thanked the gods. He reached for the thick yellow and black handle. He gripped the ring with spindly hands, tempted to pull early, if only to escape his misery. He waited with frantic impatience. On the mark, Brappa yanked, but something had already happened; a shrill humming came from overhead. His plummet was disturbed by a soft tug, his metal prison oscillated slightly, and then came a much firmer, springing jolt. He shrieked with joy as his canister fell away, leaving his booted talons dangling above a planet far, far below.

No amount of empty air would ever frighten a hunter. Through his thick jumpsuit Brappa sensed a biting chill.

Pake's breath caught in her throat. Pinpricks of flashing light, an irregular string of silver sparkles, sprinkled the sapphire sky. From far away came muted reports: *Harrump-ump-ump. Harrump-ump. Harrump. Harrump-ump-ump.* Echoes lingered in the stillness. Doors creaked against leather hinges. Frightened mothers and daughters stole into the narrow spaces between the huts, staring upward.

"Pake!" shouted Lu-Lu, her neighbor. "What do you make of it?"

Pake, her gaze searching skies now quiet, could only shake her head. There was no explanation. It was as if stars had been annihilated, their death throes marked by a soft popping. Pake was confused. The first rays of the sun bled over the jagged horizon, silhouetting the wind-tortured terrain in crimson and gold.

"Is it a miracle?" Lu-Lu asked breathlessly.

"Or more misery?" said Ho, the potter.

"I do not know," Pake replied. "It is of the heavens."

"Of the heavens?" Lu-Lu said, confused.

"Say nothing to the guardmales," Pake announced. "I will call a village meeting to discuss what we have seen. I must think on this."

"More misery," Ho repeated, turning back to her hut.

"Of the heavens," Lu-Lu muttered.

"Say nothing! Go to work," Pake said, turning one last time to the east, searching, listening. There was only a sunrise. The morning was silent except for packers chewing and the dull throb of the smelter.

Ka-thump! The jolt of his parafoil sent warm blood up Godonov's nape. The science officer exhaled hugely. He had survived his first hypermach planetary penetration. He reconsidered; he was not yet on the ground.

Godonov looked down at Pitcairn Two, perceived as a drab mottled expanse from his lofty altitude. Mountain shadows stretched over the land by dawn's low rays gave stark indication of geological relief. The parallel ranges marched north and south, their eastern flanks glowing with first light.

Godonov returned his attention to his equipment. He cleared his impact webbing and stowed his controls. Reaching up, Godonov slipped the quick release fittings on the penetrator's aerodynamic top section and slid the shell structure along a tubular backpack until it was secured on his back, like the shell of a turtle. Everything was ready for landing.

Godonov looked about. Buck's pitch-black parafoil was the farthest north and the lowest; the other foils, mottled green and black, were forming on Buck's lead. Godonov hauled on his riser, tacking into line. Once in position, the science officer enhanced the magnification on his helmet visor; the primary lenses warped smoothly, and prism deflectors deployed, impeding his peripheral vision. He searched the skies for Chastain's fire team. They were higher and upwind; Godonov counted seven more foils. All present and accounted for.

Godonov reestablished contact with the landing site. A wind shear drifted him to the east, but the touchdown point was within range. Closing on the nearest parafoil, Godonov deployed his high-lift, high-drag secondary and shook out his steering lanyards, establishing a cross-wind crab. Slowly the rusty-gold mountains rose to meet him. Godonov estimated less than thirty minutes to touchdown.

* * *

Brappa looked up to check his wind-rider. The fluted expanse of fabric was connected to the hunter's equipment pod by thin, strong shrouds. He scanned for landmarks. The mountains, flattened by great altitude, rose slowly to meet him. Between the ranges lay a long crescent-shaped lake, its bottom horn pointing to a smaller round tarn, just now turning blue in the dawn. The landing site was on the shore of the small lake, in a high valley. Brappa adjusted his wind-rider, instinctively sensing the wind drift.

Brappa's acute vision resolved other wind-riders before him and behind. He steered into line. Maintaining course, the hunter extricated himself from his impact webbing, stowing the harness in a pouch on his equipment pod. Next, he disconnected his life-support umbilical and unzipped his dropsuit. After touching his deathstick and knife, he disconnected his body armor from the harness attachments and hung suspended by one bony hand. Double-checking that he was clear of all lines and connections, he released his grip. Icy breezes filled the billowing contours of his stiff membranes. No longer stuck in a metal coffin, no longer hanging helplessly at the end of a string, Brappa was once again a free-flying creature.

The sun disappeared as Godonov descended into mountain shadows. He cleared his visor and reset optics to normal magnification. Tonto and Bottlenose each covered a flank, wheeling outward from the landing zone. Godonov tightened his harness and rechecked his riser disconnects.

Valleys and mountains, ridges and cliffs, rifts and defiles, surged upward. Godonov's speed over the ground became pronounced. The large crescent lake disappeared to the north and west behind the jagged lip of the mountain valley. The circular lake, so small from orbit, loomed large and threatening. The drop zone was on the lake's northeastern margin. A westerly crosswind rippled the lake's surface, its welcome thrust pushing him clear of the icy water.

Godonov's focus shifted to his imminent touchdown. Ahead, Buck's foil banked into the freshening breeze.

Fascinated, Godonov watched the parafoil's forward movement halt. Its inflated blackness crumpled to the planet's surface.

Humans had landed on another planet.

Godonov soberly remembered that Major Buck was not the first human on Pitcairn Two. Another marine landed alongside Buck, and then another, their feet hitting the ground with quick chopping strides. Luffing foils were frantically hauled into tight bundles.

Godonov was number five. The crosswind stiffened. The science officer pulled hard on his riser, but he had waited too long. Below him marines scurried to defensive positions. Godonov barely noticed. The boulders expanding before his eyes consumed his attention. The wind gusted and sheared left. His knees only seconds from smacking granite, Godonov hauled desperately on his risers, stalling his foil. He landed atop an immense boulder, touching down as gently as a feather. His foil collapsed and reinflated over his left shoulder, nearly yanking him from his precarious perch. Fifty meters down the rocky slope Major Buck stood watching, shaking his head.

Godonov struggled with his shrouds, at last collapsing his canopy. His gear under control, he inspected the alternatives for getting down; there was no easy way. Selecting what appeared to be the least painful route, he slid to his rump and fell twisting and tumbling onto the lesser rocks, reacquainting himself with the worst aspects of gravity. Thankful for sturdy gloves and thick jumpsuit, he shook off the cobwebs and stinging nerves and staggered heavily to his feet. Stumbling under his burden, he clambered down the tumble of boulders.

Perspiration ran down Godonov's back. His breathing was obscenely loud. The science officer disconnected his oxygen mask and allowed it to swing from his face. The breeze chilled his sweaty skin. Tentatively, he inhaled the alien atmosphere, and was rewarded with an acceptable dose of satisfyingly fresh air—as the spectroscopy readings had predicted.

A marine double-timed in his direction. Godonov recognized Private Slovak's short-legged gait. Slovak carried the laser link.

"Link's up with *Condor Three*, sir," Slovak gasped.

The marine's headup visor was over her eyes, but she had removed her mask. Her lips were bloodless, and perspiration dripped from her chin; excitement and gravity were taking their toll. Godonov pulled out his admin unit and prepared a status report, downloading it to the high-power burst transmitter in the marine's turtle-pack.

The message read: "Insertion complete. No contact. No surprises. Securing landing zone. Will advise."

Slovak verified crypto phasing and released the transmission. "Burst received," the private reported almost immediately.

"Welcome to Pitcairn Two, Slovak," Godonov said.

"Yes, sir," Slovak replied, settling under her load.

The stocky marine retraced her steps downhill. Godonov followed, scanning the barren expanse. There were no hints of animal life, but Godonov appreciated the clusters of scarlet wildflowers blossoming stubbornly underfoot. Raising his vision, he saw more of the brilliant flowers scattered across the bleak granite and was struck with their incongruity on the hard, stark surface. Slabs of flat granite dominated the landscape; the rocky surface was blemished with sulfurous lichen.

The equipment penetrators that had borne the hunters drifted unguided to the ground near the wind-thrashed lake. That body of water was about two hundred meters across, shallow and unremarkable, with a barren island nestled against the northern shore. Radar had revealed it to be shallow; an apple retro would evaporate most of its content.

Godonov raised his scrutiny. They had landed in a glacial cirque, a rounded mountain valley about eight hundred meters wide, enclosed on three sides by granite elevations footed by spills of talus. Dust-blackened scabs of snow clung stubbornly to the northern faces of the higher elevations. The bowl opened to the west. Beyond the lake the barren terrain fell steeply away, presenting a vista of mountain ridges and hazy lands flattening in the distance.

"Good site," Buck said.

The marine officer, face mask hanging loose, stood watching with professional detachment as the second fire team came to ground. Sergeant Chastain was first. The big marine hit the rocks with his legs pounding, pulling down his pea-green parafoil and trampling it into submission. The rest of the team came down in precise intervals. Within seconds of landing, each marine had collapsed his foil, disengaged from the descent harness, and secured the billowing material. Clear of their chutes, the marines established a rough perimeter, weapons pointed outward.

The hunters wheeled and tacked above the margins of the valley, losing altitude steadily. The wind was starting to lift dust. The equipment parafoils thrashed against their stall battens, dragging the heavy cargo in fits over the rock.

"Sergeant Chastain," Buck barked. "Take a team and collect the equipment pods. We'll move the perimeter behind you."

Chastain acknowledged and used hand signals to direct his troops. Buck also waved signals, and the marine perimeter moved in jerky stages down the stony incline. Godonov, gravity hauling on his heavy pack, struggled to keep up with the lanky marine.

"S'what you expected?" Buck asked, slowing.

"Expected it to be windier," Godonov huffed.

"It's early yet," Buck said.

The sun's rays poured over the mountain valley's eastern rim.

Brappa wheeled past the mountain presiding over the landing zone. The soaring hunter found a ridge burble and nosed into the turbulence, holding his position like a dolphin on a bow wave. His acute senses filtered his environment; his black eyes raked the terrain and scanned the skies; his nostrils sampled the spoors; and his sonic sensors listened to the wind and to the very rocks. He detected clutches of small furry animals. A tiny, birdlike creature flitted low over the lake. The snowmelt tarn was shallow and without fish.

He checked the other hunters. Sherrip buffeted along the valley's eastern face, and Croot'a patrolled the southern. At that moment Kraal screeched an alert from the valley's opening. Brappa's helmet amplifier processed the signal adequately, but he looked forward to removing the confining apparel. His ultrasonic reception was compromised. He sliced across the mountain bowl. The maneuver cost him dearly in altitude, but Kraal was well below him. His young cohort wheeled into the wind and luffed onto a knife-edged escarpment. Brappa drew overhead and observed what had raised Kraal's concern. In an erosion defile beneath a grime-crusted crescent of glacial-blue snow stood a herd of yellow-white animals, perhaps twenty tangle-furred creatures, including four pure white young. The male of the species carried a rack of black curling horn. Goats of the mountains. Like home.

Brappa pulled in his membranes and dove for Kraal's position. Within a wingspan of the rocks the warrior twisted acrobatically and killed his momentum, alighting softly. He stowed his membranes and breathed deeply, gathering his wind. Despite the conditioning regimen, the months aboard the long-leg star-ships had sapped Brappa of his vigor. His fur was matted with perspiration.

"They do not see us, Brappa-my-leader," Kraal chittered.

"Perhaps they do not fear that which flies," Brappa chirped.

With his talons grasping the rocks of another world, Brappa scanned the mountain valley. Viewed from across the expanse of the cirque, the long-legs were reduced to motes. Brappa pulled off his helmet and attached it to his chest armor. With his sonic receptors unencumbered, he sensed a wider range of sounds.

"I perceive no danger," Kraal, son-of-Craag, said. The young warrior had his sire's considerable height and width of shoulder.

"Remain vigilant," Brappa counseled, unfurling his membranes. "Misfortune most often strikes those unprepared for its consequences. To the air, warrior."

Brappa set his wings and glided for the landing zone. He had descended too low; there was no thermal lift in this air, and his dangling helmet dragged against his forward thrust. The warrior heaved downward with his membranes, fighting the swirling headwind. He screeched a rallying signal. Sherrip and Croot'a responded, their flights converging toward the long-leg position. Brappa's heart pounded. Stroking mightily, he skimmed the lake's surface, taking advantage of ground effect. At last the shore fell beneath his talons and Brappa touched down. Kraal was already there. Brappa, by no means an ancient, rendered youth its due.

Sherrip and Croot'a came to ground to each side. Neither hunter reported any unusual sightings. Black-face and Giant-one approached. Big-ears came next, struggling under his load.

Giant-one signed: "Is there danger?"

Brappa signed back: "We saw goats."

"Goats?" Giant-one signed, his face bunched with confusion.

"We saw goats," Brappa signed again.

"There is no danger?" Big-ears signed back, questioning.

"Where there are goats," Brappa signed, "there are eaters of goats."

TWENTY-SEVEN

SHIPS IN THE NIGHT

Carmichael stared at Buccari's status report. The decoded laser burst gave small solace.

"Insertion complete," Carmichael reported. "Condor is holding in orbit for landing zone sanitation."

"Very well," Runacres acknowledged. "Science, anything new?"

"LF transmission levels are elevating, Admiral," Captain Katz replied. "I don't think it's a coincidence."

"Something's going on, Admiral," Carmichael muttered.

"Franklin," Runacres said, "lower your orbit by thirty percent."

"Aye, Admiral," Commodore Wells replied, bending over his console.

Carmichael waited for the commodore to issue fleet rudder orders and then followed Wells's lead. The group-leader directed a shift in the screen axis. Wanda Green acknowledged with laser burst.

"Launching recovery tankers, Admiral," Carmichael added.

"Good," Runacres replied.

Carmichael issued a battery of tactical orders. Too soon was he done. There was nothing else for him to do but wait and hope.

The days since the jump exit had gone quickly for Scientist Dowornobb and his science team. Their science lab in *Novaya Zemlya*'s habitation ring was compact but quite endurable. Working with the human scientists, Dowornobb had refined his flux theory and tuned his detection network. However, without the ability to run active signal checks, the science team was exhausting new things to try. They were too frightened to be bored.

The maneuvering alarm sounded. Dowornobb floated to the primary gravitronic flux display and tethered down next to Scientist H'Aare.

"What is transpiring?" H'Aare asked.

"I know not," Mirrtis replied.

"I will inquire," Dowornobb said, fingers manipulating his panel.

Dowornobb brought up current fleet operational status and disposition vectors; Admiral Runacres was maneuvering closer to the planet. As Dowornobb deciphered the information his frame of reference began to move, firmly pressing his massive form against his station. A litter of objects lifted from their poorly secured resting places. The compartment flotsam robot commenced its darting collection voyage.

Dowornobb knew better than to inquire directly of the bridge. The scientist connected with the SDO instead. Captain Katz replaced the science duty officer on the comm-vid.

"Scientist Dowornobb, may I help you?" Katz inquired.

"Is-ah something happening, Captain?" Dowornobb inquired.

"Elevated communications are creating some concern," Katz replied. "The admiral is closing the distance to our landing party as a precaution. There is no immediate—"

"Gravity!" Scientist H'Aare boomed, jerking Dowornobb's attention from the comm-vid.

"Look! Look!" Mirrtis shouted.

Dowornobb stared with disbelief at his instruments. The signals on the gravitronic flux screen were unmistakable. Dowornobb and his scientists exchanged wide-eyed glances, brow tufts splaying erect.

"What?" Captain Katz asked.

"Please-ah wait, Captain," Dowornobb said, moving to the instrumentation console and manipulating the panels. He reoriented the grid bias and modulated the signals. The gravitronic flux lines wavered and reformed. Dowornobb measured amplitudes and frequencies and repeated the process. The results were conclusive. H'Aare's fear bladder discharged, followed immediately by Mirrtis's and then his own. Dowornobb turned and faced the impatient science officer.

"A hyperlight event-ah is about to occur, Captain," Dowornobb reported.

"A hyperlight event! You mean—"

"We must-ah tell the admiral."

"H-How long?" Katz asked.

"Ten-ah of your minutes," Dowornobb said, looking at the instrumentation. "Maybe less."

Runacres listened carefully to Dowornobb's prediction.

"Battle stations," Runacres ordered.

"Battle stations, aye," the tactical officer replied, lunging for his watch console. The general quarters Klaxon exploded.

Runacres stared at the main status plot. Dowornobb's gravitronic-flux detection system was providing exit coordinates. The projected jump-out point was disarmingly distant. Distance was no protection against the Ulaggi, with their ability to perform intersystem jumps; anywhere in the system was mere minutes away. There was still a chance the Tellurian fleet would remain undetected, if Runacres's ships maintained strict emissions controls. The humans were near deaf and blind, but going into active targeting mode would immediately give away their presence.

"Jump-ah exit is occurring," Dowornobb reported. "Flux signals have-ah disappeared."

"We are reestablished on orbit," Wells reported. "All maneuvering is terminated."

"Very well," Runacres replied, staring at the status plot, desperately seeking inspiration. He exhaled. Mothership engine blooms would be like strobe lights in the dark. He prayed his units were not detected. His only recourse would be to jump; the corvettes and the insertion team would be left behind. Minutes ticked by, all eyes on the threat assessment boards.

"Science, anything?" Runacres demanded. Time needed to

lapse before alien emissions were detected; the distances involved were great.

"Negative, uh . . . Stand by," Captain Katz replied, his gaze held rigidly off camera. Suddenly Katz's eyes clicked to the vid-cam; the science officer's voice jumped an octave. "Affirmative, Admiral, we're getting spikes. Low power megahertz range and K-band chatter. Ulaggi signal characteristics. Line of bearing is consistent with Dowornobb's jump exit projection."

"Range estimate?" Runacres asked.

"Stand by, Admiral," Katz replied, looking away. He looked back into the vid-cam. "Negative range estimate, Admiral, but we have down Doppler."

Runacres's muscles loosened. The alien ships were opening. "They aren't painting us," he stated.

"Not yet, sir," Katz replied. "At least we show no stationary energy patterns. Our shields are absorbing everything at the registering emission power."

"Admiral!" It was Dowornobb again.

"Go ahead," Runacres replied.

"Admiral, it-ah is . . ." Dowornobb struggled with his words. "Admiral, there-ah are more ships coming."

Hyperlight harmonics dampened. The planet was suddenly there. Jakkuk checked navigation references, verifying her exit point. All ship-mistresses were dendritically linked, awaiting orders; all systems were nominal. But was there something different? Jakkuk heightened her awareness and scanned the heavens. She intercepted a thought tendril from y'Map, one of her roonish ship-mistresses. Destroyer Fist a'Yerg responded to y'Map with a mind zephyr. The roons, too, had detected something peculiar, and were also unable to characterize it. The stimulation source had faded too quickly.

"Established in normal space, mother," the bridgemale reported.

"Jakkuk-hajil," Dominant Dar demanded. "Your report."

The spoor was gone.

"The cell is intact, mother," Jakkuk reported. "Setting vectors for orbit."

"Very well," Dar acknowledged.

"Pah!" hissed the slithery voice of the lakk. "Not well. There is something peculiar."

Karyai broke from her station and floated tensely across the dominant's bridge, stopping astraddle Jakkuk's dendritic station. The political probed Jakkuk's mind, but only briefly. Jakkuk felt actual physical contact on her back, warm and dry, as the lakk's molten thoughts flowed past her frightened mind and into the dendritic link. Power amplifiers surged, range selectors opened wide; the lakk was searching, using the technical amplification of the dendritic link to magnify her already awesome scanning powers.

"What is it, mother?" Dar asked.

"Perhaps nothing," Karyai at last said, pushing from the cell-control station and flowing from Jakkuk's mind like scalding water draining from her skull.

There had been something. Jakkuk pondered the political's reaction; both roon and lakk had sensed it, something untoward. Jakkuk pushed it from her mind. Ephemeral dendritic stimulation was not unusual in Jakkuk's experience; the ether was full of spurious energy, akin to vagrant odors on the wind. Sharp when first sensed, but then the senses, in straining to discern, became dulled.

The dominant's bridge remained silent. Jakkuk slipped deeper into her dendritic link, concentrating on the whispering cacophony of infinite space. She detected a searching tendril of thought, this time a familiar and persistent energy spoor. Six more ships erupted from hyperlight. Jakkuk transmitted a welcoming navigation reference and returned her mind to her duties.

"Kwanna-hajil is with us, mother," Jakkuk reported.

"Yes," Dar acknowledged, her color high.

"Execute your mission, daughter," Karyai whined.

"Jettison ore barges," Dar commanded stiffly.

"They will have a long trip to orbit," Jakkuk offered, unwisely.

"Our mission is clear," the political snapped, swirling into Jakkuk's thoughts like a barbed cudgel.

"Give the order, Jakkuk-hajil," Dar said evenly.

"As commanded, mother," Jakkuk gasped, her mind throbbing with the lakk's reprobation. But the discomfort was nothing compared to Jakkuk's anticipation. Jakkuk was also anxious to jump. The cells of Dominant Dar's frontier fleet were going to the hunt.

"Signal delay is estimated at eight seconds, Admiral," Captain Katz reported.

Eight seconds, Runacres thought. The Ulaggi would have eight seconds to initiate an attack before he knew it was coming. An eternity.

"Contact group alpha consists of at least six hyperlight ships, Admiral," Katz reported. "Contact group bravo is also estimated at six ships. We have discharge emissions characteristic of main engine plumes with ten confirmed signatures and two probables. This is the same group that hit us the last time we were here."

"Neighborhood guard dogs," Merriwether muttered over the circuit.

"Very well," Runacres said. His ships were blind, groping in the dark. The contact icons on the main threat display were encircled with huge position-error rings, but two groups of six ships was a safe bet. Ulaggi battle groups were organized in groups of six. Twelve Ulaggi ships to his eight, he was bettered on all counts.

"We have grid link!" Katz shouted into the vid-cam. The threat board seconded the science officer's outburst. The icon for group alpha glowed magenta. "They're preparing to jump."

"That was eight seconds ago," Merriwether said. "They've already jumped."

"Group alpha's off the screens," the tactical officer reported.

Runacres gripped his console. The alien killers could appear in firing range at any second. He had to do something. "All ships go active," he ordered. "Weapons free."

"All ships going active," Wells replied. "Weapons free, aye."

Expanding at the speed of light, concentric bubbles of pulsing electronics left the human fleet, reaching out for solid objects against which to dash, from which to reflect— emissions that would define the number and location of the enemy, but also precisely define their own position. There was no choice; Runacres had to see the enemy in order to engage it.

"Group bravo has also dropped from the screens," the tactical officer reported. "No active returns."

"Launching all alerts," Carmichael shouted. "Reorienting the screen."

"Keep the hounds close to home, Group-Leader," Runacres commanded. "No one leaves the grid. Commodore Wells, start your jump count."

Runacres had no choice but to jump. They would have to leave Condor Squadron and the reconnaissance mission behind.

"Hyperlight flux!" Dowornobb reported. "Jump is-ah confirmed."

"Where away, Mr. Dowornobb?" Runacres shouted. "Where?"

"Out-ah bound only, Admiral," Dowornobb replied.

"Stand by to maneuver the fleet!" Runacres barked. "Clear all primary firing arcs. I want this jump on minimum path. Clear all overrides. Jump count!"

"Ten minutes to jump," Wells acknowledged, his fingers frenetic on his watch panel.

Maneuvering alarms sounded. Ten minutes to jump. The Ulaggi would have ten minutes to tear them apart. An eternity in which to die.

"Anything, Dowornobb?" Runacres demanded.

"No-ah, Admiral," Dowornobb replied. "I-ah show no inbound signal. Flux amplitudes are-ah diminishing."

"Too long," Wells rumbled.

"Too damn long," Merriwether added from *Eire*'s command bridge. Runacres gave her vid image a quick glance.

Merriwether's eyes glowed with fire; her jaw was set like granite.

"Where are they?" Carmichael asked.

Silence reigned.

"Contacts!" the watch officer reported. "Nonthreatening!"

All eyes focused on the battle plot. A cluster of icons materialized, but many hundreds of thousands of kilometers distant. They were passive contacts, emitting no targeting or search signals.

"Those aren't motherships," Runacres muttered. "Where are the interstellars?"

"They've jumped," Katz finally offered. "They've left the system."

"Scientist Dowornobb, your assessment," Runacres demanded.

"I-ah concur, Admiral," Dowornobb reported. "The Ulaggi ships have left-ah the system. The gravitronic flux signals are-ah gone."

"Where did they go?" Wells growled.

Runacres appreciated the fleet commodore's concern. His fleet was, for the moment, safe from attack. That only meant the danger was directed elsewhere.

"Perhaps there is a way of telling," Dowornobb rumbled softly.

"Say again!" Runacres demanded.

Dowornobb's attention was not directed at the vid-cam. He spoke in konish to technicians off-camera, his eye tufts growing more erect with each passing second.

"Scientist Dowornobb," Runacres demanded, "you have something to say?"

"Our-ah calculations remain-ah theoretical," Dowornobb replied, stirring nervously. He paused again to check another console.

"Yes?" Runacres demanded.

"Admiral," Dowornobb said, "you-ah have said that in the past Ulaggi ships may have followed you from one system to another. That-ah prospect intrigued me. Resolving ripple cone-ah regressions suggested specific transit-ah bearings.

Intensity decay suggested distance. I made-ah modifications to the detection grid with that-ah purpose—"

"Your estimate, Scientist Dowornobb," Runacres interrupted.

"Yes, yes," Dowornobb said, obviously excited. "Theory can-ah wait. The Ulaggi transit line-ah of bearing passes through my home system. They-ah go to Genellan."

"Jupiter's balls!" Merriwether blurted. "Admiral Chou will be in the middle of a download."

"Scientist Dowornobb, can you be certain?" Runacres asked.

"No," Dowornobb responded, eye tufts drooping.

Runacres stared into his comm-vid. Merriwether stared back.

"Emergency recall," Runacres said. "Set jump coordinates for Kon System. Genellan lima-two. Group-Leader, get your ships back."

"The penetration teams, Admiral?" Carmichael inquired. "The download isn't completed. Shouldn't we haul the marines out, or at least take down the rest of the recon load?"

"Captain Carmichael, recall your corvettes," Runacres replied.

TWENTY-EIGHT

STRANDED

Buccari watched the orbital position bug on the tactical display. The drop window was mere minutes away.

"Skipper," Flaherty reported from the EPL cockpit. "Mission loaded and ready."

"Roger," Buccari answered. "You have permission to launch. I want you back aboard on the next orbit, Flack. As soon as you're up, we'll drop *Condor Three*."

"Roger, copy," Flaherty acknowledged. "See you on the next spin."

"Bay door opening," Thompson announced. The second officer sat at the copilot's station.

A radar detection alarm sounded. They were being scanned.

"Search lobe," Gunner Tyler reported from weapons. "It be on us."

"Took 'em long enough," Thompson said. "Do we abort?"

"We're line of sight for ten minutes, Skipper," Tyler said.

"Negative abort," Buccari replied. "Jettison the apple. We got to get the rest of the mission on the deck."

"Roger," Thompson replied. "Bay doors opening."

"Fleet zinger!" Tasker announced over the intercom.

"Now what?" Buccari muttered.

"It's a recall, Skipper," the communication technician answered.

"How much time?" Buccari demanded, checking her situation plot. How much time did she need? She would send *Condor Four*'s EPL down to augment the extraction effort.

"Immediate recall, Skipper," Tasker replied. "Imminent threat status. Weapons free. No delays accepted."

Buccari's mind reeled, desperately grasping for a plan. She opened a laser channel to fleet, breaking comm discipline.

"Group, Condor here," Buccari broadcast. "Give me two orbits, over."

The transmission delay was maddening. Suddenly Carmichael's voice was in her ears.

"Condor, you are recalled," he broadcast. "We believe the Ulaggi are headed for Kon System. Admiral is jumping the fleet ASAP. Light 'em off, Condor. Now! Over."

"Jake, I've got people on the planet, over," she pleaded, and waited. And waited. All the while her mind twisted over the implications of Carmichael's words.

Minutes dragged by. Finally a return laser comm was received.

"That's their job, Condor. Just like it was your job to put them there. Responsibility of command, remember?" Carmichael replied, rubbing her nose in her own words. "Return to ship at full emergency. Move out, Commander, or I'm leaving your ass behind. Group out."

"Condor out," she replied. The Ulaggi were heading for Genellan.

"Golly rockets," Thompson sputtered.

Duty, the instincts of motherhood, fear, all ripped at her insides.

"Hell," Buccari muttered.

"Pardon, sir?" Thompson asked.

"Nothing," she snapped. "Flack, abort the launch. Secure the apple and stand fast at your crew stations. We'll backload the mission after we're established on our vector."

"Aye, Skipper," Flaherty responded. "EPL locking down."

"Engineering, stand by for emergency acceleration."

"Engineering, aye," Chief Silva replied. "Temps and pressures are up. Ready when you are, sir."

Thompson sounded the maneuvering alarm.

"Fleet vector, Mr. Thompson," she ordered. "Get 'em lined up."

"Aye, Sir," Thompson replied, issuing rudder orders.

Buccari activated a laser link to the planet. "Landing team, Condor," she transmitted, staring at the planet.

"Go, Condor," came back a husky, young voice. A female voice.

"Patch me to Commander Godonov," Buccari ordered.

"Roger," the marine replied. Seconds dragged.

"Godonov here. We're ready, Condor. Landing site is clear."

"Nes, we've been recalled," Buccari broadcast. "We won't be bringing down your equipment. You're on your own. You copy?"

Silence.

"Nes, you copy?" she repeated.

"Rog', Condor, copy," Godonov's voice came back, thin and distant.

"We'll be back, Nes, I promise. Condor out."

"We'll wait for you, Condor."

Buccari bit her tongue and slammed her station console. Thompson twisted the corvette to its new vector.

"This is Condor!" she shouted over the squadron laser link. "Running rendezvous. We're returning to fleet. Look sharp! Eight gees on my mark. Three . . . two . . . one . . . buster!"

The kick of the main engines smashed Buccari against her acceleration station. Her tethers activated. Her flight suit diaphragms pressurized, compressing blood from her extremities. With her vision narrowed by the gee-forces, Buccari watched Pitcairn Two's vid image grow smaller by the second.

The wind howled softly.

"No need to secure the landing site," Godonov said.

"No shit," Buck spat. "Let's get off this mountain."

The marine raised one arm straight in the air. Chastain, two hundred meters away, froze like a retriever waiting for the shotgun's report. Buck dropped his arm. Chastain lunged ahead, positioning scouts and flankers with vigorous hand signals. Tonto and Bottlenose pounded into the wind-buffeted air. Notch and Pop-Eye, unwieldy packs strapped to their backs, surged after the marines, their gait a rapid waddle.

"Aren't you going to tell them?" Godonov asked.

"They ain't stupid," Buck replied. "They've figured it out. Oh, crap, Slovak, pass the word. Tell 'em we'll talk when we find cover."

"Yes, sir," the private acknowledged, moving into a shuffling double-time, her ponderous pack jiggling in counter-rhythm. Buck stepped out, his head twisting back and forth. Godonov followed.

The sun climbing over the near peaks flooded the landing site with morning light, but the gusty breeze swirling over the glacial crater offset any temperature rise. Godonov shifted his pack and settled into a hiking pace. The landing party left the wind-chopped lake behind and marched through the open end of the valley. A vista spread before them; in the distance loomed the next range of granite mountains, a lower line of ragged peaks barren of snow. Between the ranges nestled a forested watershed with a zigzagging riparian spine, its ribs formed by precipitous ridges descending from the roughly parallel geological formations. To the north, coming into view from behind the rim of their landing site, was the southern shore of the crescent lake. Farther north, above the lake, could be seen a necklace of smaller lakes, blue jewels displayed in forest-green velvet.

Godonov halted and took stock of the landmarks. "Give me a second," he shouted.

"Take your time," Buck shouted back, impatiently signaling his troops. "We got four . . . maybe six months to kill. Maybe longer."

"I got to take a fix, dammit," Godonov snapped back.

"Sorry, Nes," Buck said, moving closer. "I guess it's sinking in. We're going to be here awhile."

"Yeah," Godonov said.

"At least we got a job to do," Buck muttered.

"Yeah. A job," Godonov said, turning on his admin unit. The science officer brought up the terrain model and piped the output to a tactical display on his helmet HUD. Multicolored readouts flashed in his near vision: altitude, temperature, humidity. He used his eye cursor to select navigation mode.

He oriented himself, taking bearings on prominent peaks to calibrate his model's dead-reckoning datum.

"Terrain model checks out," Godonov said, securing his admin unit. "We've got twenty-five kilometers to the crescent lake. That's as the crow flies. Figure twice that on boots."

"How far to mission target?" Buck asked, taking the opportunity to recalibrate his own nav system.

"The transmission source is about forty klicks beyond the crescent lake," Godonov said. "But, what the heck, we got plenty of time for exploring, right?"

"Yeah, right," Buck replied.

The marine raised his visor and searched the sky. Godonov did the same. Tonto and Bottlenose, tacking hard against stiff headwinds, wheeled overhead on rising thermals. Buck lowered his gaze and studied the precipitous terrain, his jaw tight, his eyes narrowed to fierce slits. Godonov finished his readings and secured his equipment.

"You about ready, Major?" he asked. "Shouldn't be out in the open like this. Didn't they teach you anything in grunt school?"

"Up yours, shippie," Buck said, slapping Godonov's shoulder.

"Let's go," Godonov said, settling under his load.

"Yo!" Buck shouted, waving Chastain forward.

As the marines moved through the valley opening, the pitch of the ground dramatically steepened. They had no choice but to descend across a vast face of smooth, unrelieved granite. Godonov looked down and swallowed. His pack pulled heavily on his shoulders.

"Who the hell picked this landing site?" he muttered.

He stepped cautiously onto the decline. Burdened as the marines were, a slip meant certain death. Godonov moved deliberately, as often clambering on all fours as hiking on two feet. Gravity pulled on his flagging muscles. Gusting winds alternately tugged and pushed on his pack and clothes, throwing gritty dust against his helmet visor.

Godonov felt more than heard a distant rumble. He lifted his gaze and stared out over the valley between the mountain ranges. The sky was cloudless, but the horizon was now indistinct with a rising haze. The crescent lake, still far below them, dominated his attention. Its surface was no longer azure; wind-whipped whitecaps gave the lake a textured cast and a lighter tone.

"You hear something?" Buck shouted.

Godonov stopped and listened. A hunter's screech piercing the wind heightened his senses. Rising above the moaning wind, a dull, distant thunder rolled into his awareness and remained there.

"Look!" Buck said, pointing. "Beyond the mountains."

Godonov forced his focus into the dirty distance. The opposite mountain range was in clean air, but beyond, where earlier there had been nothing but indistinguished steppes, there was a veil of dust. Welling from the haze layer, its roiling tops boiling higher and higher, its awesome width spreading over a widening front, tumbled a prodigious cloud of ocher and charcoal. Jagged lightning spat upward, downward, and sideways, flickering brightly from within the black-tinted nimbus. A rattle of thunder rose above the howling wind. It was a cloud, but it was not a cloud of the heavens.

"One hell of a sandstorm!" Buck shouted.

The disturbance expanded, as if it were inhaling the atmosphere and consuming the very planet. The dun wall surged softly against the western flank of the mountain range, a titanic, slow-motion wave dashing against a gigantic sea cliff. The imperturbable peaks remained clear, but clouds of twisting dust, like ropy brown currents, claimed the lower passes. Narrowing valleys compressed the flowing air, accelerating the dingy tide past confining granite walls.

The storm's first assault spent its force scaling the elevations. The aeolian tempest fell back, pulsating at the foot of the mountains. Its complexion grew darker, more sinister. Tumbling billows of dust slowly scaled the passes, sending tendrils of grime spilling over the ridges and into the central valley. The haze in the valley bottom heightened, darkening the crescent lake with bruised light.

"Come on," Buck said, waving Chastain forward.

The members of the landing party brought their attention back to the challenge at their feet. They resumed their knee-quaking descent toward the valley floor, but the distant sand-storm and the precipitate slope were the least of Godonov's worries. The landing team was naked under the scrutiny of the enemy. Their only protection was the fragile obscurity of smallness; they were tiny animate objects on the vast face of a mountain, somewhere in the middle latitudes of an alien planet, in a star-system far from home.

TWENTY-NINE

RETURN TO HYPERLIGHT

"Passing retro marker," Buccari reported.

"Maintain your vector, Condor," the approach controller ordered. "You are cleared for full emergency retro inside the grid. Prepare your units for immediate transition to hyperlight. I say again, the fleet will jump as soon as you are stabilized."

"Condor copies," Buccari responded. She exhaled. Runacres was not going to bring her corvettes on board before jumping.

"Golly rockets," Thompson said. "Full retro inside the grid."

"And legal, too," Flaherty said. "Rock 'n' roll."

"You ever jump in the open, Flack?" she asked.

"Once," he replied, suddenly sober.

"What's it like?" Thompson asked.

"You'll embarrass yourself out of both ends," Flaherty replied, with no intent at humor. "Relax if you can. Don't fight it."

"Remember your training," Buccari said. "Don't touch anything until you hear yourself count to three."

"Y-Yes, sir," Thompson answered. "Two minutes to retro. All 'vettes phase-linked and answering calls. All thrust axes aligned."

"Very well," Buccari replied, staring into the star-spangled blackness. There was no sensation of motion, only distance. The corvettes of Condor Squadron had pivoted about, pointing main engines against velocity vectors. Buccari checked tactical; her squadron was motionless relative to her position. Speed in space was an illusion. She opened the scale on the tactical display until she could see the approaching mothership grid. Motion became evident, but not hers. She was static; icons representing motherships in formation streaked up from behind Condor Squadron.

Buccari punched up *Condor Two*. "Et Lorlyn, are you ready?" she inquired in konish.

"It-ah is difficult to prepare for that-ah which is unknown," the noblekone thundered back. "Never fear, when it-ah is over, I will be at your side, Citizen Sharl."

"Of that I have no doubt, Your Excellency," she replied.

"One minute to retro," Thompson announced.

Buccari made a last scan of her corvette's systems. Engineering verified power checks. Her crew was tethered down and waiting, not for the retro, but for the hyperlight jump to follow. The deceleration point rushed closer. Thompson counted off the seconds.

"Retro on my mark," Buccari broadcast. "Four . . . three . . . two . . . one . . . ignition."

She slammed into her acceleration couch, wrist restraints and tethers snugging like iron. Her lungs compressed, her vision tunneled.

"Nine gees . . . t-ten . . ," Thompson reported.

The corvette shook like a rat in a terrier's jaws. Buccari concentrated on the tactical display; all Condor 'vettes clung to a semblance of formation. Seconds ticked by like tiny eternities.

The deceleration timed out. Condor Squadron was in the grid, slightly past centrex. Relative drift rate for her corvette was in tolerance, but she frantically worked her thrusters, trying to kill all motion relative to the grid. Two motherships, *Eire* and *Baffin*, bright blades of white and gold, were visible through her viewscreens.

An alarm brayed.

"Fleet jumps in ten seconds," a synthesized voice reported.

"Terminate all maneuvers!" she broadcast to her corvette captains.

"Fleet jumps in six seconds," the lifeless voice warned. "Four . . . three . . . two . . . one . . ."

She pulled her hands from her controls, crossing her arms across her chest and hugging herself. Flaherty did likewise.

"Hold it together, guys," she shouted. "Hold it—"

Stars blossomed from sharp focus and then tumbled; the universe turned inside out and twisted back on itself. Merciless waves of nausea and anxiety wracked body and mind, washing her helplessly upon the shores of unconsciousness. She was thrown full-force into a nightmare. Her son thrashed in her arms, pleading for help. Nestor Godonov and Jocko Chastain towered over her, their faces twisted with insane fury. A demoniacal hunter—Tonto, talons and jaws bloody— flew from between their shoulders, his razor-toothed maw slavering. The hunter snatched her son in cruel teeth. Buccari tried desperately to protect him, but suddenly Charlie was gone from her . . . forever.

"—Condor, group operations."

The broadcast dragged her from a sweaty stupor.

"Condor here," she mumbled. Her corvette slowly tumbled. Reflexively her hands sought the controls. Within seconds the excursions were neutralized. She engaged autostabilizers. They were established in hyperlight; the stars were gone.

"Flack, you with me?" she asked. "You've got the ship, Flack. Autostabes engaged. You got it?"

"Yeah, Skip," Flaherty gasped drunkenly, "fit . . . as a frigging . . . frigate flying freight to Freeport—"

"You got the ship, dammit!" she shouted.

"Got the ship!" he snapped back.

"Condor, group operations," came the radio call.

"Condor's up," she replied. She checked squadron status; her skippers were checking in electronically. Et Lorlyn was last on line. His ship was out of position, but the konish crew was functioning.

"*Condor One* is cleared to *Eire*, direct approach," the controller announced. "Condor, report immediately to group operations. The rest of Condor Squadron is cleared to *NZ* marshal."

"Roger, Condor copies," she replied. "*Condor Two,* take them home."

Et Lorlyn, still incapable of speech, acknowledged electronically. Her squadron maneuvered about the kone's guide, all ships but hers accelerating for *Novaya Zemlya*.

Buccari's eyes blurred. Combat stimulants and adrenaline could sustain her for only so long. For the moment her struggle was over; they were in the limbo of hyperlight. No matter how horrible the future, HLA transit was a hiatus in time. Worrying, even about her son, would not move the stars closer. Her body, in daring to relax, started to crash.

"Take us in, Flack," she ordered, closing her eyes.

"Aye, Skip," Flaherty replied.

"Mr. Thompson," Buccari ordered, "go check on the crew . . . Thompson, are you there?"

"Huh?" her second pilot replied. "Eh . . . yeah?"

"You with us, Teddy?" she asked.

"Ah . . . yeah, er . . . yes, sir," Thompson stammered. "Wow! That wasn't . . . so bad. Did you say something to me, Skipper?"

"Never mind," she said, releasing her tethers. "Flack, call me when you hit the approach fix."

The physiological torment of hyperlight affected cliff dwellers less than kone or human. Toon-the-speaker, breath rasping loudly in his helmet, struggled through the malaise without losing consciousness. The nausea was worse than usual, but the ensuing rolling motion of their vessel was more unsettling than the jump transition. Neither discomfiture was severe enough to eclipse Toon's depression.

They had abandoned Brappa, Sherrip, Croot'a, and Kraal on the planet. Worry consumed the guilder.

"Are we in jeopardy?" Preet-the-speaker-apprentice chittered anxiously. The intercom circuit struggled with the range of cliff dweller speech, clipping the young steam user's rapid words. Preet's apprehension was not masked.

"No," Toon replied, interrogating his console.

The discomfiting motion of their ship steadied. Toon loosened his tethers. The two guilders were alone on the corvette's crew deck. Without the pungent long-leg warriors and haughty hunters, the compartment seemed starkly empty, a metal cell missing its raucous soul.

"What will thou tell the elders?" Preet asked.

"I know not," Toon replied. "It is not the reprobation of the elders I fear. It is Craag, leader-of-hunters, whose hard questions and harder glare I do not relish."

"The ships have jumped into the star-void," Preet said, spindly fingers working his console. "For now we are safe."

"Pray then to the gods for Brappa and his warriors," Toon replied.

The long-leg fleet had jumped back into the trackless void. Toon brought up his computer terminal. The guilder's depression was overwhelmed by his unfailing pragmatism.

The guilder was absorbed in the instrumentation when the overhead hatch moved smoothly aside. Short-one-who-leads floated to the deck, her knees flexing to absorb her momentum. As she drifted across the compartment, she broke her suit seal and pulled off helmet and skullcap. Her eyes, limpid green jewels, glowed from deep within bruised eye sockets. Her skull and eyebrows were shaded with a new growth of dark red hair, stark contrast to her ashen complexion.

"You okay, Lizzy?" she asked.

"It is for the hunters that I worry," Toon signed.

"Me, too," the long-leg replied, with words and signs. "Me, too."

Toon concentrated on the low-pitched sounds. The guilder chirped and signed: "Thou art fatigued."

Short-one-who-leads grunted, her eyes focused at some great distance, not seeing. She floated above Toon's console and stroked the guilder's neck. Her hands were strong; Toon pushed against the exquisite pressure, luxuriating in her calming caress. Too soon she stopped.

"Thou must rest," Toon signed more emphatically.

"Soon," she replied. The haggard long-leg hand-signed a salutation to Preet before pushing off for the small galley.

Toon watched her. The steam user denied superstition and magic, but the attentions of Short-one-who-leads were akin to a magic balm. As if by enchantment, the guilder's worries seemed less oppressive. Her very touch had eased his anxiety, but Toon knew that in lightening his burden, Short-one-who-leads had increased her own.

THIRTY

IN HOT PURSUIT

Carmichael checked the habitation ring's passageway. Except for the vibration of circulation systems, the curving corridor was silent. The group-leader stepped past the marine guard and back into *Eire*'s main briefing room. The mood within the compartment was funereal. Scientists Dowornobb, Mirrtis, and H'Aare overwhelmed the briefing alcove. The kones, wearing environmental suits, knelt at their stations; chairs made for humans would not accommodate their bulk. Also present, in addition to the admiral's senior staff, were eight dour mothership skippers, their science officers, and their respective corvette squadron commanders.

"Where is she?" Runacres demanded.

"Depilatory, Admiral," Carmichael replied.

"Commander Buccari just spent six days in a corvette, Admiral," Captain Merriwether said. "She's doing us all a favor."

"Things have changed since we were 'vette pilots," Runacres grumbled.

"They're a lot smarter now," Merriwether replied. "And the ready rooms don't smell like armpits."

Runacres glowered at his flagship captain. *Eire*'s rubicund skipper countered effectively with the sweetest of smiles. Carmichael gave a soft laugh, shifting the focus of Runacres's ire. Carmichael stared straight ahead. The silence grew impossibly more complete.

A shout from one of the corvette squadron skippers shattered the oppressive mood. "Merlin's ready room still stinks, Admiral."

Carmichael cringed; many years ago Runacres had been that squadron's commanding officer.

"And so do its pilots," added a gravelly voice, Wanda Green's. Carmichael filled his lungs, but the admonition died on his lips. Runacres's steely glare dissolved. The old man's eyes twinkled; his space-battered face creased. Like a gust of refreshing wind, the tension broke. The sour mood pervading the compartment was flushed away by laughter too long restrained. The kones exchanged confused glances.

At that moment Buccari walked through the hatch. She wore a gray and white underway suit, freshly creased, and a gold beret, jauntily canted. Carmichael's good cheer choked in his throat. He could only stare at the beautiful pilot.

Buccari pulled off her beret and looked about, mystified at the joviality. Her pallid, translucent skin glistened with the sheen of the depilatory's oil shower. Her presence commanded the room to order.

"Rest assured, Commander," Runacres said, "this most inappropriate levity is not at your expense. Take a seat."

Buccari moved to join the other squadron commanders. Carmichael grabbed her elbow. Her stare locked on his hand.

"Stay with the kones," Carmichael ordered. "Dowornobb wouldn't start without you."

Buccari looked up, green eyes glowing with fatigue. An uncertain smile dimpled her scar. Carmichael struggled to catch his breath. He loosened his grip.

"Yes, sir," she replied, her voice barely a whisper. She pushed for the briefing table, stumbling on her first step. The giants graced her with silly smiles. Buccari straightened and said something in their language, giving the aliens a turn to laugh at the expense of the humans. Next to the kones, Buccari seemed a child.

"Scientist Dowornobb, you may proceed," Runacres ordered.

Dowornobb lifted onto all fours and moved gingerly to the briefing station. Dwarfing the lectern, the kone squatted on his hinds and removed his helmet. His massive head brushed the overhead. A faint acrid odor signaled the kone's nervousness.

"Our-ah findings together, Admiral. Human and kone," Dowornobb thundered. "These discoveries build-ah on knowledge provided by-ah Legion science officers. Captain Katz's efforts are significant. Credit must-ah be shared in-ah equal parts."

"You are most gracious," Runacres replied. "Continue."

"I-ah must-ah provide some theory," Dowornobb rumbled, activating a holo-grid with multidimensional coordinates. He began. His presentation of hyperlight physics was intensely technical, frequently defying translation, even with Buccari's intercession. The kone lapsed into tortuous mathematical proofs, stranding most of his audience. His facts were arcane, but no one present doubted the behemoth's confidence.

"Not-ah only can hyperlight movement be detected from outside the gravitronic matrix," Dowornobb concluded, "but-ah we can now tell the universal radial of the target, both inbound and out-ah-bound."

"Scientist Dowornobb," Captain Katz said, "can you accurately resolve external HLA origin and destination points?"

"I-ah have not-ah proven this yet-ah," Dowornobb replied. "It-ah is theoretically possible. Too soon we-ah will know for sure."

The room remained quiet.

"Scientist Dowornobb, you have no doubt of the Ulaggi fleet's destination?" Commodore Wells asked.

"We-ah have remodeled the data four different ways." Dowornobb groaned, eye tufts drooping. "Our-ah worst fears are confirmed. The Ulaggi fleet-ah is headed for the Kon System. I am certain. With every passing minute the Ulaggi course and gravitronic decay rate converge on my system. Flux amplitudes remain—"

"Thunderation!" Captain Myashiro, *Kyushu*'s skipper, bellowed. "You mean to say that you are still tracking the Ulaggi?"

"You are reminded that Scientist Dowornobb's findings have been classified Top Secret," Captain Katz interjected.

"Y-Yes," Dowornobb replied. "We are trailing them on

nearly parallel flux lines. Now that-ah we know where to look, it is quite-ah easy to maintain contact."

"Can they detect us?" Captain Connors, commanding officer of *Baffin*, asked.

"Physical laws do not-ah discriminate," Dowornobb replied.

The oppressive silence returned. Somewhere a hatch clanged shut, felt more than heard.

"That-ah is all I have to-ah say."

The kone pushed away from the briefing station. Runacres stood and faced the gloomy audience.

"There are twenty thousand humans on Genellan," the admiral said. "What is more, it is likely that Admiral Chou and his settlement convoy will arrive in the Kon System about the same time the Ulaggi broach from hyperlight. Every one of those lives is in jeopardy."

"There are also four billion souls on the planet Kon, Admiral," Dowornobb rumbled.

"Forgive me, Master Dowornobb," Runacres said. "God help us all, human and kone. Together, we must prepare ourselves. This time there will be no escape by jumping." He paused, his jaw tight. "This time we do battle."

Runacres stared stony-faced about the briefing room. His ship captains and squadron commanders glared back, their countenances quarried of the same granite.

"All ships are to prepare for fleet action," Runacres announced. "We need ideas, we need tactics."

"We need luck," Merriwether interjected.

"Luck's not in the op plan, Captain," Runacres said. "But we'll take all we can. Commodore Wells, transit orders."

"Mothership commanders, use next week to complete material and system repairs," Wells announced. "For the reminder of the HLA transit, full fleet battle simulations will commence on the first day of each watch week. Be prepared for surprises. All ship commanders will be prepared to take command of the fleet."

Wells finished quickly. The ship captains remained silent.

"That is all," Wells announced. The briefing was over.

Runacres stood.

"Attention on deck!" the admiral's aide shouted.

Buccari stood to attention. Admiral Runacres and Commodore Wells walked briskly from the briefing room. Mothership captains and their science officers departed next. Carmichael, absorbed in conversation with Captain Wooden, accompanied the cadre of senior officers without looking back. Buccari was disappointed.

A heavy slap on the back dispelled her melancholy.

"Ho, Booch," Wanda Green growled. A strong arm slipped over her shoulders. Buccari looked up at the intimidating physical geography of Eagle Squadron's skipper. From her full lips and wide-set hazel eyes to her thick hips and heavy thighs, Wanda Green was spectacularly endowed, a corporeal monument to curves and cantilever. Coming up behind Green were the other squadron commanders.

"Hey, Ace," Gordon Chou said. Admiral Chou's son was skipper of the Merlin Squadron. The tenacious black-eyed pilot came from the same mold as his father, wide, thick, and with a mountainous forehead and jug ears. "Thought we were going to leave you at Pitcairn."

"Never happen," Johnny Stanton, Nighthawk leader, growled. The barrel-chested, blasted-faced pilot was by far the oldest of the squadron skippers. Stanton's colorful past was legendary; however, his exploits had too frequently diverged from acceptable professional behavior. "Sweet Sharl's our good luck charm," he crooned.

"I'm glad you are back, Buccari." Abe Feldman said. The captain of *Raven One* was as thin as a rail, with a face like a chipped meat cleaver. He gave Buccari a subtle wink. They had flown together in two squadrons. Feldman, formal and saturnine, was an old friend.

"Yeah, Booch," Mick Wong said. Everything about *Osprey One*'s pretty-faced skipper was quick and sharp, although his fingers lingered on Buccari's shoulder.

"Thanks, Mick," Buccari said.

"Yeah, Sharl," Tonda Jones said. The skipper of Peregrine Squadron was a hard charger, intensely competitive. Jones had two konish interceptors to her credit and one Ulaggi, but she had also lost two corvettes to enemy action. Her courage was not in doubt.

Max Sakamoto, the squat, wide-shouldered skipper of the Blackhawks, merely grunted as he went by. In battle against kones and Ulaggi, Sakamoto had garnered four kills, but he had also suffered at their hands. At Hornblower his corvette was destroyed; Sakamoto, seriously injured, survived but lost most of his crew. Since that action he had refused the society of his peers, relentlessly driving his squadron hard and himself mercilessly. The troubled officer was one of the best tacticians in the fleet, and his pilots loved him.

"Everyone in the simulators commencing the morning watch," Green shouted. "Screen assignments are posted. We'll be doing threat-axis shifts until we go cross-eyed."

"You've got screen command, Wanda?" Buccari asked.

"Not for long," Green said. "Big Jake says he's killing me off fast. He wants to see how we operate with heavy casualties. I expect all squadron skippers will be in the observation tank before the first day's out, while Carmichael critiques our tails off."

"Life's a joke," Buccari said.

"And then you croak," Green said. "Get some rest, Condor. You look like shit."

Green ushered the other squadron commanders through the hatch. The corvette skippers were returning to their respective motherships. Buccari was suddenly anxious to do the same. Dowornobb was at her side, his great mass moving gracefully in the light gravity.

"I-ah am greatly worried, Citizen Sharl," Dowornobb thundered. "Tar Fell's ships will-ah return to the Kon System with Admiral Chou. My mate will be in great-ah peril."

"I, too, am worried, Master Dowornobb," she replied in konish, her thoughts returning to a bleak, unanswerable future.

"Will you take us back to *NZ*?" Dowornobb said, replacing his breathing unit. "I am anxious to return to our habitat, for I am greatly fatigued. Your motherships are much too cold."

"Let's go," she said, resigned to not seeing Carmichael.

"Commander Buccari, group ops," came the duty officer's sterile voice over her multiplex unit. Her neck warmed with adrenaline. Her resignation dissolved and was replaced with uncertain expectations.

"Buccari," she said, politely turning her head. Her hopes elevated with each heartbeat, and her heart climbed into her throat.

"Captain Merriwether requests your presence for evening meal in the admiral's mess. The commander's current uniform is appropriate."

"Buccari, aye," she acknowledged. The invitation was received with mixed emotions; she dearly enjoyed Merriwether's company and counsel, but she was disappointed. Fatigue reannounced itself.

"Commander Buccari, group ops," came the same persistent voice.

Her fatigue ebbed once again. "Buccari," she snapped.

"Report to the group-leader," the voice ordered.

"Buccari," she acknowledged, her emotions jumbling. She checked her chronometer. The first dogwatch was posting; there was still an hour before the wardroom's second sitting. She was tired, and she was hungry; but most of all, she was anxious to see Carmichael.

"Friend Sharl, is something wrong?" Dowornobb asked. "You are coloring."

"No," she replied. "Captain Merriwether has requested my presence at evening meal. Friend Dowornobb, you must return to NZ without me. Lieutenant Flaherty will take command of my corvette. I'll catch the grid shuttle."

Buccari transmitted orders to her corvette crew. She escorted the kones to the habitation ring transfer station and accompanied the giants through the null gravity of the operations core. Departing the ring transfer terminus, the kones took a down-bore to the hangar bays. Buccari, emotions soaring, grabbed a tractor lug moving in the opposite direction. Once stabilized in the bore, and seeing no one in front of her, she coltishly dove upward. Nearing the bore's topmost exit on the level two, she slowed herself on a braking bungee. Twisting acrobatically, she exited the bore and careened upward to the level one, thudding against the bulkhead.

Marshaling her dignity, she stepped in front of the security station and spoke her name and purpose. The hatch opened. No one was in the flag admin office; not surprising, the ship's workday was complete. On levels one and two only watchstanders would be about, and they would be on the command bridge or the flag bridge. Buccari proceeded to the group-leader's office. The hatch opened at her approach. Light-headed and heart racing, she floated into the small anteroom.

"In here." Carmichael's deep voice carried from within, from the group-leader's underway cabin. His words carried an edge, a hint of suppressed emotion.

Buccari pulled herself through the hatch into the inner sanctum. Carmichael labored in front of an admin unit. The spartan underway cabin was no larger than a junior officer H-ring stateroom. It contained a sanitation unit, a battle armor wardrobe, and a sleep harness. The vid-screens were dark; barely audible, a Strauss waltz created a mood at once cheerful and melancholy.

"Come in, Commander," Carmichael said, stowing his admin unit. His rugged face was a record of his career; acceleration damage blemished his cheeks, chin, and nose. Battle damage from Hornblower had been repaired, but such injury left its indelible shadow. Years of duty and responsibility had also left their mark. But there was something else in his expression, an uncertainty, a fear. Carmichael's dark brown eyes brightened when their gazes met. Buccari dared to smile. An uncertain smile flickered ever so briefly on Carmichael's rugged face. It evaporated as quickly as it came, the softening of his lips replaced by a darkening fury.

"Dammit!" he shouted, the muscles in his jaw working.

She stiffened. Her intellect grappled with her emotions.

"When I recall a squadron," Carmichael snapped, his words hitting like punches, "I do not expect a debate. Do you understand?"

"Yes, sir," she replied, choking on her own words.

"Dammit!" Carmichael shouted again, releasing his tethers and pushing from his station. His momentum carried him to the low overhead. He pushed downward, pivoting away. The back of his neck was livid.

Buccari remained silent. Seconds passed awkwardly. At last Carmichael inhaled deeply, his wide shoulders lifting. He turned to face her. His actions caused him to float closer. He checked his drift, but he was still close enough to touch. She resisted the urge. The group-leader's anger would burn.

"I'm sorry," she said, fighting hot tears. She still wanted Carmichael. She wanted him more than anything in the universe, but she knew he was right. There was no room for emotion. They had a war to fight. Ironically, their roles had switched; now he was the one doing his job. She owed it to Carmichael, to her son, to her race, to do hers.

"You're right, Captain," she said, lifting her chin. "I was slow in following orders. It will not happen again."

Carmichael stared into her eyes. Fury drained from his countenance. A terrible sadness replaced his anger. "Sharl," he moaned, drifting closer. Too close.

She was confused. "I—I was wrong, Jake," she stammered.

"You've been right all along," he said.

"Jake?"

"I'm not angry at you, Sharl. I'm angry at myself. I'm angry because I was so worried. I could never have left you, Sharl. I couldn't do my job, Sharl."

"Yeah," she whispered.

Carmichael's gaze held hers. He smiled and was transformed into the self-assured young pilot she had first met so many years ago.

"Is it just me, Sharl?" he finally asked, reaching out and brushing her cheek.

"No, Jake," she whispered, taking his big hand in hers, pulling their bodies together. "It's me, too."

His other hand came down on her hip, taking possession. His body fitted to hers. She put her arms around his wide back and listened to his pounding heart.

"Oh, Jake," she said. "I'm so tired of worrying . . ."

Her fatalism, her acceptance of death, was erased. In Carmichael's arms, she wanted to live forever. He reached down and turned her face to his. He kissed her gently on the lips, and her insides stirred.

"I want you, Sharl," Carmichael whispered. "Always."

A thought came to her. "Jake . . ."

"Yes, Sharl."

"Merriwether knows everything that goes on in this ship."

"Then at the moment she's smiling," Carmichael said.

"Shit-eating grin's more like it," Buccari said.

They laughed in each other's arms.

"God, Sharl, I love you so much," he whispered.

"Not as much as I love you, Jake."

Carmichael's arms, desperately strong, intensely tender, surrounded her. She gladly surrendered. Her fatigue melted away, vanquished by a fever older than time.

THIRTY-ONE

INTRUSION

Hardwood foliage and crystalline sky reflected from the mirrored lake in a riot of azure, russet, and gold. Waterfalls cascading into MacArthur's Valley fell with muted thunder, their flowing volumes softened by seasonal drought. Winter was near, but the autumn day was still and warm. It was October extra Sunday, and the harvest was in. Genellan's four-hundred-day planetary year had thirteen twenty-eight-day months. The six days remaining were appended to even numbered months and called extra Sundays. Extra Sundays were days of much deserved rest. But not for cliff dwellers; cliff dwellers did not much concern themselves with human calendars.

At the mouth of the settlement cove a grizzled sentry master perched on a sun-bleached deadfall. The hunter's dripping body seemed too heavy for the brittle white branch. His three meter wingspan was spread wide to the breeze, drying the fine fur on his translucent membranes. In one of the old cliff dweller's cruel talons was a flopping silver fish. The black-eyed taskmaster stared with uncompromising intensity at his charges on the rocky point.

Naked as a newborn and poised like a statue on sun-baked stones, Charlie Buccari stood shoulder-to-shoulder with a squad of immature cliff dwellers. Young Buccari had grown, standing a head taller than the black-furred sentries. His boyish shoulders and back, tanned deep brown, had widened, and his chest had deepened, revealing nascent contours of muscle. His hair was collected in a queue strapped with leather.

Charlie stared deep into crystalline waters. A school of lake fish reformed and drifted closer, their green-black backs appearing magically in the silky fathoms. The boy knew to compensate for refraction; he picked out a big fish and adjusted his aim point slightly beyond its watery image. Soon the sentry master would designate the next diver. The cliff dwellers, with webbed talons and streamlined bodies, had the advantage, but the human was undaunted.

A breeze fluttered the lake surface, distorting the submerged target. Fixed resolutely on his prey, Charlie peered through the wavering reflections; he paid no heed to cascading leaves, yellow and red, falling onto the lake. He heard horses approaching. Those, too, he ignored. His concentration was total.

"Charlie's buck naked, Da," shouted a laughing young female.

Honey Goldberg's mocking taunts were impossible to ignore. Charlie broke discipline and turned. The sentry master screeched his disgust. The boy, confused, turned back to the old hunter and gave a quick bow, before clambering up the rocks to the leaf-covered bank. The sentries chittered with laughter. The sentry master screeched again, this time for order, and the sentries fell back to their task.

Charlie picked his clothes off the branches and scrambled into his shorts as the horse party came up the lake road. He little understood his embarrassment, but he knew he did not want to be seen naked by the girl. Since his first conscious memories, all children had played naked in the lake together, and frequently the adults. But something had changed. Honey Goldberg's eyes laughed at him, and she called his man-thing silly names. Charlie went to Sandy Tatum and tattled. Honey's father was Charlie's best human friend. The big redhead told Charlie not to worry. He said Honey was jealous because she did not have a man-thing. The adults laughed when Tatum said that, especially after Nancy Dawson threw a cup of tea in Tatum's lap.

Tatum and his daughter, both natural extensions of their huge golden stallions, their ponytails bouncing, came over the tree-shrouded headland and into the settlement cove. Tatum's tall, wide-shouldered form was sized well to his shaggy steed, Tank, the grandest of the studs. The one-armed man's freckled face was haloed by a bushy red beard sun-bleached to a fair match with the hide of his horse. Honey Goldberg, reed-thin and tanned dark as dirt, sat atop her thick-legged courser like a silky-haired sprite.

Charlie pulled tight his drawstring and straightened to face his tormentor with all the dignity he could muster. A third horse came over the headland. On its back were two low-bent hunters, membranes half deployed. Three more cliff dwellers glided under the tree limbs, wings whispering through falling leaves.

"Ho, Charlie," Tatum boomed, pulling up. A twittering hunter—Spitter—swerved directly at them, flaring his expansive wingspan to settle gently on Tank's ponderous flank. The other cliff dwellers glided to perches farther up the trail. Tatum's horse, unperturbed by his new rider, sidestepped closer, snorting great liquid exhalations. The snub-nosed beast recognized the boy and playfully nuzzled his shoulder, almost knocking Charlie from his feet.

"Ho, Sandy," Charlie said, recovering his balance. His small hand darted out and grabbed the beast's flaring nostril. The massive horse froze, head down, ceding mastery to the puny human. Charlie stroked Tank's wide forehead and whistled soothingly. The horse's liquid brown eyes stared devotedly at the boy. Tatum laughed deeply, and Spitter whistled approvingly. Charlie peeked sideways to see if Honey was watching, but the lanky, honey-haired girl gazed distractedly over the cove. On her face was the special smirk reserved for him alone.

"Haven't seen you up to the stables, boy," Tatum said. "Adam and Honey've been doing your chores. Even little Hope. Winter's almost here. You tired of pulling your weight, boy?"

"No, sir," Charlie said, looking up. The sun dappled through trembling golden leaves. Somewhere over the lake a hunting eagle screamed.

"He missed supper last night, too," Honey said. She looked

down at Charlie from her superior altitude, night-brown eyes glinting with satisfaction.

"Go on up to the settlement, Hon," Tatum said softly.

"Yes, Da," Honey sighed, pulling her horse's head to the trail. She took the flower-margined path along the brook, past trampled cornfields unburdened of their harvest. The other horse, with its cliff dweller riders, fell into trail.

"What's wrong, Charlie?" Tatum asked.

"Don't like being around Honey," the boy mumbled.

"Huh?" Tatum said.

"She makes fun," Charlie said.

"Oh," Tatum said. "Huh?"

"She makes fun of me."

"Uh ... okay. I know what you mean," Tatum said, the slightest of smiles crinkling the corners of his brown eyes. "All men got the same disease, Charlie, one way or the other. Sooner or later."

"I ain't sick," Charlie said.

"Yeah, you are. You ain't got a clue how to handle women, son," Tatum said, chuckling, "and you never will if you don't face 'em down. They don't bite. Well, not too hard, they don't." The redhead laughed. "Tarnation, sometimes they bite darn hard." His face grew suddenly serious. "Still ain't no excuse for you not doing your chores."

Charlie said nothing. He looked back at the cove. At that moment One-son shot out of the water onto the sentry master's perch with a fish in his mouth. The sentry master tottered on one talon but regained balance with two wind-gushing sweeps of his wings. The old hunter shook water from his body and hopped from the branch onto the log and from the log onto the ground. Two fat lake fish lay in damp shade. The inscrutable hunter slipped a bony finger behind the gill of each fish and waddled away, disappearing into the tumble of timbers and rocks. The sentries, many with their own fish, followed in an orderly file.

"I got no time for talking, son," Tatum said, pulling Tank to the path. "You be in the stables first thing in the morning, you hear?"

"Horseshit," Charlie muttered.

Tatum reined in Tank and turned in his seat. The giant of a man said nothing. He just sat there, glaring down from his great height.

"What?" Charlie said defiantly.

"Your daddy would've beat you for talking like that."

"My daddy's dead."

The big redhead's great shoulders slumped.

"Yeah," Tatum finally said, his color rising, "but you ain't. You owe it to your old man, Charlie. He always did what was asked of him. He always pulled his weight . . . and more. He was a fighter, even more of a fighter than your mom. And your old man never cussed . . . never. Well, hardly ever. Dammit, almost never!"

Tatum sucked in a great lungful of air and rubbed his freckled face with a meaty hand. Ruddy face sagging with disappointment, he sighed heavily and looked down at the boy. Charlie felt his insides twisting.

"I'll do my chores, Sandy," he said.

"Good, now I don't have to spank you," the redhead replied. "And I would have, you bet."

"I know," Charlie said, trying to smile.

"Your old man would be proud, Charlie. Damn, he would. One of these days—"

From up the hill came the ringing of the lodge triangle.

"What the—" Tatum said. "Sounds like a fire alarm."

Charlie looked through the trees, searching for a telltale plume of smoke. Seconds later, echoing throughout the valley, the Legion emergency sirens raised their horrible and unmistakable wail.

Spitter screeched and pounded into flight. The other hunters followed.

"Oh, God, no," Tatum whispered.

Charlie stared into the sky.

"C'mon!" Tatum shouted, his voice turned to iron. Charlie sprinted up the path and leaped for the horse's rump. Tatum extended his big hand and yanked Charlie on board. The boy wrapped his arms around Tatum's iron-hard midsection as Tank lunged violently into a gallop.

At least one Legion mothership remained in the Kon System at all times. *T.L.S. Madagascar*, a Second Fleet asset, was scheduled to return to Earth for an extended yard visit on the next settlement rotation. Also in Genellan orbit, slowly maneuvering into geosynchronous orbit, was the solitary konish Planetary Defense Force station. The massive PDF weapons platform was still a standard month from reaching its intended covering longitude over New Edmonton and the domes of Ocean Station.

Twelve interstellar ships materializing out of hyperspace elicited no small amount of concern from *Madagascar*'s commanding officer, particularly when all hails were ignored. That the ships were Ulaggi was too soon apparent. Unable to make the protective umbrella of the defense station, the mothership captain commenced orbital departure using Genellan as a shield. A single ship could not escape into hyperlight, but it could run. The skipper of *Madagascar* armed his laser batteries, launched all corvettes, and made ready to fight ship.

The Ulaggi main fleet did not follow the Legion mothership, maneuvering instead into battle formation focused on the PDF platform. The satellite's massive optics and tremendous power generators quickly served notice, striking out at the intruders beyond their weapons range. The Ulaggi interstellars fell back. As they retreated, the alien ships spewed a blizzard of decoys and thermonuclear probes, all of which were laid waste by PDF energy beams.

While the Ulaggi fleet laid siege to the defense station, its interstellars spawned a flurry of attack vessels. These fast-movers streamed away from the stalemate, swirling with choreographed precision around the limb of the planet. Using Genellan's gravity well as an energy sling, the streaking vessels dwarfed *Madagascar*'s escape vector, raining down upon the hapless Legion ship across a wide front. Hideous screams flooded the communications channels. The overmatched Legion corvette pilots fought valiantly; the mothership's laser batteries gave fair measure, but the result was inevitable—*Madagascar* was annihilated. Not a single Legion lifeboat was left intact.

THIRTY-TWO

CONFUSION

New Edmonton's skyline boasted a dozen buildings of ten stories or greater, all in soft shades of yellow and white, a pleasantly homogeneous cityscape in twenty-first-century art deco motif. NEd was a work in process, growing outward from its core. A flock of construction cranes and slip-frames towered above the city, but the greater construction effort over the years had been directed underground. Most major structures had at least three subterranean levels, one tier of which was heavily reinforced and connected to other structures by a matrix of interconnecting transit tubes.

The Tellurian Legion State Department's recently completed fifteen-story edifice was NEd's tallest structure. The top five floors and two full basement levels housed Legion Security Agency communications and surveillance equipment. Artemis Mather, in the absence of an appointed ambassador, occupied a richly appointed suite on the tenth floor.

The chargé d'affaires stood on her high balcony, watching helicopters fly importantly across the city center, their anti-collision beacons blinking nervously. She turned her attention to a more soothing prospect. The waning sunset was but a fading streak of orange layering the southwestern horizon. Far to the south, on the ocean's edge, where normally she would see the spaceport's blinking tower beacon and blue-lit taxiways, there was only velvet darkness. All outlying settlements in between were also blacked out, their governing managers adhering to the dictates of the invasion alert.

This was no alert, Mather reminded herself. This was for real.

Yet not all lights were extinguished. At Mather's behest NEd's central core blazed with electricity. Well-ordered blocks of residential apartments and city service facilities, preternaturally devoid of visible population, were generously illuminated. Blue-white light bars defined orthogonal streets, climbing and descending gently over the city's rolling terrain. Sharl Buccari Boulevard, in graceful contrast to the orderly north-south street grid, curved sinuously across the lighted city section, its undulations marked with parallel necklaces of amber globes. Buccari Boulevard terminated at the elegant promenade on the city's cascading river. At the boulevard's traffic circle a stone obelisk commemorating the first Kon-Earth Accord speared into the two-moon sky. Illuminated with overlapping cones of pure white light, the monument was the focal point of the vista. Mather laughed at the irony: using the lights of Buccari Boulevard to guide the Ulaggi.

Artemis Mather did not wish to hide. The very thought was ludicrous; a city could not be hidden from an adversary so technically advanced. Mather wanted not to hide from the Ulaggi, she yearned for their attention. Mather yearned for contact; diplomacy was the high calling for which she had been trained.

She retreated from the wide balcony and proceeded through a sensory door. She spoke her name, fingered the cipher optics, and stalked into the spacious security center. LSA technicians scattered from her path. A segmented holo-vid projected on a long wall. A single vid-cell depicted evacuation status. In the hissing barrels of the transportation system, far below the surface of the city, NEd's population streamed outward from the city center, each refugee to a designated disbursement camp. The evacuation was going to plan, but this interested Mather not at all. Her attention was captured by the tactical military situation plots. She studied the communication displays, searching for active links.

Et Silmarn's splayed features filled one holo-cell. The planetary governor was in unscrambled communications with Captain Quinn on board her helo, just one of many intercepts being monitored by LSA spooks. The Legion administrator's image was not on vid-link, but her strong voice was captured on audio. The kone and the human exchanged bursts of conversational konish, too rapid for Mather's rudimentary skills. She punched a button and scanned the intercept log. Nothing interesting.

"The Ulaggi are still descending," the duty officer reported, her voice flat and brittle. "They will be in ground-based weapons range within five orbits, maybe sooner."

Mather shifted her attention to the dominant display, a wall-spanning orbital plot. Hours earlier, six of the twelve alien ships had detached from action in the vicinity of the konish defense platform. Their plummeting descent to low orbit left little doubt as to their destination. The Ulaggi were about to deploy a landing party.

"They've come to us," Mather said. "Do they answer our hails?"

"No, sir," the LSA officer replied. "Other than their infernal battle screams, we've had no intercepts. All signals from *Madagascar* have terminated. We believe she's been destroyed."

A mothership destroyed! A hostile act, but *Madagascar* was a warship. Now perhaps the aliens would realize the humans meant them no harm.

"Continue hailing!" she snapped. "History is made here tonight. They will talk to us. I know it."

"Commander Quinn's helo is on final," her security chief reported. "Quinn has ordered all martial law council members to her office. The admin duty officer insists on your immediate attendance."

"Inform the administrator I'm on my way," Mather replied.

"Your tube car is ready," the security chief said.

"I'll walk," Mather replied. "It is a pleasant evening."

The helo banked sharply and flattened its descent. In the darkened cabin Quinn put an arm around her daughter and gave the wide-eyed child a desperate hug. Then she looked up at Hudson and forced a smile. Except for the square jaw clenched tight, her young husband's face was obscured in shadow. The specter of annihilation hung over their souls, heavy and dark. An hour earlier she had been gazing reverently at a fiery ocean sunset. Legion helicopters skimming over the azure waters had exploded their serenity. The settlement administrator and her family had been yanked from their idyllic wave-washed island, their extra-Sunday holiday torn asunder. Quinn had not thought it possible for emotions to swing from bliss to terror in so short a time.

"I'll take Emerald to our dispersal point, Cass," Hudson said. "I'll contact you from there. Don't worry about us."

"Take care of yourself, Nash," she said, her mind and soul torn between her duties as a Legion officer and her duties as wife and mother. The Ulaggi had left no survivors at Shaula and Oldfather. She reached across their daughter's lap and found Hudson's hand. Emerald's tiny hands covered those of her parents, completing the union.

A constellation of red landing lights rose to meet them. The helicopter grounded on the administration building's expansive helo-pad, and the roar of its hyperkinetic turbines wound down to silence. Quinn threw off her harness and stepped to the roof. The night was warm and humid. Hudson, carrying Emerald, jumped down behind her. She turned one last time. Hudson smiled and waved her on.

"Go to work, boss," he shouted. "Emmy and I are going camping."

She threw Emerald an enthusiastic wave, spun on her heel and strode across the rooftop landing surface, her mind already burdened with impending decisions.

At six stories, the new administration building was far from the tallest building in New Edmonton, but it was located at the extreme northern margin of the city, at its highest elevation. Built on a broad hill above the original PHM landing sites, the structure dominated the descending terrain. Quinn stared out at the sprawling new city, the colony that had been her responsibility since its inception. Her growing terror was replaced with incredulity. That sense of disbelief instantly transformed into black rage.

"Why are surface lights still on?" she shouted, desperately holding her fury in check. She stomped across the roof.

Quinn's military commanders and their senior aides waited at the margin of the landing pad: General Wattly, the civil defense warden, was the senior military officer on the planet; Colonel Kim was the marine commandant; Colonel Foster was the senior LSA officer. Noticeably absent was Artemis Mather.

The army and marine officers wore full hostile environment battle-suits; the marines wore forest-green, army personnel wore dun. General Wattly, his massive head improbably diminished by his bulky torso armor, held a helmet under his arm. In contrast, Colonel Foster wore the red beret and stiffly creased black jumpsuit that was the uniform of the Legion Security Agency.

There was another person there, dressed in a civilian environmental suit, helmet visor open. Tall and swarthy, Reggie St. Pierre was editor of the independent news service. Quinn exchanged understanding nods with the man. She had submitted the ex-LSA agent's name to Space Fleet as her martial law replacement, recommending St. Pierre be reinstated to active duty and promoted as necessary. She was tired of governing, and St. Pierre was trusted by settlers both north and south. And if anyone could manage the State Department's regime of LSA agents, it was St. Pierre. The civilian settlement council had also submitted St. Pierre's name as an acclaimed nominee for transition governor. The quiet widower had agreed to consider the job.

"Why are the city lights on?" she repeated, louder.

"State Department's insistence, Cassy," Colonel Foster reported.

Quinn ignored the senior security agent and glared at her watch supervisor, a bright-eyed female, a lieutenant commander wearing the field uniform of a fleet engineering officer.

"I amended your standing orders on the chargé d'affaire's authority," the watch supervisor reported. "Diplomat Mather invoked State Department executive powers per Section Sixteen—"

"Notify the assistant watch supervisor that you are immediately relieved." Quinn said, certain the watch officer was an LSA plant. Invasion emergency procedures were too explicit for any latitude. Quinn looked about the command center and wondered how many other security agents had infiltrated her administration detachment.

"Cassy, er ... Captain Quinn," the LSA colonel said in a infuriatingly calm voice, "it is not necessary—"

"Speak when spoken to, Colonel," she snapped. "Colonel Kim, I want a squad of marines in the admin command center. If anyone fails to follow my orders, shoot them. On my authority. Do you understand?" Her eyes locked with those of the LSA officer.

"Aye, sir," the marine officer replied, thrusting a gauntleted finger at an aide. That helmeted officer barked into his face-piece, while another marine sprinted for the down ramp.

"Turn out the goddamn lights," Quinn shouted, striding into the building. The settlement's martial law council followed in her turbulent wake, with aides peeling off on missions like leaves falling from trees.

"Take down the service grid and the public safety grid," Quinn ordered. "Now! All power in this city goes to transit tubes and energy battery reservoirs."

Watch personnel scattered before her as she exploded into the information center adjacent to her office suite. The assistant watch supervisor standing at the main control console snapped to attention as Quinn marched up.

"*Madagascar*'s gone, Captain," the watch supervisor reported. "Can't raise anything on tactical. There's no one there."

"Stop trying," Quinn said. "All we're doing is attracting attention. And what is everyone still doing topside?"

"The duty officer said to—" the watch officer began.

"Shift the watch to the command bunker," she thundered.

"Aye aye, Captain," the watch officer replied, hitting an alarm button. Technicians started moving from their consoles in a well-rehearsed choreography. "Captain, State's still transmitting at high power. Plain language greetings. Chinese dialects. Standard SETI text. Music, mathematics, computer chess games, flat video, you name it."

"Kill their power," Quinn ordered.

"They're off grid," the officer reported. "Independent emergency power. I can't touch them from here."

"Colonel Kim, send over some marines and take out the State Department's generators. You have my permission to use excessive force."

More marines ran to their orders.

"Status on counterbatteries?" Quinn demanded.

"All weapons manned and charged," General Wattly reported. Wattly outranked her, but Quinn's designation as settlement administrator gave the science officer broader powers. "We're tracking the aliens passively on remote array. They've knocked out all satellites. Local fire-control is in standby."

"Have you tried nuking them?"

"Yes, sir," Wattly replied. "We've deployed four dozen Steel-tips and a half dozen Mark-600s. They take out the hardware before it clears the atmosphere. It's going to be an energy weapon duel, Captain."

"Very well," Quinn replied, scanning the status boards. She thought briefly of Hudson and her daughter, praying they were safe, but her thoughts focused on the fate and safety of the other twenty thousand humans for which she was responsible.

"Reg, what's the latest from MacArthur's Valley?" she asked.

"They're buttoned up," St. Pierre replied. "Nancy Dawson says there was some panic at Hydro, but the settlers have everything under control. I have a bad feeling we'll soon wish we were up there."

"Well, I'm glad you're here, Reggie," Quinn said.

St. Pierre grunted.

"Evacuation status?" she asked.

"Except for emergency personnel, city center is one hundred percent clear," St. Pierre replied. He pointed to a holocell showing a detailed plan view of the city. "Five kilometer radius is eighty percent clear. Main tube trunks are working at max capacity. The dispersal staging areas are saturated, as are the loading queues. We're estimating ninety-five percent evacuation to ten kilometers by 0600 hours."

"I hope we have that long," Quinn said. "Status on the invaders."

"Confirmed Ulaggi," General Wattly said. "Two task groups of six interstellars each. One group remains engaged with the PDF station. The other six are descending in orbit, maneuvering to remain clear of the energy battery's firing radius. It's buying us time."

"Does the PDF station provide us any coverage?" Quinn asked.

"Negative," General Wattly replied. "Maybe in another two weeks."

"If we're still here," she said. An aide deposited Quinn's battle-armor bag at her feet. Quinn sat down and removed her field boots. Wistfully, she wished she could shower first; there was sand in her waistband and sunburn on her shoulders, souvenirs of another life, of another universe.

"Admiral Chou's due to arrive, Captain," General Wattly observed.

"Don't remind me," Quinn muttered. Another two thousand settlers, helpless in their transports. If Chou was quick enough, he could jump back into hyperspace, but to where? Not back to Sol System; that would reveal Earth's location.

"Sir, the watch is shifted to the command bunker," the watch supervisor reported. "By your leave, Captain?"

"Very well," she replied.

"Captain, State Department is off the air," the watch officer reported as she left her post.

"Good," Quinn said, stepping into her armor. She clamped shut boot and glove seals. "Colonel Kim, where's Mather? I want her in this room, where I can see her. I don't trust—"

There was a disturbance in the anteroom.

"I am in this room," Mather said. The diplomat walked imperiously through the entrance. Two burly marines accompanying her stopped at the threshold and took posts as guards.

"We have solid targeting data," General Wattly reported.

"At current descent rate, they'll be in main battery range in five orbits."

"You aren't going to shoot at them, are you?" Mather demanded.

Quinn turned and stared incredulously at the diplomat. "Not before they get in range," she replied, moving out on the balcony. She noted with satisfaction that the city lights were blacked out. There was nothing between her and the moon-jeweled ocean but absolute darkness. Her settlement was as ready as it could possibly be. There was nothing to do but to wait, to react, to fight. To die?

"If you start shooting, then they'll have a right to strike back in self-defense. I would propose—"

Quinn turned from the balcony and moved toward the communications room. Mather, fists on generous hips, stood in her way.

"We must try to make contact," Mather demanded. There was no surrender in her demeanor. They were both strong women. Quinn was taller, but Mather heavier.

"We've already established contact with this race, Art," Quinn replied. "The Ulaggi are hostile. Haven't you figured that out?"

"We have to give them a chance to—" Mather protested.

"Get out of the way, Mather," Quinn said as softly as she could.

"You call yourself a science officer!" Mather almost shouted. "We can't just—"

Mather's words froze on her lips, her eyes opened wide, terror-stricken, her dark complexion flashed white with intensely bright light. A searing splash of radiant heat struck the back of Quinn's neck. The atmosphere around her crinkled like dry paper. Her senses were overwhelmed by a discordant resonance, like a giant hand slamming the keyboard of an out-of-tune piano. The thermal front passed, and then the shock wave hit. Quinn pivoted about to see the ionized column of air still glowing. Natural lightning, radiating along the disturbance, flickered magically, it's crackling thunder a child's noise by comparison. Too late, window armor glided into place.

"I can't see!" Mather gasped.

Quinn, even though she had not been looking at the energy discharge, suffered moderate flash blindness. She blinked away ghost images. Shouts echoed through the building. Screams lifted into the night.

"Everyone below," Quinn ordered, pushing the helpless Mather before her. "General Wattly, shift the—"

Another bolt sang down from the skies, a blinding white bar of heat. Several windows were not yet shuttered, and the brilliant flash reflected into her open eyes.

"Everyone to the command bunker," she said calmly, stumbling toward the stairwell. Someone grabbed her arm.

"I got you, Cassy." It was St. Pierre. "Let's get you dressed."

She felt a helmet come down over her head.

"You ready to take charge of this mess, Reg?" she asked.

"Not yet," St. Pierre replied, his deep voice almost cheerful. "This city is still in the best of hands."

"Rome is burning," she muttered, squinting to regain her vision.

"Long live the empress," St. Pierre replied.

"Screw you," she muttered, holding onto his arm.

Outside, another energy beam struck the ground, its undeniable force vibrating the building. And another. Hot streaks of white energy pulsed their way through uncovered slits and cracks in the shielding, casting surreal shadows. Elevator power was secured, so they descended through the stairwells. Mather, seriously flash-blinded, could not move rapidly enough, so St. Pierre ordered two marines to carry the diplomat downstairs.

In time they arrived in the command center, three levels underground. With agonizing slowness Quinn's peripheral vision returned, and gradually her central vision was restored, although a resurgent pang lived behind her eye sockets. She was too busy to worry about her impairment. The Ulaggi attack steadily increased in fury. Each hammer blow was felt through layers of reinforced concrete, as alien energy beams slammed repeatedly into her city.

* * *

Nash Hudson and his daughter, their way illuminated by ghostly moonlight, trotted along deserted streets for the nearest subway station. After leaving the headquarters building, they had returned to Quinn's modest flat on Buccari Boulevard, to pick up their evacuation packs.

The subway station was just ahead. Water fountains in the central city roundabouts were still. Never had Hudson seen New Edmonton so empty, not even in the darkest hours of a Sunday morning. The city was large enough that commerce never ceased. Produce and market lorries, watchstanders, revelers, lonely people, were always about on NEd's streets, at all hours. But not tonight. The sound of a helicopter in the distance provided sober relief to the silence, deafening the sound of his footfalls. The low-pitched *thump-thump* of the helicopter's rotors disappeared and was replaced by the wail of a distant siren. And that, too, died away.

"Will Mommy be okay?" Emerald asked, needing to destroy the oppressive silence.

"She's safe in her command bunker, Em," Hudson said, trying to convince himself. There had been no survivors from other settlements attacked by the Ulaggi, but none of those colonies had been even a tenth the size of New Edmonton. Dispersal was their best option. In a colony of this many people, someone had to survive. Quinn's risk was far greater than his. He wanted with all his heart to go back to the mother of his child, to share his wife's danger, but it was up to him to take care of their daughter; she was their future.

Hudson and his daughter entered the red-lit ramp for the tube terminal. As they rounded the entrance's light baffle the lighting became brighter. Red light from the emergency lanterns transformed into a soft white illumination emanating from indirect sources. To his dark-adjusted eyes the dim lighting was garish.

From behind them a flash of incandescence scorched the air. Even the reflected light rounding the light baffles cast stark shadows past the transit station's squat support columns. The ground jumped, and a gust of air rounded the ramp chicane, swirling dust and lifting Emerald's silky hair.

They were under attack! Another beam slammed the city above them. A dull thump resonated beneath their feet, and the ramp lighting flickered. He prayed the transit tubes were still functioning. His prayers were answered. An arrival tone sounded, and he felt the air compression as a tube car approached. Arrival lights flashed; no destination was indicated on the departure marquee, only the words EVAC P1. Hudson, pushing Emerald ahead, ran for the loading ramp.

They had not cleared the ordering queues when a long cylindrical object bulleted through the station without slowing. Hudson made out the blurred forms of a few green-armored soldiers. It disappeared into the exit bore, momentarily sucking down the air pressure in the station.

"We missed it," Emerald said softly.

Hudson sagged against a column. They needed to get on the ramp where the loading sensors could detect them. But was that the last car? His concern was short-lived. The station arrival lights still flashed, even though the departed car was no longer in sight.

"There's another car coming," he shouted. "Run, Em!"

They sprinted across the red tiles of the subway station. As Hudson cleared the ordering queues, his pack strap snagged on a routing turnstile. He stopped. Emerald ran ahead, her small feet slapping the hard surface. Air pressure in the station surged with the approaching car, and then the streamlined vehicle was visible, going fast. Hudson cleared his straps and pushed forward. Emerald was halfway across the platform, waving her skinny arms. Suddenly the car's maglev brakes engaged and the tube car hissed to a panic halt. A soldier stepped through the door and motioned impatiently for them to embark. Emerald stopped and turned, waving for Hudson.

Small and blond, and so fragile, so alone in the vast, empty transit station, the towheaded little girl waved frantically with both hands. It was Hudson's last recollection. More quickly than he could formulate thought, the surface under his feet heaved upward; at the same time the ceiling collapsed in one piece. Irresistible forces struck his legs and back. Suffocating darkness annihilated conscious thought.

THIRTY-THREE

MOBILIZATION

Et Silmarn shivered under the stars. Standing on a grassy bluff, he stared across the moonlit coastal plain. New Edmonton burned majestically, bottom-lighting a scattering of western clouds with a hellish glow. Except for the trembling passage of his own exhalations within his breathing unit, there was no noise, only the stabs of light in the distance, a deluge of white-hot needles darting mercilessly from space. The night sky coruscated with an apocalyptic aurora; pulsing sheets of magenta, cyan, and coral blossomed wraithlike around the moon as lances of destruction stitched the human settlement.

To the south, darkened domes, undamaged and evacuated of all kones, glinted serenely in the moonlight.

"Why do they spare Ocean Station?" a technician asked.

"Good fortune is better left unquestioned," Et Silmarn replied.

"Governor Et Silmarn, Your Excellency, we must repair to the bunker," ordered the Hegemony's senior security officer. "It will be safer, Your Excellency."

"And warmer," someone else transmitted.

"There is nothing we can do here," Et Silmarn replied. The noblekone shivered again and took one last look into Genellan's frigid night. The Ulaggi ships were unseen on their orbital trajectories, but like the spokes of an infinite radius, their wheeling advance across the heavens was marked by razor-thin streaks of energy slicing unerringly into New Edmonton, the hub of their fury.

"The bombardment will soon stop," a scientist said. "The

incidence angle of their beams grows too steep. They no longer do much damage."

"The humans would disagree," Et Silmarn replied, falling to all fours and leading his entourage from their vantage point. The behemoths cantered to a downward-sloping tunnel and entered its moon-shadowed maw. They descended through first one armored airlock and then another, gaining increased illumination at each level. In places, moisture dripped from the ceiling, running through catchment gutters. Et Silmarn's anxiety glands bubbled. He understood the precariously thin margin of survival on this cold and cruel planet.

Et Silmarn proceeded to the evacuation shelters. The low ceiling dictated that the noblekone remain on all fours. They passed through another airlock. When the doors hissed shut, the planetary governor turned off his air compressor and removed his helmet. He inhaled the warm, full-bodied atmosphere, artificially maintained.

Energy. The atmosphere of Genellan was too rarefied to sustain konish existence. Kones needed a pressurized atmosphere with less oxygen and more gaseous carbon compounds. Satisfying that physiological need required energy. It would be the requirement for energy that would give them away; the Ulaggi would discover their bunker. The kones were not like humans; they could not just scatter into the wilds. Kones could not survive Genellan's hostile environment. And winter was coming. The humans would not be able to help them. If the Ulaggi did not kill the kones, Genellan would.

Et Silmarn looked about. Those kones in the common chamber stared back with desperate hope. They were scared, the air heavy, rank, and acrid. They looked to him for leadership.

"The bombardment has stopped," a senior technician shouted. "Ocean Station was spared."

A thunderous cheer was raised. The prevailing acrid fear smell was momentarily diluted by ephemeral wafts of bitter joy. Et Silmarn raised his tree-trunk arms and commanded silence.

"Our human friends have suffered great loss," the governor

thundered. "Respect their suffering, for our own plight is far from determined. Konish settlements may soon share the same tragic fate."

Ebullience surrendered to Et Silmarn's sober remarks. An hour passed. Word came from Kon of an attack on Goldmine Station. Ulaggi energy beams had been launched from extreme slant range. Counterfire from the PDF platform had discouraged a nearer approach. Damage to two of the five domes at Goldmine was extreme, but little loss of life had occurred. Subsequent orbits would likely result in greater damage, as the Ulaggi drew closer to the planet and farther from the PDF station's tactical range.

"Governor Et Silmarn," a technician reported. "Captain Quinn is on the land-link."

The transmission was released to the main screens. Quinn's helmet-shrouded visage materialized.

"Captain Quinn," Et Silmarn rumbled, "our relief at-ah seeing you alive cannot be expressed. What-ah is your condition?"

"Utter devastation, Your Excellency," Quinn replied in konish, her voice gravelly with fatigue. Something else was wrong. As great as was the tragedy that had befallen her city, Quinn's slumping demeanor spoke of some larger personal loss, bravely contained.

"Hud-sawn?" Et Silmarn said, horror dawning. "Where is Citizen Hud-sawn? And your daughter?"

Quinn said nothing. Her head jerked slightly.

"Oh, no!" Et Silmarn moaned. "I am sorry, my friend."

"Hudson has not been heard from since . . ." Quinn began. The human female's shoulders squared; her chin lifted. "Nash left here with our daughter just before the attack started. They haven't mustered at their evacuation center . . . but of course there is still reason to hope."

"Of course," Et Silmarn said. "They will be found . . ."

"I'm told Ocean Station is still intact," Quinn continued, her voice gaining timbre as she changed the subject.

"We are thankful," Et Silmarn replied. "And mystified."

"May good fortune stay home," she said, using an old

konish saying. "Needless to say, Governor, we cannot accept any more of your refugees. Our facilities are overwhelmed. Perhaps I should be sending you my refugees."

"Of course," Et Silmarn replied. "Anything we can do to help."

"We will be in contact," Quinn said. "I must sign off now."

The holo-vid darkened. Et Silmarn contemplated their fate, humans and kones. Even though the domes of Ocean Station were intact, he did not feel liberated from fear. Inescapably, the Ulaggi ships would come over the horizon again. It was a matter of time.

Those agonizing minutes passed quickly.

"Ulaggi ships are in line of sight," a technician reported.

Another energy squall descended upon the planet, and the governor's worst fears were answered. This time the domes of Ocean Station were not spared. Midway through the orbital pass, the targeting point altered from the battered human settlement. An Ulaggi beam found a dome at Ocean Station, and then another, igniting the gases within the habitats. The energy beams did not stop—a timpani from hell. Ulaggi energy beams hammered at the boiling scab until their marauding ships had rounded the heavens on their ever-lowering orbital passage.

On planet Kon orange-leafed *kotta* trees were in full flower. The Hegemonic capital's buttermilk atmosphere should have been sweetly redolent with the essence of the giant white blossoms, but botanical odors were overwhelmed by the collective bladder discharges of an entire civilization engulfed in panic. Invisible clouds of pungent fear, heavy and acrid, roiled across the city, and mobs of watery-eyed *trods*, moaning like thunder, swarmed the streets like three-hundred-kilo lemmings. Soldiers wielding power bludgeons struggled in vain to keep the city's wide thoroughfares and mass transit systems clear.

King Ollant piloted his shuttle craft across the metropolis, its navigation systems probing the yellow haze. Planetary Defense Force Headquarters, protruding from layers of brownish-gold methane smog, materialized on his landing display. Ollant established visual contact and reduced power to begin his descent. A powerful, splendidly buttressed edifice, at twenty stories, the PDF Headquarters numbered among the tallest buildings in the hemisphere. On final approach Ollant looked down from his hovering shuttle and witnessed the mindless exodus of the masses. He prayed his regional governments were functioning, but he refused to waste precious mental capital on issues no longer under his control. Ollant no longer governed.

The king grounded the shuttle on the commodious PDF landing dock. General Talsali was there to meet him.

"Your Highness," Talsali said, "you are far from your palace."

"The scourge has returned," Ollant said. "Status, sir."

"So it would seem," Talsali replied, leading the king to the power lifts. "New Edmonton and Ocean Station are destroyed. Goldmine holds on only because the defense station remains in operation."

"Any news of the humans?" the king asked.

"Their distress calls have ceased," General Talsali said.

Ollant exhaled. His anger surged and his bladders discharged their full fury.

They plunged many levels in silence, to the subterranean strongholds of PDF operations. The initial salutations completed, the PDF commanding general paid the king little deference. The Planetary Defense Force command center enjoyed extraterritorial status. It was neutral ground, subservient to no crown or regent, answerable only to the Vows of Protection.

They debouched from the lifts and came to a low railing overlooking the command center's operations amphitheater. Activity boiled below them as the resources of an entire planet were marshaled to meet a common enemy. Unit dispositions were updating on a status panel. A major PDF fleet was staging off moon Kreta.

"The Genellan defense station remains under fire by six Ulaggi interstellars," Talsali reported. "Its batteries have so far managed to hold them at bay, not without difficulty."

"Any threats to this planet?" Ollant asked.

"There are no alien ships in the vicinity of Kon, Your Majesty."

"What are your plans, General?"

"I have imposed a full alert," Talsali replied. "All heavy defensive platforms are on line. Secondary battery platforms are being brought on line as crew availability permits. Three full waves of interceptors are fueled and staged."

"Of course, you have my full cooperation in whatever you need," Ollant said. "All Hegemonic ships are at your disposal."

Talsali bowed his forehead to the stone floor. "May I ask your personal status, Your Highness?"

"I have resumed command of the Hegemonic fleet," Ollant said. "As I just stated, I place my fleets and my commission in your hands."

Ollant detected the old spacer's gratitude wafting gently on the air currents.

"Who governs in your stead, Your Highness?"

"Et Kalass is a most capable regent."

"Of course," Talsali replied.

"Your orders, General?"

"King Ollant," Talsali replied, "in Tar Fell's absence, you will assume the rank of armada-master and take command of the PDF battlefleet. Report to me daily. My attentions will remain on the readiness of orbiting defenses."

"General, I beg you," Ollant protested. "I wish no gratuitous appointment, if others are better suited to the task."

"Your appointment is genuine, Armada-Master," Talsali replied, more sternly. "Permit me the discretion of my authority. Say no more, and attend to my commands."

"Well then, General," Ollant thundered, "I request permission to mobilize for attack."

"Permission to mobilize is granted," the old general replied. "But for now there will be no attack."

"The alien fleet numbers only twelve," Ollant said. "I will field near ten times that number of heavy ships."

"More alien ships may appear at any moment," Talsali replied. "It will take three moon cycles to haul down the enemy, that is, if the enemy stands to fight. No, Your Highness, the PDF armada will not yet be drawn out. Our Vows of Protection are first designed to protect the home planet from invasion. Marshal your forces, Armada-Master, but remain within the perimeter of the primary energy batteries. Ours will be a defensive posture, at least until the foe is better understood."

"What of Genellan, General?"

"At the moment, Genellan is untenable."

THIRTY-FOUR

NIGHT OF TERROR

The children of the Survivors were brought into the lodge, where they camped on the wooden floor atop thick buffalo hides and silky nightmare pelts. Leslie Lee and Nancy Dawson took turns lying on the long couch, sternly admonishing any untoward activity. In the great stone fireplace an old fire danced, casting wavering shadows. Charlie Buccari rolled over in his sleeping bag, his senses tuned to the excitement. The brooding autumn night, redolent of wood, fur, and fire—and fear—seemed to last forever. The shouting from outside and, worse, the whisperings at the lodge doors were too much for a child's imagination. And yet, despite his efforts to forestall sleep, Charlie at last succumbed to fatigue.

In the dark hours before dawn Charlie came hard awake, alert to a lurking presence. Dying embers cast an impoverished glow. Out of the shadows materialized a hulking shadow. The towering specter stopped next to the couch. Charlie's initial flush of adrenaline was stilled by recognition of the phantom's smell and movements. It was Sandy Tatum. Slung over the one-armed man's shoulder was a big assault weapon, bigger even than the huge rifle he used for hunting superdragon and bear. The tall man stared down at Nancy Dawson for an eternity. At last he stooped and kissed his wife soundlessly on the cheek. Dawson grunted softly, then rose stiffly from the couch and followed Tatum through the weather doors, leaving the children unattended.

Charlie, still warm from his adrenaline surge, slipped from his sleeping bag. His knee rolled onto Adam Shannon's hand, buried deep in the silky furs.

"Huh?" the older boy moaned.

"Shh," Charlie hissed, creeping toward the door.

"Where ya going, Charlie?" Adam whispered, burrowing up from the nightmare pelts, his wide face a fuzzy white blur framed by a thatch of pitch-black.

"Shh," Charlie pleaded.

"I'm coming," Adam said thickly.

"What . . . you doing?" came a sleepy voice. Honey Goldberg's slender form was silhouetted against the embers, her long disheveled hair fired with dim highlights.

"Huh?" Hope Lee mumbled.

"Stay in your sleeping bags," Honey ordered, more loudly. "I'll tell."

"Shh," Adam hissed. "You'll wake up the twins. They'll cry."

"Don't tell me to shush," Honey chided, lowering her voice.

Charlie left the others behind and slipped through the weather door. In the mud room he grabbed his jacket and stepped into his sandals. Adam caught up with him. Honey and Hope followed. Out of enlightened self-interest, the girls remained silent. With stealth natural to inquiring youth, they opened the outer door. A helicopter taking off from the settlement pad masked their noise. The four escapees slipped along the moon-shadowed porch to the corner railing, taking cover behind a rough-hewn planter.

The settlement was dark. Solar-powered trail globes and gate lights normally providing nighttime illumination for the settlement common were extinguished. Even the wooden bridge over the gurgling spring was unlit. But it was not too dark to see; both moons were up, the big moon, approaching full phase, was lowering to the western mountains; the little moon was high in the night sky at first quarter.

Nancy Dawson and Sandy Tatum stood on the steep steps talking in low tones to a collection of settlers and Survivors. Bits of whispered conversation lifted to Charlie's ears.

". . . damn bugs . . . *Madagascar* destroyed . . . NEd's burning . . . Shaula all over again . . . Ocean Station's melted down . . . Let's get going. It's time . . ."

It was cool and damp; the whispered words, haloed with misted exhalation, were delivered with fervor. At the front of the small crowd stood Sam Cody. With him were Chief Wilson, Terry O'Toole, Toby Mendoza, and white-haired Beppo Schmidt. Leslie Lee and Mrs. Jackson, walking from the cabins, joined the crowd. Moonlight painted everyone ashen-faced. They looked scared.

Noises came from up the hill.

"Hsst, look!" Honey whispered.

"Tookmanian's coming!" Mendoza shouted.

Charlie looked past the corner of the lodge toward the back sally-gate. A procession of people and horses rattled and squeaked down the hill. Some horses had riders, but most beasts were burdened with pack frames and household goods. A few refugees carried flashlights, their beams coalescing into a cluster as they approached the elevated porch. A baby cried. Tookmanian, tall and foreboding, walked at the head of the column. Colonel Pak, short and deceptively slight, strode at Tookmanian's side.

"Morning, Tooks. Colonel Pak," Sam Cody said softly.

The procession halted before the lodge.

"Good morning, Sam," Pak replied. "The situation's grim, is it not?"

"God's will," Tookmanian replied, his voice deep and resonant. The tall, hawk-nosed man's eyes were lost in moon-shadowed sockets, lending his somber face the aspect of a death's head. "Retribution is His. We are punished for our sins."

"Praise God," shouted one of the farmers.

"Good evening, Reverend Tooks," O'Toole said. "Nice night for sinning, ain't it? Why don't you bring your crowd down to the tavern after the invasion and have a little Took Juice nightcap. I haven't changed your recipe one bit."

"God forgives our sins," rumbled the scarecrow of a man.

"Make up your mind, Tooks," O'Toole said. "Will we be punished or forgiven?"

"Cut it out, Terry!" Dawson snapped.

"You're determined to go, then?" Sam Cody asked.

"Colonel Pak, you've got more sense than this. Dammit, Han, you're our mayor."

"Ex-mayor, Sam," Pak replied. "I have resigned. I must go with my wife and her family . . . and my conscience. As Tookmanian says, it is God's will."

"You're all putting your wives and children into danger," Dawson said.

"If we are invaded, the greater danger will be here," Tookmanian rumbled.

"High Camp is not large enough for all of us," Pak added. Becky Pak, black hair glinting in the moonlight, grabbed her husband's arm.

"It is God's will," Tookmanian replied. "The invasion is a clear signal. There are rich valleys to the south. The winters will be gentler there. The alien pestilence will pass, and we will make a new beginning."

"Gentler my ass," Wilson mumbled. "You can't outrun the weather, Tooks. Winter's only a few days away. If the bugs don't kill you, the cold will."

"Is there another choice, Gunner?" Tookmanian asked softly. "We cannot sit and wait for the Ulaggi. As Colonel Pak said, there is not room enough nor sufficient provision at High Camp for my flock and yours. I will not desert them. There is a large valley a hundred kilometers south, with many caves. Tatum knows the valley. That is our destination. We carry our harvest and our future on our backs."

It was a long speech for the taciturn man. The small crowd was silent.

"Pray for us," Pak begged, putting his arm around his young wife's shoulder. Her furs could not mask the swelling of her abdomen.

"You know we will," Dawson said.

"Use Fenstermacher's old raft," Wilson said with sudden inspiration. "You can move your supplies down the river and free up the horses for riding."

"Thank you," Tookmanian said softly. "It is a good idea."

"Good luck," Tatum said.

The procession moved out. Tookmanian's congregation, the

faithful following their minister, some of the oldest settlers in the valley, many of the best farmers and their families, all leaving their land and homes. Women sobbed; children cried. Horses, impatient with the pace, snorted and pranced, their breath shooting out in jets of moonlit vapor.

No sooner did Tookmanian's procession clear the palisade's main gate than an armored ATV came racing through, lifting dust in the moonlight. It bounded over the brook bridge and skidded to a stop before the lodge. Six Legion marines jumped from the lorry bed. Billy Gordon and Captain Kowolski, the thick-chested officer in charge of the marine detachment, exited the driver's compartment.

"Dammit," Kowolski shouted. "I don't have enough marines to protect all of you if you're going to be spreading out all over the countryside. Sergeant Gordon told me you're heading into the hills this morning. I came over to try and convince you to stay put, and I find Tookmanian already heading out."

"Give it up, Ski," Sam Cody said. "You best be worrying about protecting Hydro and the Legion personnel. We're breaking camp within the hour."

"We're breaking camp now," Tatum rumbled.

Kowolski turned belligerently to Tatum. The marine officer was a powerful man, but Tatum was a head taller and wider of shoulder.

"We're leaving, Captain," Tatum said.

"Oh, man!" Kowolski said.

Charlie, his ears sensitized to cliff dweller signals, heard a subtle sonic pulsing. He turned to locate its source. Peeking upside down from the eaves, a sparkling pair of black eyes reflected the moonlight. Charlie slipped around the porch corner as Captain Two and Bottlenose parachuted on cupped membranes silently to the ground. Charlie went under the railing and dropped from the porch. The hunter leader chirped and Bottlenose darted away; the scarred old hunter flowed like black water across the common.

"Come, Thunderhead," Captain Two chirped, moving through the shadows. The boy followed.

* * *

Nancy Dawson detected movement on the lodge porch. Moonlight through the porch railing illuminated several pairs of small knees and ankles. More movement on the roof peak caught her attention. She glanced up and saw half a dozen hunters perching like misbegotten gargoyles.

"What's it like in Hydro, Billy?" O'Toole asked, recapturing Dawson's attention. "Is my tavern still standing?"

"It's still there, Terry," Gordon said, "and you've got a good crowd. Trouble is, no one's paying."

"Why do people riot?" Lee asked.

"Nothing to lose. No hope for the future," Dawson said.

"Hell, this isn't Earth," Sam Cody replied. "We're on Genellan. The future is ours for the taking."

"It's the contract laborers," Kowolski said. "They were pissed off and half bagged before the invasion started. They got wind of the attack on *Madagascar*, and they tuned in the bar's receiver. Turned up the volume, and broadcast a play-by-play of the massacre. Everyone on Lake Road heard the gory end. They went berserk."

"It's calmed down," Gordon said. "We kicked some butt."

"We're wasting time," Tatum shouted. "Nance, get the kids dressed. I'll bring down the horses."

"You coming with us, Billy?" Wilson asked.

"I'd like to, Gunner," Gordon said, "but I got a job to do."

"Damn right you do, marine," Captain Kowolski snarled.

"Move 'em out," Tatum bellowed. "Split up and take your assigned routes. Stay as far from town as possible. The last thing we need is a panicked stampede following us up the mountain."

"Sounds like a plan," Kowolski said. "I'll hold the townies until sunrise. Most of the settlers will probably hunker down on their farms. Who knows what will happen—"

"Is the hospital okay?" Leslie Lee asked.

"Yeah, Les," Gordon replied. "The fires are at the other end of town. The worst injuries so far are hangovers."

Dawson sighed with relief. She moved to the lodge steps.

"How long must we hide?" someone asked.

"As long as it takes," Tatum said.

"The freighter rotation!" Lee exclaimed. "The freighters'll come out of hyperlight without a chance. All those people!"

"Let's hope Admiral Runacres gets back before then," O'Toole said.

"Assuming his fleet hasn't been destroyed," Wilson said quietly.

"Always the optimist," Dawson said.

"Move!" Tatum thundered.

The crowd dispersed. Dawson mounted the steps. Movement in the shadows confirmed her suspicions.

"What are you kids doing?" she asked. A knot swelled in her gut; Charlie was missing. "Inside, now. We're going on a hike."

"We heard lots of noise," Hope said.

"Told them to stay inside," Honey said, "but they didn't listen."

"Are we going to High Camp?" Adam asked.

"Yes," Dawson said, looking around desperately. "You need to dress warm. Where's Charlie?"

"He's right here," Adam said, turning.

There was no one there.

Charlie followed the ungainly hunters, squirming through the brook portcullis beneath the palisade wall. Challenged by human and hunter sentries, the hunters on the ground exchanged screeches with their cohorts on watch, never halting. The cliff dwellers moved fast, but the boy could run like a deer. Black shadows hissed overhead, membranes blotting out moon and stars.

At the cove peninsula they were joined by more hunters and sentries. Charlie answered the chirping hails of One-son and Two-son with a whistle. Bottlenose brusquely silenced them. With little ceremony and less noise, the troop scuttled along the lakeshore, avoiding the forest road. All around them heavily burdened cliff dwellers, guilder and hunter, male and female, moved through the trees.

The direction of their movement was fortuitous, for when

the first energy beam came down, the refugees were looking away from its impact point. The noise was deafening. Secondary lightning rippled over the valley ridges. Charlie's ears rang and static electricity lifted his hair out from his head. The hunters, with their hypersensitive hearing and night vision, were stunned into motionless stupor. Charlie, with duller human sight and hearing, was less incapacitated, but it still took several minutes before he could hear the valley's waterfalls or see clearly in the night.

His first perceptions were of the conflagration at the lake's far southern end. Hydro exploded, its dry wood structures sucking air and exhausting leaping flames and billowing ash. The big yellow cube housing the hydropower facility glowed brightly at the end of the lake, tinted orange by flames. A column of smoke, ghostly white in the full moon, spiraled into the skies. Shouts and the sounds of thudding hoofbeats lifted from the settlement cove. Charlie stopped and stared through the trees in the direction of the palisade.

"Thunderhead!" Captain Two whistled. "Come!"

Bottlenose, groping with one hand, pulled Charlie along. The hunters, undaunted by their incapacitation, stumbled gamely forward, chirping and tweeting into the subsonic. Unable to see, they resorted to ultrasonic ranging, literally using their brain sensors instead of their eyes and ears. They moved deeper into the forest. It was slower going, but when the next energy beam struck Hydro, its debilitating effects were attenuated by thick foliage. A third blast, and a fourth, came to ground in front of them. Charlie guessed the landing facility on the high cliffs across the river was under attack.

By the time they reached Longo's Meadow, the hunters had regained the full range of their senses. The broad stretch of moon-washed grass on the lakeshore looked peaceful enough, but a hunter would not traverse such an exposed area with impunity. Captain Two halted the determined migration. Charlie moved out from under the canopy of the forest to a position behind a fallen tree. All along the forest's edge, eerily silent, hunters and guilders massed, waiting.

Charlie heard scouting signals on the edge of his sensory

awareness. Captain Two chirped another command. Bottle-nose prowled forward, leading a troop of hunters across the meadow. The warriors scattered, their dark fur blending with the dull light of the moon, until they disappeared in the near distance.

A soft, warm hand touched Charlie's hand. He looked down to see Greatmother. The old huntress carried a small parcel of goods in a leather rucksack.

"Thunderhead," she chirped, slipping her bony hand into his.

"Long life, honored huntress," he squeaked, struggling to form the tight sound groups. Greatmother chittered good-naturedly at his efforts and squeezed his hand with near painful pressure. She was no taller than the boy's shoulder, but her presence was powerful. Nothing else was said; there was no need. The human child and the old huntress stood close together, waiting to venture forth.

The signal came, a distant shriek lifting into the ultrasonic. Captain Two whistled another command, and a thousand cliff dwellers surged from the forest, turning the meadow into a field of flowing fur. Greatmother, still holding Charlie's hand, waddled forward, and together they trotted out onto the meadow. The temperature had fallen. A delicate patina of frost crunched underfoot. At first the sweet scent of crushed field mint drifted into the night air, but that fragrance was overcome by drifting wood smoke.

A meteor streaked overhead. No, it was too bright, too persistent. The moving creatures stopped as one to follow the falling star. A second meteor slashed the sky, its course curving unnaturally. And another. Not meteors. The arcing slices of silver did not dissolve into memory. Instead they grew larger, blossoming.

Finally, one after the other, the ersatz falling stars faded away, their friction-heated glows extinguished, but they did not completely disappear. Three ear-splitting *ba-booms* shuddered the ground. Hunters shrieked in dismay and threw hands over ear openings.

Charlie's tumultuous thoughts came into sharp focus: the

Ulaggi were coming. Coming to attack. To kill. The cliff dwellers had to get out of the valley. They would be murdered.

Charlie pulled away from Greatmother and placed the fingers of both hands in his mouth. The boy whistled the hunter command as loudly as he could.

"Move!"

Cliff dwellers, many still dazed and half blinded by energy beams, remained in the trees. Charlie pushed the creatures into action. Captain Two and Bottlenose followed his example, pulling guilders from the forest and setting them in motion across Longo's Meadow. Charlie, with One-son and Two-son at his side, returned repeatedly into the woods, searching for cliff dwellers and ushering them across the meadow. The cliff dwellers' journey back to the plateau would take three days, but they had to get out of MacArthur's Valley as soon as possible, or they would never leave. They would die.

At last the stream of cliff dwellers dwindled to stragglers. These were ushered safely across the meadow and into the hardwoods beyond. Captain Two whistled softly, ordering his warriors to retreat. Charlie turned and looked back toward the palisade.

"Thunderhead!"

Greatmother was at his side. Her hand grabbed his.

"Come, Thunderhead," she chirped. "The signal."

Charlie gently pulled his hand from the huntress's wiry grip. The lovable and fearsome huntress had dominated Charlie's emotions since first memory. She had been his most constant parent. Never had he deliberately disobeyed her direct command.

Until now.

"No, honorable huntress," Charlie chirped.

She opened her mouth and hissed. Moonlight glinted from rows of snow-white teeth. Her old eyes were angry black mirrors.

"Must come," she chirped. "Danger."

Charlie signed: "Must return my people."

"Great danger," Greatmother chirped, louder, insistent.

He stared down, at once frightened by authority and determined to disobey. Chirps and whistles caught his attention. Captain Two, Spitter, Bottlenose, and a half-dozen battle-hardened warriors approached, the rearguard, their countenances impatient and hard.

"Leave us, honored huntress," Captain Two ordered.

The huntress expelled air in a long, low whistle. She turned abruptly and waddled away, not looking back.

"Thunderhead has plan?" Captain Two signed.

Charlie bowed low to the scarred warrior. Spitter spat into the grass and growled his displeasure. His guttural noises were interrupted by an intermittent pulsing, a warbling exhaust, more often throttled off than on. Human and hunter faces jerked upward, eyes scanning the night, ears ranging to the noise. There! Something reflecting moonlight arced smoothly overhead, its underside pitch-black. An engine pulsed. A needle of flame shot backward. It skimmed overhead and was gone from sight. The manic warbling faded away. Waterfalls beyond the lake rumbled back into Charlie's awareness.

"Danger is here. We leave now," Captain Two signed.

Charlie looked to the south, toward the settlement. A column of smoke tumbled across an ash-reddened moon.

"I stay," Charlie signed. "This my home."

SECTION FOUR

THE BATTLE OF GENELLAN

THIRTY-FIVE

INVASION

"Captain Quinn."

A voice from far away.

"Captain Quinn, sir," the voice nagged.

It was all a dream; she was having a bad dream. Nash and Emerald would be there when she awoke. They would play in the surf, and later go snorkeling in the cool green lagoon. Why did it hurt? Swimming. Quinn swam upward, struggling reluctantly to consciousness. Her eyes opened. The red ambience was dim, yet bright enough to overstimulate her nerves. Pain throbbed behind her forehead. Her tortured eyes slammed shut, but the pain did not recede. She tried again, forcing her eyes open, blinking with discomfort. It hurt, but at least she could see. Quinn did not recognize the woman standing over her.

"Sir," the army officer said, "I was told to wake you before the bugs came over the hill."

Quinn jolted upright, memory gelling. "How long before?" she groaned, holding her head.

Quinn had spent an endless night giving orders. Her staff had set up emergency hospitals and quelled evacuation riots. With heart-stopping regularity her city had been pulverized by orbital bombardments. At dawn she had surrendered to the unavoidable demands of a spent body.

For an hour's sleep.

Her mouth tasted of hot metal. Perspiration trickled between her breasts, and her blouse stuck to a sweaty back. Her neck ached, but the pressure behind her eyes overwhelmed all other sensations. Not a dream, it was a nightmare.

313

"Line of sight in four minutes," the officer reported. "Estimated firing declination in sixteen minutes."

Grunting an acknowledgement, Quinn pushed from the bunk and stumbled forward on unsteady legs. The officer seized her elbow.

"Get me something . . . headache," Quinn ordered, pulling away and straightening her shoulders. She willed away a wave of vertigo.

"Mr. St. Pierre wanted you to know that the preliminary evacuation census is complete," the officer reported.

"St. Pierre?" Quinn asked. "Is he back?"

"Command center, sir. He just heloed in from Evac Two."

"Good," Quinn said. "Headache," she repeated.

"Yes, sir." The officer pivoted for the dispensary.

Quinn moved with begrudging steadiness down the low-ceilinged corridors of the deserted bunker. Emergency lamps, sullen and sanguinary, cast a forlorn glow. The air was rank; the cloying smell of urine and sewage hung heavy. There was no air-conditioning, no running water, and very little hope. Quinn caught herself thinking of her daughter. She forced the vagrant prayer back into the iron box of her will.

Bypassing the disabled lifts, she plodded up a steep, narrow stair to a guarded landing. A marine corporal triggered cipher locks and swung aside a vault door. A flood of white light poured forth, abusing Quinn's tender retinas. She walked squinting and blinking into the multitiered command center. Air currents brushed her sweaty face; warm humid air, but at least it was circulating.

There were two dozen watchstanders, mainly army and spacer technicians. At the bottom level of the command center, on the operations pier, Reggie St. Pierre looked up from a civil defense landform model, his jet hair lank with sweat, his handsome face furrowed with concern and darkened with stubble. Quinn descended the shallow companionway. Both the admin watch supervisor and the command duty officer stepped away from their watch consoles, poised to report.

"Damn my head," Quinn cursed, shading her eyes. She

tried to blink away the fuzzy glow in the center of her vision, but it persisted. A medical officer came forward.

"You have retinal burns," the doctor said, handing Quinn a powerbottle and several pills. "It'll take a couple of days for your optic nerve to settle down. We can clear up the scarring, once we . . . repair our medical facility. Please take the pills, Captain."

Quinn slugged down the pills with a mouthful of tepid nutrient.

"How much power has come up?" she asked, dismissing the medical officer.

"A couple meg," St. Pierre reported. "Reactors are fail-safed. Tech Corps has two secondary generators turning on kerosene, and the engineers have deployed a solar array."

St. Pierre had taken charge in her absence. She took stock of the command center. A few status panels were back on line, although the holo-vids remained dark. She looked at the digital landform model, a three-dimensional scalable civil works representation. NEd was demolished, melted down and glassed over, but Quinn was surprised at how little damage was apparent in the seaward defensive sectors. The spaceport was unscathed.

"Evacuation status," Quinn said. "Casualty reports."

"As good as could be expected," St. Pierre replied. "Emergency power is still out on the major trunks, but Phase One evacuation is complete. We're clear out to twelve kilometers. General Wattly's troops are moving civilians from the dispersal centers into the foothills as fast as transportation becomes available."

"Casualties, Reg," she demanded, feeling her throat constrict.

"Two thousand dead," St. Pierre said, his voice clipped and sterile. "Eleven thousand injured, mostly burns and blindness. Another eight hundred people unaccounted for."

Ten percent of the settlement dead; sixty percent casualties. The silence was deafening. Quinn forced herself to breathe. Nash Hudson and her daughter were unaccounted for. Unaccounted for—such a sterile, ambiguous term.

"Anything from MacArthur's Valley?" she asked.

"No communications since before midnight," St. Pierre replied.

Quinn stared down at the terrain model and pondered what she saw.

"The spaceport," St. Pierre hinted.

"They're going to use the runways," she said.

"Apparently so."

"What are we doing to stop them?"

"General Wattly has a dozen counterbatteries still operating," he answered. "Colonel Kim is moving what's left of a battalion to the high ground above the spaceport. Wattly's adding a company of military police. I ordered Colonel Kim to blow the bunkerage, Cass."

"I'm going down there," she said.

"They need you here, Cass!"

"Where's my gear?"

"Here, sir!" A marine officer in full field armor lumbered down from the main entry alcove.

"Captain Quinn," the command duty officer said. "The chargé d'affaires is waiting to see you."

"I'm busy," Quinn replied, turning to meet the marine.

"It won't take long, Captain," Mather said, stepping down from the command duty tier. Quinn's first instinct was rage. That the duty officer, no doubt another LSA plant, had permitted Mather into the command bunker was infuriating. She took a deep breath and counted the pulse throbbing at her temples.

"What is it, Art?" she asked, turning to face the bureaucrat.

Mather removed glare goggles from a pair of watery, tortured eyes. One of her arms was in a sling.

"The chargé was injured helping with the evacuation, Cass," St. Pierre said.

"It's been a tough night," Quinn said, exhaling.

"Excuse me, Captain Quinn," Mather said. "I apologize for overriding your orders. The city lights should not have been kept on. I was only attempting to fulfill my mission. You must realize—"

"Apology accepted, Art," Quinn said, turning away.

"Please, Cassy," Mather remonstrated. The diplomat's pudgy features were drawn with appropriate sincerity. "I was wrong. I have ordered all State Department staff and all Legion Security Agency personnel to cooperate fully with the martial law edicts. That said, is there anything you want me to do?"

"Get out of the city," Quinn snapped. She turned back to the marine. The hard-featured, bruised-eyed major stood at attention, helmet under one arm, Quinn's heavy field bag held effortlessly in his other gauntleted hand.

"Duty officer, make ready a helo!" she shouted.

Watch personnel jumped to her commands. Mather, lips tight, marched up the opposite companionway and out the main vault exit.

"Your field gear, Captain," the marine officer said.

"Who are you?" she asked, relieving the marine of her equipment.

"Major Becker, sir. Colonel Kim said I was to stay with you wherever you went, sir."

"Lucky you," Quinn said wryly.

"Yes, sir," the marine thundered.

Becker's enthusiasm was good medicine, either that or the drugs were taking hold. Quinn's headache faded as she checked readouts on the bag's systems annunciator. Suit power was down to forty percent. Outside, the sun was elevating; she would get some solar charging.

Quinn lifted the stiff shoulder yoke over her head and adjusted the projectile armor around her torso and rib cage. Then she slipped into the shielded overalls. They smelled of sweat and grime, vestiges of her frantic trips outside the night before. The slick fabric's wicking interior felt cool against her sweaty skin; the suit's coolant system was low. She checked her sidearm and ammo load. Lastly she pulled her helmet from the bag.

"Radiation levels?" she asked, inspecting the seals.

"Some pockets, but less than level two for the most part,"

St. Pierre reported. "Cass, you should go north with the command center. I'll go into the field."

She glared up at St. Pierre's haggard visage. "Any more advice you'd care to impart?" she asked.

St. Pierre's features hardened. Not for long; the handsome countenance smoothly regained control. "You were hard on Mather," he said.

"I've seen her act before," Quinn replied, searching through the suit's survival pocket. Her ration pack was empty. "You got any food?"

He reached into his battle bag and pulled out a field ration. Quinn popped the wrapper and pushed the carbohydrate load into her mouth, washing it down with field nutrient.

"Send me down to the spaceport," St. Pierre said. "You should stay here—"

"You keep telling me you're a civilian," she replied. "Besides, I'm placing you officially in charge here."

"If I'm a civilian, then I should be—"

"You've just been reactivated and reassigned your old rank. Now do as you're ordered, Major," Quinn snapped, pulling on her helmet.

St. Pierre's reply was muffled by her helmet's sound-proofing, but Quinn had no trouble reading his lips. The physiologically impossible retort was mitigated only slightly by a resigned grin. Major Becker's eyes widened and an uncertain smile flickered on his hard mouth. Quinn concentrated on her system checks, activating helmet sensor and filtering systems. Satisfied, she secured power and opened her visors.

"Lead the way," she ordered.

Quinn followed Becker from the command center into a decontamination airlock. Outside the lock a steep ramp led into the staging bay, a heavily buttressed cavern housing the few remaining operational vehicles. A light breeze danced on her cheeks. The vaulted ceiling was caved in at one end. At the other end a doglegged tunnel had been excavated to the surface.

They walked into the glare of a cloudless morning. Light-active camouflage netting fluttered above the site, except where it had been retracted over the helo pad. Quinn reactivated her helmet systems. Her visor darkened; temperature readouts on her headup revealed a warm, humid morning. Radiation and contamination levels were negligible.

Where the admin building once stood there was nothing but fused debris. A traction-dozer was at work clearing away rubble, creating a blast bulwark around the command center perimeter. Fifty meters upslope, a medium caliber laser battery was being rehabilitated. Surrounded by brown-suited weapon techs, it was elevated into firing position, its power dissipation coils sparkling in the bright sunlight.

Under the open netting, a Legion combat helo waited, turbines running, its main rotors not yet engaged. Quinn stepped on a skid and was about to board when an alarm burped. The alert was quickly quelled.

"What's going on?" she asked. Her helmet was not receiving the sentry unit's tactical frequency.

"Someone just came up the hill," Becker said, signaling for his marines to board the helo. "A survivor from the bombardment."

An entry into the blast bulwark had been plowed through the eastern debris wall. Standing at the entrance, face in shadow, slumped a tall human, wide-shouldered yet slim. Quinn's heart vaulted into her throat.

She jumped from the helo and sprinted across the crater. Drawing near the bedraggled man, she slowed and pulled off her helmet. The tall person was mantled with dust, the color of his hair indistinguishable from the color of skin and clothes. His face was a chalky gray mask, streaked muddy with dried tears. From above those tragic blemishes radiated red-rimmed eyes of blue. Familiar eyes.

"Nash!" Quinn shouted.

"Cassy," the specter moaned, raising clenched fists.

"Where is Emerald, Nash?"

"I lost her, Cassy," Hudson cried. "I lost her."

THIRTY-SIX

SERGEANT GORDON

The morning broke clear and cold.

Charlie awoke to find the hunters gone from their sleeping nests. The boy crouched, shedding his blanket of dry leaves. Frost crunched delicately underfoot, but the boy's concentration was total; he did not feel the chill on his bare legs. Lake Shannon, green and placid, was visible through the hardwoods. Farther out the lake became a blue mirror reflecting the valley's glacier-hung western wall. In the purpled distance snow-draped granite speared upward from the planet's shadow, catching the first light of dawn.

Charlie lifted a tentative whistle: "I am here."

He listened. There was no answer. In the near shallows a fish plopped sideways, marring the lake's silky perfection with concentric ripples. The jeweled motion rolled hypnotically outward.

The stillness was broken by a distant, muted *carrumph*. Charlie's knife-edged alertness was heightened as the report echoed across the lake. A hunter shrieked—a cautionary signal.

Charlie's stomach growled its own imperative. A warrior eats when able. Searching away from the lake, the boy found abundant fungus on old trees. He disdained the convoluted black growth favored by the hunters; its pungent chalkiness upset his stomach. Instead he broke off chunks of a waxy parasite growing in the crotch of an ancient sugartree. He stuffed the substance, bland and dry, in his mouth. Acorns lay on the forest floor. Charlie ground the bitter nuts between his strong teeth, spitting out fibrous husks. Late sprigs of forest lettuce, flowering and no longer sweet, moistened his mouth, but not enough. He crawled into a thicket-shrouded gully and put his lips into the narrow rivulet running at its sandy bottom. He sucked gently, deliciously filling mouth and throat with icy wetness.

A hunter screeched—closer! More urgently. Charlie wormed his way along the gully, following the gurgling rill to the lake. One-son, ravishing a fish, waited. The sentry offered the human a strip of silvered flesh, gratefully accepted. Spitting bones as they moved, human and cliff dweller crept down the shadowed shoreline, returning to the edge of Longo's Meadow. At the forest's verge Captain Two and Bottlenose stared intently across the broad expanse. High clouds above the valley's eastern flank announced the coming day with swirls of pink.

Charlie clicked to gain attention. Bottlenose signaled impatiently for silence. The hunters were angry at the boy's stubbornness. Yet they refused to abandon him.

Charlie settled onto his haunches and hugged his knees, warding off the chill. One-son slipped into the thickets. Charlie scanned the treetops and counted a half-dozen hunters perched in vantage points along the meadow's rim. Spitter, bent-necked and sinister, hulked overhead on a weathered snag. The only sounds were the innocent melodies of morning.

As the gloaming surrendered to sunrise, a herd of toy deer emerged from the wood to graze. The toy deer jerked as one, sharp snouts and tall ears focused to the same point. The hunters stirred. A noise rose to Charlie's awareness! A familiar noise; a cargo lorry or a troop carrier at high rpm was coming from the direction of the ferry landing. He crept forward, hardly breathing. Spitter, knife in hand, pointed across Longo's Meadow, toward the road. Charlie looked up and sighted on Spitter's point. The deer bolted into the wood. The chirping of birds ceased.

More noises! Strange noises! A humming vibrated the air, a warbling buzz oscillating in pitch and volume. Charlie lifted his head higher, trying to see over the grasses. A strong, spindly hand smacked the back of his head and pushed his face into frost-crusted dirt.

"Down," Bottlenose hissed.

A large object whistled across the treetops and out over the lake, whiplashing the boughs and exploding flocks of water-fowl into tumultuous flight. The sky filled with panicked ducks and geese, their collective wing beats muffling all other noise, their swerving trajectories providing a kaleidoscope of color and texture. Charlie's attention was focused not on the rising flocks but on the unnatural object flying over the lake. The source of the pulsing noise stood on a short, rounded wing and pulled into a turn. It pointed back at shore, lowering altitude and whisking past them, so low and close that Charlie could see a pilot profiled in the bubble canopy, human-sized, wearing a black helmet. It streaked over the meadow, its engine warbling menacingly. The hunters rose from the grass to better follow its flight. So did Charlie.

An armored personnel carrier emerged from the forest, speeding along the ferry landing road. The truck threw up a rooster tail of dust as it whined in front of the alien airplane's sights. A star-spiked barb of energy blurted from the flying machine. Simultaneously the APC's traction engine exploded, and the stricken vehicle slammed abruptly onto its side. The warbling airship banked hard over, climbing above the trees at the far end of the meadow. Marines tumbled from the smoke-belching APC. Some sprinted to either side of the meadow. Some staggered, others crawled. One marine lay where he fell.

The alien flying ship positioned itself for another run. A second tortured engine rose above the sound of exploding fuel. Through the billowing black smoke of the destroyed truck careened a high-speed all-terrain vehicle. A marine sitting in the back of the bounding ATV fired a laser blaster. The attacker, impervious to the laser's impact, barrel-rolled for the hapless vehicle. The flying ship changed colors as it moved across its background. Over the lake the craft had been a light mottled gray. With trees and ridges as a backdrop, it became darker, a shimmering green; and as it barrel-rolled, color transitions flowed over the craft's exterior.

The alien aircraft tracked the swerving vehicle. Suddenly, a hair-thin coruscation from the attacker's nose sliced through the ATV. Its driver lost control; the all-terrain vehicle left the road and flipped over and over before coming to rest on its back, rear wheels racing. The marine at the back station was catapulted violently to the ground. By some miracle he was able to get to his feet. Grotesquely bent and dragging one leg, the marine staggered for the forest.

The alien flying machine gained altitude but slowed to a hover, as if stalking, its humming engine screaming up and down the tonal scale. It moved sideways, crabbing parallel to the forest's edge. From across the meadow an assault rifle fired, and then another. The alien craft peeled off and gained altitude.

"Alert!" Spitter chirped. From his vantage point the hunter extended a bony hand and swept it across an arc of thirty degrees and then flashed four fingers five times.

Aliens were approaching! Twenty!

Captain Two trilled a command. Hunters stationed in tree limbs launched themselves toward the lake, gliding low. Captain Two shrieked ultrasonically. Bottlenose darted for the shore. Charlie followed. The cliff dwellers moved rapidly along the stony beach, some sprinting on bandy legs, others skimming gracefully over the mirrored lake. Charlie followed, easily keeping up with those hunters on foot. The band of warriors sped along the shore toward where Lake Shannon outflowed into the Great River valley.

The yodeling vibration returned, growing louder. A hunter screeched. As one, the fleeing troop dove for the safety of the forest. Charlie darted into a skin-ripping thicket.

A warbling shadow erupted above the moraine marking the valley's end. From the brambles Charlie glimpsed its silvery form darting overhead. The alien flyer swept over the lake, turning steeply to reconnoiter the lakeshore. At Longo's Meadow it banked sharply and disappeared behind intervening trees. Captain Two shrieked a cautionary signal. The hunters scurried from their hiding places and resumed a more furtive movement along the shore.

A hunter trilled an alert, freezing the hunters in mid-stride. A panicked crashing lifted from the thickets. Grunts and heavy breathing lifted above the thrashing. Bows, knives, and short pikes were brought to bear. Captain Two and Spitter, brandishing Legion service pistols, took position at the front of the phalanx of warriors.

Charlie drew up abreast the noise and, fighting the explosions from his own lungs, listened intently. There was something familiar about the urgent exhalations.

"Make haste, Thunderhead!" Spitter shrieked, pushing the human.

Charlie avoided the hunter's grasp and ducked under a thicket branch. Whatever was approaching crashed heavily to the ground.

"Help me!" sobbed a human.

Charlie knew the voice. "Billy!" he gasped. It was Billy Gordon, his friend. Charlie dove into the underbrush, toward the labored breathing.

"Thunderhead!" Spitter shrieked. "Caution!"

"Billy!" Charlie whispered loudly. "Billy, over here!"

The moaning in the underbrush halted. "Charlie? Charlie Buccari?" came the astounded reply. The crashing in the brush resumed, and suddenly there was the marine, crawling through creepers and intertwined thickets. Billy Gordon pulled himself erect. He had lost his helmet, and one leg dragged uselessly.

"Billy, you okay?" Charlie whispered.

"Geez, you're alive!" Gordon gasped. "Everyone's worried sick, Charlie." He was sweating profusely and bleeding from the scalp. The frightened marine glanced over his shoulder.

"What happened, Billy?" Charlie asked.

"Cut a tram line," the marine said. "Attracted their attention, don't ya know."

"What . . . do they look like?" Charlie asked.

"Ain't seen any up close yet," Gordon gasped. He grimaced and sat down.

Spitter, eyes slit fiercely, hissed at Charlie's side. Captain Two and six warriors materialized from the brush.

"Come, Thunderhead," Captain Two chirped, his pistol ready.

Charlie glanced at the stricken human and then back at the hunter leader. "No," the boy pleaded.

Captain Two signed: "Warrior badly injured."

Charlie understood all too well. His brain spun, searching for an answer. He was with hunters—he was a hunter. In battle, hunters killed their own wounded. The cliff dwellers raised their weapons.

"Billy," Charlie pleaded. "You gotta get on your feet, Billy. Go back the other way. Please, Billy!"

The injured marine looked up. His frightened expression was replaced with a look of slump-shouldered resignation.

"Yeah, sure, Charlie," the injured marine said. Eyeing the menacing hunters, Gordon turned and crawled back into the thicket, his unsteady progress marked by cracking leaves and twigs.

An iron grip seized Charlie's forearm. The boy turned to confront the scarred countenance of the warrior leader. Captain Two's double-lidded anthracite eyes drilled into his. An ultrasonic blast emanated from Captain Two's gaping maw; grating vibrations blasted Charlie's sinuses and inner ears, yet he heard no sound. Spitter hissed his disgust, ragged white teeth displayed in fury. Captain Two chirped sharply. The angry warrior lowered his bow and melted soundlessly into the foliage.

"Flee now, Thunderhead!" Captain Two shrieked.

Without a word the boy dashed into the brush, crawling and squirming. Gunfire sounded behind him, and the pulsating noises of the alien flying machine persisted in the distance. Hunters stalked around him, rarely visible, occasionally chirping signals.

A scream, ghastly with triumph, eclipsed all other noises, all other sensations. Not human, the murderous wailing erupted into the skies, echoing from the valley walls like rending metal. The small hairs on Charlie's neck lifted, but it was the accompanying subtone that mortified the young man. A horrendous bellowing, a plaintive beseeching, lower in pitch and volume than the victory scream. It was a human crying in anguish.

Shuddering, Charlie acknowledged Billy Gordon's last mortal exhalation.

THIRTY-SEVEN

T.S.P. NEW EDMONTON

"I'm coming with you," Hudson protested. The grime-covered wraith transformed. He stood defiantly erect and filled his lungs.

"No," Quinn said.

Conflicting emotions ripped at her soul. The fates had stolen her daughter, but they had spared her husband. She wanted him at her side, yet her duty was clear; Hudson was another settler in her charge, a soul to be protected.

"Give me a nutrient hit and a stim dose," Hudson said. "I'm not leaving you, Cass."

"Enough," she shouted. "I'm ordering you to join the evacuation. Don't make me use force, Nash."

"Cassy," Hudson pleaded.

"Take this civilian into custody," she shouted.

Hudson's shoulders slumped. Combat-rigged marines surged forward. A medic at Hudson's side took him by the arm. Hudson yanked free and pulled Quinn into an embrace. She waved off the lunging marines and threw her arms around the father of her child, bemoaning the unyielding barrier of her field armor.

"B-Be careful, Cassy," he stammered, eyes welling.

"I gotta go, Nash," she said, pulling away. She lifted her hand in farewell. Hudson touched her fingers and turned away, striding ahead of his escorts. Would she would ever see him again? Heart heavy with premonition, she boarded the helo. Major Becker and his marines were already tethered in. The marine signaled the pilot, and the main rotors engaged. The sleek craft surged up and forward, pressing Quinn into a hard-panned jump seat.

The pilot lifted skyward only high enough to hurdle the bunker's rubble heap. Following the nap of the terrain, the helo streaked down the rolling topography, across blasted landscape. Quinn checked her helmet annunciator for contamination and radiation levels. Nothing. She rebelliously pulled off her headgear and stared out at the ruins, the pummeling slipstream drying her tears and thrashing her greasy hair.

The humid air stank of burnt metal and evaporated plastic. Road grids were unrecognizable. A few blackened buildings stabbed upward, their facades crumpled, their materials fused with buckled rubble. Scattered conflagrations still burned, tumbling gray and white smoke into the air, but most fires were reduced to smoldering hot spots. The helo curved between clouds of acrid embers; Quinn's eyes burned. Reluctantly she returned the helmet to her head, dropped visors, and engaged environmental filtering. Her comm light immediately illuminated.

"Captain Quinn," Major Becker said over the intercom. "Mr. Hudson commandeered an ATV. He's driving south."

"Didn't waste any time, did he?" she replied.

The helo cruised beyond the southern limits of the city, flying over undamaged cultivation and isolated agrarian hamlets. Beyond the grain fields and rice paddies vast expanses of wild grass spread across their course. The helo's rotor-wash whipped an emphatic wake through the savannah, scattering scarlet-hued flocks of grain egrets, exploding coveys of yellow swallowtails and multitudes of other birds. At less frequent intervals, herds of black-antlered gazelle and white-eyed antelope burst from their path. Memories of hunting trips with Hudson came forward, memories of stalking grass dog and popper on the teeming savannah, of camping under constellations delineated not with a few meek stars but rather with brilliant slashes of galactic energy.

All that had changed, Quinn thought. A day ago her life held so much promise. She possessed a family; and she had

Genellan—an entire planet to explore. Hudson had begged her to resign from the Legion space force, to start living her own life—at his side, of course. For Hudson it was an easy choice: family was the highest duty. Quinn knew better; she had a higher duty. Her daughter was lost, her family shattered. But her problems did not matter; all human families on Genellan were threatened, and it was her duty to protect them.

The helo approached the ocean. The pilot tracked along the spaceport road, making a sweeping turn along the shore. Below, a convoy motored parallel to the rolling sea cliffs, past the quarry and concrete processing plant.

"Where are we going, Major?" Quinn asked dully.

"Command post is on the promontory west of the airport," Major Becker reported, his stolid features animating.

"You sound almost happy, Major," she said.

"My troops are down there, sir," Becker replied.

Quinn nodded and watched the bluff grow nearer, her own resolve burgeoning. The young men and women defending the planet were her troops, too.

The coastal road curved inland, beginning a switchback that would take it over the promontory. The spaceport, still obscured by the elevation, lay beyond the high ground. Quinn knew the vantage point well. The helo climbed the craggy, tree-crowned rib of bedrock protruding into the ocean. The pilot curved into the wind and planted his craft on the landing zone, a flat expanse below the ridge line.

Major Becker and his marines leapt from the hatch and sprinted across the landing zone. Quinn followed. No sooner was she clear of the helo's spinning blades than the sleek aircraft lifted skyward. As the thumping of rotors receded, her aural sensors detected the endless crashing of ocean breakers. She opened her visors and inhaled briny vapors. A wind-carved copse of cypress gracing the point of land added its perfume to the euphoric blend. It was a beautiful day.

Perspiration rolled into her eyes. Sagging under the weight of her battle armor, Quinn hiked to the top of the promontory, traversing into the shade of gnarled and twisted cypress trees. Engineers had thrown up defenses along the ridge line, defiling the land. A mobile CCCI unit and a brace of missile pods were bunkered into the lee of the high ground. A shallow trench curved inland along the ridge. Extracted dirt, red as blood, and shattered stone, white as bone, formed a telltale breastwork. Marines manning field blasters were spaced at intervals along its length.

A lusty cheer lifted along the line. Major Becker raised a hand to acknowledge his welcome. Colonel Kim emerged from the CCCI bunker to confront his returning officer. The marines exchanged salutes and a few brief words. Kim turned to Quinn as she approached the crest. In the distance, lifting into her view beyond the ridge, spread T.S.P. New Edmonton. The spaceport's primary rollout runway was bordered by luminous green tidal marshes, beyond which rose a narrow string of barrier islands. Low dunes, soft and textured with sea grass, gently repulsed white-curling breakers.

Quinn searched the expansive landing facility. The regimented, multihued tanks of the spaceport's fuel farm were still intact.

"Good morning, Captain," Colonel Kim said, his stern tone and brusque saluting belying the salutation. The marine did not want Quinn there. She was a science officer, not a line officer—a complication in the warrior's chain of command. Line officers led warriors into battle, not science officers.

"Why have you not blown the bunkers, Colonel?" Quinn demanded, returning the marine's salute.

"My demolition teams are withdrawing as we speak, sir," Kim replied stiffly. "They'll be clear in less than three minutes. You may give the destruction order if you wish, Captain."

"No, Colonel. You're in command," Quinn said. "What's your plan?"

"Aye, sir," Kim replied, his demeanor softening. "General Wattly's energy batteries will interdict the entry vessels as they penetrate the atmosphere. If any landers reach the runways, we will engage with tactical laser and artillery from enfilading positions on this high ground. Should any aliens leave their ships, there are four autonomous attack units in full kill mode deployed on the spaceport grounds."

"Only four?" Quinn asked, analyzing the terrain.

"All we've got," Kim replied. "Four AAUs can do a lot of damage."

She grunted. The spaceport was situated on a wide tide-water shelf, uncontained to the west and north. The curving high ground on which Kim's marines waited melded into grassy hills less than five kilometers to the northwest.

"Your flank isn't supported," Quinn said.

"My marines will adjust to the battle if it should break out of the spaceport. But yes, sir, you are correct. My right flank is vulnerable."

"Do you have a fallback, Colonel?" Quinn asked.

"Earth, sir," Kim replied evenly.

"Right . . . Earth," she answered.

"You will excuse me, Captain." Kim said. "Major Becker, rejoin your men."

Becker rendered a razor-sharp salute. His chiseled face bore a grim smile as he pivoted for the trench line.

"Captain Quinn," Kim said, "I'm returning to the command center. Will you join me?"

"In a minute, Colonel," she replied.

Kim nodded curtly and departed. Left alone, Quinn moved back into the cool shade of the cypress trees. She walked out onto the headland and stared out to sea. A shining white fish eagle, backdropped by the ocean's translucent blue depths, swooped below her elevation, riding fresh breezes welling upward against the face of the rocky cliffs. A day too brilliant for war, she thought. No one should die on such a day.

A ready alert pulsed over the tactical frequency, synching communication protocols. Quinn adjusted her helmet receiver to the designated antijamming code. A technician, his monotonic voice purged of all emotion, commenced an abbreviated countdown.

"Fire in the frigging hole!" someone else bellowed, as if to punctuate the sterile reporting.

Quinn activated her visors, shutting out the odors of the ocean. She turned to face the sprawling spaceport. The seaward bunkerage went first. The stuttering explosion jolted the ground underfoot as the low volatility hydroxide tanks went up in rapid sequence. The thermocatalyst tanks to landward went immediately after, blowing in two mind-numbing detonations. Thermal pulses darkened Quinn's faceplate and baked her chest armor. A ripple of turbulence tugged at the thick fabric of her battle suit and clipped branches from the twisted tree limbs. She went to her knees behind a tree trunk.

Recurring shock pulses clapped the air. Quinn watched the demolition in resigned frustration. So much hard work gone. Where once there had been orderly rows of bunkering tanks, there were now only sheets of rolling flame gouting skyward, fanned by the freshening offshore breeze. A twirling, slashing blizzard of smoking debris rained down, clattering madly on the runways and splashing insanely into the ocean. An obscene column of oily black smoke billowed across the network of runways and taxiways, tumbling reluctantly skyward.

Someone whistled over the tactical circuit.

"Cut the crap," the voice of authority admonished. Quinn recognized Major Becker's stern tones.

With the tank fires still rumbling, Quinn got to her feet and headed inland. Emerging from the cypress grove, she trotted behind the trench line, nodding encouragingly to the young warriors, returning their frightened smiles and gestures with uncertain smiles of her own. What were their odds? There had been no survivors at Shaula or at Oldfather, and only a fortunate few at Hornblower. Genellan was different. This time they would give the Ulaggi a little heartburn.

But the nagging question remained: Who would survive?

Quinn came to the trenched ramp that led into the CCCI center. She marched past the headquarters guards and through the command center's environmental lock. The unit's airconditioning registered immediately. In the confined service alcove, she opened her visors and mated an umbilical with the power unit of her battle armor, recharging her suit systems and purging waste reservoirs. Lining one bulkhead of the cramped main compartment was a row of technicians, their integration helmets softly bottom-lit by luminescent data units. Colonel

Kim paced behind the technicians like some Mephistophelian demon, his helmet visor glowing red with reflected light.

"Captain Quinn," came a voice from behind her.

"Yes," she replied, turning to confront a military police officer.

"Security has intercepted a civilian in a stolen ATV," the MP reported. "Name of Hudson. Says you're expecting him, sir."

Quinn closed her eyes. He had made good time. She wanted so badly to see Hudson again, to touch him. Perhaps for the last time.

"Send him north. In custody," she replied, growing furious with her own weakness. "He doesn't belong here."

"Ah . . . yes, sir," the officer stammered. "Sir, I'm afraid he talked his way past the sentries. He's on his way up the hill."

Quinn had to laugh—at her own misplaced joy. She would touch Hudson, one last time, and then she would load him into his ATV and send him north, under guard.

Unplugging from the charging unit, she marched up the trench ramp into bright sunlight. Her vantage point on the backside of the promontory gave her a clear view of the coastal road. A convoy approached the marshaling area in the grassy valley below. A single ATV trailed the military vehicles. The personnel carriers and supply lorries pulled off the road into a staging area, but the ATV was waved through. Quinn watched the ATV climb the gentle traverse to the top of the promontory. Two hundred meters short of the crest the vehicle pulled into an unloading area.

A tall individual dressed in full battle armor and carrying an assault rifle jumped from the vehicle. He jogged uphill, glancing frantically about. Quinn lifted an arm. Hudson pulled off his helmet with a flourish and broke into a sprint. Unable to stop herself, Quinn ran down the hill. Hudson's sandy blond hair whipped about in the rising breeze; his radiantly blue eyes, blazing with pitched emotion, caught the sun. The tall man stumbled to an uncertain walk as he drew near, bending to peer through Quinn's helmet visor. She fought to keep the smile from her face and the tears from her eyes.

"I should have you shot," she growled.

"Sure . . . okay," Hudson said, smiling sadly. "Later we could go for a swim."

"Idiot," she whispered, fists on her hips.

"I had to be with you, Cass," Hudson said, moving closer.

His handsome face bore a tragic expression. They had lost their daughter. Now, more than ever, they needed each other. Quinn opened her arms, and Hudson came to her. They embraced—like turtles, their chest armor clanking dully. Hudson backed off and touched her through her open visor. Quinn held his hand to her cheek for several seconds. Reluctantly, she pulled away.

"Put your helmet on and get off—" she said, stepping back.

Her words died in her throat. A low rumbling intruded on her awareness, distant thunder from ominously clear skies.

"They're coming down," Hudson said.

Quinn started running uphill. She felt Hudson on her heels and wheeled on him. "Get out of here, Nash," she shouted.

"You've got more important things to do than yell at me," Hudson replied, hefting his assault rifle. "I'm not leaving, Cass."

She glared; anger, fear, and love exploding in her heart.

"Follow me," she ordered. "You belong to Major Becker. You do what he says, or I will have you shot."

"Lead the way, Captain," Hudson replied.

She found Becker in the middle of the trench line. Hudson's reputation in the konish battles was legend among the marines. Becker wasted no time detailing him to a reserve infantry platoon. Hudson, rifle in hand, jumped enthusiastically into the trench with his new dirtmates. He threw Quinn a kiss before donning his helmet.

She ignored him, returning her full attention to the tactical situation. The radio chatter on the fire-control circuit was picking up.

"Securing all radars," the monotonic technician ordered. "Acoustical and optical tracking systems only."

"All units report," Colonel Kim boomed on tactical.

Quinn's helmet scanner picked up the chain reaction of

acknowledgments. Radio chatter was curt and businesslike. She looked around. The marines, hugging their weapons, stared intently at the razor-sharp horizon.

"Secure your visor, Captain," Major Becker ordered.

"Yes, of course," she replied, embarrassed. Taking a last deep breath of ocean air, Quinn deployed her helmet visors.

An alert sounded.

"We have optical acquisition," the sterile report sounded.

All heads turned seaward. Two more muted sonic booms drifted in from the sea; and then three more. Agonizingly long minutes dragged by.

"Estimate twelve minutes to touchdown," the technician droned.

Ocean waves pounded the shore. Sea birds screeched with innocent arrogance. Quinn increased visor magnification to maximum.

"There they are," Becker said, pointing out to sea.

Quinn studied the horizon, moving her scanpoint in short increments. Her stomach sank. She resolved a rapidly descending object, too distant to discern its shape. And then another. And then a third.

"What's General Wattly waiting for?" Quinn asked.

The words were barely out of her mouth when the remaining Legion batteries opened fire. From emplacements on highlands far to the north, Wattly's civil defense lasers discharged, rending the air overhead with low-angled bolts of energy. The beams were invisible, but the atmosphere rang with their passage.

Far out to sea, against a perfect blue sky, the closest alien penetrator blossomed into a crimson and black fireball.

"Kill the frigging bastards!" someone shouted.

Fists and weapons lifted along the line of troops. A helmet-muffled cheer rose over the pounding of the surf. Exhilaration rose in Quinn's throat as the lurid fireball tumbled in slow motion from the lustrous skies, trailing black smoke.

"Yes!" she screamed, jumping from the trench to better view the downward plunging enemy.

Her exultation lasted mere seconds. With heart-stopping

resonance, the skies exploded in incandescent yellows and golds. Quinn's brain throbbed with the vibration. The very atmosphere blossomed with calamitous energy as answering counterbattery fire rained down from orbit. Relentlessly, murderously, beam after beam, columns of hot death pounded the planet, seeking to quash its defenders.

Quinn's visor darkened instantaneously to pitch, shutting out the nerve-burning luminescence, but the high magnification of her optics caused immediate flash blindness. Disoriented, she fell to her knees and groped blindly for the trench line. She knew she had only to crawl up the gentle grade, but after several eternal seconds of scrambling and not finding the excavation she knew to be only a few meters away, she realized she could no longer tell up from down.

"Help," she shouted, her ears deaf to her own voice.

Gale force winds blasted sandy soil against her visor. Heat lightning crackled the ether, more felt than heard. Thunder shook the ground. The reek of ozone overwhelmed her filtering system. Fear began to suffocate. Panic seized her heart, but then a strong hand grabbed her arm. Quinn scrambled along the ground, aiding her rescuer's insistent tugging. With exquisite relief she was pulled tumbling into the ragged ditch. Recovering her sense of direction, yet still deaf and blind, she pushed herself into a sitting fetal position and cowered against the lee of the breastwork. Her shivering hip pressed against a hard-muscled thigh. A powerful arm fell over her shoulders, and she was comforted. Huddling in a dirt ditch was no protection against the devastation of alien lasers, but touching another human being calmed her racing heart and connected her to life. Alive. She was still alive.

It only seemed like hell.

THIRTY-EIGHT

LOST AND FOUND

"We've lost contact with Colonel Kim," the communication officer reported.

"Dammit!" St. Pierre shouted, his frustration building to rival his burgeoning fear.

Decked out in battle armor though still bare-headed, St. Pierre monitored the remote sensing outputs and the passive frequency filters, trying to get a fix on the descending aliens. Energy beams thundered overhead, each moaning impact punctuated by flickering lights. At last surrendering to the power surges, the lights dimmed and died, as did the air-conditioning. Emergency systems kicked in, flooding the command bunker with an oppressive red glow. Primary lighting flickered back on, but the circulation systems remained inoperative. A wispy layer of smoke and dust formed, heightening St. Pierre's desire to leave the concrete hole in the ground, to flee from the pulverized city.

"General Wattly reports all civil defense batteries destroyed," the admin duty officer reported.

They were officially defenseless.

"Goldmine Station is taking hits," an intelligence tech shouted.

The alien motherships had dropped low enough in orbit to fly under the umbrella of the konish defense station. There remained no sanctuary on the surface of Genellan.

"Communication with the kones is gone," the communication officer reported. "Land line is dead."

"Aliens on the ground," the intel technician reported.

"Confirmed communication intercepts all around the konish evacuation centers."

"How the hell'd the bugs get on the ground?" someone muttered.

Nine alien large penetrators had tracked in from the south. One had been destroyed, two others were aborting back to orbit, but the others were still descending. Numerous smaller contacts, coming in from all points of the compass, flickered ephemerally on the passive screens. Mysterious craft, their trajectories defied analysis.

"We now have unconfirmed reports of aliens on the ground to the north," the watch officer reported. "Evacuation area two."

St. Pierre prayed it was mass hysteria.

"The evacuation command center is operational," the communication officer announced.

St. Pierre glanced up at the functioning holo-vid. General Wattly's dark image glared back.

"Go," St. Pierre shouted.

"Manned and ready," Wattly pronounced.

"Shifting operations to the dispersal bunker," St. Pierre ordered. "General Wattly, you are in command."

"I relieve you," Wattly replied. "Secure your station and report in as soon as possible. Good luck and God bless you, sir. Wattly out." The carrier signal terminated and the holo-vid went blank.

"Shut her down!" St. Pierre shouted, pulling on his helmet. "Report to the marshaling area for muster. I want everyone in their vehicles and ready to go the second this bombardment stops! Let's move!"

At least it was warm.

Et Silmarn slumped against the wall, straining to listen, his hearing impaired from innumerable concussions. The popping of electrical fires created static, difficult to resolve from the nagging buzzing in his skull.

The Ulaggi attack came suddenly. The konish sensors had been focused on the energy bombardment over New

Edmonton. Mesmerized, the kones watched the alien ships gliding in from the sea. A clever misdirection. Ulaggi ground troops, mysteriously delivered to the planet's surface, took out the konish laser batteries and attacked the tunnel entrances without overture, annihilating the Hegemonic security forces and breaching the environmental locks within seconds of the first alert. Video systems in the tunnels revealed images of squat, wide-shouldered monsters scurrying with coordinated ferocity into the primary bores, blasting and murdering the defenders. Their faces were obscured by dark visors. Thin beams of scarlet twinkled from the middle of each helmet, malevolent pinpricks of light—sensors of some sort.

A different noise! Something heard, a patterned scraping. Footfalls perhaps, or was it just disordered signals from his battered brain? White-blue sparks danced insanely in the blackened corridors of the konish evacuation shelters, providing a desultory, stroboscopic illumination. Et Silmarn peered into thick blue smoke and imagined terrible death stalking the murky shadows. With indomitable will the noblekone forced himself calm. Rippling emanations from his tortured fear bladders quieted, if only for brief seconds. Fear served little purpose now. Et Silmarn's breather unit purged contaminants from the air, but its filters could not remove the redolence of his own terror.

Another explosion jolted the ground. Et Silmarn collapsed to all fours and remained there, fatigue overwhelming courage. He wanted so badly to yield, to lay down and rest. The noblekone, crawling on all fours, pressed ever deeper into the maze of maintenance tunnels, desperately seeking a place to hide.

The soldiers of the Northern Hegemony had fought valiantly, but they were too few. The Ulaggi warriors, chopping through the dead defenders and attackers clogging the tunnels, were automatons, not overtly brave, rather insanely indifferent to their own survival, resigned to death, programmed to kill. Powerful grenades, fanning energy rays, and flaming gases were employed profligately. Imperial Guard detachments fought back with blaster and shoulder artillery, exacting a terrible toll from the aliens. In desperation, the few remaining security officers had moved the governor from the administration area, pushing Et Silmarn on his flight into the bowels of the tunnels. One by one his soldiers had died, trying to buy time. Time.

Et Silmarn had chanced to be in an interchamber airlock when the air had exploded. The last of his guards perished with that blast. Et Silmarn struggled through a debris-clogged breech and found himself crawling over dead and dying kones, their Genellan suits blasted into shreds. There were aliens among the carnage, too, their horrible countenances, moist and gray, made unspeakable in death.

Et Silmarn regretted not compelling more of his charges to evacuate. Less than a hundred kones, out of six thousand in the bunkers, had volunteered to brave the elements, to join the humans in their flight into the planet's cold, cruel hills. Had it not been for his responsibilities, Et Silmarn would willingly have gone with the humans. To remain holed up underground was certain death. Genellan's climate might kill, but the planet destroyed without malice. Perhaps for those kones courageous enough to go with the humans, rescue would come in time.

Precious time.

The last transmissions from Kon indicated that King Ollant had launched the fleet. There would be a great battle in space. The Hegemonic space fleet and the Planetary Defense Forces would engage the invaders. Perhaps the humans, too, would arrive in time, with Tar Fell's ships. Tar Fell was due back within the moon cycle. Rescue was coming, but time was running out. Et Silmarn knew it was too late for him.

At least it was warm. He would not die cold. Foolish thoughts.

Et Silmarn leaned against the wall. Something moved in the acrid, stagnant layers of smoke. Red beams pierced the blackness, lancing scarlet tubes dancing with motes of destruction. Et Silmarn rose to his hinds, his helmet brushing the overhead. He had seen the squat, broad-shouldered aliens. Had seen them on the vid images hurtling down the tunnels. Had seen them dead in the corridors, their gray faces distorted with death. Something different stood before him now, a horror, knife-thin, tall and cruel. The noblekone stared into the visage of a dagger-faced alien, its gibbous silver eyes on a level with his own.

There is no mercy in those eyes, Et Silmarn thought. A seeping chill flooded his being. He would die cold after all.

Artemis Mather stared out at the energy-devoured slopes, her indignation long ago given over to a mood as black as the land. The convoy of Legion security vehicles bounced across the tortured terrain, at last reaching unscathed road eight kilometers beyond the northernmost edge of the city. The road was undamaged, but the surrounding environs were devastated. Climbing grasslands scorched to crumbling carbon gave way slowly to foothill chaparral singed rusty brown. In the near distance, tall, russet-trunked trees formed a horizon-spanning barrier. Whole companies of redwoods were enveloped in flames, pillars of flickering yellow fueling gray and white pillars of smoke.

Whooom! The atmosphere flared yellow with the onset of another Ulaggi bombardment. Mather's anger was transformed instantly to fear. Beam after beam slammed down. The all-terrain vehicle bucked with each brick-hard shock wave; its windshields darkened instantly to leaden opacity. Mather was suffocated in darkness. Buffered by the protective structure of the ATV, her visors cleared quickly, revealing only the green luminescence of the command vehicle's instrumentation. She looked forward, into the driver's compact station.

"Sonic guidance is saturated," the driver shouted into his radio.

"Switch to road radar," the convoy commander ordered.

"Won't they detect us?" Mather cried.

"No choice, sir," the driver shouted over his shoulder. "Unless you just want to sit here and hope the beams don't walk over us. There's a tube station a half kilometer ahead. We can get underground. Convoy commander's set in coordinates. That's where we're heading."

The blinded vehicles rolled along, tracking their position

with radar. The forward windshield, in the lee of the energy blasts, lightened somewhat, giving a forward view. The trucks accelerated for the tube terminus.

Tall trees drew closer, the southern-facing foliage uniformly brown and heat-shriveled. The road brought them to a settlement on the forest's edge, prefabricated homes and admin structures supporting a logging mill and military training facility. Battle-armored marines guarding the roads waved them into the tube terminal's parking area. The terminus structure was standard Legion architecture, art deco, yellow and buff composite construction, an unnatural edifice nestled against the towering forest. A lake flashed blue beyond the trees.

The bombardment abated as they pulled into the parking lot. The convoy halted next to three konish all-terrain vehicles, bus-sized, with huge, soft tires and articulating waists. Mather leapt leadenly to the ground and made her best effort to dash for cover. Her portly physique was not designed for anything faster than a dignified stroll. A squad of armored marines sprinted from the tube station to assist the new arrivals. Black-suited Legion security agents spilled from the convoy vehicles, lugging communication and security equipment. Mather joined the flow of people moving to safety.

"What is that?" someone shouted.

People had stopped, staring and pointing. Mather pulled up and followed the fingers. Streaking low over the charred landscape to the south were three ovoid aircraft, visible only when silhouetted against the smoke-filled sky.

"They ain't ours," a marine shouted.

A stuttering spasm of energy slammed to ground beyond the alien flyers. Mather's helmet visor went pitch-black. Recoiling, she lost balance and stumbled to the ground.

"Move!" someone commanded.

She was blinded. Thudding feet pounded past on both sides. Strong hands grabbed her arms and legs, and she was carried bodily across the square. Echoing footfalls and shouts announced their entrance into the tube station. After a short distance she was dumped unceremoniously onto smooth tiles, bruising her hips and elbows.

"Help," she pleaded, more indignant than injured. Her aches and dented pride were quickly displaced in her hierarchy of discomfort by an overpowering stench. Gagging and near panic, she imagined herself suffocating in the noxious odors. Mather mewled louder, but her pitiful alarm was overwhelmed by a greater threat. Aboveground the bombardment continued with renewed fury, and her pleas for help were drowned in the manic resonance of the singing ether. Abandoned, her heart grew dark with fear.

In time the thundering bombardment ended. The strobing pulses ceased and her vision improved. She detected people moving.

"Is that you, Art?" an excited voice called out.

A familiar voice. Jadick Jones-Burton.

"Jad!" she cried. Never could Mather have imagined his whining voice would be so welcome to her ears. Her visors were clearing and she discerned her assistant's pear-shaped form silhouetted by the tunnel's entrance. The man slid to the ground at her side.

"I just finished talking with General Wattly," Jones-Burton said. "St. Pierre has evacuated the primary command center—"

"Why do they attack?" Mather raged. "Why won't they talk to us?"

"Oh my, who knows," Jones-Burton replied.

"Somewhere . . . sometime," Mather said softly, "humans must have done the Ulaggi some unspeakable wrong. Something happened that we don't know about, Jad. The admirals are keeping it secret."

"If something happened, it happened at Shaula," Jones-Burton surmised. "The AC fleet was slaughtered for some reason. Maybe a human committed an unspeakable cultural crime. Raped the bug king's daughter, or some such."

"Mankind's history is filled with militant transgressions, Jad," Mather said, her mind finding solace in debate. "That's why you and I are here, to talk, to communicate, to prevent the military from bulling in where they don't belong. There has to be a reason, Jad. A highly technical race like the Ulaggi just does not attack another race for the pleasure of murder."

"Absolutely right, Art," Jones-Burton said, stifling a yawn.

"It stinks in here," she said, her febrile thoughts displaced by her olfactory discomfort.

"Kones," Jones-Burton said, pointing.

Mather followed his finger into the terminal's dark interior and discerned the source of the stench. On the lower level were two score or more of the mountainous, gray-suited creatures. They huddled against the walls like monstrous, helmet-wearing slugs.

"Whew!" Mather exhaled, her fear dissipating.

"We should talk with them, shouldn't we?" Jones-Burton said.

"Yes," she replied, pushing to her feet.

She was a diplomat; it was her place to communicate with the hulking aliens. The kones, after all, were allies. She limped down the ramp. Widely spaced emergency lanterns, splashes of garish yellow in the shadows, illuminated the walls. Dark though it was, the security of the tube terminal's thick walls was sorely welcome.

Beyond the circles of light, faintly aglow with eldritch strips of emergency luminescence, were the pitch-black bores of the transportation tubes. Tube cars had stopped running, but a steady trickle of refugees, hunched specters, straggled up from the bore. Military police and civil defense personnel with glowing armbands assisted the injured.

Mather shifted her attention to the kones. The giants watched her approach, rumbling among themselves. The stink increased with each downward step.

"Who-ah is in charge?" Mather asked in konish.

"I am," said a giant, speaking Legion.

A kone loomed up on all fours and bowed; a noblekone, Mather discerned, vaguely familiar. Grunting, she bowed in the konish fashion, dropping to her bruised knees and touching forehead to the cool tiles.

"My name is Artemis Mather," she said, struggling back to

her feet. "I am the Tellurian Legion chargé d'affaires. Is there anything I can do for you?"

"We have met, Diplomat Mather," the noblekone said. "I am Et Joncas, assistant to Governor Et Silmarn."

"Ah, yes," Mather replied.

"Have you heard anything from our bunkers?" Et Joncas asked, eye tufts drooping. "There were rumors of an attack."

"More than rumors, Your Excellency," Mather replied. "The konish evacuation bunkers were under attack when communications were cut off. I regret to inform you that their security was breached. I am sorry."

The noblekone slumped onto his haunches, his slab features sagging with worry. A putrid wave of emotion suffused the area. Mather looked away, laboring to control her disgust. Refugees staggering up the ramp from the tube tunnels captured Mather's attention. A sooty-faced, shell-shocked urchin shuffled near. Her filthy blond hair was spiked with oily grime. The little girl stopped abruptly and stared dumbly at the kones. There was something familiar about the child's walk, the thin neck, the angle of her head.

Mather knelt and took hold of the little girl's hand. "Emerald?" she asked uncertainly.

The urchin looked up.

"Emerald Quinn," Mather repeated, taking the child into her arms.

"Y-Yes, ma'am," the filthy little girl mumbled.

THIRTY-NINE

ALIEN LANDING

The bombardment stopped.

"What's next?" the person next to Quinn exhaled. It was Major Becker. The marine stirred and moved abruptly away. She felt abandoned.

Quinn brought her breathing under control. She dared to lift her head. Her visors seemed clear, but her vision was still scarred with glowing orange after-images. She squinted out the sides of her eyes, desperately trying to regain her sight. Her tongue tasted metallic, and the odor of burnt copper filled her sinuses, but at least she could still taste and smell. And hear; the pounding of surf and the roaring of fuel fires reasserted themselves.

"Flash Condition Alpha, people!" Becker broadcast. "Set battle visors. Periscopes only. Scouting personnel only. Everyone else keep their brains below their butts. Anybody not know the difference?"

Quinn's vision slowly improved, but the accumulated punishment was having increasingly persistent effects. Becker's image was haloed as he moved down the trench line, issuing orders. Quinn pushed to her feet to squint over the breastwork. Her eyes accommodated distances better than the near field, but colors were washed out. The once livid sky was now faded to a destitute blue. The tank farm fires raged, spawning greasy black columns of smoke that merged into a single prodigious cloud. The wind had strengthened and veered to its prevailing westerly flow, pushing the noxious, billowing obscuration directly down the runway's final approach course.

"Get back in the frigging hole, dammit . . . sir!" Becker barked.

Quinn dropped obediently into the trench, satisfied that she could still see. The lee rim of the trench was lower than the breastwork, and she marveled at her view of ocean and beach, of grassy hills and blue sky, the tints slowly enriching. The bombardment had been so overwhelming, so terrible. She had expected to witness utter devastation, but except for the fuel fires, her surroundings were unscathed. The energy bombardment had evidently impacted to the north, targeting General Wattly's energy weapons.

"One reentry vehicle confirmed destroyed," the exasperatingly calm voice reported from the command center. "Six bogies remain active in the atmosphere. Three are continuing their approach to this sector. Five minutes to alien landing."

"Hold fire until the first bug ship is over the numbers. Firing sequence as briefed." Colonel Kim's clipped tones came over the tactical frequency. "Report readiness."

From down the line came a well-ordered sequence of status reports. The voices revealed a curious mixture of fear and courage. Intrepid humanity against the horrible unknown.

"Keep your thick skulls down." Becker's raging command brought Quinn the rest of the way back from fear to anger. The officer worked his way back toward her, positioning assets and exhorting his men. He stopped at her side.

"I'm calling up an ATV to get you out of here, Captain," Becker said. "Colonel Kim is ordering your immediate departure."

"Negative," she countermanded.

"Sir, this is no place—" Becker protested.

"I leave when you leave, Major," Quinn said. "Colonel Kim may be on-scene battle commander, but I'm still in charge of this settlement. Do your job. I'll do mine."

The frustrated marine looked into the sky.

"I leave when you leave, Major," she repeated.

"Aye, sir," Becker replied, bringing his gaze back down.

"Bogie at five kilometers," the fire-control technician reported.

Becker turned to look. Quinn lifted up to do the same. The first alien penetrator soared down the glide slope, growing ominously large, a black delta-wing planform heading right for the oily smoke tumbling thickly along the runway. The alien ship would have to fly into the billowing cloud in order to land.

"Maybe it will wave off," she said.

"Bogie at three kilometers," fire-control reported.

The Ulaggi landing craft slid undeterred onto final, disappearing into the tumbling obscuration.

"Optical acquisition lost," came the report over the tactical frequency. "Touchdown in twenty seconds."

"Stand by," fire-control reported.

"Wave off, you bastard," Becker whispered.

The roiling black cloud held its secret. For a brief moment Quinn imagined the smoke had magically consumed the lander, that the cruel enemy had been transported far away.

"Weapons ready," Becker shouted over the command circuit.

"Four seconds to touchdown," the voice on tactical frequency reported. Quinn observed black smoke curling with sinister laminar fluidity over some fast-moving object, like the bow wave on a shark making its approach.

"Weapons free!" fire-control announced.

The alien lander exploded from the smoke plume trailing streamers of pitch, its matte color a perfect match to the greasy black shroud. Laser blasters and artillery barrage-fired from the trench line, taking the alien craft under murderous fire. It was made of sturdy stuff. Laser impacts engraved the ship's black flanks with silver scars like cat claws. Artillery detonations buffeted the vessel, heaving it up on its wing; but still the Ulaggi ship kept coming, visibly damaged, wing tips and empennage shredding into the smoky slipstream.

Quinn peered over the breastwork, awed by the alien ship's vitality. And horrified by the courage of its audacious crew. The large ship contacted midway down the runway in a crunching salvo of direct hits. The blunt-nosed, delta planform collapsed on its near wing and ground-looped off the runway, throwing up sod and sand. There were no viewing ports on the craft, but at the wing root of each wing was an ominous blister from which emanated a murderous sparkling.

"Incoming!" came a shout over tactical.

Lurid bars of energy raked the high ground, burning the air, melting the dirt, killing marines. Like a steamrolling blast of hot air, a coruscating beam swept straight for her, expanding as it came. Quinn, mesmerized, watched the grassy upslope turn black and wither on a razor-sharp approaching front.

"Down!" Becker shouted. He threw himself at Quinn, knocking her to the dirt. The air crinkled. Blades of grass whispered into white puffs. Trees on the sea cliffs exploded in flame.

Quinn regained her senses and pushed herself from under the marine and into a sitting position. Major Becker stayed down, writhing on the trench bottom. The back of his helmet was heat-blasted. His battle armor was cauterized silver and bronze across the shoulders.

"Medics!" Quinn shouted into her transmitter.

Keeping her head below the breastwork, she looked about. On the higher slopes behind them, grass fires burned furiously. She dared to touch the marine, examining his helmet. The armor was mangled, but it was not pierced. Becker moved. Groaning, he pushed himself unsteadily upright. In vain, Quinn tried to hold him down.

"I'm . . . okay," he mumbled, pushing Quinn aside. He struggled unsteadily to a kneeling position. A marine mortar battery behind the ridge coughed out a barrage, pulsing the ground with low frequency thuds. Air pressure pulsed around them.

"Report!" Colonel Kim demanded.

"Stand by," Quinn replied. Her slowness to react had caused Becker's injuries. She pushed aside a wave of incapacitating guilt and forced her brain into action. A banshee whistled overhead. The air crinkled again as another thermal wave swept their position.

"Second lander at four kilometers," the monotone reported. "Touchdown in fifty seconds."

Quinn peeked through a breastwork periscope. Mortar fire covered the spaceport with rippling detonations. Many of the rounds exploded harmlessly in the air, intercepted by antiordnance lasers, but a few struck their target.

"Major Becker's down," Quinn broadcast. "All units report."

"I'm . . . okay," he insisted. The officer staggered to an unsteady crouch and pitched forward on his face. Quinn crawled to his side just as a medic arrived.

"Report!" Quinn shouted.

Surviving sector leaders gave their reports: nine marines killed, including four officers; thirty-one incapacitated by injury, another nine injured but still capable of holding their weapons.

"Move the dead and wounded from the line," Colonel Kim ordered. "Bring all reserves forward. Captain Quinn is now in charge of line sectors one and two. Lieutenant Harper, sectors three and four."

Quinn took stock of her position. Whenever a Legion weapon fired, it gained heavy attention from Ulaggi lasers. Half of her line emplacements were knocked out. Legion missiles and mortar rounds roared overhead. Ulaggi lasers knocked most of them from the air.

"Second lander touchdown in twenty seconds," the technician droned. "Third lander at ten kilometers."

She returned to the scouting periscope and surveyed the distant spaceport. The Ulaggi lander slumped on the side of the cratered runway, its wings and fuselage shredded, but its powerful laser blasters continued to blaze at the human positions. The front of the lander had clamshelled open and engines of destruction were deploying onto the spaceport's ramps. Over the distance Quinn could discern three varieties: large, sleek vehicles with faceted turrets fore and aft; smaller vehicles with studded wheels, each with an articulating grappling device; and a fleet of darting beetles.

Another thermal disturbance distorted the air, momentarily darkening her periscope optics. Grass fires flared to the rear. To her left what was left of the cypress trees reignited.

Legion defensive fire was having an accumulating effect. Gouts of dirt blasted into the air around the grounded alien lander as mortars and remote artillery pounded the crashed ship with direct hits. The structure collapsed. Its wing-root lasers ceased spewing death, but the robots it had loosened on the land scuttled outward.

"AAUs are attacking," the technician announced.

Quinn searched the distant terrain, seeking the autonomous attack units. The Legion robots were fantastic killing machines, but there were only four on the spaceport grounds. The alien robots were responding in concert to something, but the distances were too great to resolve what was happening.

"Attack units are engaged," the technician reported.

Inside the CCCI bunker, technicians monitored the telemetry of their mechanical assassins, but Quinn's attention was on the second lander. The black, snub-nosed penetrator, its wing roots already blazing deadly coherent energy, disappeared into the black smoke. A third lander, wing roots sparkling, curved behind the second.

Someone jumped into the trench next to her. Quinn turned to see Hudson, assault rifle in hand.

"Are we in trouble, Boss?" Hudson asked.

"Keep your head down," she ordered, returning to the periscope.

The second lander exploded from the black cloud, its ebony lines silhouetted against a turquoise ocean. The remaining Legion weapons took the ship under fire, but the Ulaggi defensive systems gave more than they took. The large black craft pancaked onto the cratered runway, shearing its landing gear. The impact should have disabled a living crew; Quinn estimated it to be another robot ship. The craft shuddered and bounced to a stop. Immediately the front clamshelled and more robots debouched from its gaping maw. All the while the ship's wing roots spewed yellow bars of death.

Legion mortars found their range, and the robot ship took a direct hit. Ulaggi robots rolled about like tenpins, but many of them immediately uprighted and continued on their programmed missions.

The third lander disappeared into the smoke plume. It was larger than the first two. Quinn felt certain it contained living aliens.

"Unidentified aircraft inbound from the east," Colonel Kim reported over tactical.

Quinn jerked from the periscope and searched the skies behind her. Her helmet sensors picked up a warbling sound emerging from the crashing surf. She saw three fast-moving aircraft, spread into a wedge, streaking along the shoreline. They blended perfectly with their backgrounds, but their raw speed over the ground gave them away; vortices of sand and dust swirled in their wakes. They were after the mortars.

Twinkling starbursts emanated from their noses, taking the mortar positions under fire. Ammunition on the ground exploded, and the three warbling craft streaked through the resulting cloud of debris and tumbling smoke. Two of the craft banked hard out to sea. The third one kept coming. It gained altitude as it approached the ridge, its weapons redirecting and fanning the back side of the breastworks. Mobile missile radars captured it, their missile racks training and depressing to track its sand-burning trajectory. Marines raised weapons to their shoulders, some kneeling, some prone. The alien machine was again distressingly visible, getting larger and more ominous. It dipped a wing, slightly wavering around a twisted ocean tree.

A Legion missile fired with a *whoosh* of gray smoke. It sprang from the racks, accelerating out of its own ignition cloud. Another missile fired, and another. The alien flyer danced over a rise in the road and dual white-hot streaks of energy shot from the craft's wing roots, laying onto the missile emplacement like the frozen strings of a puppet. The emplacement exploded in a yellow ball. A panicked heartbeat later the proximity fuses of the first two missiles detonated. The flyer screamed through concentric smoke rings. A large chunk of one blunt wing, clipped by the expanding rods of the missile warheads, flipped crazily into the slipstream. The third missile streaked to its self-destruction limit and detonated in a distant golden puff.

The alien flyer warbled insanely past the exploding emplacement, rolling languorously. Quinn stared open-mouthed at the engine of destruction, its pilot struggling to regain control. Marines scattered as the alien craft, careening gracefully onto its rounded wing, nicked the breastwork and pinwheeled violently out of sight. An explosion lifted into the air from beyond the ridge line.

Quinn let loose a scream of brutal joy, an uplifted cry reveling in the death of another mortal creature. It was kill or be killed, nature's highest level of competition, humanity's most developed talent.

The celebration was short-lived. A massive lander retro exploded into her awareness. Quinn scrambled back to the periscope. The third alien vessel was on the ground. A great cloud of debris was blowing out to sea, and the surface beneath the lander was streaked carbon-black. The ship had used its retro engines instead of risking the cratered runway. Quinn knew with certainty that this lander contained Ulaggi.

"All autonomous attack units have been eliminated," the CCCI technician reported, as if reporting the weather. "Sensors indicate enemy scouting robots approaching sector five."

A stuttering line of energy impacts walked up the ridge and along its top. Ulaggi lasers, fanned wide, scoured the air overhead. Quinn pressed her head against the breastwork and listened to the frightened reports filtering in. Casualties were over fifty percent. The marines were helpless; all Legion weapons emplacements on the breastwork were destroyed. Desultory artillery and mortar fire continued to rain down on the spaceport, but the reinforced Ulaggi defenses intercepted the incoming munitions well before they struck home. The Ulaggi beachhead was established.

Quinn peeked into the periscope, enhancing its magnification to maximum. On the largest of the landers a belly hatch blew down, and dozens of wide-shouldered, two-legged aliens rapidly deployed. Scattered in their midst were a half-dozen lithe, long-legged creatures, each with a gait like a two-legged spider, an extremely quick, two-legged spider.

"Bugs on the ground," a deep voice reported. Quinn turned

to see Major Becker crawling along the breastwork. He moved close and took a turn at the periscope. The marine wore a new helmet. His head was bandaged and one of his eyes was covered with a patch.

"I see them," she said. "Are you okay?"

"Been better, sir," Becker replied. "I'm not talking about these bugs, sir. Word just came in. Ulaggi have been reported on the ground behind us. We're surrounded."

She fell against the breastwork, speechless. All hope was vanishing. All was lost. She stared up the gently climbing elevations to the north. Sheets of brown smoke footed with yellow flames blanketed the terrain as far as she could see.

Her helmet buzzed, notifying her of a personal message. She opened the channel.

"Captain Quinn. Colonel Kim here."

"Quinn," she replied, her head spinning.

"I thought you should know, sir," Kim reported. "Your daughter has been found. She is alive and well."

FORTY

THE GREAT RIVER

Charlie Buccari, trying to escape the wretched wailing, ran hard along the forested moraine. Leaves of red and gold cascaded from the trees. His sandaled feet rhythmically crunched the forest's carpet. The morning chill had given way to an unseasonably warm day.

The low end of the valley was just ahead. Lake Shannon outflowed from MacArthur's Valley over an expanse of sloping granite into the deep, broad valley of the Great River. At this time of year the lake outflow was only a modest sheet of water. Beyond the moraine the Great River rumbled majestically, vibrating the air as it thundered down from the northern cataracts.

Neck-chilling screams rose above even the river's roar. Horrible, predatory screams, they were not human, nor cliff dweller. Charlie braved a backward glance. A flight of hunters soared along the uplift, wings hissing the air.

"Thunderhead, danger!" Spitter chittered as he went by.

The boy accelerated into a life-or-death sprint, past the last few golden-leafed trees. The forest ended. His only shelter was a red-barked scrub supporting a waist-high canopy, and that cover ended at the outflow. Once over the valley's lip, Charlie would have to traverse the naked granite to get down into the boulder-tumbled river valley.

A leaf-choked driftwood jam marked the lake outflow. Beyond the outflow a fine mist floated in the air, spawning rainbows that drifted with the angle of the sun. Charlie topped the moraine, and the din of shattered water invaded all thought. Lungs heaving, he stopped and glanced backward.

Bottlenose, screeching frantically, flew into the boy and tackled him to the ground. Charlie, breath knocked from his lungs, tumbled beneath a thicket of red-barked brush. Other hunters came to ground around them.

"What?" Charlie wheezed. The warrior slapped a bony hand over the boy's mouth. Spitter joined them, flashing signs to his cohort. Sucking air, Charlie moved to his knees.

"Danger!" Bottlenose hissed, staring toward the outflow. Keeping his head below the low foliage, Charlie peeked through the thick leaves. He detected movement. Just beyond the outflow, black helmets and wide shoulders lifted into view. They were cut off.

More hunters flew in high figure eights overhead. They screamed warnings. Captain Two flew across the sun, and the bright backdrop illuminated his distinctively scarred wings.

"Stay!" Spitter signed emphatically.

The hunters disappeared into the scrub, skulking downhill. Once clear of Charlie's position, they audaciously struggled into the air, spreading apart so their massive wingspans would not conflict. The hunters seized burgeoning thermals and gained altitude, yet they still flapped their membranes. They were attracting attention to themselves.

A breeze ruffled Charlie's hair. He lifted his nose and sniffed the air. A tangy odor sifted into his consciousness, not unpleasant, a blend of spices. His eyes followed his nose upwind. Another platoon of Ulaggi emerged from the woods. Man-sized, if stockier, two legs, two arms, gloved hands, and wearing helmets, they walked along the edge of the forest, their suits blending with the autumnal colors and shifting shadows. One alien directed an apparatus at the winging cliff dwellers, not a weapon, an instrument of some kind.

The hunters, still flapping like stupid ducks, knifed into the grain fens favoring the northern side of the lake. The alien with the instrument turned from the hunters and waved his tool in a short sweeping motion encompassing Charlie's position. The Ulaggi technician started walking in that direction. Two hunters crashed from bushes along the shoreline. Instead of thrashing into the air, they folded their wings and dove into the leaf-layered water, submerging behind a thin wedge of bubbles.

Charlie slid lower. The two groups of aliens merged on the lakeshore below him, their chameleon suits shifting smoothly. They carried black clubs, prods of some type. The one with the instrument continued to stare intently in Charlie's direction, moving his helmeted head from side to side, as if to sift between the branches of the underbrush. Charlie sank deeper into the bushes, barely breathing.

"Remain still!" Captain Two, soaring overhead, screeched.

Charlie glanced upward. Something was wrong. The hunters were reacting to something unseen. Shrieking, the cliff dwellers pulled in their membranes and plunged downward, disappearing beyond the moraine. Over the crashing of the river, Charlie heard the pulsating engine again—growing louder at each pulse. The flying machine *whooshed* low across the moraine; the stiff scrubby bushes vibrated with its turbulence. The craft descended nearly to the lake's surface and banked sharply, rippling the placid waters. It disappeared behind the trees.

The aliens, merged now into one group, started walking toward the forest. The alien with the instrument did not move. It pointed emphatically in Charlie's direction, its darkly shielded eyes staring straight at him. The alien wended his way through the thickets. Three other troopers followed.

Captain Two flapped above the moraine. "Flee!" the hunter leader screamed.

Charlie scrambled upslope and rolled over the crest of the moraine into a thicket of rockberry. A hot charge of energy ripped the pale green foliage over his head, blasting a clean hole through to the azure sky. The boy leaped to his feet and sprinted like a deer along the steeply descending terrain, away from the outflow.

Beneath him the Great River coursed, still frothy from its tumultuous passage over the cataracts. The riparian valley spread wide and deep, the river current slowing and its glacial sediment settling. From this point south for almost a hundred kilometers, the river ran deep, dark, and smooth.

Where roots could gain purchase on the steep banks, hardwood forest resumed. A thousand shades of red and gold filtered out the sky and obscured Charlie's view of the river. Leaves sifted downward. He flushed a toy doe and her fawn. The miniature animals vaulted over fallen logs, lithe legs pointing straight down with each powerful leap. He bounded after them. The underbrush grew thicker as he descended. Over the river, hunters flew past, even with his elevation.

Charlie traversed the steep terrain, using the slope of the land to increase his speed. Through thickets and hardwoods he saw the river, brown and green in the near shadows, blue as the sky farther out. The river made a gradual bend, and the rumble of the cataracts quieted, yet he still sensed their power vibrating the air.

A hunter signal brought him up short.

Charlie listened. A bird sang nearby. Insects hummed and clicked. Perhaps he had lost his pursuers. His hope was short-lived; the distinctive warbling, coming from upriver, lifted once again to his hearing. The flying machine was suddenly visible, two hundred meters from shore. As it came abreast of his position, it banked steeply to the river's edge and slowed to a hover. Charlie rolled behind a log.

The flying machine continued downstream, slowly, its spine-chilling warbling diminishing in intensity. As the engine noises subsided, the thrashing of heavy feet crashing through the underbrush took its place. The valley floor was near; the open expanse of rocky river shoreline was only a stone's throw away. Current pushing pebbles over a gravel bar below lifted to his ears. Charlie rolled onto his feet and resumed his downward slant. The bank steepened, undercut by high water and eroded by old floods. He was forced to climb a defile, or to descend. He chose the easier route and leapt out onto smooth river stones, leaving behind the protection of the forest.

The river was immense, the far shore over a kilometer distant. A hunter screeched, and then another. Danger signals. If he kept going downriver, he would eventually come to the ferry landing, and no doubt to more aliens. If he stayed where he was, his pursuers, with their instruments, would find him. He was trapped.

Charlie looked to the river and spied a crotched log awash on a gravel bar. An idea formed. He would escape down the river; he would float past the ferry landing. He splashed out to the branch-studded log and pushed it fully afloat. It rode high enough to support his weight. Not that it mattered; he intended to swim in the river, using the wood as cover. The gentle current tugged at his sandals; the water in the shallows was almost warm. He knew it would be much colder out in the current. Then he got another idea.

Charlie beached the log and ran back to the woods, where he broke off several branches still endowed with yellow leaves. He carried them to his erstwhile raft and interwove them into the tangle of bare branches, creating a canopy of foliage around the main crotch. The frightening yodel of the alien flying machine echoed once again over the river. Charlie slipped under the camouflage and pushed against the rocks, propelling his raft into the moving current. The log moved steadily from shore, and he settled into the shaded branches.

The Ulaggi flyer came around the bend and pulsated up the river, far out in the channel. It disappeared downstream. Charlie's concerns were closer; his raft spun slowly in the current. The symmetry of his foliage shield was imperfect. The opposite shore was too far away to worry about, but he had assumed the thickest collection of leaves would stay oriented to the near shore, and it had not. He slipped into the water. The current moved faster; the water temperature grew colder.

The river pushed him from the curving shore. In the distance Charlie could see the concrete jetty jutting out from the ferry cove. The tram lines from the spaceport came to ground at the ferry landing. He looked for the lines. Only two of the four catenaries were visible. Two of the cables were broken. Billy Gordon had left his mark.

The current pushed the log and its passenger steadily southward. The jetty grew larger. The gray slash of steel-reinforced concrete was new, built in the previous spring. In previous years the jetty had been constructed of concrete and boulders, but the spring floods ripped it away annually. Sandy Tatum said the river would eventually take out the reinforced jetty, too. The Great River was too powerful.

The river was not cooperating now, either; the current swerved directly for the man-made cliff. Movement caught Charlie's eye; a lone alien, its garb blending with the background, walked the jetty, its black-visored helmet pivoting diligently. Charlie tried to hide as much of his body under the log as possible. His feet made contact with shoaling boulders. He gently frog-kicked, trying to propel the log out into free-moving water.

The current was stronger as the main river channel swung against the concrete surface. The raft slipped under the eye of the Ulaggi sentry. Charlie, clinging to a branch, went underwater. Opening his eyes in the sun-shafted water, he watched the ponderous concrete structure retreat upstream. At the jetty's tip the current eddied strongly and the raft swerved shoreward. To his relief, the water temperature increased. Charlie watched the bottom rising to meet him. His lungs ached. Slowly, still under his leafy blind, he pushed his nose and eyes above the surface.

His raft was trapped in the rockbound cove sheltering the ferry landing. With his knees on steeply slanting sand, his head just clear of the river, Charlie peered through dead leaves. He had a dismayingly clear view of the landing. A dozen or more black-helmeted Ulaggi soldiers stood at their guard posts. It seemed each of the bugs was staring straight at him. He slipped low in the water.

All about him, cluttering the cove, was the sundered wreck of a wooden ferry. He tucked in between a pair of massive timbers and slid slowly along their protective length, easing his log with him. Once positioned in the middle of the flotsam, he rose into his leaf-depleted blind and lifted his eyes over the floating debris. Five meters of shallows and ten times that of sandy riverbank lay between him and the forest. He would have to climb the bank and run across the ferry landing road to get into the woods—an unlikely prospect. His only viable escape route was back into the deeper river, but he would not move his blind until nightfall. The boy shivered.

The autumn sun was already settling behind the soaring skyline of the western mountains, limning the windblown crags with glittering auroras of gold. There were several hours of daylight left, but the air and the water temperature would quickly grow colder without the direct rays of the sun. Movement on the shore displaced the temperature in Charlie's list of worries. Walking toward him on the road, guarded by black-visored Ulaggi soldiers, came a file of human beings. From the boy's low perspective, only the hostages' heads appeared at first. As they drew nearer, the rest of their bodies rose above the obstructing rocks. They shuffled and stumbled along with their eyes cast down, their shoulders drooping. They were all men, and they were all naked.

Charlie's frightened wonderment was interrupted by a mechanical noise. The tram line was moving! He looked over his shoulder in time to see the approaching car. Slipping lower in the water, he pulled a bough over his upturned face. The yellow and white car trundled overhead and eased into the terminal structure. A portion of the terminal's steeply pitched roof was missing, and the rest was blackened—more of Billy Gordon's work.

The arrival of the car was significant. Something was happening. Every black visor on the riverbank fixated on the tram landing. The guards who had been lethargic to that point, spurred the straggling humans into the terminus with frightening animation.

The men were being loaded onto the tram. To what purpose?

After several minutes the tram clutch engaged and the tram car eased from the darkly shaded terminal structure. The car hesitated and then stuttered forward, oscillating to the screeching sounds of metal carving metal. As it lifted past the river's edge, the tram screeched to a halt, swinging and bouncing gently, no more than twenty meters from Charlie's position. The boy saw wide-eyed prisoners peering through the tram's window. These quickly disappeared, and the black visor of an alien took their place. Charlie slid lower in the water, slipping between his blind and the floating timbers. He tucked his legs under a timber and gently patted the bottom with a flat hand, stirring up silt.

A loud commotion rose from the tram terminal, flashing and loud clapping sounds, a scream, shouts, and then rifle fire. Charlie ducked from under the timbers and dared a peek. A pathetic grunting sound emanated from behind bushes bordering the bank. Those bushes were suddenly bent back and parted, disgorging two bodies. The corpses tumbled down the rocky incline, rolling to the riverbed like rag dolls. Limp and gore-covered, they were not recognizable as human, but one wore the shredded green jumpsuit of a spacer marine.

Noises continued. A burst of rifle fire! Another! More loud claps accompanied by flashes of light. And then silence. Silence.

Charlie lowered his head. It was too quiet. A platoon of Ulaggi guards lumbered along the road. As one they stopped short, their weapons offered in salute to another creature that stalked almost delicately into view from the tram landing. It was grossly different! Its clothing did not shimmer and fade into the background. It was garbed in vivid red, with black and white trim on shoulders and breast. It was extremely tall and lithe, taller than a kone. One of the stubby aliens, hands clasped beseechingly, stumbled backward, retreating before the graceful being.

The tall being moved unbelievably quickly, taking the nearest stubby alien into its embrace and lifting the broad-shouldered soldier from its feet. The red-garbed creature screamed the same unholy refrain heard earlier in the day, a horrible sound beyond description. Goose bumps covered Charlie's skin; his scalp crawled.

The nightmare scream faded to a hiss, and the lithe alien cast the limp and bleeding soldier to the ground. With animal savagery, the tall alien swung its boot, kicking the fallen one in the head. Two of the stubby soldiers ran forward and collected the limp and sundered form of their cohort, dragging it toward the jetty.

Charlie recoiled. His spasm created a splash and wiggled the leaves of his blind. The tall alien's head snapped up. Charlie lowered his head until only his nose and eyes were above water. He peeked sideways to check the jetty sentry. That alien was running to the beach end of the concrete pier, to assist the others with their gory burden.

Charlie heard a chirp. He glanced up at the tram car. Two hunters, like pelican-beaked buzzards, perched on the tram cable. Then he saw a human face in the side window gaping down at him. It was a familiar face, a settler or laborer, someone he had seen before. The man's mouth shut slowly as he glanced nervously to the side. Then he waved. Slowly, Charlie lifted his hand in tentative acknowledgment.

The liquid grumble of a ferry engine vibrated across the water. Charlie peeked around his blind and saw the blunt-nosed craft approaching. A powerful bow wave surged in front of the ferry. He realized that the calm cove of the ferry landing was about to be transformed. The massive timbers floating about him would soon be colliding against each other with bone-crushing force.

He risked a peek at the riverbank. The tall, red-garbed alien, accompanied by dozens of jogging troopers, strode imperiously along the jetty. The ferry's motor shifted into reverse; the heavy raft entered the cove, commencing its approach to the wharf.

The wharf! He would hide under the wharf. With his eye at water level, the approaching bow wave looked taller than the western mountains. Charlie sucked in a lungful of air and submerged in a bottom-hugging dive. He frog-kicked and stroked in slow, easy motions, hoping not to attract attention with jerking movements. Wave turbulence washed over him. Gravel rattled on the shore and wave-thrashed timbers collided in a low-pitched timpani as the bow wave vented its energy. The boy swam doggedly forward. His lungs grew hot. A darkness moved across the surface, just over his head. He looked up to see the silvery sky blotted out by the ferry's mass, its engine screw rotating at idle.

The screw missed, but the rudder post slammed Charlie

sideways as it shifted to the opposite position. The engine was gunned in reverse. Cavitation bubbles frothed everywhere. His lungs burned; his momentum was lost. The current and engine wash pushed him away from the wharf. He felt himself surrendering, drifting upward.

Something grabbed his arm! Charlie jerked in horror. It was a hunter—Spitter! Membranes spread and webbed talons thrusting water, the cliff dweller yanked the boy powerfully down, back into the bubbles of the ferry. Charlie, fighting panic, stroked with his free hand and kicked violently.

Finally, finally, the hunter angled to the surface. After interminable seconds, Charlie clawed the warmer nothingness of the atmosphere. He inhaled hungrily, greedily, his lungs in command of his being. Water streamed from his hair and ran into his mouth; he gasped and choked, but his lungs demanded their due. He breathed deeply and, realizing where he was, submerged again to cough violently.

In control of his lungs, he surfaced, red-eyed and raw of throat. Spitter floated easily at his side. They were under the wharf, a floating pier to which the raft had been docked. The waters within its timbered bays were choppy and confused. The ferry engine bubbled at a fast idle, and the thudding of tromping feet pounded overhead. Within minutes of docking the engine revved high and the ferry moved away. It nosed back into the river, straining at top speed.

With the ferry gone, Charlie could once again view the opposite side of the cove. The Ulaggi remaining on the beach maintained a nervous vigilance. Only the short, broad-shouldered ones were visible; the tall terror had evidently departed on the ferry. A group of soldiers returned to the tram terminal, in an effort to get the tram mechanism to reverse itself. There were aliens still in the tram car, along with their prisoners.

Unable to free the bound gears, six aliens walked along the rocks and through the shallows, stepping over Charlie's wave-grounded blind. Gesticulating emphatically, the aliens on the shore exhorted the aliens in the car to jump. There were three bugs in the car. One at a time they stepped from the door and plunged ten meters into the deep river. Each thrashed to the surface, and each was retrieved with a line.

One of the prisoners jumped, and then another. The clapping reports heard earlier came in salvos as the aliens on the bank fired their weapons point-blank at the surfacing humans, erupting the water with pink, steamy geysers. The remaining prisoners stayed in the car. Not satisfied, one of the aliens fired at the swinging tram door, blowing it cleanly off and causing the tram car to rock against its cable guard. The same alien blew a fist-sized hole straight through the car's middle. The car bounced violently, and human cries drifted over the river. As other aliens were taking aim, they jerked their heads in unison toward the beach. Lowering their muzzles, the aliens jogged over the river rocks and ascended the bank, taking positions on the perimeter.

Charlie, shivering with cold and horror, discovered a niche in the wharf timbers, a small alcove not visible from the riverbank. He climbed from the water and crawled trembling into the dead space. He could no longer see the riverbank but did not much care. He needed badly to dry out and warm up. Spitter pulled from the water. There was barely room for the two of them. The warrior moved close and lay down, draping a fur-covered wing over the boy's shivering body.

FORTY-ONE

IN FULL ROUT

An Ulaggi laser burned the air overhead as Quinn crawled frantically down the line. Carbon-black slopes behind the lines reignited with the laser's passage, like a napalm hose jetting over the countryside. Shell-shocked marines watched Quinn pass. Hudson saw her coming and started crawling. Behind his flash-darkened visor his expression was frightened. And worried.

"Emerald's alive, Nash," Quinn gasped.

Hudson's eyes opened wide; his features twitched with disbelief; his arms fell to his sides.

"She's alive," Quinn repeated, putting her helmet against his.

"What? How?" he stammered, incredulous. His arms closed around Quinn with desperate strength.

"In the tube tunnels. Art Mather found her, of all people." Her laugh was choked off by a planet-jolting detonation. A hundred meters down the line a gout of dirt erupted. Quinn and Hudson collapsed in each other's arms. Debris showered down. The deep-throated singing of heavy caliber lasers filled the air. Brilliant flashes of white and gold scintillated through the haze as their positions were raked by energy weapons. Another explosion clobbered the breastwork to seaward. Quinn lifted her head. Where the command and control bunker had been, there was now only a smoking crater. The infuriatingly calm drone of the CCCI technician was forever extinguished.

Over the cacophony of the barrage came the unmistakable sound of a lander retro. Another alien ship was on the ground, and the Ulaggi were making certain the humans did not contest its arrival. Of that there was little threat; all significant defensive weapons had been neutralized; the surviving marines huddled at their positions like slugs under stones.

Quinn looked into Hudson's eyes. He managed a smile.

"Big trouble, Boss." He had to shout. She held him tighter.

"Line sector five, fall back by platoons!" Major Becker commanded, filling the void. "Muster and proceed to designated LZs. Get the wounded in the helos."

Quinn pushed away. "Becker needs my help," she shouted.

She started to move and then abruptly turned. Hudson ran into her. Alien energy discharges resonated around them.

"Nash!" she shouted. "We have to separate. One of us has to make it back. You have a better chance alone."

"No," Hudson protested.

She had no time for arguments. She scuttled down the breastwork, looking for Becker. Behind her another ground-jolting explosion ripped the human defenses. And another. She was afraid to look back, afraid she would see Hudson's position in ruins. As the thundering reverberations cleared, she heard the air-chopping sounds of helicopter rotors.

The first two Legion helos came in low, below the silhouette of the high ground. There was activity in the staging areas; a convoy of all-terrain vehicles and armored troop carriers moved out. The vehicles departed the prepared road, bouncing overland. The retreat had begun.

A familiar warbling lifted from the bedlam. Quinn watched in horror as two Ulaggi aircraft, invisible over the ocean, rolled in on their targets. With two efficient bursts of light, the Legion helos were destroyed.

Missiles from marine defensive batteries opened up on the swift flying ships. One warbler was hit, but the pilot kept it airborne, steering it on a wavering course over the ridge and out of sight. The other yodeling demon tracked in on the convoy and ran its lasers down the line of vehicles like a searing sword stroke. It banked hard left and followed its wingmate out of sight.

"Line sector three and four, fall back," Becker shouted.

She joined Becker where the command center used to be. The headland was cauterized. Not even a stump remained of the stand of cypress. The major conferred with the remnants of his company leadership.

Becker looked up. "I'd say it's time for both of us to leave, Captain," he said.

"Concur," Quinn replied. "What's your plan?"

"Run like hell," he said. "The coast road is interdicted. There are robot scouts and an undetermined number of bugs approaching from the west. Can't go east. Due north, uphill and through the coastal savannah, is our only way out."

"Thirty kilometers of open grasslands," Quinn said.

"There are places to hide."

She nodded and looked north. She knew the area. The broad sweep of savannah was deceptively featureless, but the rolling terrain hid countless drainage defiles and ravines. In the depressions could be found willow stands and alder thickets. High up the slopes tall cedar forests started, if they could make it that far.

Becker dispatched the officers and noncoms.

"All sectors pull back to marshaling areas," he broadcast. "Move out through the gullies and ravines. Stay beneath the plane of the lasers, if you can. Look for areas that aren't burned. Every marine for himself. Good luck, and I'll see you in hell. Becker out."

The air over their heads wrinkled in a vertical line. Another mighty explosion wracked the ridge. Marines staggered from their positions, gaining momentum as they sprinted down. Officers tried to maintain order, but the rout was on.

"You ready, Captain?" Becker asked, his face distorted with frustration.

"For a muster in hell, Major?" Quinn replied.

"Aye," Becker said. "We'll have plenty of company."

A barrage of heavy weapons erupted on the ridge. The marine rearguard was pulling off the line, many supporting wounded comrades. Something was coming up the other side. Major Becker did not hesitate; he sprinted for the action.

Quinn attempted to keep pace with the marine, but fell farther behind with each step.

An Ulaggi robot breasted the ridge, a beetle-shaped machine, high-slung on six wheels. It ripple-fired a laser and cast out grenades that exploded with an immense flash and a monumental blast. Three more robots came into view, all dispensing concussion grenades. The marines fought valiantly, but they could not match the ferocity of the alien firepower.

A salvo of explosions detonated in front of them. Becker, almost to the trench, left his feet as if he had been shot. Fifty meters behind the marine, Quinn ran into an invisible brick wall. She staggered backward, trying to reengage a faltering consciousness. Marines still on their feet scattered from the area. One came running straight at her. Quinn's brain struggled to process what she was seeing. She realized that it was not a marine; it was Hudson.

"Go back!" Hudson screamed. He lifted her and turned her around. Quinn's muscles hesitantly regained control. She concentrated on running. Panic seeped into her awareness, effectively clearing away the fog.

The explosive exhaust of an alien lander taking off rose above the din. The big craft stood on its tail and screamed skyward, spewing a white column of smoke. Quinn was sprinting hard now. Hudson, running at her side, pulled on her arm, trying to make her go faster. The terrain descended sharply as it approached the headland. There was nothing but empty air ahead of them, a precipitous drop to the ocean.

Hudson steered them downhill, parallel to the brink, and slowed. Quinn struggled to catch her breath. She glanced back, across the valley behind the promontory. Some Legion vehicles climbed the sloping terrain, but many were immobile and burning. Individuals and small groups staggered up the burned-out slopes.

"There's a ledge," Hudson gasped, jogging along the brink. "I've climbed this cliff. It's got some crevices and overhangs that'll give us cover."

"They aren't going to make it, Nash," Quinn wheezed.

Hudson looked up to see what she was talking about. "Neither are we," he replied, dropping onto his stomach and throwing his legs over the side, "if we don't get out of sight."

She looked up. The Ulaggi lander returning to orbit arrowed straight overhead. It arced backward, as if doing a loop, but the top of the loop disappeared in the upper atmosphere. The thunderous sound of the orbiter drifted away—to be replaced with the all too familiar pulsating scream of a flyer. Quinn's gaze jerked from the zenith and searched the lower skies. The flyer swooped across the ridge, targeting marines. Needles of white heat darted through the haze.

"Come on," Hudson shouted. "I found it . . . I think."

"Right behind you," she said. Taking a deep breath, she moved to the cliff edge and fell onto her stomach, groping downward with her boots. Hudson guided her feet onto a ledge no wider than her hand. She knew if she looked down, she would freeze. Hudson, one hand on her waist, pulled her along the steeply descending ledge. Thankfully, it grew wider. As her head fell to the level of the cliff, she glanced up. An alien robot was halted on the ridge crest.

"Do you think it saw us?" she gasped, ducking against the rock.

"What?" Hudson asked, tugging her along the precipice.

"There's a robot up there," she exhaled.

"I'm not going back to ask," Hudson gasped, yanking on her suit.

She wanted to scream at him to stop pulling. Her gloved fingers clawed at the rock, her fear of heights overcoming her fear of the aliens. Her muscles locked up.

"Look down, Cassy," Hudson huffed.

Gritting her teeth, she peeked. They had reached an outcropping almost a meter wide, a comfort compared to what they had traversed. She exhaled, forcing her muscles to loosen. Her fingers were cramped into claws. She straightened them, painfully forcing blood to circulate.

"Come on, Cass," Hudson exhorted. "We gotta get under cover."

He lowered himself to a protruding boulder and stood with

his arms up. Quinn glanced down. Beyond Hudson, silky blue waves shredded against emerald tidal pools and crushed softly into the grottoes at the base of the guano-stained cliff. Streamers of kelp waved hypnotically in the backwash.

"Can't we hide here?" she asked, leaning against warm stone. Her head spun. Wheeling sea birds, objecting to the presence of the two-legged interlopers, did little to help. She closed her eyes and breathed deeply.

"Come on, Cass," Hudson panted. "Just a little farther. There's an overhang below us. There're some places to wedge into. We won't stand out so bad."

"I'm coming," she gasped, dropping to her knees and lowering her leg. Hudson guided her down to the boulder. He let go of her hand and moved out across a precarious ledge.

"Follow me," he said. He pressed against the rocks, his long arms spread wide.

"S'fraid you were going to say that," she groaned.

Hudson sidled along the sheer face, his boots moving from one small foothold to another. Less than four meters away there was a ledge escarpment. The four meters seemed like a light-year. Beyond the escarpment the cliff face broke into stair-stepping terraces.

"You can do it," he gasped.

She had to. She inhaled and took hold of a rocky protuberance. Without looking down, she reached out with her foot and took a toehold.

"Doing great," Hudson said. "There's good footing right— *aggh!*" His foot slipped. He pedaled his flailing leg against the rock, trying to regain purchase.

"Nash!" she shouted, extending her arm.

Hudson looked up, his expression filled with fear, but also with an element of resignation. The brittle ledge shattered. His fingers, stretched by the full and sudden onset of his mass, could not contest the elemental persistence of gravity. He slipped down the rocky face and bounced off an outcropping, arms and legs flailing. His eyes and mouth opened wide as he fell backward and out of sight.

Quinn screamed into her fist, gagging back the noise—but

not the tears. She buried her head in her arms and leaned against the rocks, sobbing. She clung desperately to her handholds.

The wailing pulses of the alien flyer intruded into her stunned misery. The ululations grew steadily louder. Extremely loud. Horrifically loud. She turned her head. Hovering over the ocean at eye level, no more than twenty meters away, rock steady, its energy weapons trained on her, was an Ulaggi flying machine. Too exhausted to be frightened, Quinn stared at the black-visored pilot.

"Go ahead and shoot," she sobbed, turning back to the cliff. Her helmet struck unyielding rock. A grating noise close at hand dominated her senses. She peeked sideways; adrenaline pulsed once again through her wracked system, boiling the back of her neck.

Taking purchase on the cliffside next to her face was an obscenely wide boot. Quinn willed her clawed fingers to loosen their grasp, to let her join Hudson in death. Her hands refused; her daughter was still alive. Quinn knew she could not die. Not now.

A brutal, iron-hard grip yanked her up.

FORTY-TWO

MANEUVER TO BATTLE

Jakkuk trembled, near ecstasy.

Enmeshed within her dendritic interface, she reveled in the resonant swelling of her cell's collective *g'ort*, an exquisite symphony of fear, a glorious expectation of violence. The emotions of her ship-mistresses, especially those of y'Trig, the roon, intertwined in delicious harmony. The screams of a'Yerg's roonish attack pilots, fear rampant, sang across the tactical frequencies.

"Again," Dar commanded breathlessly. The dominant leered at the status projections, a lover stalking naked prey.

Jakkuk's mind surged with the requisite empathic commands. Her cruiser cell, with nerve-tight coordination, loosened another energy salvo at the orbiting station, all six star-cruisers firing in discrete plasma frequencies. The satellite's shield signals wavered majestically, struggling to offset the wide-spectrum assault. The massive weapons battery would not last much longer.

Ever closer Jakkuk's interstellars approached, guided by their ship-mistresses in a disciplined dance of death. Cautiously, cautiously, for the commander of the orbiting platform played the game well, feigning weakness and then making Jakkuk's cell pay with massive, asymmetric blasts of energy. Inexorably, the energy platform's discharges grew weaker; the satellite was nearing defeat, but the defense station's imminent collapse was not the sole source of Jakkuk's glorious euphoria.

There were stirrings from the distant second planet. Rising on orbit arced a wave of formidable vessels. Jakkuk's sensors detected no fewer than thirty capital ships, in three battle groups, accelerating upward from the massive golden world. Nine of the alien units were behemoths, easily thrice the mass of Jakkuk's star-cruisers, larger even than an Imperial battleship or a rebel dreadnought. A second wave of ships marshaled in lower orbit. There could be little doubt the powerful ships were preparing to do battle. The cell-controller vibrated with sensual expectation.

Ineffable fear pervaded all Ulaggi chemistries, an exquisite emotional state of being. Jakkuk's thoughts joined the ethereal chorus. Honor would be theirs. Great honor. Jakkuk presented her mind for orders. Dominant Dar glared at the battle display.

"The first battle group is sufficiently clear of the planet's gravity well," Remac, the dominant's ship-mistress, said. "Angular momentum is negligible."

"Gravitronics?" Dar snapped, her color high.

"No indication of gravitronic emission," the primary bridge-male reported, deep voice trembling at the rising cloud of passion. "Linear b-battle f-formations. Negative grid-linking."

"Their dispositions do not conform to grid matrix," Jakkuk reported.

"Pah! These are not interstellars," Remac said.

"Savages!" Dar snarled, brown-gold eyes firing with disappointment. "Still plodding between planets with impulse engines. It will be three moon-cycles before they close our energy batteries. Jakkuk-hajil, rescind the recall. Kwanna-hajil may finish her collections, while we continue our contest with this impertinent satellite."

"No doubt there is ample time," a whining voice pronounced. Karyai, the political, floated wraithlike onto the bridge. "Nevertheless, expedite the harvest, daughter. We have had enough surprises. That is a large fleet, and even though its units cannot jump, its very presence is disturbing. I am anxious to report these findings to the Empress."

"As you direct, mother," Dar replied. "Cell-Controller Kwanna is to terminate operations at first level objectives."

Jakkuk issued orders. Kwanna acknowledged rapaciously, swelling Jakkuk's envy. Kwanna's cell had been chosen to descend to penetration orbit; to investigate the aboriginal settlements and to harvest its denizens. Humans! There were humans on the third planet, soft and egg-worthy. More *kar*-like than *kar*.

Jakkuk suppressed her vagrant thoughts, returning full attention to the orbiting defense station. Her star-cruisers relentlessly harried the imposing satellite, the first surprise offered by this system. The defense station's power levels were grievously diminished. Its largest caliber optics were discharging less frequently, and Ulaggi energy weapons were scoring telling strikes. The infernal piece of engineering would not frustrate her ships much longer.

"What is this? Wait!" the political hissed.

The lakk's normally inscrutable *g'ort* was suddenly palpable. Torrid thoughts thrust through Jakkuk's consciousness, to preemptively connect with the cell's dendritic interface. Jakkuk, taken prisoner in her own mind, felt the lakk's hunger as if it were her own. Lonely. Bitter. Sensual.

Helpless to prevent it, Jakkuk's attention was ripped from the satellite and drawn to the political's vibrant focus. Jakkuk's entire emotional being, like that of a child standing next to an enraged adult, was overwhelmed by that of the powerful lakk. She sensed the intrusion, more ships arriving from hyperlight. She also sensed the collective pulsations of Ulaggi fear, including her own, through the vast emotional lens of the political's mind.

"More ships. Human," Karyai said, her tone shrill and wheedling. As abruptly as she had intruded, the lakk withdrew, leaving whip welts in Jakkuk's mind. "Definitely interstellars these."

"Human ships jumping from hyperlight, defensive sector three," the bridgetalker verified, eyes white-margined with fear.

Jakkuk, still reeling from the political's violation, forced her focus to the threatening presence. More targets! Liberated from the lakk's rasping mental embrace, Jakkuk's *g'ort* ascended in exquisite waves, delicate and yet powerful. She trembled deliciously.

"Cell-Controller, your assessment," Dar demanded. Jakkuk's *g'ort* retreated into the shadowed recesses of her mind.

"Ten ships," Jakkuk reported, nerves still tingling, raw and sharp. "Six hyperlight signatures and four cell ships, transports or freighters."

"Prepare all units for attack by maneuver," Dar ordered. Jakkuk acknowledged.

"From where do they come?" Karyai snarled.

"Backtracking trace," Jakkuk replied. A strong vector was evident, the tenuous signature of a very long jump. The cell-controller logged the coordinates for analysis and exploitation. Before Jakkuk could report, the lakk's presence was once again blasting down the corridors of her mind, bludgeoning aside the cell-controller's thoughts.

"Yesss!" Karyai hissed. "More! Still more. Yes!"

Jakkuk also sensed the second batch of arrivals. She analyzed the hyperlight path; it retraced the Ulaggi's own track perfectly. This alien fleet had followed them. Were they in a clever trap?

"M-Mother," the bridgetalker blurted, nearly hysterical. "Hyperlight exit. Sector t-two!"

The hapless bridgemale's fear signals were too much. A young roon screamed and pounced for the pathetic male, mating organs squirming free of her bridge suit. Karyai was quicker. The political locked minds with the *g'ort*-stricken female, and the silver-eyed officer was rendered catatonic in mid-leap. The incapacitated roon soared past her recoiling target and slammed into a bulkhead. She rebounded in dazed semiawareness. Her gossamer hair, pitch-black and longer than she was tall, billowed free, partially obscuring her obscene display. Another roonish officer glided forward and pulled the disheveled sister from the bridge.

Bloodshed averted, Ship-Mistress Remac assumed control. Wielding her command rod, the ancient hajil, unsexed by age, bludgeoned the bridgetalker from the bridge. A replacement male pulled himself reluctantly forward, assuming duties as bridgetalker.

The delectable taste of mayhem in her throat, Jakkuk

shifted her focus to the designated coordinates and analyzed the signatures, blossoming sharply and tightly grouped— familiar gravitronic signatures these. Very familiar.

"Eight more, mother," Jakkuk reported, breathing heavily. "The same star-ships encountered at Ore Source Two-ten. They followed us. Their hyperlight trace directly maps to ours."

"Blood," whined the lakk. "We were not alone there after all."

"They followed us," Dar snarled. "Then we are under attack."

"Attack?" Karyai repeated softly, eyes shutting. "Perhaps this time they will remain to fight. Terminate the harvest."

Karyai's powerful *g'ort* swelled once again into Jakkuk's mind. Jakkuk recoiled at the lakk's attention. After several eternal seconds, the lakk withdrew, enmeshed in her own thoughts.

"Terminate the harvest," Dar ordered. "Jakkuk-hajil, bring your cell to grid-support positions. Prepare to execute a battle jump."

"As directed, mother," Jakkuk replied, attending to her duties with enhanced concentration. "It will take a watch cycle for Kwanna-hajil's ships to elevate from low orbit."

"We cannot wait," Dar said. "We must seize the initiative. Kwanna-hajil will join us when she is able. Permission to attack, mother."

"Choose well your victim, daughter," the political replied.

Runacres forced his mind to alertness, shedding the cobwebs of hyperlight. Threat-warning Klaxons blared. Detection systems groped outward. Electronic pulses blossomed spherically, searching the limitless vacuum. Targeting systems cycled, hungrily scanning for opportunities.

"Exit complete, Admiral," Commodore Wells reported. "Stable grid. All units alpha-alpha. All main batteries at combat temperature. All ships ready to engage."

"Very well," Runacres barked. "Formation One-one. Maintain one-half battle spread. Double overlap on the vertical axis."

"Form One-one, double overlap the vertical, aye," Wells echoed, manipulating the operations console. "All ahead flank impulse."

"All corvettes ready to launch," Carmichael reported.

"Hold launch," Runacres barked.

"Holding, aye," Carmichael replied.

Tactical status still updated; the onset of data arriving from great distances flooded all receptors. Icon's representing Runacres's own motherships, maneuvering in good order, materialized first. The system star and the planets resolved next. An icon representing the orbiting PDF defense station blossomed into being.

"Defense station is in distress!" the tactical officer reported. The icon pulsed with an emergency beacon.

"We have ident on Legion transponders, Admiral," the tactical assistant reported.

"*Madagascar?*" Runacres asked.

"Negative. Clear return on *Malta*, Admiral," Wells reported. "Admiral Chou is with us."

"Ident on Second Fleet units. Also motherships *Vancouver* and *Hawaii*," the watch officer verified. "Also *Hispaniola*, *Kodiak*, and *Honshu*. Also auxiliaries *Darmstadt*, *Anchorage*, *Kent*, and *Oslo*. Standard Sol-Sys arrival coordinates."

Two thousand helpless settlers thrust into the middle of a war.

"They-ah have also just-ah arrived," Dowornobb reported. "Their gravitronic emissions are yet-ah strong. Their incoming track disturbance is still measurable. But, Admiral Runacres, Tar Fell's ships are not present."

Runacres studied the output screens displaying this newest technology. Scientist Dowornobb and Legion technicians had fully integrated a gravitronic mapping array into the fleet's combat information systems. The Second Fleet's hyperlight emission patterns were marked with icons, their positions faithful to transponder outputs on the main tactical display.

Tar Fell's absence was troublesome, but Runacres's attention was dominated by another realization.

"God save us," Runacres whispered.

Also displayed on the gravitronic map, with fading but undeniable clarity, was the Second Fleet's entry track from hyperlight. Their derived origination coordinates were also displayed—Sol System. Earth!

"Where are the Ulaggi, Scientist Dowornobb?" Runacres demanded.

"They-ah are here, Admiral. I have gravitronics."

Dowornobb's apocalyptic announcement boomed over the science circuit. Runacres glanced down at the kone's vid image. Dowornobb's great cow eyes stared back at him with frightened wisdom. If Legion instrumentation could track the Second Fleet's inbound trajectory from Earth, then so could the Ulaggi.

"Where?" Runacres demanded.

"Hostile contacts!" the watch officer reported. "Contact group alpha: six ships in siege around the konish defense station. The station is under heavy fire and is requesting emergency assistance."

Runacres's eyes snapped to the resolving icons. Only six!

"New hostile contacts!" the watch officer barked. "Contact group bravo coming around the planet's near limb in low orbit. Six more motherships and numerous fast-movers. Ulaggi emission signatures."

"There . . . they are," Runacres said.

The second flight of bogies solidified on radar, six more hostile icons in low orbit tracking rapidly across the surface of the planet. Runacres discounted the low ships; it would take them hours to break from the planet's gravity well. The six alien ships in high orbit moved slowly across the screen, clustered around the konish defense station like vultures on carrion. Those ships could jump as soon as they recovered their attack force and formed a grid.

Runacres felt *Eire* gaining momentum. The flagship surged gently, rotating into her mission vector. The admiral was pressed into his command chair. Gravity flotsam loosened during the hyperlight transit drifted through the larger voids, pursued by collection robots. Acceleration continued unabated, cinching tethers and inducing a fractional gravity.

"Admiral," Captain Katz reported from science, "intercepts indicate a fleet lifting into high konish orbit."

"Planetary Defense Force armada," Dowornobb said. "I-ah detect King Ollant's command signal."

"Mighty crowded in this system," Wells said.

"Damned crowded," Merriwether interjected from the flag-ship's bridge.

Runacres exhaled, staring wistfully at the tactical plot. The konish ships, so powerful and numerous, were irrelevant. Their great number and firepower would not be a factor for at least three months; by then the battle for Genellan would be long decided. The game pieces were set: fourteen fleet motherships against twelve Ulaggi interstellars. Runacres knew he had the smallest of numerical advantages. Could he capitalize?

"Second Fleet is requesting instructions," Wells reported.

"Engage and destroy the enemy," Runacres replied. "Order Admiral Chou to jettison settlers."

"Aye aye, Admiral," Wells replied.

It would be a tough haul for the PHMs, commencing their drop that far from the planet, tough on the men, women, and children, four days strapped to their landing harnesses. But there was no choice.

"Estimated time to engage the enemy?" Runacres demanded.

"At flank impulse, seventy-six hours to main battery radius," Wells replied.

An eternity.

"Admiral," Dowornobb boomed. "More ships! More ships are arriving from-ah hyperlight. Estimated arrival in-ah twenty minutes. They come from Earth, Admiral. Konish gravitronic signatures. It-ah is Tar Fell."

Tar Fell!

Runacres stared with renewed hope and heightened fear at the gravitronic plot. Tentative imaging signals displayed the imminent arrival of the konish task force, more reinforcements in battle, but yet another road sign defining Earth's galactic position. On fate's ledger Runacres was now credited eighteen warships to the enemy's twelve. Was it enough to counter the Ulaggi maneuvering advantage?

"Tar Fell is only four hours from rendezvous with Admiral Chou's units," Wells replied.

A battle was in the offing, and soon, but Runacres also saw a far distant future. Scientist Dowornobb's crude instrumentation allowed Runacres to see beyond the hyperlight warp. The admiral knew with profound certainty that Dowornobb's discoveries were auguries—to a future of hyperlight warfare.

"The bugs are breaking off their attack on the defense station, Admiral!" the tactical officer thundered. "They're maneuvering."

Runacres commanded a magnified image of the region. The six Ulaggi ships were opening, making course away from the satellite, on a vector that offset orbital angular momentum. The Ulaggi were preparing to jump. They would attack Admiral Chou first, Runacres guessed.

Runacres's attention shifted to the Ulaggi units in low orbit.

FORTY-THREE

INTO THE FRAY

Tar Fell shuddered, nauseated to his soul.

"We're out!" Captain Ito announced triumphantly. Behind their environmental partition the human technical crew moved with extraordinary animation. Tar Fell envied the humans their vitality. How could their constitutions be so indifferent to entering and departing hyperlight?

"Oh, yes!" Ambassador Kateos cried.

Her mellifluous voice, albeit weak with dizziness, was a tonic to Tar Fell's misery. The armada-master forced his wambling physiology through the miasma of transition vertigo. His vision begrudgingly cleared, but his thoughts were still jumbled. He chastised himself. This was a great moment; his ships had just completed the first hyperlight voyage in konish history. Tar Fell wanted to vomit in his helmet.

"Stable trajectory," General Magoon reported tremulously. Tar Fell was not alone in his misery.

"Admiral Chou's fleet is in position," General Otred gasped. Neither was the commanding officer of *House Ollant* immune.

"Something's wrong," Ito announced.

Threat alarms exploded into life. Tar Fell's mal de mer dissipated like feathers in the wind.

"What is amiss?" Kateos demanded.

"Admiral Chou maneuvers away from-ah the planet," Ito said. "Engagement commands are being intercepted. We have jumped into a battle."

"We are detecting emergency signals," Magoon reported. "The defense station is under attack by Ulaggi ships."

"Battle stations, General Magoon," Tar Fell ordered.

More alarms sounded. The flotilla commander issued orders, and *House Ollant* heeled smartly to her impulse engines.

"First Fleet transponders," Ito reported. "Admiral Runacres is also here. He is transmitting to us on laser link."

"Laser link?" Tar Fell said. "How were our coordinates resolved so quickly? That transmission was initiated before we exited hyperlight."

"My mate saw us coming," Kateos said proudly.

"Of course," Tar Fell gasped.

Admiral Runacres's space-battered countenance was suddenly on holo-vid, watery blue eyes glowing like icy coals. Tar Fell struggled to understand the human's words, but the officer's expression and somber tone were eloquent.

"Armada-Master Tar Fell." Kateos translated as Runacres spoke. Tar Fell studied the human carefully. "I ask you to join up with Admiral Chou at best speed. The Ulaggi are about to perform a tactical jump. I anticipate an attack first upon Admiral Chou. He has been instructed to stand and fight. We must defeat the Ulaggi here. All humanity pleads for your help."

Tar Fell took his eyes from Runacres's grim visage and scanned the tactical plot. Admiral Chou's formation sagged in his direction, working desperately to minimize time to rendezvous.

"Emergency flank speed," Tar Fell ordered. "Set course for join-up with Admiral Chou."

He inspected the increasing amounts of information available on the status boards. Icons representing six more Ulaggi ships in low orbit were revealed. The marauders of history had returned to the konish system. Tar Fell's great resolve welled within his massive chest, and his emotion bladders exploded with incessant fury. Battle was at hand—battle with the timeless enemy.

"Inform Admiral Runacres we join battle," Tar Fell roared. "Our Vows of Protection demand nothing less."

"Armada-Master," General Magoon said, "the Ulaggi ships have jumped."

* * *

Buccari, on the flight deck of *Condor One*, leaned into her tethers, stretching neck and back. She felt her corvette compressing its docking cradle dampeners as *Novaya Zemlya* strained against its own acceleration. Persistent gee on a mothership was unsettling. Admiral Runacres was going to war in a hurry.

"What are we waiting for?" Flaherty demanded. "Launch 'em!"

"War is defined," Thompson said, "as endless boredom interrupted by split seconds of utter terror."

Buccari studied the tactical display, set at maximum range. Chaos reigned, yet one thing was certain—there would be battle. Her heart pounded in her throat. She imagined what Runacres was contemplating: somehow, the admiral needed to combine his forces against one of the Ulaggi battle groups. Which one? And what was happening on Genellan? No reports from the planet had been received. Buccari feared the worst, and that fear swelled in her throat, suffocating her.

"Get this show on the road," Flaherty grumbled.

"It's pretty ragged out there, Flack," Buccari said, desperately holding her emotions in check. "Admiral's trying to get us some easy pickings."

"Target board be showing plenty of meat," Chief Tyler offered. "Can't hardly be missing with that much to shoot at. Weapons be ready, sir."

"Engineering, anything to report?" Buccari barked, diverting her anxieties.

"All systems turning and burning, Skipper," Warrant Officer Silva reported patiently.

Yet again Buccari went down her squadron status annunciator, electronically interrogating her squadron's tactical systems. All pilots, all crews, all corvettes signaled readiness to launch.

Et Lorlyn responded verbally: "Commander, there will be a great battle. I speak-ah for all pilots of Condor Squadron. We are proud-ah to fly on your wing."

"Thank you, Your Excellency," she replied. "And I'm glad

you're on my team. All of you. You're the best pilots in the universe. Now knock off the bullshit and stand by for launch orders."

"Hoot-ah, hoot-ah," Et Lorlyn thundered.

Condor flight was ready. Buccari, using her eye cursor, punched up group ops.

"Group, Condor. Launch status?" she asked.

Carmichael's broad countenance materialized on her commvid. His glance darted about the flag bridge, brown eyes slit with fierce concentration.

"Holding launch, Condor," Carmichael replied, bringing his fatigue-shadowed gaze down to hers. His adamantine features softened. "Stand by," he said.

A secure channel phased in. Buccari linked up. "What's happening, Jake?" she asked.

"Crap just hit the fan, Sharl," Carmichael said. "They've jumped."

FORTY-FOUR

DESPERATE MEASURES

"Where away?" Runacres demanded. His gaze darted between the radar plots and the gravitronics map. He clenched the station railing, wishing desperately for more speed, more power.

"Master Dowornobb, where are they? Tell me something."

On the comm-vid, the kone's massive countenance stared down at his instrumentation, brow tufts rigid, immense brown eyes unblinking. Runacres looked about the flag bridge. All hands fixated on the gravitronics plot, all movement frozen. His gaze moved to the flagship's command bridge. The tableau was the same; all eyes locked on the gravitronics map and the radar plots. Except for Merriwether; hands clasped to her breast, she stared up at him. Runacres exchanged nods with his old shipmate.

"There!" Dowornobb thundered, pointing.

Runacres's attention snapped to the gravitronic display. Delicate electronic signatures blossomed on the screen in the anticipated sector. The Ulaggi battle group was indeed attacking Second Fleet.

"Contact group alpha is on radar," the watch officer reported.

Six hostile icons materialized on the main sensor plot, frighteningly close to Admiral Chou's right flank. Runacres marveled at their maneuvering accuracy.

"How do they stay in one piece?" Merriwether asked.

"Main battery engagement imminent," the watch officer reported.

Until Tar Fell could join up, it was six alien interstellars against six Legion motherships. The numbers were even, but the alien commander had executed a classic maneuver; the Ulaggi salient was positioned to broadside Chou's flank. Runacres gave a silent prayer. There was little else he could do. His ships were at max impulse, and still he was three days from engaging. Like the vast konish armada rising from the second planet, his ships were irrelevant.

"S.O.S. from Genellan." Captain Katz came up on his screen.

"Go," Runacres said, almost grateful for a diversion, anything to take his mind from his frustration.

"General Wattly reporting," Katz continued. "*Madagascar* was destroyed with all hands, Admiral."

Runacres's frustration was eclipsed by anger.

"New Edmonton . . . destroyed," Katz went on. "Ocean Station destroyed. Nothing heard from MacArthur's Valley. No fewer than two thousand humans and possibly as many as six thousand kones dead."

"Eight thousand dead!" Carmichael gasped.

"Admiral," Katz continued, "an estimated four to six hundred prisoners have been taken off the planet."

"God damn them!" Merriwether spoke for all.

Eight thousand dead. Prisoners taken! Runacres stared with boiling fury at the icons. And yet his rage could not mask his horror, the horror that the Ulaggi might know the location of Earth. Frustrated fury provided desperate inspiration.

If the Ulaggi could do it, then so could he.

"*Hawaii*'s taking ranging fire." Wells reported.

So soon! Runacres shifted his attention to the developing battle. Status board resolution was enhanced; six ominous red squares signifying enemy ships were arrayed in an attack line against Admiral Chou's right flank, the blue and white icons of Chou's convoy less than fifty thousand klicks distant from the aliens. The intervening space contained a fast-moving corvette screen swinging to meet the oncoming threat. Admiral Chou, from his flagship *Malta* on the far side of the battle line, commenced a wheeling maneuver in an effort to match up with the Ulaggi ship-to-ship, but the formation intervals were too great;

perceptible ship movement was glacial. Chou would not cover his exposed flank soon enough. The four yellow icons representing Tar Fell's task force were still hours from engagement range. Could Admiral Chou stave off the assault long enough to gain Tar Fell's support? Runacres wondered. He must.

"Commodore Wells! Master Dowornobb." Runacres barked. "I want to execute an in-system jump . . . to engage the enemy."

"Sir?" Wells replied.

On *Eire*'s command bridge, Merriwether's helmeted head jerked upward. Runacres locked stares with his flagship captain.

"Yes-ah, Admiral," Dowornobb replied, hunched down, his image on the comm-vid absorbed with concentration. "How close-ah to Admiral Chou should-ah we attempt?"

"No, Master Dowornobb," Runacres replied. "I want you to put me dead in front of the Ulaggi ships coming off the planet. They're vulnerable. They will not be able to maneuver."

"Ah . . . ah, yes, but-ah, Admiral," the konish scientist's grainy image filled the comm-vid, brow tufts spiked like iron. "But-ah we jump directly into Genellan's gravity well. There is grave-ah risk of overshoot. Of a reentry, Admiral."

"Master Dowornobb, how soon will you be ready?" Runacres demanded.

"Uh . . . uh," Dowornobb said, scanning his instruments, his fingers flying. "I-ah am ready now, Admiral."

"Commodore Wells?"

"All hands, jump stations!" Wells shouted.

Jakkuk cleared her mind. Fist a' Yerg's destroyers, their crew's battle screams penetrating the ether, rippled from the holds of her star-cruisers.

"A good exit, Jakkuk-hajil," Dar commended.

Indeed. Jakkuk's cell had erupted from hyperlight at the intended coordinates, with the correct vector, placing her star-cruisers in position to roll up the alien's flank. The cell-controller issued maneuvering commands. Her ship-mistresses broke from grid matrix and accelerated to their line of battle. The dominant gave orders to engage.

The human ships returned fire, but the hapless interstellar on the flank was taken under simultaneous fire by three Ulaggi star-cruisers. Its shield signals were quickly burned away. With their interstellar in extremis, alien screening units tried in vain to distract the Ulaggi battery focus. Caught between the defensive systems of Jakkuk's cruisers and the coordinated fury of a'Yerg's destroyers, the alien attack ships were vaporized like mist striking magma.

"That ship is incapacitated," Dar said. "Shift your battery focus, Jakkuk-hajil."

As the dominant spoke, the alien interstellar gave up its ghost, detonating near its core with a glorious super-critical ionization. Roonish battle screams filled all tactical frequencies.

"Ah, yesss!" Karyai purred.

Jakkuk adjusted target priority. The full weight of her line joined in enfilade on the next two ships in the human line. So great was the directed firepower that Jakkuk commanded Ship-Mistresses y'Trig and Kapu to direct their barrage onto the human interstellars maneuvering intrepidly toward the killing zone.

"They do not run," Ship-Mistress Remac snarled.

"No," Jakkuk replied, transmitting a stream of dendritic orders. "They chase us to their death."

Jakkuk's cruiser cell hammered against the exposed elements of the human formation, at the same time moving laterally to offset the alien commander's wheeling maneuver. Another alien ship was taken under fire and a third, but at a cost. Ship-Mistress Kapu reported her cruiser taking shield-warping impact energy. Jakkuk directed Remac to move the dominant's ship into Kapu's sector, to provide supporting fire. At that moment the second human ship ruptured. A subtle orange glow flared from its central core. Its energy weapons were stilled.

"Yesss," Dar whispered. "They die well."

Jakkuk rolled her star-cruisers along the human line, but her attention was now on the four interstellars last to arrive from hyperlight. These were larger ships, emitting peculiar signatures, different from the humans. Their mass was worrisome, and their engagement velocity was considerable; it would be a short encounter, and likely fierce. Jakkuk took note of their shifting disposition; their commander was not divulging her battle formation. Competent perhaps, but could she fight? Would she fight?

"Hark!" Karyai barked. "What is this?"

Jakkuk also detected the gravitronic signal anomaly. The cell-controller shifted her attention to the other human ships, eight interstellars plodding into battle at impulse speed, still three watch cycles from weapons range. Jakkuk detected gravitronic warp. Amazingly, the distant human task force disappeared into hyperlight.

"Blood, they have jumped!" Jakkuk shouted.

"Jumped," Karyai whispered.

"Where?" Dar demanded.

FORTY-FIVE

FALLING

Split seconds lasted an eternity.

Runacres clutched at his tethers. The turbulence and the spatial disorientation were severe, but the uncertainty was horrifying. The proximity of Genellan's gravitation field affected HLA field properties, and the hyperlight translation was too short; it was as if the jump exit started before the entrance had been completed. Had his fleet physically been in two places at once? Runacres fought for consciousness, second-guessing his decision. His ships and crews were experiencing stresses never before imposed. Would their systems be functional? Could his fleet fight?

"Grid marginally stable," Wells gasped, almost a sob. "All ships reporting. *Baffin*, *Kyushu*, and *Corse* single-linked. All other ships alpha-alpha. Threat assessment is saturated."

"Jupiter's balls, what a ride!" Merriwether exclaimed over the command circuit. Runacres looked down upon the flag bridge. His flagship captain leaned into her tethers, shouting orders to *Eire*'s underway watch, her hands punching the air.

"Launch the screen!" Runacres commanded, struggling for command of his brain.

"Aye aye," Carmichael shouted. "Standing by for threat axis determination."

"Maneuvering to modified line of battle," Wells boomed.

Runacres stared at the mysteriously blank status screens. He desperately needed a reference point from which to launch his attack. Data points materialized and shifted in gravitronic flux, laboring with time delays engendered by great distances.

Threat warnings warbled and clanged. He needed the enemy's location.

Genellan bloomed into resolution, enormous, universe-filling; its magnificent proximity sucked the air from his lungs. Runacres concentrated on his instrumentation. Systems adjusted, filtering the onslaught of data. Preliminary returns sparkled into life, faded, and resolved.

"Critical vector!" Merriwether shouted on the command circuit. "We're on the fall line and accelerating past emergency limits. Permission to deflect trajectory?"

"Stand by," Runacres ordered. He stared at the status plots.

"Navigation systems are resetting," Wells reported. The big man was all business. Runacres would miss his presence.

"Commodore Wells, you will immediately cross deck to *Novaya Zemlya*. Take command of the second division and proceed immediately to a covering orbit under the protection of the defense station. Scientist Dowornobb and the technical teams are to be removed from the battle. Their knowledge must be preserved. They are your responsibility."

"But . . . Admiral?" Wells responded.

"You have your orders, Franklin," Runacres snapped.

"Aye aye, Admiral," Wells replied, relinquishing his position to a senior watchstander. His large body shot across the flag bridge.

"Admiral, I say again!" Merriwether was shouting. "Request permission to deflect trajectory."

"Stand by, Captain!" Runacres shouted back.

Surprise. He needed the advantage of surprise. He held superior gravity position, but he needed surprise.

"Come on," he growled. "Information. Give me a pointer."

"Contact group bravo!" the watch officer reported. "Bearing one-one-five. Engagement range."

"Threat axis established!" the operations watch officer shouted. "Targets designated."

"Commence firing," Runacres commanded.

Oh, man!" Flaherty gasped. "My brains are coming out my nose."

"Crank it up, Flack," Buccari shouted, shaking off the fuzziness.

They were out. It had been, by an order of magnitude, the most turbulent jump in Buccari's experience. Through bleary eyes she checked instruments; launch alert lights were already illuminated.

"Rog'," Flaherty replied, gloved hands flying over his console.

A secure interrogation brought Buccari's attention back to the comm-vid. Carmichael was staring at her, his countenance at once tragic and proud. She linked in.

"Pretty nasty ride," she said.

"Come back to me, Sharl," the group-leader said. The secure channel dissolved before she had opportunity to answer.

Buccari stared, unseeing, at the tactical plot. A premonition of death stole over her. She surrendered to a great sadness.

"All systems go," Thompson shouted.

Buccari's eyes refocused. The screen plot updated as she watched, reestablishing threat axis. Launch lights illuminated. *Novaya Zemlya*'s corvette bay doors swept aside, revealing a star-splattered blackness.

"Launch all corvettes!" Carmichael's steel-hard command penetrated her tumultuous thoughts, shutting them off. Her conditioning took over, and she transformed instantly into an extension of her corvette.

"Hoo-o-o-ot!" Flaherty yodeled.

Launch authorization illuminated. Buccari used her eye cursor to acknowledge release. Flaherty sounded the maneuvering alarm. A hollow sound vibrated her ship as docking grapples fell away. Sequencing diodes flashed with the countdown.

"Launching," she broadcast over the intercom.

Condor One jolted into motion, propelled by its launch piston into the yawning abyss. Clear of the hangar bay, Genellan loomed to starboard, a glittering crescent, opalescent against fathomless blackness. It was huge! They were gut-wrenchingly close to the planet's night side, and they were plunging directly into its star-occluding, black-satin depths.

"Good frigging grief!" Flaherty shouted. "We're in the trees—"

At that instant *Novaya Zemlya*'s main battery discharged; a silent, diaphanous bolt of white gold disappeared to a perspective point just above the planet's limb. The electronics in *Condor One* resonated with the energy weapon's field effects.

"Whooee!" Flaherty shouted. "Big dogs are barking."

"Setting vector!" Buccari shouted, hammering in a power coupling, pivoting the corvette to its rendezvous course. In the great distances, left and right, mothership energy weapons discharged like golden razors slashing black velvet. She checked trajectory; the fleet was falling into the planet at a breathtaking rate. What was Runacres doing?

"Admiral better pull out," Thompson said.

"Clear angle," Flaherty announced.

Buccari met the swing and positioned the corvette's nose on screen course with heavy-handed squirts of power. She checked tactical and would not credit her eyes—six large-mass hostile contacts were arrayed before the fleet, six alien interstellars, two by two, straining to clear Genellan orbit.

Runacres's strategy was suddenly clear. And brilliant.

The Ulaggi interstellars had no choice but to climb out straight ahead, seeking a velocity vector that would null their orbital momentum. The konish defense platform, badly damaged but still deadly, severely restricted their maneuvering options. Runacres had them in a box.

Legion mothership batteries blazed in all quadrants. Her corvette's shielding rendered the alien return fire invisible, but Buccari's detection systems indicated columns of destruction flaring up from the Ulaggi energy weapons. The bugs were targeting the Legion motherships; the corvettes posed an insignificant threat in comparison. There were no Ulaggi attack craft on the screens; the alien fast-movers were being kept in their hangars, enabling the Ulaggi interstellars to jump to hyperlight at the earliest possible moment. Runacres was not going to let them.

"*Condor Two*'s up and out. And linking," Thompson reported. *Novaya Zemlya*'s main battery discharged again, resonating her corvette's detection systems. Prudence dictated opening distance from the Legion heavies, and quickly.

"Six gees," Buccari broadcast, setting throttles.

"Three's out. Four. Five and Six. Condor flight is hard-linked to the screen."

"Kicking it!" she barked, hitting her main ignitors. Condor flight leaped forward as one, flattening all crew members against their acceleration couches.

"Hoot . . . h-hoot," Flaherty grunted.

"Condor's up," Buccari broadcast on laser link.

"Take the point, Condor," Wanda Green's gravelly voice replied.

Buccari checked tactical. *Eagle One* was screen commander, and six Eagle 'vettes were established at the focus of the screen disposition. Johnny Stanton and his Nighthawks struggled for position on the center right; Gordon Chou's Merlins maneuvered to center left. Max Sakamoto's and Mick Wong's squadrons streaked outward, covering the flanks. Peregrine and Raven squadrons, in reserve and escorting a gaggle of fleet-fuelers, brought up the rear.

Buccari, as fleet ace, acknowledged her preeminent assignment on the point of the spear. She lifted her scan outside. Rising on orbit above the planet's sunlit limb, sparkling like a diamond, was the battered konish defense station.

"All units remain above the firing plane," Green ordered. "We got no business in the middle of this fur ball. Let the heavies hammer it out. As long as no fast-movers come out, we'll stand by to collect lifeboats."

Buccari's six corvettes, in advance of and spread above the primary plane of the screen, streaked across the void. She acknowledged Green's sobering command and settled back to watch the mothership battles unfold, one below them, backdropped by Genellan's threatening mass, and the other far above.

"Tasker," she said over the intercom, "any reports on Admiral Chou?"

"It's bad, Skipper," her communication technician replied. "*Hawaii*'s gone. Lost at least a dozen 'vettes, far as they can tell."

Buccari's soul imploded. Her anger blossomed.

"Geez, Skipper, it's happening again," Tasker said. "Check button six. I got a plain voice intercept from the Second Fleet battle."

Buccari used her eye cursor to select the designated frequency. From across the great distance came an all too familiar scream:

"Booocharry! BOOOO-CHARRY!" the horribly familiar voice wailed. *"A'Yerg hai doe, Booocharry. Lay aw doe chow sei."*

"Translation," Buccari demanded, already knowing.

Tasker piped the translation text over Buccari's headup.

"Ahyerg is here, Buccari. Come to me and die."

FORTY-SIX

ATTRITION

PHM-16, one of twenty planetary habitation modules being jettisoned by Admiral Chou, broke loose from fleet auxiliary, *T.L.S. Darmstadt*. One hundred settlers, stacked within PHM-16's passenger containments, cowered in their acceleration harnesses, listening wide-eyed to the clanking and groaning of their emergency separation. An agonizing hour crawled by as their module floated in a marshaling queue. Occasionally a child complained, a fragile, futile noise, but for the most part the distraught settlers waited in panicked silence.

The grappling clamps of the orbiting maneuvering tugs slamming against PHM-16's flanks exhorted a feeble cheer from the lander's hapless occupants. The rough acceleration that followed transformed the cheers to nervous shouts and screams as the OMTs jolted the ponderous lander roughly onto its reentry vector. Once the habitation module was established on course, the tugs disconnected and returned to the marshaling area for fuel, to repeat the process with another waiting habitation module filled with frightened settlers.

A steady stream of PHMs was being propelled planetward. Four days hence the habitation modules would enter Genellan's atmosphere, using their precious fuel and monstrous retro engines to establish correct atmospheric penetration angle and to retard their touchdowns on the planet's surface, but for now they plummeted directly for the planet, with no force other than their original impetus and no acceleration other than that afforded by planetary gravity.

* * *

Destroyer Fist a'Yerg led her roonish attack force on a sweep through the outer defense perimeter. The human fast-movers, suffering grievous punishment, had retreated from the engagement zone. They would be back, a'Yerg was certain, after salving their wounds and reorganizing their shattered ranks. Humans had proven nothing if not intrepid.

Above her in the gravity well, human and Ulaggi interstellars danced their languorous ballet of death, their great energy weapons flicking out, stingers of piercing incandescence. Jakkuk's cell of star-cruisers continued to pound the shifting human flank, outmaneuvering the human commander. Jakkuk-hajil's disciplined mind wove a strong command web, despite her inhibited libido. A'Yerg sensed the cell-controller's feeble *g'ort* flickering among the dendritic signals, feeble yet still provocative.

The alien fleet was being crushed, nevertheless a'Yerg gave the beleaguered ships respectful berth. The roonish attack commander's attention was drawn to the downpour of unpowered ships heading from the battle and toward the planet. Targets of opportunity. Targets of value, possibly holds filled with humans. Intercepting the downloads would likely bring the alien escorts out to battle.

The strategy was effective; as a'Yerg's formation of destroyers arced downward, four fast-movers streaked from behind the battle line, intent on interception. Six more followed. The human ships held intercept position; a'Yerg could not ignore them. She directed three destroyer triads to engage the first flight and steered four triads more at the trailing attackers. A'Yerg increased power and established an intercept vector on the nearest of the unpowered vessels. Her two wing-mates assumed attack spread.

There were so many targets. As her magnificent *g'ort* swelled in ecstasy, a'Yerg gave the raging animal within license to scream its fury.

Jakkuk brought her attention away from a'Yerg's attack. A third human interstellar had died. Combined fire from four Ulaggi star-cruisers reduced it to a glowing radiation cinder, still spewing lifeboats, lifeboats filled with the dead and the dying. The engaged enemy fleet was defeated, its number reduced to three. As Jakkuk watched, one of the remaining ships wallowed from the line, shields stripped, its return fire reduced to desultory spasms. The engagement was in hand, yet Jakkuk's exquisite fear was not abating.

The large ships hurtling down upon Jakkuk's battle line fueled her emotions, but what concerned her far more was the dire predicament of her sister cell-controller. Kwanna's cell was caught in low orbit by the human fleet commander's outrageous gambit. Her sister's glorious fear had risen beyond ecstasy. A peculiar emotion in Kwanna's dendritic transmissions ripped at Jakkuk's being. Kwanna's thoughts hinted strongly of imminent death, of glorious death in battle. Jakkuk's envy spiraled upward.

"Kwanna-hajil's cell is under fierce alien fire," the cell-controller reported.

"Yes," Karyai snarled.

Jakkuk sensed the political's awareness working within her own, very close, frighteningly gentle. Perhaps even aroused.

"Blood!" Dar snarled. "The human commander is insane."

"We have underestimated these humans," Karyai said, withdrawing from the interface and from Jakkuk's mind.

"No longer. Bring the attack force back to grid," Dar commanded. "We must consolidate, or we will loose Kwanna's cell."

"Fist a'Yerg is attacking, mother," Jakkuk said

The political hissed with contempt. Roons, once committed to attack, did not relent. Aborting a'Yerg's thrust, even employing the most penetrating dendritic interface, would challenge the full measure of Jakkuk's powers. The cell-controller's self-doubt was evident.

"I will recall the roons," Karyai snarled with contempt. "Mind your cell, Jakkuk-hajil."

"Yes, mother," Jakkuk replied, quelling her cowardly relief.

The lakk's mind slipped once again into the interface. Karyai's powerful essence projected an imperious wrath, tightly focused, intensely textured. Except for the rise and fall of her breast, the lakk sat immobile at her station, long chin elevated, eyes tightly shut. Bruised lips, thin and hard, traced a beatific smile.

Almost immediately the enraged screams of a'Yerg and her pilots erupted into the attack frequencies, not battle cries, but a wretched whining, an enraged imprecation. The political increased the unfathomable powers of her dendritic projection, brutalizing the roons into hateful obeisance. With formations wavering and ragged, the destroyers changed course, breaking away from the curious human activity.

The roonish attack had been broken; a'Yerg had been recalled. The lakkish presence slipped from the interface. Jakkuk allowed her mind to explore the control system's confines; its neural chambers echoed with a slow, fading resonance, the shuddering taint of emotional power.

Jakkuk·forced her full attention to the advancing line of battle. It would take a watch cycle to retrieve a'Yerg's attack force, and Jakkuk's cruiser cell was still engaged with the enemy. A fourth wounded human mothership died as she watched, shriven by a blast to the power cores, a glorious death in combat, its death throes marked with a majestic golden energy flare. And yet the humans seemed undaunted by the enlarging massacre. Hopelessly outnumbered, the two remaining human interstellars pressed into engagement with mindless ferocity. Even their fleet auxiliaries moved forward into the line of battle, adding their feeble calibers to the raging fury. One of the transports collapsed immediately under withering bombardments, and then another, both ships atomizing into nothingness.

"Two interstellars left," Dar said. "Honor is ours."

"No, there are still six," Karyai said. "Four more are coming to play. Shift your pressure, Cell-Controller. The remaining two must await their annihilation."

Jakkuk nodded. She wanted nothing more than to exterminate the targets at hand, but the fast approaching large-mass ships could not be denied. Maintaining standoff fire on the human ships with only two of her cruisers, Jakkuk shifted weapons focus onto the approaching formation. Her cell maneuvered to the impending encounter, small motes drifting slowly in the vastness of the universe. The actual engagement, unlike the stately overture of maneuver, would be brief, much like the arrival of glorious death.

Tar Fell was in awe. Admiral Chou continued to press the attack.

"Laserburst from Admiral Chou," a watch officer reported.

"Report," Tar Fell replied.

"Signal reads: 'Will hold the enemy in place until you arrive.' "

Tar Fell's respect rose impossibly higher.

"Targets are assigned. Firing sequences are established," Magoon reported. "All is ready, Armada-Master."

"Deliver me mine enemy," Tar Fell boomed the timeless prayer.

The armada-master floated above the command bridge's observation deck, staring into star-washed infinity. General Magoon and Captain Ito drifted at his side. Their strategy was defined, their options few. Beyond the circular transparency of the observation window, Genellan and her moons, sublime spheres fully illuminated, dominated the ebony expanse. On the deck below, silhouetted against the planet's ethereal radiance, Ambassador Kateos also stared outward.

"It is time to take battle stations," Ito said, his konish without accent. The human's anger smoldered beneath his words.

Tar Fell looked down at the fragile, helmeted human. Ito's countenance was as impassive as iron, except for the glaring caldrons of his black eyes. The little man was angry beyond judgment. Is this how humans fought? From anger?

"Casualties, Captain?" Tar Fell asked.

"Motherships *Hawaii*, *Hispaniola*, *Vancouver*, and *Honshu* destroyed. Transports *Darmstadt*, *Kent*, and *Oslo* destroyed," Ito spat. "*Malta* and *Kodiak* continue to press the engagement."

"Admiral Chou will be a great hero," Magoon pronounced.

"Admiral Chou will soon be dead," Kateos said, turning

and wending her way upward along a perimeter companion-way. She joined them on the hyperlight bridge.

"The Ulaggi formation has ceased maneuvering," Magoon reported. "Four ships have aligned to our approach. Two ships remain in contact with Admiral Chou. The humans are holding their own."

"Perhaps we have arrived in time," Kateos said.

Time. An eternity had passed as they watched Admiral Chou's motherships die. Cruel time always passed slowly.

An alarm sounded. On the command bridge Ship-General Otred commissioned the battle watch.

"Armada-Master, permission to return to my station," Ito said.

"It is time," Tar Fell boomed.

Ito saluted and pushed resolutely across the bridge for the human section of the hyperlight bridge.

"This is torture," Kateos said.

"Such is war," Magoon rumbled.

Tar Fell looked upon the comely ambassador, proud of her indomitable spirit, yet sad that she must be here, exposed to mortal danger. The Ulaggi might well prevail over his ships on this day, as they had over the humans.

"Mistress Kateos, you will leave the bridge," Tar Fell commanded.

"I would like to remain," Kateos replied.

"On this bridge you have my respect, Ambassador," Tar Fell said. "But you have no authority. Report to your emergency station."

Kateos bowed, donned her helmet, and departed.

Another alarm. The observation port sealed over. Tar Fell floated across the hyperlight bridge and took position behind his command console. Enemy fleet dispositions solidified. Acquisition and targeting designations held firm. The game board was set. Tar Fell's ships and crews were about to be tested, as was his leadership. The armada-master pulled his helmet over his great head and secured the seals.

Tar Fell's tactic was to attack the two units harrying what was left of Admiral Chou's fleet; those Ulaggi ships were least prepared to defend themselves. The desired outcome: to provide a diversion enabling Admiral Chou's surviving units to separate from battle. Tar Fell hoped to rescue the humans, but his first goal was to destroy alien ships.

"Positioning maneuvers are complete," Magoon reported. The flagship was now in the lead position of a four-ship oblique line abreast. Next in the line of battle, on *House Ollant*'s left quarter stepped back at standard battle interval, was *Star Nappo*, followed by *Thullolia*. Star-cruiser *Mountain Flyer*, with the smallest energy optics, brought up the rear wing. Ito had beseeched Tar Fell not to take the van. Human battle doctrine dictated that flagships operate from a less exposed position. Tar Fell was not to be denied.

"Our primary batteries will have opportunity for but one discharge," General Magoon confirmed. "Assuming we strip the Ulaggi shields, our secondary batteries may have a telling effect; they will be fired at extremely close range."

"Inform the battery masters that our fate is in their hands," Tar Fell said. Magoon acknowledged.

Timing was everything. Firing prematurely and failing to exact significant damage might allow the enemy to counter with an overwhelming response. To wait too long would court destruction without inflicting damage. In battle, timing was everything.

"All ships are ready, Armada-Master," Magoon reported.

"Kill the enemy," Tar Fell said, issuing the traditional order.

The armada-master concentrated on the main status plot. The Ulaggi and human ships were racing directly at them, the dimensions of the battle area expanding like a blossoming *kotta* flower.

The time for contemplation was over. It was time to react.

"Engagement radius counting down," a watch officer reported. "Ten . . . nine . . . eight . . ."

Tar Fell cinched his acceleration harness and took a last look around his bridge. All was ready. Battle was at hand.

". . . four . . . three . . . two . . . one—"

House Ollant trembled. Violently. The flagship's main

energy batteries discharged simultaneously, making the superstructure sing with high-pitched vibration. But the manic report of his weapons was overwhelmed by the jolting shudder of a shield collapse.

Alarms brayed.

"We have been grievously hit," Magoon reported.

Tar Fell's flagship had absorbed three first-order energy blasts. The flagship's screens were pulverized; only the aft shields remained in place. Pressurization alarms warbled. The temperature dropped; Tar Fell's visor fogged over. The environmental systems in his battle suit activated, clearing his vision. A frosty haze sublimated from the air. A slippery patina of moisture covered all instrumentation surfaces.

"Damage control reports!" Magoon shouted.

They had survived. Tar Fell's slicing tactic had blown by the Ulaggi task-force, driving his flotilla far beyond the realm of battle. The armada-master's piercing gaze scanned the status plots, surveying the aftermath. His fleet had been reduced by one.

"*Mountain Flyer* is destroyed," Magoon confirmed.

"Bring your ships about, Flotilla-General," Tar Fell commanded. "Prepare for another strike. Advance at full power."

Magoon acknowledged and issued signals. The big ships strained against their own inertia, as main engines opposing their headlong attack vector were fired in retro. Tar Fell relaxed against the mounting gee-force. His heart thundered in his great chest, but his mind was clear. His remaining ships might be damaged, but all were under full power, and all were still capable of fighting. Fight they would.

"Partial shield repairs are being affected," Magoon reported. As the flotilla-general spoke, environmental systems reengaged; pressurization levels returned and temperatures elevated. The annoying moisture evaporated.

"What is Admiral Chou doing?" Tar Fell roared in disbelief.

Admiral Chou had not broken from conflict. Tar Fell examined the battle plot; six Ulaggi ships still maneuvered in formation, two in mortal embrace with *Malta* and *Kodiak*.

Admiral Chou had rejected the opportunity to flee. *Mountain Flyer* had been sacrificed to no benefit.

With infuriatingly slow pace, Tar Fell's impulse-blasting ships were reversed on course and accelerated back along their attack vector. Tar Fell analyzed the status plots, trying to develop a new tactic.

"We have hurt them, Armada-Master." Ito's excited voice came over the command circuit. "*Malta*'s batteries are not being answered. Admiral Chou is taking the upper hand in his engagement."

Unbelievably, the beleaguered human ships accelerated toward their tormentors. Astoundingly, the Ulaggi ship nearest *Malta* blossomed with the unmistakable emissions of a catastrophic reactor failure.

Ito shouted in his own tongue.

An enemy mothership was destroyed. *Mountain Flyer* was avenged.

Muffled cheers rose above even the screaming alarms.

"Now it is five to five," Magoon said.

"And we have them between us," Tar Fell thundered. "All ships ahead, emergency flank, General Magoon. Commence firing in range."

"Armada-Master," Magoon reported, "the Ulaggi attack craft are returning to their launch ships."

"Tar Fell," Ito shouted, "the interstellars are forming an hyperlight matrix. They are preparing to jump."

"So it would appear," Tar Fell replied, analyzing the battle plot.

"We have beat them," Magoon said.

Tar Fell only grunted.

FORTY-SEVEN

TURNING TIDE

Runacres pounded a gauntleted fist into his palm.

"Override your firing lockouts!" Merriwether shouted. "Keep their shields loaded."

On the ship's bridge, *Eire*'s underway watch danced to their captain's orders. The flagship's energy batteries erupted with unchoked power. And again. Two more hits! The enemy answered in kind. Powerful beams ripped at *Eire*'s deteriorating shields.

Runacres returned his attention to the data screens. Sun angle, photon currents, magnetic and gravity field flux, radiation levels, shield strength parameters, were displayed—the elements of the battle equation. *Eire*'s shield strength was critically diminished, her energy batteries operating above critical temperature tolerances.

Runacres lifted his gaze to the main operations plot. Icons representing *Eire*, *Kyushu*, *Tierra del Fuego*, and *Shikoku* knifed downward, straight for the vanguard of the alien formation. He intended to cross the enemy's bow with as much firepower as he could afford to risk. Weapons panels danced with the furious discharge of the fleet's main batteries. On the main navigation display, looming magnificently beyond the icons representing his rising targets, was the near limb of Genellan, too large to fit within his sensor screens. Runacres doubted his own sanity.

All eight motherships fired upon the enemy, but the trajectories of *Novaya Zemlya*, *Baffin*, *Britannia*, and *Corse* veered from the precipitous plunge, defying the planet's implacable attraction. Commodore Wells, still in transit, had taken command from his shuttle. Wells's division of motherships, en route rendezvous with the orbiting defense station, was too quickly elevating out of range, their delivered energy rapidly fading to nondestructive levels. This Runacres noted with grim satisfaction; those ships would fight again, and, more importantly, Scientist Dowornobb and the technical teams were safe.

The four Legion ships remaining on the descending battle line fired in phased sequence, punishing the shields and systems of the lead Ulaggi ships. Runacres's tactical advantage increased with each passing second, for as his motherships plunged planetward, firing angles prevented the trailing enemy vessels from firing on the humans without jeopardizing their own ships.

"Admiral, if we don't deflect in the next few minutes," Merriwether said, "we are committed to reentry."

Runacres stared at the battle plots. What price victory?

"*Shikoku* and *Kyushu* break off now," Runacres barked. "Join with Commodore Wells at best speed."

The operations watch officer relayed the admiral's orders. The two motherships labored away from the line of battle, still firing at the enemy, desperately seeking to stem their descents.

"Admiral!" Merriwether shouted. Shield warnings blared constantly.

"Press the attack, Captain," Runacres ordered.

Merriwether glared up at the flag bridge. *Eire* took a first order energy strike; the dispersed power buzzed through the ship's structure like a swarm of two-ton hornets.

"Aye aye," Merriwether replied, turning to her bridge crew and shouting orders.

A different set of alarms sounded. Merriwether had ordered all nonessential crew to their lifeboats. *Eire* took another vicious hit; electrical systems fluctuated drunkenly. A blue haze suffused the environment. Emergency power generators kicked on line and secondary systems became inoperative. *Eire* was in trouble.

"Your status, Captain," Runacres demanded.

"Propulsion systems are degraded," Merriwether reported.

"Very well," Runacres replied. "Can you still fight?"

In answer, *Eire*'s main battery discharged. One of the lead Ulaggi ships flared majestically, a blossoming aura of destruction.

A kill! A mothership kill!

"New target!" Merriwether screamed. "Maintain firing rates!"

Eire and *Tierra del Fuego* passed directly in front of the climbing aliens, their coordinated firepower focused on the Ulaggi van. The other Ulaggi lead ship, now under the combined weight of mothership energy cannons, died even more spectacularly than did the first. Another kill! The bridge crews cheered wildly.

Celebration was short-lived. *Eire,* her precipitate trajectory now streaking below the orbital altitude of the aliens, was taken under fire by the next two Ulaggi ships. The flagship's wavering shields were stripped away. The mothership's mass shuddered. Her wallowing oscillations grew more extreme.

"*TDF* and *Eire* deflect course to orbit," Runacres ordered.

The operations watch officer acknowledged and issued signals. *Tierra del Fuego*'s plunging trajectory showed a small alteration. Telemetry revealed all *TDF* main engines in radical overboost, straining to maintain a parabolic deflection through the increasing effects of atmospheric drag.

Eire's course remained unchanged.

"Captain Merriwether," Runacres boomed. "Make best course to orbit."

"Main propulsion is down," Merriwether reported quietly.

"Estimated time to repair your casualty," Runacres demanded. He stared at the status plots. The Ulaggi ships rising on orbit were well above his altitude now, accelerating from Genellan's orbital imperative. Runacres needed to rejoin his fleet, to consolidate his forces. Perhaps he could marshal one more attack. If only Tar Fell—

"*Eire*'s out of the game, Admiral," Merriwether said, her back to him. Her bridge crew looked up from their consoles.

Runacres stared down at his flagship captain.

"It's over," she said, turning and staring across the void.

"Admiral!" the watch officer shouted. "Contact group alpha has jumped. Gravitronics indicate a local jump. They're coming our way."

"New targets!" the tactical officer shouted.

Five hostile icons materialized on *Eire*'s battle plot, but only five! Admiral Chou and Tar Fell had exacted some retribution. The Ulaggi ships emerged from their local jump with all the advantages; they were above him; they had energy, numbers, maneuver, and firepower.

"Commodore Wells has raised his flag on *Novaya Zemlya*, Admiral," the operations officer reported.

Runacres was out of the game, too. At least for now.

"Inform Commodore Wells that he is task force commander," Runacres announced. He turned to look at the vid images of Genellan. Its black-velvet girth blotted out the stars. His dying flagship plunged into utter darkness.

Abandon ship alarms brayed.

"I've given the order, Admiral," Merriwether replied.

"Very well, Captain."

Most of *Eire*'s crew had long ago departed for lifeboat stations. Runacres stared up at the radar plot. Jettisoned lifeboats' beacons twinkled in a steady stream. Transponder IDs for fleet tugs and corvettes moved among the emergency craft, propelling the unpowered vessels into stable orbits as fast as they could be collected.

Runacres dispatched the flag watch to their lifeboats. He was alone on the flag bridge. On the ship's bridge, *Eire*'s battle watch secured from their posts with professional expediency. Within seconds only Merriwether and her officer-of-the-deck remained. Satisfied with the final muster, Merriwether excused the watchstander, and then she was alone. She stared up at the flag bridge.

"She was a fine ship, Sarah," Runacres said.

Eire thrummed with reentry vibrations, a meager hint of the violence to come. Stabilization systems were failing; the mothership was wallowing, making movement across the voids increasingly perilous.

"A damn fine ship," Merriwether replied.

"Will you join me in my barge?" Runacres asked, moving to the mezzanine railing.

The flagship captain nodded, releasing her tethers. "A moment, sir," she said.

Merriwether ordered all remaining lifeboats jettisoned. Damage control logged off. Seconds later all emergency status lights blinked to red. All boats were away. The flagship captain took a last long look around. Satisfied, she pushed off from her command station and arrowed upward. Holding firmly to the railing, Runacres caught her hand in his and pulled her to the deck. She clung to him, and Runacres took comfort in her familiar touch. For a few seconds they embraced.

Carmichael was at their side. "Your barge is waiting, Admiral," the group-leader said.

"Very well," Runacres exhaled.

"She's precessing, sir," Carmichael said. "We only have—"

Runacres silenced the well-meaning officer with a glare. Carmichael saluted and pushed through an overhead battle hatch.

"Captain Merriwether," Runacres said. "Are you ready?"

"After you, Admiral," she replied.

"Certainly," Runacres said.

Jakkuk's cell broached from hyperlight, a difficult translation; the planet was near, the entry vector precipitous. Once established in normal space, Jakkuk's navigation concerns were immediately displaced by an immense discomfiture. Something was dreadfully wrong. Kwanna-hajil's dendritic link was missing. Her sister cell-controller's powerful mind, so recently raging to ecstasy, was no more. A black hole thundered silently in Jakkuk's mind—no echoes, no vagrant impressions, only a loss beyond measurement.

Jakkuk surveyed the field of battle, seeking links with the surviving ship-mistresses. Alien ships, in three groups, were scattered in various orbits, with the main body climbing for shelter under the umbrella of the tenacious defense station. One alien ship labored at extremely low altitude, struggling to clear the atmosphere, its impulse signature radiating profligately. Jakkuk detected another ship, even lower, its impulse engines quiescent. Doomed, its skin glowed with impending destruction. Cell-Controller Kwanna had not perished alone.

Jakkuk located the remaining Ulaggi ships—only four.

"Status, Jakkuk-hajil," the dominant demanded.

"Two more star-cruisers have been destroyed," Jakkuk reported.

"Blood!" Dar muttered. "Three cruisers lost in battle."

"Honor is ours," Karyai said, sneering.

"Cell-Controller Kwanna has perished," Jakkuk continued. "Ship-Mistress y'Lante and the remaining cruisers are elevating to grid formation."

"Blood and blood!" Dar shouted. The dominant's features twisted with rage, her copper-tinted skin blue with anger.

"Permission to attack?" Jakkuk asked.

The alien interstellars were running for the cover of the orbiting weapons platform. Jakkuk rued having not earlier eliminated the miserable machine. Without its protective umbrella, the scattered human ships would have been pitifully vulnerable. Even with the satellite lurking over the battlefield, three of the alien ships were easily intercepted.

"What will we tell the Empress, Dar-hajil?" Karyai said. The lakk laughed cruelly.

The dominant remained silent. Jakkuk sensed her fury.

"Permission to attack?" she repeated.

Neck-crawling threat alarms exploded into life.

"Holy smokes!" Thompson shouted. "Hostiles coming out of hyperlight, sector two. Transponder matches—it's contact group alpha coming down on us."

Buccari analyzed the tactical display, watching the alien interstellars blossom, their icons garish with threat-assessment haloes. At current closure rates, the Legion corvette screen was less than three hours from contact radius. Ulaggi targeting systems lit up her threat warning panel.

"There are only five," Flaherty said. "Admiral Chou scored."

"Yeah, but the cost," Buccari said, her stomach tightening.

The enemy had consolidated. There were now nine alien main interstellars in orbital proximity, against six functioning Legion ships; Tar Fell's task group and Admiral Chou's decimated fleet no longer figured in the battle equation. Admiral Runacres's ships were scattered on wildly different orbits, while the ordered Ulaggi formations remained in position to coordinate an overwhelming attack. There was only one obstacle between the Legion motherships and an Ulaggi onslaught. Buccari's worst nightmare had come true. The corvettes stood squarely between the hammer and the anvil, fleas against tigers. Buccari knew the odds. All corvette pilots did. She forced herself to breathe.

Screen chatter exploded on the screen frequency. There were no orders forthcoming from group operations. *Eire* had been taken out, along with the corvette command structure.

"Attack formation one-one-delta!" Wanda Green roared, blasting over all other transmissions. "We're going after the high five. Condor has the point. Eagle's on the hook. Tanker call."

Brickshitter was taking charge. Buccari's operations annunciator updated, squadron position signals were assigned and attack precedence established. Buccari would lead the attack, taking Condor, Nighthawk, and Merlin squadrons down the throat of the beast. Wanda Green would bring Eagle, Grayhawk, and Osprey squadrons in behind Buccari's thrust, hoping to saturate the enemy's defenses.

"Where's our tanker?" Buccari snapped.

She commenced programming the attack profile for the squadrons under her lead, forcing her mind onto the job at hand. Too many delinquent thoughts trespassed on her concentration.

"Fueler section maneuvering our way now," Thompson replied. "Et Lorlyn's issuing tanking assignments."

"Very well," she replied, struggling to keep her voice steady.

The tactical display coruscated with a ripple of main battery fire, commanding Buccari's attention. The four low Ulaggi ships continued their climb out, trading desultory energy exchanges with the orbiting defense station. Commodore Wells's division had commenced a maneuver away from the station, as if to engage the Ulaggi ships. *Shikoku* and *Kyushu* were over the horizon, established in a climbing counterorbit that would bring them perilously close to the Ulaggi track.

"Attack vector is set," Flaherty reported.

"Very well," she replied, her lurking fear struggling with her burgeoning impatience. The fueling rendezvous was still a half hour away, an eternity of worry. She changed scale on the tactical display, focusing on the plight of Admiral Runacres's flagship. *Eire,* emergency beacons flashing, was beyond hope.

"He'll get out, Skipper," Flaherty whispered.

Buccari did not acknowledge. She stared helplessly as the mothership plummeted for the planet, trailing a diminishing stream of winking transponders. The lifeboats were in critical danger of reentering the atmosphere; OMTs, tenders, fuelers, and reserve corvettes worked feverishly to collect those most in jeopardy, but many of the fleet tugs had broken away from lifeboat rescue in frantic effort to reach *Tierra del Fuego. TDF,* also jettisoning lifeboats, was still caught in the planet's gravity well, her overboosting engines in danger of going critical.

"Yeah, Skip," Thompson said. "Don't worry."

"Right," she replied. Her prayers went out to the crews of the doomed ships, but her hopeless heart went out to one man. She knew Jake Carmichael would wait till the last possible moment before he left a ship.

"Tanker's calling us in," Thompson reported.

Flaherty hit the maneuvering alarm.

Buccari diverted her thoughts to the refueling operation. A section of fuelers had accelerated onto the attack vector. Ready-tanker icons illuminated on her headup. Grabbing her flight controls, she hammered stern thrusters to initiate a closure rate, thankful for the plotting task, thankful for anything to take her mind from her worries. Rendezvous and hookup with the tankers went smoothly, all ships topping off and marshaling into attack formation. Crew chatter was subdued, the normal ribald tanking banter nonexistent. All the while the corvette formations accelerated on their attack vector, closing on the enemy.

Engagement range was less than an hour away.

"Skipper," Flaherty said as they broke away from their fueler. "There's one thing I always wanted to tell you."

"What's that, Flack?" she asked, setting her throttles.

"I . . . just wanted to . . ." Flaherty stammered. Flaherty never stammered. "I just wanted—"

"Shut up, Flack," Buccari replied. "We're going to make it."

"Yeah," her copilot replied, without conviction.

She struggled to purge her mind of death's dark image. She could not afford the luxury of fear. Nor could she waste time thinking of the future. There was no future.

"Attack formation is set," Thompson reported.

All corvette commanders signaled readiness to attack. Messages flew over the fleet laser net.

"Time to go to work, Condor," Wanda Green broadcast.

"Attack vector!" Buccari called, moving her throttles to military.

Flaherty hit the maneuvering alarm.

"Buster!" she shouted, engaging ignitors.

"Hooot-ah! Hooot-ah!" Et Lorlyn's deep voice rumbled.

Acceleration slammed Buccari against her headrest. Vision tunneling down, she stared at the tactical display. An obvious component of the battle equation was missing.

"Where are the fast-movers?" Flaherty asked, reading her mind.

"Yeah," Thompson seconded.

Only alien motherships, still in grid matrix, were revealed on the tactical display. The Ulaggi attack units were not in the game. Buccari was strangely sorry. If she was going to die, she would have preferred to go in a dogfight with Ahyerg, rather than getting vaporized at long range by an interstellar's main battery. Ahyerg was out there. She wanted another shot at the Ulaggi pilot.

"Ahyerg! Wh-Where are you, Ahyerg?" Buccari shouted

into an open frequency, breaking radio discipline. "This is Buccari, Ahyerg. Come out and fight, you son of a bitch."

The silence of the universe was her only reply.

"Damn your soul, Ahyerg!" Buccari shouted.

Minutes dragged by. The Ulaggi formation grew larger on her weapons displays. She designated primary and secondary targets, not that it mattered, at least not for her and her squadron. They would not get close enough to fire weapons.

"Alien battery range in twenty seconds," Flaherty reported.

"Weapons check," she barked. Force of habit.

"Kinetics be on line, Skipper," Gunner Tyler responded. "Seeker's tracking. Cannon's hot; storage point eight and accumulating."

"Decoys?" she demanded.

"Ready," Flaherty answered. "Let's get 'em, Skipper."

"We are weapons free," Thompson reported.

"Rog', weapons free," she replied.

The first Ulaggi energy discharge struck her corvette, out of range yet still powerful enough to resonate her ship's hull.

"Shields eighty percent," Thompson reported, his voice up an octave.

"Engagement radius in ten seconds," Flaherty announced.

"Roger," she acknowledged. Involuntarily she thought of her son, and with brutal discipline she forced those thoughts back into oblivion. Hope was an emotional luxury she could ill afford.

Threat alarms warbled. Main battery designators from at least three Ulaggi ships tracked them, firmly locked. Another Ulaggi discharge enveloped her ship, making its electronics sing.

"Shields sixty percent," Thompson reported.

"Decoys now, Flack," she ordered.

"Rog'," Flaherty replied, wiggling spasmodically against his tethers, gloved hands pounding his console.

A screamer left *Condor One* with a dull *thunk* amidships, and then another. The jamming modules diverged on random courses. The other corvettes were doing the same. Buccari checked tactical; the attack formations blossomed with false targets.

"Jinking," she shouted. Her flight commenced a programmed maneuver, thrusters and main engines simultaneously slewing all corvettes in coordinated evasive maneuvers; anything to confuse the Ulaggi targeting systems.

"Eng-gagement r-range," Tyler reported, fighting the effects of the violent maneuvers, "five seconds . . . four . . . three . . ."

Buccari took a deep breath, possibly her last. She forced all thoughts from her mind and allowed her training, and her hate for the Ulaggi, to drive her onward.

She prepared to die.

"Hyperlight activity!" Thompson reported. "Contact group bravo has jumped."

"L-Look!" Flaherty blurted, pointing to the tactical display.

Disbelieving, she stared at the holo. Her attacking force was in perfect order, but they were no longer designated with threat circles. Ulaggi fire-control radars and targeting lasers no longer painted them.

"Group alpha's gone, too!" Thompson shouted.

The Ulaggi ships had disappeared.

"Look sharp!" she shouted, opening the scale on the tactical display. The enemy could reappear anywhere. Eternal seconds marched by.

"Negative contacts," Thompson reported "They're gone, Skipper."

All nine Ulaggi ships had jumped into the timeless void.

FORTY-EIGHT

AFTERMATH

Charlie, parting black, icy water, surfaced under a bloated moon. Spitter swam ahead, his wake rippling like disturbed mercury. Charlie breaststroked cautiously, listening. An object flamed across the skies, outshining even the garish moon. The fiery green-yellow streaks disappeared behind the southern mountains. Many seconds later a chain of muted sonic booms drifted over the river.

Shrieks pierced the night. Silhouetted against the moon, a calling hunter took flight, membranes cracking chill air. The cliff dweller settled into a silent glide as Charlie's sandals found sandy bottom. Shivering, the boy slogged from the river and trudged up the moon-silvered beach until the steepening sand gave way to a jumble of boulders.

Ebony specters prowled the blue shadows.

"Come, Thunderhead!" Bottlenose chirped. The warrior was close at hand, startling the boy. Hunters assembled on the road, scores of them, hundreds, carrying bows and pikes. More flitted wraithlike through the moon-shadowed woods. The boy climbed, dripping, onto the road, joining the massing warriors. Captain Two and Spitter appeared. Under hoary light Charlie walked down the landing road, a hunter warrior at each shoulder.

Tendrils of fog lifted from the forest, and with the sinister ground vapors arose a frost-muted stench. Ruptured bodies lay along the road, limbs locked in grotesque postures, no longer recognizable as human, their features forever frozen with fear. The boy's heart hardened with each step, his innocence

417

forever lost. Hot blood coursed through his veins, dispelling his gooseflesh.

They came to Longo's Meadow. The open expanse lay misty under the silvered light. Charlie saw living humans, shadowy forms stumbling across the fields, some alone, some helping the stricken, some carrying the dead. Mostly they straggled along the road, toward the settlement.

A warrior screeched. A trio of tall men approached. The tallest had only one arm. Charlie stopped as they drew near.

"Charlie Buccari," Tatum whispered.

Terry O'Toole and Beppo Schmidt stood at the big red-head's side.

"Ho, Sandy," Charlie managed, his anger tempered with relief. Suddenly he was cold. He shivered.

"Damn, it is him," O'Toole said.

"H-Have you seen Billy Gordon?" Charlie asked, already knowing.

"He's dead, Charlie," Tatum said.

The boy looked up at the stars, wanting to sing the death song.

"Damn, his face glows," O'Toole whispered.

"Like an angel's," Schmidt said.

"Like his father's ghost," Tatum replied.

Charlie looked down at his bare arms; he had lost his jacket. In the moonlight his skin was brightly pale.

"I b-been in the river," he said. "I'm real clean."

Tatum laughed. The sound lifted across the quiet glade. People turned toward the unlikely noise.

"You worried us sick, boy," Tatum sighed.

"Yeah," Charlie mumbled.

The one-armed man, still holding his assault rifle, lifted Charlie from the ground. The boy threw his arms around the adult's warm neck.

"Where did the Ulaggi go, Sandy?" Charlie asked.

"They're gone," Tatum said, turning for the settlement.

"For now," Beppo Schmidt added.

"Is my mom okay?" the boy asked.

"Yeah, Charlie," Tatum said, looking up. "We got word a couple hours ago. She's still up there, watching over us."

The current carried Hudson out to sea. He drifted through the moon-washed night, expecting at any moment to become sustenance for an ocean denizen. Genellan's seas boasted a plenitude of carnivores.

Shortly after the tired moon dropped below the horizon, the tide brought Hudson in. The injured man struggled to keep his head above water as breakers tumbled him shoreward. He brushed land three times, but each time the teasing backwash hauled him out. Finally he dug his hands into firm sand and held his position against the clinging waters. In the murky dawn he dragged himself from the ocean. His left ankle flopped loosely at the end of his leg. He felt no pain. He felt nothing below his waist. Using elbows and arms, and the onshore wash of the waves, Hudson wormed across the wide, shallow beach. After an eternity he found dry sand.

"Cassy," he whimpered, his salty sweat mingling with the briny water dripping from his hair. Death was near, courting him. Hudson no longer cared, and he stopped fighting.

A noise penetrated the pall of darkness.

"Daddy."

It was a tiny sound, a crystal bell ringing in the distance.

"Daddy," the sweet voice repeated.

Hudson's consciousness retreated from oblivion; one eye eased open and the other quickly followed. There stood his daughter. Close, too close to be a dream. Silky white-blond hair glowed with an inherent luster, and innocent eyes of radiant blue blinked in wonder. Behind Emerald, hands on his daughter's shoulders, stood Art Mather, a dark, uncertain presence. Hudson considered the apparition and chose to investigate, leaving death behind.

"Daddy!" his daughter whispered, her face peering into his.

"Emmy!" Hudson croaked. His head swam with narcotics, but his heart welled into his throat. He attempted to reach out, but he could not. His hands would not move; his limbs were restrained. It was a cruel nightmare after all. He wished for death to reclaim him.

"Daddy!" his daughter shouted, truly the shout of a delighted child. He reconsidered his wish.

"C-Come here, Emmy. Touch me," he begged, desperately needing physical contact to confirm his hallucination.

"He's with us!" Mather said softly. She spoke to someone he could not see. Mather's voice had always grated on Hudson's nerves, but for once it was welcome. If Mather was real, then so was his daughter. Hudson needed physical contact with his daughter. Emerald leaned onto her father's bed; the mattress moved to her weight. Her soft touch on his cheek was exquisite. His daughter was real. Hudson strained to make the soft touch more substantial, but with his efforts came a white-hot pain in his lower back. He groaned in distress. Alarmed, Emerald pulled away. An unfamiliar face hove into view.

"Pain is good," said the person, a doctor by her garb.

"I . . . want a doctor, not a masochist," Hudson panted through gritted teeth. The pain had shredded his narcotic stupor.

"He's definitely back," Mather said.

"Your spine needs reconstruction," the doctor said. "You and your daughter will be going back to Earth with the fleet."

"We're going to Earth, Daddy!" Emerald said.

Certain now that his daughter was real, there was only one thing on Hudson's mind—an obsession.

"Where's Cassy?" he demanded.

"Take it easy," the doctor admonished, looking over his head.

"Art," Hudson said, desperately seeking succor. "Where is she?"

"We're still looking, Nash," Mather replied softly. The challenge normally resident in the diplomat's voice was gone; her features were sorrowful, without guile; her eyes welled with tears. Hudson's opinion of the bureaucrat was forever altered.

"Cassy," Hudson whispered, closing his eyes to stem his own tears.

"We'll find her, Nash," Mather replied. "General Wattly's conducting a personal search. We're still picking up survivors."

Hudson opened his eyes and tried to smile. A tear trickled down his cheek, and then another. A hand reached out to wipe them dry.

"Our patient needs to go back to sleep for a few hours," the doctor said. Mather took Emerald and started to lead her away.

"Art," Hudson said, sniffing.

"Yes," Mather said, turning.

"Thanks."

"For what, Nash?"

"For finding Emerald," Hudson said, his voice breaking. "And for taking care of her."

"She found me," Mather said.

"Still, thanks," he said.

"You're a lucky man, Nash. You have a wonderful daughter."

"I know, Art," Hudson said. "I know."

The doctor cleared her throat.

"Bye-bye, Emmy," Hudson said.

"Bye, Daddy," Emerald replied.

Mather and Emerald disappeared from view.

Hudson's cries turned to sobs.

Arc lights, their garish beams filled with dust motes and diesel smoke, overpowered the flat light of the moon. The air around Reggie St. Pierre vibrated with the chugging power of straining bulldozers and traction graders. Jackhammers and demolition charges, tearing into fused plastic and stone, punctuated the night.

Nash Hudson was not the only person bereft of Cassy Quinn's presence. St. Pierre desperately missed the science officer. Quinn knew New Edmonton and its recovery capabilities better than anyone. NEd was Cassy Quinn's settlement. St. Pierre's respect for Quinn's calm, rational intellect rose ever higher. Over the years, St. Pierre had provided Quinn with opinions and advice, but the science officer had made the decisions. Now those decisions were his to make. His alone.

St. Pierre laughed at his overwrought sense of ownership. He knew all too well that the Legion Council and the State

Department would insist on participating in any decision. He would not succumb; he would govern; he would lead. He was Quinn's appointed successor; the settlers were behind him. So were the kones. He turned toward his helicopter; there would be no rest on this night. In less than thirty-six hours twenty planetary habitation modules would descend on Genellan.

St. Pierre noticed the running lights of a konish all-terrain vehicle approaching from the devastation that once was the city center. The big-tired vehicle halted and a bulky shadow bounded from its forward hatch. Et Joncas, the leader of the konish survivors, moved into the dome of construction light. The young noblekone, surefooted on all fours, trotted over the hard-shadowed debris. St. Pierre picked his way down the incline, stepping carefully, stumbling frequently.

"I bring-ah tidings from King Ollant," Et Joncas rumbled in Legion, easily eclipsing the jackhammers. The ground crunched under his great mass.

"As-ah always," St. Pierre shouted in halting konish, "we-ah are honored with the king's regards."

"So you will rebuild on this site?" Et Joncas asked.

"Yes," St. Pierre said.

St. Pierre had considered rebuilding to the west, on the untrammeled savannah, but he decided the sooner the scars of invasion could be eliminated, the sooner the emotional scars of NEd's population would heal. Besides, much of the subterranean infrastructure was still in place. The tubes were a mess, but at least one transit artery was already back on line.

"There is much to do," Et Joncas said.

"And so little time," St. Pierre replied.

The landing zones had to be prepared immediately, but St. Pierre had to plan carefully, for the habitation modules would be the key to the city's reconstruction. They would form its new core. Four of the PHMs would have their retro engines converted into power stations. Others would serve as living quarters and commissaries. At least one would become a hospital.

The modules were bringing down two thousand settlers, two thousand more human beings escaping Earth's hopelessness. To what end? These hapless souls were not escaping anything; they were descending into hell. Genellan was no haven; Genellan was the front line of a galactic war.

St. Pierre laughed bitterly. As bad as it was, Genellan was still a more hopeful place than Earth. He would not give the settlers time to worry. He would put them to work.

All the news was not bad: the agricultural survey was positive; the fall grain crop, assuming they could harvest in time, would come in at seventy percent of preinvasion expectation. They had ample natural reserves. Genellan was an endless store of protein. They would not starve.

Shelter would be another matter. The masses of evacuees were slowly returning from the disbursal centers, and the monsoon season would soon be upon them. Those whose homes were in the outlying agrarian hamlets would be permitted to resettle first, the autumn harvest their first priority. The city dwellers would live in underground tube stations for the foreseeable future.

"Will-ah you rebuild Ocean Station?" St. Pierre asked.

"Only as a memorial," Et Joncas said somberly.

St. Pierre had flown over the devastated konish bunkers. He had seen thousands of corpses being prepared for interment. He had volunteered manpower to help the kones bury their dead, but Et Joncas had politely refused. More kones and their equipment were brought in on suborbital flights from Goldmine. A small environmental dome was already in place.

"Will-ah you construct another settlement?" St. Pierre asked.

"I have discussed this with King Ollant," the kone said. "Perhaps we should-ah consider building a single community."

"It-ah is a good idea," St. Pierre replied. "If only for self-defense. We must-ah get the engineers together immediately."

"It will be done," Et Joncas said. "But Governor St. Pierre, I have more news. Extremely good news."

"Yes?"

"King Ollant is deploying an Hegemonic defense platform to Genellan orbit—immediately. The PDF has also agreed to send a defense station, though it will not leave Kretan orbit for four moon-cycles."

"That-ah is wonderful news," St. Pierre replied.

With three orbiting defense stations, the Genellan settlements would have a markedly increased chance of survival against invasion. But how much better? The Ulaggi would attack with more ships the next time, and St. Pierre was certain there would be a next time.

He looked up. The konish defense station rose higher in the sky every night, a comforting sight. Soon it would take a stationary position at the zenith. St. Pierre's gaze moved slightly south. On lower orbit, difficult to see in the full moon, minuscule points of light moved sedately across the starry sky—Admiral Runacres's battered fleet.

St. Pierre sighed. Sharl Buccari was up there.

"Five hundred meters," Flaherty reported.

"Rog'," Buccari replied, sharp-eyed and rested. Her worries had been answered in the hours after the battle; she had received word her son was still alive, and Carmichael, broadcasting from the admiral's barge, had resumed command of the corvette group. During the twelve-hour dash back to the motherships there had been little else to do but rest. It was that or worry about the Ulaggi. Sleep was more productive.

Buccari brought *Condor One* down the approach chute to *Novaya Zemlya*. Following her at precise intervals were the ships of Condor Squadron. Buccari's scan lifted from her instrument panel. She checked out the mothership's battle damage. *NZ*'s hyperlight shields were warped, and her habitation ring was brazed with moderate laser damage.

She noticed something else; pennant data emanating from the signal bridge repeaters indicated Admiral Runacres had shifted his flag to *NZ*. That meant Carmichael was also on board.

"Cleared to dock," Flaherty said. "Docking checks complete."

"Roger," she replied, concentrating.

Lineup and glide slope were dead on. Buccari looked outward again. Beyond the scarred geometry of the mothership, beautiful and indifferent, loomed Genellan. The planet, a massive blue-white limb across her viewscreen, beckoned. She wondered if she would ever again see its skies painted with sunset.

"Cheated death again," her copilot added.

"Stow it," Buccari replied.

"Aye," Flaherty replied. "Wouldn't want to piss off the gods."

"Whose side are they on anyway?" Thompson muttered.

"The gods?" Flaherty said.

"So many people died," the second pilot moaned.

"Easy, Teddy," Flaherty said. "There ain't no gods; there's no good and evil. It's all dumb luck . . . statistics."

"Look sharp," Buccari commanded, considering her copilot's words. Was there, in fact, a greater purpose to their struggle? There had to be more than just galactic timing and coincidence. But could it be as simple as good against evil? Who then was good, and who evil?

"Hundred meters," Flaherty reported.

"Rog'," she replied, centering her mind.

The hangar bays expanded and slipped around her corvette; yellow and black docking grapples reached out for her ship's hardpoints. *Condor One* settled against the cradle's braking pistons. Lock-down levers thunked dully against the hull. *Condor One* had landed.

Buccari relaxed and looked about the mothership interior. The hangar bays were almost empty. All fleet tugs and fuelers were turned out, their crews trying to restore order to the fleet. *Tierra del Fuego,* its thrusters catastrophically overboosted, was still being gang-towed to a viable orbit. That massive effort, plus ongoing lifeboat collection and battle repairs, was absorbing all available auxiliary craft.

Alone in the great void of Hangar Bay Two sat a Schooner Class EPL. A burgee decorating its tail identified the large penetrator as the fleet admiral's flag barge, reminding her again that the admiral and his staff were on board. Jake Carmichael was once again the focus of her thoughts. Her emotions roiled.

She was still alive. So was Carmichael.

"Commander Buccari." The order came over the command circuit. "Report immediately to the main intelligence briefing room. Negative depilatory. Admiral Runacres sends."

"Buccari," she acknowledged, laughing at the admiral's preemptive order. Humor only made her emotional state more confused.

"Secure the ship, Flack," Buccari ordered, breaking loose from her tethers. "I've been summoned."

"Aye aye, Skip," Flaherty replied.

She floated from the flight deck, through the main access tube, and onto the crew deck. She moved rapidly to her locker, stripping off her helmet and battle armor in favor of an underway suit and docking hood. *Condor One*'s crew was coming off station, their voices loud with transparent relief. When they saw Buccari they quieted and slid against the bulkheads, careful to stay out of their skipper's way.

"Carry on," Buccari said, checking the integrity of her docking hood. "We've work to do. I want this 'vette ready to go before the watch changes."

"Aye aye, Skipper," they shouted as one.

"Thankee for bringing us back, Skipper," Gunner Tyler said.

"Again," Fenstermacher added.

"Get to work," she ordered, pushing off from the boatswain's shoulder. She sailed through the aft hatch and into the EPL bay. Buccari emerged from the corvette's personnel lock and soared across the hangar bay. At the quarterdeck the watch officer saluted her through the battle locks and into the mothership's main environment. She arrowed into an upbore, emerging at level five, the communication and intelligence deck. The corvette skipper floated down a putrid pink and gray passageway until she came to a guarded hatch.

The main intelligence briefing room was darkened to enhance the holo projections. Scientist Dowornobb's towering presence dominated the primary briefing station. Captain Katz was at Dowornobb's side. The fleet science officer, not a small man, was dwarfed by the kone. Admiral Runacres was tethered front row center. He was flanked by Commodore Wells and Captain Merriwether. Jake Carmichael also occupied a front row station.

Tar Fell's image projected from the primary real-time holo-vid. Kateos and Sam Ito sat beside the armada-master. Admiral Chou's blocky countenance and a montage of mothership captains projected from the secondary holo-vids.

"We must now assume the Ulaggi know the position of Earth," Captain Katz was saying.

The Ulaggi know where Earth is! Runacres's strategy must certainly change, Buccari thought. Earth would need the fleet for its own defense. Did that mean the end of galactic exploration? Buccari remained in the darkened entry alcove, trying to determine how to reach a briefing station without being noticed.

"Citizen Sharl has arrived," Dowornobb rumbled. The assembled officers turned at their stations. On the holo-vids Tar Fell's eye tufts fanned out. Kateos smiled hugely. Ito snapped erect in his tethers.

Buccari flushed. Et Lorlyn, still in battle armor, was suddenly behind her, his great mass pushing Buccari into the compartment. She halted her momentum by grabbing an overhead railing. She made eye contact with Carmichael. The group-leader floated only meters away, his visage tragically saddened.

"Ah, Buccari," Runacres said. "I'm afraid I'm going to leave you behind again, Commander."

"S-Sir?" she said.

"I'm ordering all Tellurian units back to Sol-Sys," Runacres replied. "Except *TDF*. She's too damaged to jump. Captain Ito will take command and move her to the PDF yards off Kreta for overhaul and upgrade. Tar Fell's going to put konish cannon on her."

"Yes, sir," Buccari said. "But—"

"I have asked Admiral Runacres for you to remain," Tar Fell boomed in his own language. "King Ollant has seconded that request. We have much left to learn."

"The honor is mine," Buccari said in formal konish.

Briefing robots verbalized the translations. Printed translations marched across the briefing monitors.

"Commander Buccari, you and your corvette crew are hereby assigned to the Planetary Defense Force," Runacres said.

"Your first mission is to transport Master Dowornobb and his staff to my ship," Tar Fell ordered. "The Hegemonic ambassador has requested the presence of that estimable scientist."

Buccari smiled at Kateos. She would enjoy that mission.

"I am immensely anxious to see you, too, friend Sharl," Kateos's smooth baritone pronounced in perfect Legion. "After you and my mate have arrived, we will go to Genellan together and embrace the living and pay our respects to the dead. We have lost many good friends."

"Yes," Buccari said. The list of the dead grew daily.

"Commodore Wells," Admiral Runacres commanded. "Issue fleet orders. We jump in seven days."

"Aye, aye, Admiral," Wells replied.

"We are done here," Runacres announced.

"Attention on deck!" an aide barked.

The admiral and his staff departed. The other officers followed. Except for Carmichael and the kones. The group-leader moved in her direction. Blood rose in Buccari's neck.

"Commander Buccari, may I have a word?" Carmichael said.

"Of course, sir," she said.

Carmichael used an overhead grip to halt his forward motion. Buccari stared into the group-leader's sad brown eyes. Neither spoke.

"Excuse me," Dowornobb said, pushing off. "I must-ah transfer my data files. There is much to analyze. We have discovered some interesting anomalies during all these local jumps."

Et Lorlyn stood nearby. Dowornobb's great bulk pushed straight for the pilot, herding the noblekone ahead of him. Like two elephants in parade, they floated across the compartment and through the hatch, leaving Buccari and Carmichael alone. The briefing room seemed immense.

"I knew you were going to die, Sharl," Carmichael said.

"I thought you were going down with *Eire*," she replied.

"What are we going to do?" Carmichael moaned.

"Jake . . ." she said.

"Yes, Sharl?"

"Marry me . . . before you jump."

"Oh, yes," Carmichael replied, pulling her to him. "Yes, my love."

In that instant all Buccari's worries vanished. The width and breadth of her universe was defined by Jake Carmichael's strong arms.

EPILOGUE

BITTER SALVATION

Little One came home. Pake helped the girl to her pallet, covering her trembling body with packer hides. Little One would be allowed a day to recuperate, and then she would wet-nurse the infant daughters of working women. Her milk would not go to waste.

"I never saw him, Mama," Little One whispered.

"I know," Pake said, holding her daughter close. Little One's sobs did not last long; the child-mother was too excited.

"He cried so loud."

"A good sign," Pake said. "A healthy baby."

Red dust sifted into the glow of their flickering lamp. The door rattled softly in the wind.

"Yes," Little One said, a proud smile stealing onto her face. "And strong. He kicked and squirmed. I named him Yung Gum."

"A good name," Pake said, gently rocking her daughter. The mother fought back her own tears. The name meant "brave." Pake's first grandchild would need courage.

Little One drifted off. Pake slipped free. The mother admonished her daughters to attend to their older sister and then shuffled outside. A rusty dervish swirling up from the valley bottom brought with it the chugging aspiration of the smelter. The village was empty; the women were at the mines. Pake pulled her hood tighter and allowed the gale to push her along the path. The guardmales would be angry at her for being so late. They would beat her, not hard. Hard enough to hurt.

She climbed the footworn path, leaving the huts in the

blowing dust. It was a dark day and cold. Perversely, she looked forward to entering the mines. It was warmer in the mines, and there was no wind.

The path narrowed and became a ledge leading upward. The terrain dropped precipitously on her left and climbed vertically on her right. Neither gully bottom nor ridgetop were visible in the sideways-driven red-textured atmosphere.

Ahead of her something moved.

Pake pulled up, questioning her senses. Nothing was there, only the wind and the rocks. There was no reason for anybody to be about. Yet she was certain something had moved. The wind moaned. She stepped forward cautiously. A guardmale may have come looking. Forced to come after her in the cold, he would be angry.

Familiar landmarks materialized in the dust-hissing gloom. Nothing was there. Confidence returning, she pulled her scarf higher and walked faster. The trail rounded an escarpment.

In the path loomed a giant.

Pake at first thought it was a guardmale hulking close, but then her eyes recomputed the distances. The giant was as wide as a guardmale but much, much taller. It raised its arms and lunged. She turned to run.

Her escape was cut off by two winged creatures descending onto the path behind her, horrible, batlike monsters. Wicked talons grated on rock. Black-veined flight membranes encompassed the horizon and stole away the dim red light. The hissing monsters had pickax heads split with scarlet maws and jagged teeth. Pake's heart seized in terror, her lungs sucked in gritty air, but the scream never left her mouth; a huge glove clamped her face with suffocating force. A brutally strong arm swept her from her feet and clasped her in an iron-hard embrace. Her back pressed painfully against the giant's rough garment.

The giant began running. The trail widened as it approached the ridge. Three furtive beings appeared from the turbulent haze, smaller than the giant but garbed identically. Lithe creatures and quick of movement, they communicated with their hands, waving the giant onward. All carried formidable weapons.

The giant, with Pake clasped to his chest, gained the crest. He did not follow the path to the mines; instead the huge being continued over the ridge and along its back side. The giant made a short sliding downhill traverse and then started climbing once again. Black shadows on the wing flitted past.

After an eternity of jostling and pounding upward, the giant's pace mercifully slowed. He jogged into a wind-smoothed defile, its narrowing surfaces blasted smooth and striated by eons of wind. The defile twisted crazily, becoming a shoulderwide crevice, with its opening to the sky obscured by warping, slanting walls. The wind surged and sucked, moaning like a pipe organ.

The giant stumbled onward, climbing all the time, at last rounding a sharp corner and stepping into a wind-sheltered chamber. One of the hideous, mattock-headed bats, its wings folded, waddled from the rust-shadowed gloom. It whistled and flashed hand-sign. The giant staggered past the black-furred monster and collapsed. He slid to the ground, holding Pake in his lap like a doll, one hand still over her mouth, but lightly. The creature's chest heaved magnificently; its breath rasped in her ears. Strangely, she was not afraid. The monster's grip was gentle, his embrace warm. The giant was immensely strong; had he wanted to hurt her, he would have done so. Strangely, she felt safe.

The fearsome bat squeaked, startling her.

Climbing into the wind-sheltered chamber were three more helmeted creatures. They uncovered their faces and uttered terse words, hushed and conspiratorial. Their tone was deep, resonant—not unpleasant to her ears.

The giant replied, his voice deeper yet. But soft.

Pushing back against the wide shoulder, she dared to turn her head. The giant's mouth and jaw were covered with dark hair, and yet Pake thought its large rounded features becoming. The giant turned soft brown eyes on her. Its full lips turned upward in a jolly smile.

Another one of the creatures spoke, seizing Pake's attention. In a voice deep and firm it spoke uncertain sounds. Yet familiar.

"Aw tei hai . . . pun yau," the creature rumbled.

Pake's brain processed the strange, rumbling tones. Dully, she realized the creature had spoken a dialect of her language. She ran the syllables through her mind again, adjusting pitch and inflection.

We are friends! the creature had said.

Words from her language, but the accents were wrong. The words were spoken too deeply. The words were—

It was not a female's voice.

"Friend?" Pake replied.

"Friend," the smaller one said.

"Are you . . . a man?" Pake asked.

"Yes," he replied.

"A man!" she exclaimed.

"We will take you away," the man said.

Pake was thunderstruck; before her was a man. A man. With difficulty she pondered his words. Take her away? Her imagination had never held the prospect of escape. Even her dreams knew no alternative. Leaving her mud hut was beyond the pale of comprehension.

"Huh?" she replied.

"Yes," the man said. "You come with us."

Pake looked around, suddenly frightened. "No, I must go back," she begged. "To my children."

"You cannot," the man replied.

SATISFACTION GUARANTEED

We at Del Rey believe in our books. In fact, not a single Del Rey book is published unless somebody here loves it and believes in it. We are so sure that you'll agree with us that we guarantee your total satisfaction! If you are not 100% satisfied with this book, fill in the form below, then return it, together with the entire book, to us at the address below. (Be sure to send in the completed form and book before the expiration date noted below.) Photocopies of forms or forms submitted without books (or submissions after the expiration date) will not constitute acceptance of this offer. *Please note that you should not return the book to the store where you bought it— you must send it directly to us together with this form in order to take advantage of this offer.* We'll send you a list of alternate Del Rey titles to choose from—and you can pick any book from the list. Your new book will then be sent to you completely free of charge!

Name:_____ Age:_____

Street:_____ Apt. #:_____

City:_____State:_____Zip Code:____

I did not like this book because:
[ ] of the plot or story line   [ ] of the characters
[ ] of the wolfwalker world [ ] of the writing style
[ ] other_____

Number of books you read per month: [ ] 0–2 [ ] 3–5
    [ ] 6 or more
Preference: [ ] fantasy [ ] science fiction [ ] horror
    [ ] other fiction [ ] nonfiction
I buy books at: [ ] superstores [ ] mall bookstores
    [ ] independent bookstores [ ] mail order
I read books by new authors: [ ] frequently [ ] sometimes
    [ ] rarely

Send completed form and book to: Del Rey Guarantee
                                 201 E. 50th Street
                                 New York, NY 10022

[Expiration Date: 11/30/98]